Praise for
BODY OF KNOWLEDGE

"At its comedic best, *BODY OF KNOWLEDGE* reads like a collaboration between a team of talented soap-opera writers and the romantic Brontë sisters. . . ."
—Autumn Stephens, *San Francisco Chronicle*

"An important contribution to Southern, American and world literature . . . a major novel . . . [a] marvelous story."
—Tom C. Armstrong, *Nashville Tennessean*

"A magical, multigenerational, utterly mesmerizing struggle between good and evil . . . Once again, Dawson proves herself an astonishingly accomplished novelist. . . ."
—*Kirkus Reviews*

"Dawson's control over her material, her gift for metaphor, description and structure and the vivid nature of several of her characters make spending the time worthwhile. . . . She is a master of the light, suspenseful touch. . . ."
—Fredric Koeppel, *Chicago Tribune*

"A book you will want to read over again several times."
—Betsy Lindau, *The Pilot-Southern Times* (NC)

"Downright hypnotic . . . extraordinarily rendered characters, whose passions and sadness and craziness and essential goodness will remain with you, perhaps forever."
—Nan Goldberg, Hackensack (NJ) *Sunday Record*

Body of Knowledge

Carol Dawson

WASHINGTON SQUARE PRESS
PUBLISHED BY POCKET BOOKS
New York   London   Toronto   Sydney   Tokyo   Singapore

This book is a work of fiction. Names, characters, places and incidents are products of the author's imagination or are used fictitiously. Any resemblance to actual events or locales or persons, living or dead, is entirely coincidental.

A Washington Square Press Publication of
POCKET BOOKS, a division of Simon & Schuster Inc.
1230 Avenue of the Americas, New York, NY 10020

Copyright © 1994 by Carol Dawson

Published by arrangement with Algonquin Books of Chapel Hill

Dawson, Carol, 1951–
    Body of Knowledge / Carol Dawson.
        p. cm.
    ISBN: 0-671-53572-2
    1. Overweight women—Texas—Fiction.   2. Family—Texas—Fiction.   I. Title.
    [PS3554.A947B63   1996]
    813'.54—dc20   95-47122
                                                           CIP

First Washington Square Press trade paperback printing May 1996

10 9 8 7 6 5 4 3 2 1

WASHINGTON SQUARE PRESS and colophon are registered trademarks of Simon & Schuster Inc.

Cover design by Robin Gourley and Lisa Sloane, art by Lynne Buschman, calligraphy by Jeffrey Stern

Printed in the U.S.A.

This book is dedicated to Lura May Lewis
and Elizabeth Hale Calderon, in memoriam

And with love to Justin, Nikos,
and my father

With heartfelt gratitude to Mark Bentley Adams,
Robert A. Rubin, Dona Chernoff, Bettye Dew,
Marilyn Sainty, Dori Gores, and all those friends
who have, through their patience, generosity,
and vision, helped me to persevere.

Also by Carol Dawson

The Waking Spell

Contents

BOOK ONE

How the Ransoms
Made Their Pile

First I cite physical conditions: I am the last of the Ransoms. There is no one left but me. Since earliest childhood I have remained immured within these grounds, concealed from all but the most private of viewers. This is because a freak's nature admits only limited future social prospects. My destiny lies here. For the last few years I have been isolate; for certain reasons, almost inviolably so. Except for Nyla. And the fact that Nyla is here at all, and is someone I could not get rid of even if I could get along without her, has reinforced my solitude.

In order to explain how I came to be, to track the full, glorious preponderance of my incarnation, it is necessary to revel in history. Otherwise, what could possibly justify the quality of such a life?

I want to know. By God, I do.

It was Viola, of course, who told me about the ice money. It was Viola who told me everything. But I was the one who found this, the letter from my great-grandfather that began it all.

Planters' Hotel
Saint Louis, Mo.
July 8, 1908

My Dearest Arliss,
You cannot conceive of the beauty that greeted my tired eyes on this sultry July day in Saint Louis, after a morning spent combating misery and a taste like cotton on my tongue. Upon finishing a poorly cooked luncheon, I retired to the hotel's gallery

to try and catch what little breeze there was in the street. There I called to the boy and told him to bring me a drink: "Any kind," I said. He returned from the bar with a tall silver cup, adorned with a sprig of mint. But the loveliness lay in the way the sides of the cup misted over, as if it had passed through a chilly fog. Droplets stood out on the metal, reminding me of a cool spring bubbling from rocks, or the kitchen window during a frosty spell. In other words, the cup was cold! and held a mixture which I can only compare to Ambrosial Nectar. Holding it in my hand led me to think. Now, I know that Texans imbibe such drinks. I have often heard Governor Deloache praise them, in midst of our work on some civic project, and I have wondered what a mint julep could be like. But Bernice lacks one of its prime ingredients. And let me assure you, my dear wife, that the result was what saved your husband's spirit on this hot day in a distant capital. Gone was the searing summer bane—or if not gone, then appeased. By what? Ice! The drink was made with ice. Now, we in Bernice have forgone this luxury. The town has been civilized such a short time that I don't think anyone recognizes what a deficiency marks our way of life, relying on the spring houses as we do. It may strike you as a trivial concern to spend one's energies on, when, as you so very often remind me, we have our chores cut out for us in the planning and governing of our town. But such concerns become colossal when used to oppose our oppressor, the Texas summer. Why has not some enterprising person taken it upon himself to institute ice's charity? Certainly, during the winter, we get an occasional supply of it; but we don't require it then, it is redundant. That mint julep was one of the happiest experiences of my forty-five years. I understand, from what Mr. Lawrence, the manager here at the hotel, tells me, that ice is a commonplace in eastern cities. Even in Dallas they have a factory! On my return, I intend to investigate this frigid haven with all haste, and to bring its balm back to Gilead.

I catch the four-fifteen back home tomorrow. I trust you and the children are well.

Your loving spouse,
Garner Ransom

P.S. I will inform Governor Deloache of my success regarding our transactions on my return. If you happen to see him beforehand, *Please Do Not* avail yourself of the opportunity to do so, as this is men's business, and falls within my duties as Bernice's City Clerk. I know that you, my dear, dear Arliss, with your wisdom and intelligence, will understand my plea.

This letter, written by my great-grandfather during the sole journey he ever made away from his wife's side, arrived at his small shotgun house on Bois D'arc Street on July 10th, 1908.

A few hours later my great-grandfather himself followed it. He kissed his three children hello, went straight to Governor Deloache's house to tell him the results of their "men's business," and then drove out into the country to have a chat with his old acquaintance, Mr. Archibald Macafee. At Mr. Macafee's ranch, as he sat in the pine-board parlor and sipped a tepid bourbon-and-branch water, my great-grandfather shared his brainstorm. "Come to Dallas with me," he urged Mr. Macafee. "Let's take a look at this ice house." Apparently Mr. Macafee too was hot and thirsty. For Archibald Macafee, who had stuck to cattle all his life, agreed to accompany my great-grandfather without delay.

Thus the initial partnership, pilgrimate in its overtones (balm to Gilead!), began on that steamy thirty-five-mile train ride. As they traveled together over the yellow dust-cloaked plains, Garner Ransom outlined his design in greater detail, and touched Archibald Macafee for the cash. Thus the poetry of ice was made manifest. And thus, a union with far-reaching implications was formed, which has connected the two families in arcane and arctic practices of the soul forever since.

My goodness. How one mint julep changed the destiny of my family, not to mention the entire town.

Within a year, my great-grandfather and Archibald Macafee had built two factories to supply not only Bernice but three nearby communities as well. The ice business caught on like a prairie fire, changing customs, altering the habits of everyone from the milkman to the local undertaker. All at once the meat stopped turning green in a day. Ice cream could be cranked before dinner and still eaten with a fork for dessert, and for the first summer in memory matrons saw the point in setting the table with butter knives. By 1909, when ladies got the afternoon flutters they could soothe their heads with an ice pack. Babies drank yesterday's milk before it curdled. Children grew bilious on cold sarsaparilla. In short, the "trivial concern" that a hardnosed wife might have condemned became the RanMac Chill Company, providing an invaluable service.

"YOUR GREAT-GRANDDADDY made a lot of money when he started off, but it was nothing like what he made after he let his imagination loose on the world," said Viola. By that, she meant the oil money, and the Ford dealerships. The oil came after the ice venture. What excited my great-grandfather about it, as he paced the floor of his new office downtown, was its pedigree: from ancient forest and rotting dinosaur to befouler of well water to fuel for locomotion. When oil was discovered in West Texas, he was romantic enough to decide that the fields of Bernice must yield it, too, despite the reports of his geologists. He hired a team of drillers to probe a few acres of land he had bought on spec. Soon the black prehistoric soup was spouting from the ground, just as he had predicted, into the tanks he had ready for it. That same year he bought the woods, meadows, and pastures that became the Ransom estate, and, deep inside the post oaks at its heart, he built this house.

I live in a palace of white rock. Limestone from the Hill Country, slabs from Carrara, the columns of feldspar that front the porch: these rose up from the scrub landscape at my great-grandfather's command until now they stand three stories tall against the blue sky. When I stroll along the porch, looking at the lawns pooled like green water between the azalea beds and the tangled rose gardens, watching the lake ripple under its arched bridge, and I run my hand over a pillar, or knock against the rough cheek of limestone, and hear the doves call from the woods beyond, I know what work and vision it took for him to impose this emerald isle set in its dry brush sea. Even so, it was not for himself. His birth home — the two-room log house with the dogtrot, the corncob mattress and frayed quilt and the patch of gilt on an old picture frame, his first glimpse of gold — did not goad him. This house on the still-raw frontier was not built for his tastes.

He built it for Arliss.

"I SWEAR this house been quiet as a tomb ever since Miss Arliss died," Viola said in the kitchen, watching Bessie make cookies. Bessie was strictly the cook, but Viola did everything else in the house. "Was a time she use to have parties every weekend."

"Law, yes," said Bessie.

"Ladies wearing long white dresses, carrying little umbrellas they called parasols. I recollect Miss Arliss hollering at me one morning, 'Now don't you forget this time to give me my parasol, Viola, before I go call on Mrs. Deloache. I must have it or the sun will sap my strength.' What a woman need with a parasol when she got on a hat the size of a laundry basket I sure don't know. But 'Viola!' she'd holler. 'You bring me my card case and hurry up about it, the trap's waiting this minute.' Them cards — everybody in town know perfectly well who Miss Arliss was, she don't need to advertise. Ladies sure made me laugh in those days."

"Mm-mm!" Bessie agreed, dropping some molasses snaps onto the sheet.

"Was she sickly, to need to keep off the sun?" I asked.

"Shoo! Miss Arliss was strong as a mule. She wore a long string of pearls down her bosom, even in the bathtub. Chock-full of pride, too."

"In what way?" I loved to hear her tell it.

"Getting rich done gone to her head. She sassed over her old friends like the Queen of Sheba. She come in the first place from an old cotton farm out Tyrone way! From nothing but dirt-scratchers. She didn't like to recollect that."

"Why not?"

"Because it burned her up, that's why. She wanted to pretend she been born to plenty. She didn't like to recollect the time her husband was nothing but the city clerk, neither, or how the money come."

"Do you recall that time?"

"Why, I reckon I do. I was living in her kitchen pantry room five full years before Mr. Ransom got the money."

"Five full years. Sleeping in the kitchen pantry," I repeated, pondering. "On the old wooden army cot." Since the day she turned eleven years old Viola had worked for the Ransoms. One month before she came knocking on the back door of the shotgun house on Bois D'arc Street to ask for a job, her entire family, parents, brothers and sisters, had burned to death in a grease fire inside their shanty on the east side of Bernice. Viola had been spending the night helping an aunt in childbirth at the time. Her surviving relatives told her afterwards she was now going to have to go out and earn a living; they could not afford to keep her, and had no extra room in their homes. It was she who took over the care and raising of Arliss's three children, playing with them in the back yard through the long afternoons, listening out for the cries of their bad dreams at night, teaching my grandfather William to slick down his hair with spit, trundling the toddler Sarah around in the arms that were still cocked open and ready for her own younger siblings. All this while she was still no more than a skinny little girl herself.

I was seven years old, and she had told me all of this. But Viola so completely made *my* world that I could not yet begin to imagine hers.

"What *did* Arliss like to recollect?" I asked instead. I closed my eyes, trying to conjure the living, breathing Arliss, my great-grand-mother that Viola described so well and often, to bring her forth there before us.

"How rich she was."

"Ain't that the truth," said Bessie.

"How did she do that?"

"She bought things! Miss Arliss had fifty different party dresses from New York City," explained Viola. "She had twenty-four pairs of satin shoes, and three fancy capes and a fur cape. The fur cape was out of chili fur or something like that. It ain't raccoon and it ain't mink."

"Chinchilla?" My own mother had a chinchilla stole, which I had seen. Mentally I draped the cape around Arliss's wide white shoulders.

"Yeah," Viola answered. "She wore that one in the winter. And when we moved to this here house, she got all the furniture and the china and the glass from Europe. She put on the dog, my land! She told your great-granddaddy how she want this house to be, and he have to do it, just like before he got rich and she told him how to run the courthouse."

"That was when she told him to give the hunting parties, and invited people all over Texas," I said. Viola nodded, smiling grimly. I had already gathered many details of these parties, and Arliss's pre-siding over them. She would go into the fields with the men to shoot birds, while the other ladies remained back in the house, eating little sandwiches and drinking lemonade. They tried to imitate Arliss on some things, but not that one. She fished as well. She would instruct

9

Ezra to bear champagne to the hunting field, or down to the river if there was a fish-meet, in the manner she had understood was used throughout aristocratic England and Scotland.

"Bernice was too dull for Miss Arliss," Viola added. "She get mean when she get her money, but she was a mean woman anyhow."

"Surely was," growled Bessie. "Remember that time Dandy still work for Mrs. March?"

"Yes, yes. Mrs. March, she was a Baptist lady from Mississippi," Viola said to me.

"She told me the same thing, Dandy do," Bessie said. "She say she never met a meaner white woman than Miss Arliss. She act just like a hurricane when she got mad. One time she go call on Mrs. March, when the Ransoms still in that house on Bois D'arc Street, before the ice house, and she say that boy what done the gardening had been taking Dandy out behind Miss Arliss's woodshed. 'Just like a bitch in heat!' Miss Arliss hollered. She was madder than a rattlesnake caught in the corner. 'You keep that gal of yours in your kitchen, Mrs. March, or I'm going to whip her myself.' Dandy hear it all, but she wasn't scared. Mrs. March was sweet as could be, she treated Dandy good. Mm-mm! Miss Arliss was mean, all right."

"That was before Dandy left Mrs. March's house to go work for You-Know-Who," Viola said. Then she shot me a sidelong look. "You know what Bessie mean? About that Dandy and the woodshed?"

"No," I lied.

"That's enough of that, Bessie. You hush about Dandy, now. Victoria remembers her good, from the time she come to visit us when Victoria was a tiny. She always talked too much anyhow."

"May I have another biscuit, please, Bessie?" I asked.

"So Miss Arliss give a lot of parties when she got rich," continued Viola. I buttered my biscuit and waited. "Yes, she surely did." She leaned back and shut her eyes. Soon she began to whistle through her nose. I ate three more biscuits. Bessie measured the ingredients for pecan cake into a bowl, and began to beat the eggs. She did it gently, so as not to make much noise; Viola hated to be jerked awake.

By the time Bessie was pouring batter into the pans, Viola's lids had begun to flutter. "Oh, law," she sighed. "Miss Arliss give parties that folk come from the whole state to dance at. And barbecues and all kinds of food parties. Luncheons and dinners. We sure worked a lot harder in them days than we do now."

"Huh. I don't know about you, you best talk for yourself," Bessie muttered.

"Your mama, she have her little party sometime, but child, they ain't nothing like Miss Arliss's. And she never let Miss Mavis come to them, neither. Not till Miss Sarah went away."

I had always watched Mother's dinner parties, and her bridge afternoons with cocktails, from my place on the staircase landing. It was an amenable arrangement. But I could understand how it would certainly have galled Mavis.

"When Miss Sarah have a luncheon or a tea for her friends, she let Miss Mavis come. But she still not allowed to dance. You guess why! Yes, though, Miss Arliss was tall as a soldier, and she danced to beat the band. What time is it, Bessie?"

"Two, two-thirty," Bessie mumbled around her snuff.

"Time for my rocker in the sunshine. If folk ask me what Miss Arliss doing today, I say, 'Miss Arliss up in heaven, telling Gabriel the right way to hold his fork, when he's doling out the manna.' And then I say, 'And he better listen good.'"

GARNER RANSOM'S partner, Archibald Macafee, loved to remember what Arliss preferred to forget.

"Wasn't that one whale of a day, when we climbed on that train, Garner?" he said at a hunting breakfast one morning, as they sat around the huge mahogany table sipping coffee over the remnants of scrambled eggs and toast and fried quail. Among the guests present were the lieutenant governor, three businessmen from Connecticut, and a minor German count. "I tell you! And didn't we have us a time in Dallas, going through that factory like a couple of cowhands on a Saturday night spree?"

"Yes, we sure did," said Garner, smiling in reminiscence.

"And I declared I'd never dream of investing in anything so far-fetched and high-faluting."

"I believe the price of beef is predicted to climb this year, isn't it?" said Arliss, turning to the neighbor on her right, although talk of cattle or cotton bored her silly.

"And then, you old coon dog, you poked me and said it was going to cost me ten thousand dollars and a mortgage on my ranch to taste the same damn drink you had for ten cents up in Saint Louie. By God—by God!" And he laughed and chuckled, thumping the table with his fist. Then he reached an elbow over and nudged Arliss.

"That's the truth, Archibald," said Garner. "It was one hot afternoon, too, I can recall."

"Whooee! Was it ever! All the more inspiring. Or should I say 'perspiring'? Haw, haw." And Archibald stood up, and proceeded to regale the whole table with the story of how he and his friend got rich.

That was the first occasion. But Archibald enjoyed himself so much telling it that soon he developed the habit. Every time Arliss and Garner would go to a party, there he'd be, talking and talking, catching every ear he could with his one big adventure, and roping my great-grandfather into it as well. Then one day Arliss could take no more. In the middle of an important formal banquet, right at the point when he said, "How about that train going Dallas way, Garner?" Arliss shoved back her chair, stood up, whirled around, and stomped out of the room. The trouble was, it was her own party, and they had only just started the soup. Everybody began talking and whispering, commenting on what a powerful strength of mind Arliss commanded, and how adroitly she could make her feelings plain without one word. Archibald cocked his head at the dining room doors, and looked puzzled for a moment. "Why, Garner," he said, "is Arliss troubled about something?" My great-grandfather sighed. "Wind, I think, Archibald." All the guests fell deathly quiet for the remainder of the meal.

Perhaps that was the beginning of the terrible split between the Ransoms and the Macafees. In any event, it was the last time Archibald Macafee was ever invited to this house. I regard it as a pity, because he was a widower. His wife had died many years before, and he must have grown lonesome, living out on the old Macafee ranch, companioned only by men, with not one good cook among them. But if he missed coming to Arliss's parties he was too polite to say so. Her stomach trouble grew and grew in his mind, until it swelled to an affliction of Job-like proportions. He would come up to this house with one express purpose, wait until Viola opened the door, and then ask in a whisper loud as a squeaking hinge, "Tell me, Viola. How is Mrs. Ransom? Is that poor lovely woman still a martyr to her food?" And when Viola replied, "Oh, Mr. Archibald, the doctor say he can't do nothing at all," he'd shake his head, make a *tch-tch* sound with his tongue, exclaim "Such a tragedy!" and go away again without disturbing anyone. The fact that Arliss possessed a digestive tract like an iron foundry never entered his head. It nearly drove her mad in the years to come how her snub missed home. She had to put up with his kindness for the rest of his life, and she often complained to Viola that it was ten times worse hearing about it than hearing any malice he might have spread regarding her, because all of Bernice came to believe in her malady, and every time she would choose to pursue some unorthodox whim they excused her by saying it must be her belly made her do it. If there was one thing Arliss detested, it was to get misunderstood.

Archibald Macafee's innocence failed to pass down to his only son, Grant.

His mother died when he was six years old. She had come from Scottish stock, followers of John Knox, as had her husband. But whereas Archibald Macafee exemplified the shrewd good will of a pioneer, and left religion to those less rooted in the soil than he, his wife pursued God and His predestined plans with a fanatic's zest. From what little I have heard of her, she was primarily known as the first figurehead of the Bernice Presbyterian Church, a woman noted for her good works, stern nature, and inexorable dogma. She had been poor when she married; the legacy she left to her son was an abstract one. But her heritage remained imprinted on his features, graven in his personality. Everyone always agreed that Grant was his mother's boy.

"Grant Macafee always reminded me of the boy loitering at the open windowsill, sneering at the cooling cherry pie he couldn't have," Grandfather once told me.

My grandfather William and Grant Macafee attended school together. There they kept out of each other's way. The Bernice elementary school was small at that time, the classrooms uncrowded. But apparently Grandfather, and Grant also, marshaled the intuitive wisdom to avoid contact. Otherwise their profound difference was sure to lead to trouble.

At the time my grandfather said to me what he did concerning Grant, they were both well into their fifties. He then added, "When we were boys, Grant Macafee was hell with a rock in his hand. We used to have rock fights in the schoolyard after class. Grant grew notorious as a dead shot." Grandfather bore a faint silver scar on his temple, above the cheekbone, which he touched ever so lightly as he said this. Perhaps that, rather than Arliss's banishment of Grant's father, was where the enmity began. Or perhaps it came from some later battle. Grandfather could have been a network of scars inside, all inflicted by life among the Macafees, and he would not have let me know it.

When the ice partnership crystallized, however, the two boys, now in early adolescence, suddenly found themselves thrown together.

Viola said to me: "Some folk are born all in one piece, and they stay that way for all their days. Ain't nothing they can do about it. They're never even babies."

In Viola's opinion, Grant came out on his birthday the way he meant to stay.

As a child he was apparently friendless. Nobody invited him anywhere or solicited his company; chances were he would have refused them had they done so. Then the partnership bloomed between his father and Garner Ransom. "We want you two to be chums," the fathers urged. "Come on, boys, it's Saturday. We're going to take you out hunting." So the two children marched through the cornfields together for their parents' sakes. But a David-and-Jonathan intimacy failed to evolve. Grant shirked it, William shrank from it, and according to Viola, the best they could manage was to eye each other askance, shuffle their feet and speak with good manners. The dynamics changed somewhat when they were grown. But only for awhile, before the real trouble began.

"But my Mr. William, he was the soft one," said Viola. "It ain't no fault of his that Mr. Grant got born with a hole where his stomach ought to been. You listen to me, child, it's the stomach from where we get the juice of human love. Most people think it's the heart, but it ain't. You look at Mr. Grant Macafee. His pieces all stuck together like a scarecrow. He's so dried out that if you blow on him, he fly away." She turned to me. "That's why I'm glad my lamb here is so nice and round. It means you busting with good juice."

"I am?" I stared at her longingly.

"Well, naturally. What else you think? Look at you! But Mr. Grant, now—the only time *he* ever plumped out a little was when he got to mooning over Miss Sarah, and look where that landed us all. He dried back up after she gone. Yes, you could pour the cooking into his mouth, and it just disappeared, he'd squeeze it all out again like bile."

My grandfather William Ransom was short and compact, built like a nail keg. His sturdy red neck, rising above the white constriction of his collar, is one of the features I recall best about him: I can see that head like a burnished block, set squarely on its pillar, as he peers down and levels brown eyes dim with reserved tenderness to my hands where they clutch at his trouser leg. He does not smile, but seats himself wordlessly in an armchair, so that he can then invite me into his lap—for at that time I am already too "round" to hoist into anyone's arms. He does not sigh. He does not say anything. He runs his palm over my shoulder, and then pats it. The formality of his caress is in keeping with the rest of him: nothing out of place, nothing wasted, no extravagance. This kind of love suits me. I do not expect any more than the confirmation he gives, before I slide back to the floor and go off to the kitchen.

But Grant Macafee's thrift was of a different order, expressed in the attenuated limbs, the mouth like a blade, the scoured eye sockets and furrowed brow. The word "spare" evokes him well. He spared nothing and no one, least of all himself. So it was a fierce and disturbed focus he gave to his one anomaly, the desire that ate into him as truly as any corrosive eats into the pit of a cast bronze, and I am surprised at Viola's description when she said it was this very flaw that fattened him up for awhile during his early manhood. I would have assumed it would make him leaner. But then, what can I know of physical passion, except for what I have absorbed from these people, my kin?

One thing Archibald Macafee and Garner Ransom agreed to do was to send their sons off to college together. The old men died while their sons were away—Garner a victim of the influenza epidemic of 1918, Archibald of a "choleric seizure." By the time Grant and William had reached the age of twenty-one, in the year 1921, they had both attended Yale, and spent much time in each other's company when they came home for vacations. Grandfather—William—was now the man of the Ransom house. Grant Macafee, his college fellow and sometime friend, was the head of Archibald's ranch and ice business, and alone.

Grandfather's two sisters, Sarah and Mavis, had been born several years after he was, back in the shotgun house on Bois D'arc. They too went to school in Bernice, following their brother's footsteps. Sarah was beautiful, in a dark and Indian way, with shining brown hair, a full, deep lower lip, and long, slanting eyes. But Mavis was frail and stunted, with a slight hunchback—a sort of gnomic changeling who interfered in everyone else's business because she had none of her own. There is, in Grandfather's library, a photograph of all three of them together, taken one day in the summer of 1921, under a sun that absolves no grace or misfortune. The shadows of the photograph stand sharp, as if chiseled, and line every curve and corner with blackness. It is mid-July. William and Grant have both been home from Yale for about a month, and the four children of the ice enterprise (along with a fifth companion, the photographer) are on a picnic. The Ransom siblings are sitting on the ground in front of a large touring car. They wear the exalted look a photograph confers, as if invaded by unearthly spirits. Sarah has on a wide-brimmed hat that hides her forehead. Grandfather looks stiff, and at the same time lazy, as if his feet hurt inside tight shoes which he cannot be bothered to remove. His face seems abnormally bleached next to Sarah's swarthiness. He grins and scowls at the camera. Mavis is half-reclining against his arm, like a cat oozing up to be rubbed. Her features are huge in her small face, and she looks stricken with self-conscious doubt. She is the deformed one, the one soothed and tolerated and unloved. The photograph would have told me this, even if I had never known her later on. She is fifteen years old. Sarah is seventeen, Grandfather twenty-one. Grant Macafee, although present at the picnic, is not in the photograph.

I have always been intrigued by the riddle of this grainy talisman. Sometimes, when I was still a child, I would take it down from its place among a nest of silver frames, and watch it. Not study it, but watch it, as if it was going to come alive. I had the feeling that if I watched long enough, Grant Macafee would come striding out of the shadows behind the touring car, dressed in his Arrow shirt and striped tie and boater, his lips a knife edge below his bony nose. He would come and sit down beside Sarah, slowly, as if moving through water. She would not turn to look at him. She would ignore him completely, and continue to stare at the camera, dark and immobile, except for her hand, which would creep sideways, like a bird, and slip into his.

I still watch the picture occasionally. Sometimes I think I can just catch sight of his hat brim, beyond the car roof, or see the pale fingertips through the glass of the other side of the windshield. He never comes further than that. Even now, when he would be allowed by me. I suppose that time is too fixed in that picture, and Sarah will never permit him, through all the ensuing events and sacrifices that her decision set in motion, to come forth and take his place.

How Business and Pleasure
Did Not Mix

"That's your aunt Sarah, that you never seen, gone and run away before you was born," said Viola when I was eight, searching this same photograph. She pondered a moment. "Law, that day was one the devil raise the sun. The Lord, he must've spent that day under the covers resting."

"Why?" I asked, although I already knew.

"Because Mr. Grant took it into his head to go on that picnic. And then he found he had to speak his mind or bust. And the devil's been playing the tune ever since."

It had begun the Christmas before. Grant and William had come home from Yale for the holidays, and there, at a ball given by Arliss, under the splintery light of her best French chandelier, Grant discovered how Sarah Ransom had grown up.

It so happened that this was Sarah's first ball. She spent a great deal of it sitting on a chair, rejecting offers to dance—not out of shyness, but from a natural self-possession. Occasionally some of the more lively young guests would jig by and call out and try to snare her into their circle, but Sarah merely shook her dark head and smiled. Even when Arliss sent her reproving looks from across the room, she kept her seat.

At some point during the later hours, Grant Macafee approached her and sat down. Viola, upon whose report I rely, was roaming to and fro among the guests with a tray of punch cups. She saw him speak, earnestly and with an austere frown, and she stepped behind the row of chairs in order to hear better.

"I went to see an exhibition of paintings in New York on a week-end from Yale in October," he was saying. Sarah bent her head, tilting her ear toward him. She was staring down at her gloved hands, which lay loosely folded in her lap.

"I didn't know you liked art, Grant."

"I had not seen it enough before. In order to fully appreciate it."

"And do you like it now?"

"You have stepped out of a picture by Goiter."

Sarah sat there like a deer, not moving. He leaned towards her. His expression looked like a preacher's delivering a warning. Viola almost expected smoke to escape from his eyes, he was drawn up so tightly, staring into Sarah's face. Viola jumped back, suddenly unnerved. Then she sneaked forward again.

"Sarah, do you know who Goiter is?" he whispered. Sarah did not say a word, but kept her eyes trained on the dancers' feet, whirling around out beyond where she was sitting, and she smiled ever so slightly.

"Goiter was an artist from the land of Spain," he said. "He lived a hundred years ago. You have become as lovely and mysterious as a lady from one of his pictures." Then he added, "You have changed, Sarah. You've changed very greatly since the last time we met."

It was then that Viola saw what had bit him. "He gone dizzy, just like he fell off a gully head. I seen then what most folk don't ever have to suffer in their livelong days, which is a thing like a sickness that I only witnessed once or twice since I been on this earth. Not love, mind. It look like love, but it ain't. It make the man do things he wouldn't ever do if he had his sense, and the woman either likes it or she don't. And if she don't like it—But my baby was still a child, she didn't know what grabbed Mr. Grant by the hind leg and shook him until he went crazy."

She sat there, watching the dancers spin around. Grant kept trying to explain to her, repeating himself two or three times, as if he was trying to work it out in his head and convince her at the same time.

"Yes, Sarah. You have changed. I'm telling you, you have changed."
And then his face went hard. Sarah, for a moment, seemed troubled.
At last she parted her lips. She said only one thing. "Grant—you
haven't."

Then she rose from her chair, and without looking back, glided
out the door, climbed upstairs, and did not come down again.

Arliss was furious with her for leaving the ball before the guests
went home. But Sarah did not seem to care. When she appeared at
breakfast the next morning, on Christmas Eve, she was as quiet as a
possum, her eyes as sleepy and half-shut as a possum playing dead.

She did not say anything to Viola about what had happened the
evening before. It was not until the next time, when summer came
and Grant and William returned home for good from Yale, that she
told Viola the truth. But Viola knew already, from seeing Grant with
her own eyes, the evening of Arliss's Christmas Ball.

"My heart was just full of lamentation, that it was that sickness
that cast itself upon my baby. And all through Mr. Grant getting it,"
Viola said. "No good ever grew out of being like a starving man with
craziness. That's why I reckon Mr. Grant ate like he did. He was
starving fit to die for Miss Sarah. And because he had no stomach,
nothing but a hole, he wouldn't ever get enough. Like the devils in
the Bible, that Jesus turned into the hogs."

Even though Grant Macafee's obsession was plain to her and Sarah,
no one else seemed to notice. Arliss said nothing, and did not change
her policies towards Sarah's freedoms, which she would have done
instantly had she played her mind towards Grant's frequent appear-
ances on her doorstep. His closer association with William she
accepted as manhood's estate. They were now business partners,
after all—a sacred if unpleasant bond. Nearly every morning
throughout the months of June and July he appeared, narrow, severe,
and fastidious, just after breakfast, and offered his company to
William for the rest of the day. William seemed to accept his presence, although he must have wondered at it. Their mistrust of one

another, the dislike Grant had shown for so long towards William's flippancy and light-heartedness, was in abeyance that summer. Sometimes William even took advantage of the truce to poke fun at Grant's seriousness. Grant rarely responded. He continued to avoid Sarah's eye and shovel food down his throat. "That knob in his craw was big as a turkey gizzard, bumping up and down while he swallowed Bessie's squash and okra," Viola said, "just like it was tapping time to some music other folk couldn't hear."

But he never spoke to Sarah.

It could have been that he failed to apprehend just what it was that had struck him. He did not come out and express anything. He was simply drawn to the house every morning as regular as the sunrise. But Viola knew. And Sarah knew by then. She lost weight, grew as skinny as a buggy whip, fell silent upon her own feelings, sat and waited. Viola saw how she flinched from Grant when he came over, hurrying up from the dinner table once or twice when he gave her his look. Then Viola began to dread and worry, because she assumed Sarah was frightened out of her mind by him. But later on she found out: that was not the case at all.

ON THAT day, in the middle of July, when the three Ransom progeny decided to have a picnic in the country with two friends (the second, our photographic archivist, to this day unknown), Grant finally summoned the grit to speak his heart. Or perhaps the dam had burst.

I do not profess to comprehend carnal love. But that Grant Macafee was unhinged by Sarah's image, and pursued it during every waking moment, that much I know. I cannot say whether he was actually insane or not. I myself am familiar enough with certain conditions of the spirit that cause it to exclude itself from its worldlier surroundings, and therefore I think I can provide what is missing from the photograph: the portrait of a youth, enclosed, already bearing the bitter, indelible marks of his imprisonment, and wearing an expression of surprised self-reproach. He is aghast at his own renegade emotions; his asceticism rails against them. Lust has made him a puppet. In a few moments, he might emerge from his station behind the touring car. Those moments have decided him on the only course of action he can take. From what Viola told me, I can now conjecture the meaning of his lust for Sarah—the deep mindless peace he saw in her face and body, her innocence, which he could not fully feel merely by staring at her.

On the day of the picnic, he took her walking down by a cow pond, close to a clump of live oaks. She wore her hat sloped over her face, so that he could see only a dense shadow above the arch of her nose. The grass was dried brittle under the blue shade from the trees. Grasshoppers thumped against his trouser legs, and they could smell the rank air of the pond mud.

"Sarah?"

"Yes, Grant."

"I want to marry you," he said.

He stopped and turned. His eyes burned at her from their deep-set sockets. He reached out one hand and gently touched her sleeve. His fingers were shaking.

"I think about you all the time," he said.

"Yes. I know." She felt a swooping sensation as their eyes met. She smiled.

"I think about you too much. Maybe if we were married, it might cure me. I wouldn't be so caught up with the idea of you then. I'd have you."

So startled was she by the way he framed it that she felt knocked off balance, and took refuge in self-defense. Swatting a gnat under her hat brim, she blinked. "Why, Grant! Whatever do you mean?"

Choked by this coy sidestep, he jerked his hand back. "I am asking you to marry me." He stared at her. She felt as if he had scalded her.

"You are wrong. You don't want to marry me," she answered gravely.

"How do you know?"

"Not *marry* me."

He frowned. His eyes grew bewildered. Then they hardened once more, and he said, "Anyway, I have to. That's all there is to it. I have to. You don't have any idea of it." He looked away.

"I won't have you."

"You mean you won't marry me?"

"I won't marry you."

He did not ask her why not. He turned around and left, and she stayed in the live-oak clump, fending off the gnats absently while her heart pounded and she thought about what had just happened, until Grandfather came searching for her, to take them all home. Grant had already started hiking the four miles back to town.

BY THE time she reported the proposal to Viola that night, her eyes were blacker than usual, and luminous. She said, "What he wants is what I want. But I won't marry him. I won't let Grant 'have' me." And when Viola threw up her hands, jabbering warnings, and moaned in Sarah's ear with foreboding, Sarah said nothing more.

Late that summer, long after Grant had ceased to arrive at the house for meals and companionship, and had to all intents and purposes abandoned the Ransoms, Arliss complained to Viola: "I can never find Sarah when I want her. She has spent the past month either moping around in her room or disappearing just as somebody comes to visit, and I'm mighty sick and tired of her bad manners. Do you have any notion of where she gets to? She tells me she goes on 'nature walks'! Which is of course ridiculous. She knows nor cares less about nature than I do."

"Nome," Viola answered. "I don't know where she go or what she do, but I reckon it must be just growing pains."

ONE NIGHT at the end of August, when the stars blazed overhead and the moon sliced like a sickle through the blue-black reaches, Viola wandered outside to try to find some fresh air. It was about eleven o'clock. The day had been baking hot. Now crickets sang in the lawn, and from the lake shore came the throb of the frogs. Scraping through the bleached grass beside the stables, Viola felt the bushes pull at her skirt. She was dead tired; she had been on her feet all evening, serving the members of the Ladies' Social Auxiliary planning committee. She headed towards the woods, where the shade had been deepest during the day, and where the breeze blowing across the surface of the lake cooled down before it hit the trees. But she had only reached the rear corner of the stables when she heard a noise, rising clear of the night clamor.

The voices sounded close by. They were so near that at first she thought they carried through the air itself. Then she realized that they came from around the corner, in the hay bales behind the stable. They paused. There was a silence. A rustling floated towards her. Under the fringe of distant oaks she caught a metallic gleam, and as she peered through the darkness, straining and listening, she distinguished the boxy outline of a Nash, parked back at the woods' edge. At that instant the first voice spoke.

"Say it," it said. "Say it. Now."

"No." The reply was breathy, and so faint that Viola almost did not recognize it.

"Please."

"No."

"Please, I *want* it, Sarah." The name broke on a ragged gasp.

"Don't stop. Oh, God, no, don't stop now." Her entreaties swelled louder, trebling from a whisper to a groan. "More. Keep—oh, more, please, God, oh, Grant."

"I will keep you. *Say it!*"

Then the cry tore up from the hay, in such a mixture of pain and triumph that the hair rose on Viola's neck. Her blood ran cold.

She craned around the stable's corner. The arc of white flashed like phosphorous in the moonlight as he surged, and the ivory limbs wrapped and convulsed. Sarah's head was thrown back, her eyes shut, mouth open. Grant's eyes closed, also. His face lifted blindly to the sky. In the clasp of union it lay bare, shorn of all qualities except helplessness. The stern features relaxed. A great relief slid over them, filled with wonder. He dropped his head to her breasts, and then slumped downward, covering her whiteness with his own.

For a moment there was no sound but the crickets and the far-off frogs.

"You must go now," she whispered.

She reached for her clothes.

Viola ran back to the house.

FIVE MONTHS after that picnic day in July, Sarah went away for a visit to a distant cousin in San Francisco, and never returned.

I had reached womanhood before Viola finally described to me those months preceding Sarah's departure for the home of an amiable, if elusive, San Francisco relation. The tale of Sarah and Grant grew as I grew. At first Viola's hints and headshakes and sudden silences when she neared the sexual parts puzzled me and left me with an impression of obscure rites, presided over by a demon prince and a dark maiden. My coming of age was marked by the revelation of actual physical magic between the two lovers; a while later, I learned that they had "done something together." And when I chanced, still later, to find a book of famous reproductions in Grandfather's library, the likening of Sarah to a Goya painting struck me freshly; but they were copies of some madhouse etchings, and I was bemused as to the resemblance between an ephemeral girl inmate and my lost aunt. Only when Viola had repeated the story to me many times did I understand exactly what it meant. But throughout the tellings the characters of Sarah and Grant stood clean, burnished with a terrible purity of emotion and intent, shining more brightly as the particulars became clear; and eventually, when Viola decided I was ready for the facts of that August night when she had stumbled upon their congress, I felt I had known both man and girl myself: they were misty figures of my earliest memories; they were real people with skin and hair and blood and sweat.

Their story was mine.

Then suddenly the story leaped completely out of legend and into the domain of the everyday.

"A month go by," Viola explained, "and Miss Sarah didn't give me her rags to wash when the time come. So I worried some. But I thought, well, my baby's young, and she been troubled. Maybe she just skipping. So I don't say nothing. But the next month come, and go by, and she still didn't have a rag soaking in her little bowl like usual."

Viola started prowling about in her mind when the thing she expected to see did not appear. Day by day her trembling increased as she considered the matter. Then it was the third month. Still Sarah gave her nothing. Viola studied her carefully: was she filling out? She looked as plump and sweet as an apple, but her complexion had gone the color of house dust.

One afternoon Viola went up to her room, where Sarah had taken to sitting most of the day. No longer would she come down to the family meals; nor would she consent to entertain Arliss's callers, any more than a bird living in the trees. Viola sat down next to her chair where she was reading, and gazing out the window. "Child," she said, "I got something to say."

Sarah looked up. Her face went flat, pale as a turnip. She did not allow her thoughts to show; she breathed no word, but sat there waiting. Something appeared in her eye, however, piercing cleanly through the calm. When Viola saw it, her arm began to shake, and she dropped down on her knees. "I wanted to hug that baby, just hug her to my breast like I done when she was a tiny child," she told me. "But I wasn't able to do it. I was so full of trouble, and the sorrow of Jesus. I feel like she was my baby lamb, but there wasn't no person able to touch her no more. Her eyes shone so black, it made me scared. They had stubbornness in them. And they had another thing: the kind of look some creatures get before they're killed. 'Oh, child!' I moaned, 'Don't tell me. Don't tell me!' It was too hard to keep the sorrow in, I couldn't just set there quiet and ask. It was plain as tap water, there in her black eyes.

"'Yes, Viola,' she answered.

"'You ain't had no flow for three blessed months,' I said.

"'No,' she said, 'I haven't.'"

Sarah sat there stiff as iron. She had gone dead, it seemed.

Then Viola crouched down on the floor by her chair and grabbed Sarah's knees. Sarah did not move. There was only one thing to say.

"Oh, child! What you gone and done with yourself? What we going to do?"

They sat there for a time before Sarah spoke at last. "Viola," she said, "you're going to have to help me."

Viola was too full of sorrow to ask her how. "There's only one thing I can do," Sarah went on. "I need your help." Her voice sounded hard, and braver than Viola had ever heard it. "I've got a plan, but I need you to help it happen."

"What you want me to do?" Viola said. The cold blossomed suddenly along her backbone. "Oh, child! You want me to go to Mr. Grant? Is that what you asking me to do?"

Sarah set her lips tightly in a lock. Her face was white as a chicken breast, straining down towards Viola where she knelt and held her knees. "Viola," she whispered, "you must not tell Grant about this. Promise me. Promise you'll never give him the truth, no matter what he ever asks you, for as long as you live. No matter what."

"Oh, my poor baby-lamb."

"Promise me. Give me your word."

"I give my word," Viola said. "You know I don't never break no promise to you. I promise on the Lord Jesus," and then Sarah sank back into the chair. Her face closed in, withering up like a leaf. But Viola felt the fear leave her. Then she knew: it was better that Grant

Macafee did not find out about his baby. It was he she was so frightened of for Sarah's sake. If Sarah had to pay for what she had done, then God would wash her sins away. But if Sarah paid by giving Grant her hand, then nothing would forgive her. She would have died already. That was what that kind of man did, what that sickness leads to in the end, Viola thought. He would burn her up to ashes.

But of course the long-term consequences of this promise, the penalty of loneliness and horror it would exact from Viola throughout the years to come, could not possibly have been foreseen. Even if it could have, she would not have dreamed for an instant of doing anything other than what she did.

So they rested a while, rocking and waiting for Sarah to clear her mind. And Viola was hurting so, she thought she would break clean in two.

Then Sarah told her what she wanted. "Viola, I have to go away. Mother can't ever know."

"That's the truth," Viola said. "You got me here beside you."

"Then listen. I have written a letter. It's got to look like it came from somewhere else, somewhere far from Bernice, and far from Texas."

"Where does it come from, honey?"

"It comes from Cousin Marion Ransom, my daddy's cousin that lives way off in San Francisco. She sent me a letter, and invited me to come and visit her. I'll go on the train," she said, "but first you've got to say you threw the envelope away, so Mother won't get the chance to look at it, and see the postmark. I mailed it already. I'll get the letter tomorrow. Then I'll tell Mother I want to see that city, and visit my daddy's cousin awhile. I'll tell her I want it more than anything in the world. But I think she'll be glad. Cousin Marion's rich and knows people there. You've got to fetch the mail yourself, Viola. Then you bring this letter to me. You bring me the mail, I'll be waiting downstairs. That way Mother won't see it first.'

"Oh, child," Viola cried, "San Francisco! That's way on the other

29

side of the country. That's out by the ocean! How am I going to take care of my lamb if you go so far?"

But Sarah just looked at her hard. Then she set her mouth again, and said in a hushed, dreary tone, "Viola, nobody is going to be able to help me. I've got to do this all by myself." When Viola tried to object, she added, "I'll show the letter from Cousin Marion to Mother tomorrow. Will you do what I ask, to help me? You don't have to if you don't want to. But then I've got to slink away from the house and go anyhow, and if Mother sends me away to Cousin Marion deliberately, she'll give me the money I need to go. Otherwise I've got to go with only my pocket money, and it isn't enough."

Viola bowed her head. Tears dripped from her eyes. "I reckoned this was the last time in my life I'd feel so bad," she said to me now, "because there's nothing no worse than sending my baby away without me. But there weren't a thing I could do. It was time to lay down and die, but I didn't say it out loud. My baby's trouble was too big for that. 'I'll fetch the mail, and give you the letter,' I said, and it seem like my mouth didn't move hardly. 'I'll give it to you tomorrow, and then you show it to Miss Arliss.'

"'Yes,'" Sarah muttered. "'That's how it goes.'"

"So that was what we done. May Jesus rest my soul for it, and give me mercy when my hour arrives to lay in His blessing arms."

VIOLA'S HISTORIES so colored my childhood, infusing it with layers of light and hue the world will not see again, that it is difficult to distinguish between the long narrative chants and my own perceptions, the memories I cannot possess but do: I am granted a strange new kind of omniscience. Enveloped in this house, I see the flickers of its former life pass to and fro, and of course at night hear them reverberate with a fuller series of voices. I see Sarah in her room, packing a valise and a small portmanteau to take with her on the train. Viola is there. She assists in the folding, the laying out of silk teddies and muslin camisoles, the rolling of stockings into small sheeny bundles on the bedspread. Mavis is there, too, hanging against the headboard, watching and sniveling a little.

The autumn sunlight fell pale as a lemon. It filigreed the lace window curtains, and touched Sarah's hair with a mahogany-brown glint. The furniture in the room stood heavy and dark; a monstrous highboy loomed behind Mavis, dwarfing her further than nature had and spilling from its drawers gentle frilly things that made her sallow face look like a kid boot.

"Why do you get to go and I don't?" she asked. "It's not fair. You couldn't claim it's fair, could you, Sah-sah?"

"I don't know."

"I don't think it's fair. If Papa was alive, I could make him let me go, too."

Sarah moved to the closet and lifted a maroon dress from a hanger. "You would only try to make him feel sorry for you. You must get out of that habit, Mavis; it won't be forever that people feel sorry for you. I don't even now."

Mavis wiped her nose with the back of her hand. "What do you mean by that? Are you so high and mighty that you can just not care about other people when you feel like it? I don't give a darn if you're sorry for me or not. I just care about what's fair."

"Exactly," Sarah said quietly, folding the dress into a length of winey velvet. She smoothed it against the bedspread, doubled it over, stroking it lightly with her fingertips. Her face was mask smooth.

"Mama says I haven't gotten my full growth yet," Mavis cried in a high shrill voice. Arliss had said no such thing. There were times when she confided to her friends that she thought Mavis must be a changeling. "And when I do, when I'm full grown, I'll get Mama to send me to finishing school up East. Then I'll marry whoever I feel like marrying, and you can bet one thing. You can bet I won't invite you to be a bridesmaid."

Sarah said nothing, but took down another dress from the closet and carefully tucked its organdy ruffles into a neat spray. She sighed. "I don't think I'll take this one. It's not very practical."

"You might need it for parties," Mavis observed. Her hand slipped towards the dress; she fingered an embroidered garland of poppies on the bodice, covetously.

"I don't think so." Sarah lifted it so that the ruffles spread and trembled, and hung it back in the closet. (It hung there still when I was a child. The white organdy had gone yellow as foolscap when Viola first gestured towards it and elaborated its place in the scheme of things.)

Mavis followed Sarah with her eyes. Then she grew sly. "I'll bet you have somebody here in Bernice who'll be mad you've gone off to San Francisco. I'll bet I know something that you don't know I know about."

Sarah did not reply, but sorted through the hangers, choosing, rejecting.

"You think you have secrets nobody knows about," Mavis threatened eagerly. "You think I can't see with my own eyes, when you go off on long walks."

Viola stopped in the middle of a fold.

"You shouldn't follow people about, Mavis," Sarah said. "Someday you might hear or see something that will make you unhappy."

"Who said I follow you? I didn't follow you!"

"Then don't imply that you do. If you have done so, then you should know you were behaving rudely."

"I don't follow you, or spy on you," protested Mavis, unsure of her ground. "If you and Grant want to meet each other, and I just happened to see you in the distance, then so what?"

"If we did, then it was our own harmless business."

"You know what Mama would have said, if she knew."

"What makes you think she doesn't?" asked Sarah. Mavis stared, nonplussed.

"Well, then . . . suppose Grant decided to marry somebody while you're gone?"

Sarah brought out a crushed-satin coat with a fox fur collar, and folded it over the armchair. It was as if Mavis had not spoken. But Viola now felt ridden with dread.

"That might bother you some, mightn't it?"

She awaited an answer. It did not come.

"I think he will," Mavis said. "I hear he's already been paying some attention to Sophie March. What if he starts courting her, what will you do then? Away in San Francisco? I wouldn't leave, if I were you, to go off to San Francisco to parties and beaux, and leave Grant behind. He won't follow you, will he? He can't."

"I should hope not," Sarah said, smiling. "I think you'd better go study your Latin now. I've got to finish doing this."

"My Latin is boring. I want to talk to you."

Sarah sighed.

"Will you write to me from San Francisco? Write to me about the people you meet, and the men who call on you, and the parties you go to, and the places you see, and Nob Hill and Union Square, and everything! I'll write to you faithfully, I promise."

"We'll see," said Sarah.

"There'll be no one left here except Wicky and me. And I'll miss you so." Mavis's irritating habit of rechristening people with nicknames no one else used was born, perhaps, of a feeling that this would endear her. William allowed himself to be called Wicky. "Just us, all alone. What will I do, Say, what'll I do?" she wailed. "Wicky won't take me anywhere."

"You'll have William and Mother here. That's the whole family. And William will take you anywhere you want to go, and give you anything you want to have. You know that." She sighed again, resigned now, filled with a forced pity for one so cunning and lost as Mavis. "You're really a very spoiled girl," she teased, to make amends for lovelessness. "I won't forget about you, I promise. Come in here before dinner, I'll give you something nice. A surprise."

33

Mavis smiled tremulously. Her eyes lighted with greed. "Oh, dearest Sah-sah, what will I do when you're gone?"

"Run along now. Study your Latin."

Mavis walked slowly to the door, passed through, and shut it behind her. When she had gone, Sarah took a coral brooch from her valise and placed it on the bed. Then she turned wordlesly to Viola.

"What in the world are we going to do if that child tells your mama what she's gone and seen?" Viola breathed. Her dark hands, blanched the tone of gray flannel, retreated across the rows of silk and ribbons. "I'm a mess just thinking about it."

"I don't think she will," whispered Sarah. "At least not until I'm gone, and maybe not even then. I don't think she realized half of what she was saying, or what it meant."

"Um, um. Don't you know that child is sharp as a snake? And contrary! Honey, she knows exactly what she's doing."

"Mother hasn't noticed anything special about me. She doesn't have time for it, thank goodness. And she would probably ignore anything Mavis says." She mused. "Yes. The things Mavis says, even when she tattles, are not much use to Mother. She has too many other ideas on her mind to pay much heed to a tale from that quarter. Poor Mavis."

"Watch and pray," Viola whispered fearfully. "Watch and pray. The Lord provide us all."

IT WAS perhaps foolish of Sarah to underestimate the extent of Mavis's spite, or to imagine that a coral brooch would heal Mavis's burns. Pure shortsightedness. How well I know the practice of monsters! There are few gifts more calculated to excite the ire of the ugly than the ornaments of the graceful, the delicate, the feminine.

And where was Arliss all this time, while the plots and future counterplots were afoot? Arliss was preoccupied, as Sarah had said.

"JUST LOOK at this!" Arliss said to Viola, three days after the train had left Bernice, bearing her daughter away.

She sat at the dining room table, opposite her guest Mrs. Deloache. Although Mrs. Deloache was an entity in her own right, a former governor's first lady, she had this day to concede Arliss's preeminence. The relics of a rich luncheon lay before them. Mrs. Deloache's was practically untouched, the sherried doves arranged beautifully by her listless fork. Arliss's plate gleamed, unsmudged by a single drop of sauce. Everything about the room, in fact, seemed a reinforcement of Arliss herself: the damask drapes she had selected, the meal she had consumed with gusto, the dry joviality that now radiated from her. Her thick white skin was opaque under its powder, her hair coiled in a strong pompadour knot. She sat erect, the heavy bracelets chunking lightly together as she rested both arms against the table edge.

"Viola."

"Yessum?" Viola paused from removing the chafing dish.

Arliss knocked one fist on the table beside her plate, and then thumbed a yellow paper. She gave the impression that she could push it right through the table, were she so inclined. Her satisfaction was only emphasized by her control. "Here are some tidings that I think might interest you. I have received word from Sarah! Two wires, no less. Not one, but two!"

"You don't mean it!" Viola said, and nearly dropped the chafing dish.

Arliss flattened the paper out on the tablecloth. "She is safe and well and ensconced in San Francisco. That child is just the soul of considerateness. She must have known how hungry I was to hear from her."

"Well, glory, Miss Arliss. I surely am glad to hear that." Viola settled back on her heels, beaming at the two ladies, trying to still the frantic internal questions. Had Sarah really gone all the way to San Francisco in order to send her mother telegrams? How long would she stay there? It wouldn't be long. Where would she go afterwards? How much money did she have left, making that extra, expensive journey? They had talked about Arizona; they had discussed New Mexico as a stopping place. How would she pay for herself? Perhaps, after all, she thought this the safest thing to do, to confute suspicion. Perhaps she wanted the train ride, putting empty space between herself and her past, carrying her so many miles away from them all. Viola waited. It was clear that Arliss had more for her.

Mrs. Deloache, having placed her knife and fork across her plate to indicate she was finished, smiled remotely into the middle distance; the back-and-forth between Arliss and a Negro was none of her business. But, "Viola has had a hand in raising my Sarah, you know," Arliss murmured, and the smile then turned a few degrees in Viola's direction. "What would we do without her! Well, I just don't know. I think we'd be a lost cause."

Arliss's look of satisfaction stayed motionless on her face as she picked up one of the telegrams. The brawny shoulders, mantled in black peau de soie, thrust back, and she hoisted the telegram high, squinting at it. A moment of suspense, before the voice began, a deep contralto that nevertheless held a glancing quality.

" 'Dear Mother, Just off train.' "

Mrs. Deloache hid a yawn.

" 'Tried telephoning Marion from station. Number not listed. Taking taxi to Pacific Heights address. All well, wonderful trip. Wire again tonight.' That's why there're two telegrams at once. Those lazy slowpokes at the Bernice Post Office delivered them together." Arliss grinned at the yellow papers. "Here's the second one." Mrs. Deloache lolled back in her chair, gazing at her half-empty coffee cup.

"Now, Viola, listen to what she says. That darling booger! Have we raised a social butterfly between us? 'No telephone at Marion's.' Probably doesn't believe in them, knowing her, Ransom that she is! 'Welcomed warmly. Nob Hill for dinner. Opera tomorrow. Too busy to write.' See there! All caught up in the giddy whirl already, and dodging her duties. But I expected nothing less, frankly." She gave Viola a coy nod. "That's the girl you changed didies on! 'Very thrilling. Much love. Sarah.' Well, what do you think of that, Viola?" She put the telegram down. Mrs. Deloache sighed. "Does she sound like she's sitting in the lap of pleasure, or what? The little minx! Can't write, my foot! Well, it's plain as day that San Francisco hath charms for our girl that we can't provide in Bernice. I'm glad to hear Marion is doing her justice. I've a good mind to give her three or four months out there and then go join her myself."

"Yessum, that sure is good to hear. Surely do thank you, Miss Arliss."

"I think you can finish clearing this away and bring us our dessert now. Some fresh coffee too, Viola."

"I wonder what's playing at the Opera?" Mrs. Deloache said languidly, as Viola took up the plates. "When Henry and I were there we heard *Aida*. Real horses they had, trampling across the stage and all." She grimaced and leaned sideways, so that Viola could reach her plate. "They were a mistake, I thought. One of them—can you imagine?—delivered a . . . you know . . . right in the middle of the Triumphal Procession. The Prince or General what's-his-name stepped in it. Thank goodness we had a box. Most unpleasant for those sitting in the first circle. The smell."

"They will be doing something more restrained, I imagine," Arliss said coolly, as Viola headed for the kitchen door, thinking to herself that Arliss had probably dabbled in animal dung or worse in her time, and that Sarah had never been afraid of work, or getting dirty. "Get out of here, Ezra," Sarah would shout to Bessie's husband when she was thirteen; "I'm taking over this chore for you now." And she would grab a shovel from the wall and scrape out the layers of hay and manure, her face rapt, her arms swinging with regular thrusts. Viola's heart hurt as she dumped the cutlery and plates on the kitchen counter and returned to the dining room. How Arliss used to scold, how she had a fit, seeing Sarah's shoes dottled with muck on the drawing room carpet.

". . . or *Carmen*," Mrs. Deloache was saying. "Although that one is a mite racy for a girl Sarah's age. Don't you think, Arliss?"

"Oh, I hope Sarah is up to anything with some culture in it," Arliss said. "Some Gilbert and Sullivan might be nice for her to hear. Now that's what I call a musical education."

"Is it? I suppose . . ." Mrs. Deloache said doubtfully. "I hope she gets a chance to hear Mozart, at any rate. And Strauss. My favorites, you know," she trailed off with exhaustion, and then closed her mouth.

"Oh, yes indeed. Yes, I should say. I have no doubt that Sarah will enjoy *those* operas. And think of how sweet she'll look, all eyes on her, sitting in the box. I imagine she's already got swains lined up outside the door, nice San Francisco boys." She stirred her hot coffee complacently, filling the room with a vigorous force of certainty as perceptible as a perfume. "Yes, I think I might just up and catch an express out there myself in a few months, after my big Easter fish-meet, of course. Can't let the men down, just because Garner is no longer with us to supervise. Bass—you know Henry, for one, would hate to miss it, and so would I. I managed to catch fourteen big mouths last year. That's lovely, Viola, that'll do. Offer the cream to Mrs. Deloache. You must have cream on that lemon souffle, Mrs. Deloache, it just begs for it."

When Viola got back to the kitchen to help Bessie with the dishes, the feel of Sarah was as immediate as if she were just outside the door. What was she doing now? Had she already left San Francisco, wandering through a gray place of indifferent people? The stillness of her dark eyes lingered in Viola's recollection. Remembering her childhood strength, Viola's hands faltered as she rinsed a glass: "You can have this sugar egg for Easter, Mavis, since you broke yours. But don't throw a tantrum and break this one too," holding her head back, revoking her own desire for the pretty village seen through the peephole, the tiny world she would enter if she could, merely by putting one eye to it and staring for hours. And when Mavis broke it anyway: "No, Viola. I'm not crying. I don't mind that it's gone." The dark eyes lifted and tearless, regarding the wreckage of sugar, the fragments of icing and cardboard castle that had been the world she loved. "Don't blame Mavis. She can't help it." Her strength reached out across desert and mountain. Viola stood under the kitchen window in front of the sink, weeping quietly, holding the glass high and staring at the rainbow within before dousing it under the water to wash the soap away.

How Sarah Vanished

Nine weeks after Sarah boarded the train to San Francisco, eight weeks after the telegrams came assuring Arliss of her safe arrival, Viola opened the door to Sarah's room to find Mavis there.

She stood, hunched and intent, reading a piece of paper. The highboy drawers yawned open, spilling a mess of scarves, beaded bags, camisoles, and sachets onto the floor. Viola observed the rifled possessions, the paper in Mavis's hand, and knew immediately what it was and where Mavis had found it, nestled under an orange stuck with cloves.

"Miss Mavis!"

She jerked. Then, as she peered aggressively at Viola's frown, her face convulsed. There was an oddness about her clothes. Something, Viola saw, sat bunched around her short neck, something white and filmy, draping her shoulders like an ill-fitting shawl. As Viola squinted towards it, Mavis, with one motion, ducked her head and flung it off, sending it sailing onto the floor behind her. Not until then did Viola identify it, the organdy ruffles turned inside out and nearly obscuring the chain of stitched poppies looped down the front.

Mavis giggled self-consciously.

"Viola!" Then, in a rush, "Look at this very strange thing I've come across."

"What are you doing, child, going through Miss Sarah's drawers?"

"Oh, I was just looking for something."

"What were you looking for?"

"Don't worry. I wouldn't take anything of hers. I was just search-

40

ing around for that letter Cousin Marion Ransom sent. And look here! I've found it!"

"What you want with that letter?" Viola felt a tightness in her chest.

Mavis spread it flat on the bed and pointed to it dramatically. There was about her manner something rehearsed. "I swan, I just can't seem to understand it. Isn't this the strangest and oddest thing you ever saw, Viola? Do you understand it?"

"What do you mean, do I understand it? What are you talking about, child?" Viola strode to the bedside. Staring first at the unfurled letter, then back to Mavis, she stooped downward. But Mavis anticipated her and snatched the prize to her chest.

"Why, just look at this!" Mavis drew an envelope from her pinafore pocket. "See what I mean? This letter here is from Cousin Marion Ransom, in San Francisco. See? It's addressed to me!

"Yessum," Viola said slowly. "I see the letter. But you know I can't read."

"Well, it is. See? That postmark says 'San Francisco,' plain as day. And it's addressed to me. See? Here's my name. 'Mavis Ransom.'"

"Uh—"

"I wrote to Cousin Marion myself. I said to her, how nice it was that she'd invited my dear sister Sarah out to California like she did, and how lovely it was to think of her, and how I just hope that Sarah will write to me and tell me about all the wonderful things she's doing and the nice people she's meeting out there, because I don't have an invitation to go out and see for myself. And I told her how I'd written three letters to Sarah already, but Sarah hadn't written back. And how I hope I'll be old enough soon to spend some time visiting my dear long-lost Cousin Marion, my daddy's first cousin, if she would like to meet the rest of her family. And Viola!" Her eyes widened. The pupils contracted. "Do you know what she said?"

"Nome," Viola whispered.

"She said the most astonishing thing!" Mavis's stagy astonishment contorted her face. "She said she was so very pleased to hear from the Ransoms of Texas, and it had been too long since they'd corresponded with her! But Viola! She didn't comprehend what I was writing about, Sarah visiting her. She said she'd got the letters addressed to Sarah from me, and thought there must have been some mistake. And she sent them back to me in this very same envelope. And she said she would be delighted at any time to have us as guests in her home, and to show us the city and society out there, although she doesn't get out much these days because she's old and retiring—rheumatism, she says. But Viola! Sarah isn't there at all! She never has been!"

The silence hung a moment.

"Now, Miss Mavis—"

"She has never been there at all," Mavis repeated wildly. "Not at all! Now what do you think of that?"

"I—I don't—"

"And the most curious thing is, I've come up here and found this letter from Cousin Marion Ransom, that Sarah received with her own two hands. And look! The handwriting on it is utterly utterly different from the letter Cousin Marion Ransom sent me. Now isn't that the strangest thing you ever saw in your life? What on earth can it mean?" She leered meaningfully.

Then, before Viola could say a word, she folded up the culprit letter, crammed it into her pocket, and whirled in a pirouette. Her toe caught the organdy dress, scuffing it, but she did not notice.

"I must run down quickly and catch Mama before she goes off on her shopping! I must show her this mystery. And Viola," she cried out over her shoulder as she neared the door, the finishing touch, "where, oh, where in the wide world is Sarah?"

And she tripped away triumphant to her mother's side.

I HOLD open on the promontory of my lap an edifice as complete as a small manor. It is a scrapbook, with foundations laid fifty years ago, and built slowly year after year, like a stately home situated on a

Continental headland, by the doings, comings, and goings of the Ransom family. Mavis began it; Mavis, with her carpenter zeal, assembled the newspaper clippings that compose its structure. Our family rests in stasis within its pages, frozen as they were when they moved through the rooms of this house, the locus of many of the clippings' subjects. This scrapbook contains my life; this is what I am. Most of the material for it came from the society column of the *Bernice Sun*. I thumb back a heavy leaf, much pasted, and read:

The most glittering event of this holiday season has surely been Mrs. Garner Ransom's Christmas Ball. Presented in her own home, which many outstanding Texans uphold as a paragon of beauty and good taste, Mrs. Ransom last Saturday evening entertained some of the best-respected members of our grand old families, including Governor and Mrs. Deloache, Attorney-General Madison and Mrs. Madison, who traveled from Austin to attend the lavish fete, and several young beauties from San Antonio homes who we were proud to have grace our own Bernice for the occasion. Mrs. Ransom gave us the privilege of witnessing her daughter Sarah's formal introduction into the mainstream of fashion, and your humble correspondent would like to say that, in her opinion, Miss Ransom more than matched her contemporaries in decorum and loveliness. Bernice can be proud of our starry flowers of young womanhood!

Mrs. Ransom, gowned in green watered silk worn with an emerald parure, conducted the festivities herself, as the setting of new styles in entertaining and etiquette has, we all know so well, become her trademark. The sumptuous dinner included whole smoked salmon, fried quail, consomme, roast beef, asparagus in aspic, rice done in the Italian mode, and several desserts. After dinner, the party adjourned to the grand drawing-room, where an orchestra brought by train from Waco . . .

For my further delectation (oh, Nyla, if only you could cook such a meal) there is a reprint of the same article, which appeared also in the *Dallas Times Herald*.

On the opposing page, I descry:

. . . a tea honoring Miss Sarah Ransom, daughter of Garner (deceased) and Arliss Ransom, held in Bernice House. Also present were Mrs. Lutrell March, Miss Sophie March, Mrs. Henry Deloache, and many others. Miss Sarah Ransom wore a lovely dress of white organdy, embroidered with posy garlands, and her sister, *Miss Mavis Ransom*, doing the honors among the punch and sandwiches . . .

The underscoring, in heavy red pencil, annotates the scrapbook compiler's relief.

Here, then, is documented the skeletal framework within which my ancestors furnished their lives: the hidden fascia, the sinews of private collusion, and the decorous heart-muscle pumping, pumping out blood to the rhythm of Grant Macafee's ardor.

I flip back a few pages, and read of the Ransom family's rise, this time culled from the business page:

The corner of Bois D'arc Street and Main will be the location of the first new Ford Automobile Distributors. Mr. Garner Ransom, of Ransom-Macafee Ice, Inc., has purchased the site, and will start preparations for the erection of the Ford Emporium in early October. According to Mr. Ransom, "The Ford Automobile is unique in its position as a means of furthering American Democracy. I foresee a time when every man, woman, and child in Bernice, Texas, and the United States of America will be equal to his or her fellow through the offices of a Ford Motorcar. The genius of Mr. Henry Ford has seen to it that what can and will unite us all is locomotion. He is our benefactor; now we are blessed with this wonderful machine at prices the common man can afford. Let me say, as the first

proud perpetrator of this ideal here in Bernice, that soon I
expect to see all Berniceans waving a howdy to one another
from the front seats of their new Model T."

I uncrease a folded yellow column, and in the very next clipping
discover this heady rhapsodist's obituary.

But canvassing through five years' activities, in another few pages I
find this paragraph:

Mrs. Garner Ransom notifies us of the departure of her daughter, Miss Sarah Ransom, on Tuesday, to the city of San Francisco
where she will spend several months with her second cousin
once removed, Miss Marion Ransom. Miss Sarah Ransom will
travel on the Houston and Texas Central Railway to Dallas,
where she will catch the Southern Pacific. We are saddened by
Miss Ransom's leaving of us, but hope to receive an account of
her exciting trip when she returns.

Sic transit gloria.

How Detectives
Came to Bernice

Viola stood frozen in the noontide January glimmer of Sarah's empty bedroom. Her mind pivoted back and forth; she glanced in appeal at the highboy, the armchair which she herself had months past smoothed of Sarah's indentation, the neat antimacassar no longer scented with pomade. No help waited there. Her lips moved without breath. The seconds ticked by, swelling to minutes. Sunlight dimmed as a shadow crossed the yard; the cloud slid on, the sun glowed again through the lace curtains.

"Viola!"

She leaped, galvanized, and crushed her apron in her fists.

"*Viola!*" The cry took on a shrill note, wheeling throughout the house, rebounding on stone.

"Coming, Miss Arliss!" She bolted through the doorway and down the staircase.

Arliss reared, foreshortened first from the landing, and then angling into rage as Viola took the turn.

"Hustle!" Indeed, Viola hustled so that she nearly tripped on the carpet runner. The letters, held stiff out in Arliss's hand, like a semaphore, did not so much as flutter. Mavis cowered just beyond their white signal. Her eyes gleamed.

As Viola stopped, gasping, before Arliss, Mavis crept a few inches backwards.

"Viola," Arliss said in a clenched voice, "what do you know about this letter from Cousin Marion Ransom?"

Viola tried to speak. She could not.

"Don't try to tell me you don't know what I'm talking about. Mavis told me you were with her in Sarah's room just now. If there is one person in the world Sarah confides in, it's you." Then she gripped the letters tighter, as if to seize their secret meaning from the paper. "Viola," she warned hoarsely, "I am very outdone with you."

Then she clamped both her strong arms, letters and all, like a vise against her breasts. "Now talk!"

When Viola told me the story of the discovery of Sarah's deceit, there was always a point at which mere narrative failed to suffice. I would stare up at her as my only contact with the theater broke into action, and Viola reentered that time of day, that hour of consternation, when she envisioned the consequences of her loyalty: jail, prison farm, perennial unemployment, starvation. Enacting herself, Arliss, and Mavis (even imitating Mavis rehearsing her drama up in Sarah's room before delivering the letters), she would assume several faces at once, and the sensation of watching a play within a play visited me more surely than any later reading of *Hamlet*. Viola would become Arliss, standing royally immobile, her gray hair gathered in the pompadour above her swinging earrings.

"If you don't quit rolling your eyes at me like a golliwog, I'll turn you out of the house this very minute. I'll haul you down to the sheriff's office, and see what *he* can get you to say about this disgraceful business."

"Oh, Lordy, Miss Arliss." Viola became herself again, as she was in January 1922—a thin, small woman who walked bent-shouldered over her tasks.

"Miss Arliss, I swear I don't know nothing about no letter. You know I can't even read."

"Where is that envelope? There should have been an envelope to this letter. Where did it go?"

"Oh, ma'am, I sure don't know. It was a long time ago now. It must've got thrown away."

Arliss stared, tapping her index finger against the letters. With her eyes she raked Viola up and down.

"Miss Sarah is missing."

"Oh, Lord, Lord! I know it. My baby, my child what I nursed from the day she's born! Gone disappeared into the yonder!"

"*My* child," Arliss reclaimed evenly, and Viola quickly subdued herself.

"Oh, Miss Arliss! Where can she be?"

"Where has Mavis gotten to? *Mavis!* Come here this minute!"

"I'm here, Mama," Mavis murmured, and tiptoed back into the foyer.

"You must both understand this right now. Mavis. Viola. Are you listening to me?"

"Yessum."

"You must not breathe a word of this to anyone. Do you hear me? To anyone! You must not open your mouths about anything to do with Sarah, not so much as mention her name, until we get to the bottom of this. You must behave as if nothing at all has happened, if I catch *either* of you telling so much as the time of day in San Francisco to a soul, you will wish to heaven that you'd had your tongue torn out of your mouth. Is that understood?"

"Yes, Mama," whispered Mavis.

"I don't yet know what this portends, but it could be something terrible. The Pinkerton people have experience with things like this. I do not."

"Yessum."

"My Sarah," she murmured. Her mouth twisted. Then she turned. "Viola, call Mr. William. Tell him I want to see him in the library. I think he's out in the stables, fooling with his car."

THE PINKERTON Detective Agency supplied two men for Arliss's service. They arrived the very night of the discovery, driving down from Dallas in a taxicab which William paid off at the front door. One of the men trailed always two steps behind the other, as when Viola ushered them into the library; when they left it two hours later, after interviewing the household and making their guarded promises, and stopping in the kitchen for a late supper and coffee before William drove them to the Harrison Hotel, the second detective again followed the first with a precise martial pace.

Viola always described the two detectives as "those Pinkymen."

"The front one," she said, "he was more pinky-looking than the back one. That hind-leg man look kind of high yellow to me. But I don't say nothing about that to Miss Arliss, of course. Only to Mr. William. I could say anything to him. He just laughed. Even when he was worried plumb out of his mind for his sister, that boy still be laughing."

They both came in wearing big coats, and the second one did not remove his the entire time they were interrogating the household staff. Arliss had ordered a big fire to be built in the library hearth, where the servants all stood in a row, waiting their turns. Of course nobody knew anything, except Viola, but she merely began to squawk like a terrified chicken about her "lost lamb," and soon the Pinkertons tried to dismiss her.

"I would prefer to have Viola involved in the proceedings," said Arliss. "I think it would edify her to hear the possibilities of my daughter's fate that you might offer us. Viola, sit down on the settee." Then she gave Viola a look that nearly cooked her liver. So Viola hastily went over to the settee, and then heard all the questions as, one by one, each member of the staff, down to the boy who dug up the weeds in the flowerbeds, passed through that gauntlet as if it were the Day of Judgment, and the first Pinkerton was Saint Peter.

Arliss then presented a range of speculations that chilled Viola to the bone. She must have exhausted every bogey that a mother's paranoia could invent, not to mention some of the "penny dreadful" scenarios popular during Victorian England. Viola squirmed and winced, while Arliss watched her narrowly. "These men are here to help us," she told her. "If you tell them all you know—all you can *remember*—you will be helping Miss Sarah get saved."

"Tell me, ma'am," the tall thin detective, seated at Arliss's desk, asked gently, "has there been any kind of trouble in the house?"

"Trouble? Certainly not!"

"Could this original letter have been forged by a member of the family? Perhaps the girl herself—"

"Don't be ridiculous!" Arliss snapped. Silence fell.

"She has been lured away." Arliss lifted her lip. "There is also the distinct possibility that our cousin Marion Ransom, who I have not seen or spoken with in quite a number of years, has become senile. She is about sixty-five years old or so by now. She could have written the letter and then forgotten she ever did it. And she says herself she has arthritis—that can change a person's handwriting from time to time, can't it?"

The detective glanced up with surprise.

"Ma'am, you haven't really known this cousin in—how many years did you say? Not to say *known*, don't you know."

"Cousin Marion Ransom," Arliss intoned, "has always been an eminently respectable woman. My husband grew up in her close vicinity. She moved to San Francisco after receiving a legacy from an aunt who married one of the San Francisco Cuttles. That should speak for itself."

"It was only that you said—"

"I was venturing into the realms of wild surmise. I believe you often do that yourself, in your business. Leave no stone unturned?"

"Well, yes, ma'am."

"It could account for the outlandishness of her reply to my daughter Mavis's letter. But I am sure and certain that Cousin Marion Ransom, no matter what streak of fantasy runs in the Ransom blood—and my dear husband was gifted with a *surplus*, which he of course turned to interesting ends—has all her born wits about her."

"That's all right, then." The detective retrenched. "Now, this letter, the one to the relation. Your daughter Mavis was the one who wrote it. That right?"

"Yes."

"Can I talk to her? Where is she now?"

"In bed, where she ought to be. She has no call to hear any of this, she's a mere sixteen years old."

"We'd really rather ask her about it. Sisters often confide in each other."

Arliss gazed at him dryly, hemming her words as if they were a delicate handkerchief. "They are not close." Then she added, "I have all the facts and documents you need in the case. Mavis has only been the—I believe the term is 'model operandum.' She has nothing more to do with it."

Suddenly William spoke for the first time.

"She's an innocent little thing, if you understand me, sir. With a physical encumbrance. It'd be better for her—" He halted after receiving a curt nod from Arliss, but not before the second detective leaned forward. Even though the fire burned hot in the grate, he still wore his overcoat. His silence remained unblemished. He patted his upper overcoat pocket as if feeling for something, and then settled back in his chair.

The spokesman, despite his Texas Ranger chivalry, looked slightly irritated. "So: what we have here is a case of missing person, whereabouts unknown, misrepresentation conducted through the medium of the U.S. Mail, subject gone from these premises a total of two months and four days, relation in San Francisco, California—we will check that—envelope enclosing the letter of invitation unfortunately disappeared, subject eighteen years old, very pretty, to judge from this photograph. Who are the other people in this picture, ma'am, if you please?"

"One, as you can see, is my son, William, who sits before you," Arliss said thinly.

"Yes, ma'am."

"The girl I pointed out to you is Sarah. The other girl is my daughter Mavis."

"Um-hm." He pondered the photograph. Once more the second detective leaned forward, as if he would rise and look, fell back again.

"I have another picture of Sarah here." Arliss motioned to William, who went to the desk and opened a drawer. "This," as he handed a heavy frame to the expert, "is Sarah in her Christmas Ball gown. She was a lovely 'subject,' as you can see."

"Yes, ma'am, thank you. This picture is a little more useful. Shows more of her face."

Arliss nodded composedly.

"How much money did the subje—did your daughter have with her, when she boarded the train to go west?"

"She had some loose change, pin money. Also a fifteen-hundred-dollar bank draft, to be drawn on the Wells Fargo Bank in San Francisco. My bank telegraphed the Wells Fargo today. The draft has never been cashed."

Suddenly the second detective came to life.

"That's another indication she never got there."

It was because of these words that Viola discovered for the first time an unnerving fact about his identity, which caused her to feel a qualm where before she had been lulled into a sense of safety: he was a Yankee.

"But there's been no ransom note, remember." He chuckled, tucking his chin inside his overcoat collar. "No note addressed *to* the Ransoms *concerning* ransom. Heh heh! Anyhow—that always leaves white slavery."

"What about white slavery?" Arliss cried, outraged by the disrespectful pun. "Are you saying my daughter could have been caught by—"

"It was something that had occurred to us," the Texan said. "But don't worry, ma'am. It's very unlikely, very unlikely indeed." He shot a glance of reproof at his colleague, who shrugged.

"They may as well know the possibilities."

Arliss bristled. "It is inconceivable. Other forms of kidnap, yes. That I expect."

"Did this young woman have by any chance a sweetheart?" The Yankee glanced at each person in the room, and Viola thought that she might faint.

"Absolutely not," Arliss hissed to the Texan. "There can be no question of it. Unthinkable."

"I'll make a note of that," the Yankee said. "It won't hurt to ask around, in town."

A quiet fell. "Mr.——," Arliss murmured. "I do not think I recall your name properly, sir."

"Wheelis, ma'am," the Texan answered.

"Mr. Wheelis"—her jawbone had gone rigid—"is it the custom of your head office to send persons out to important clients who will be bent on giving offense? If so, please tell them I resent it extremely. There is no reason for me to put up with crudeness and mistrust at a time when I am hiring their services for help. Do you understand?"

"Ma'am, I'm most terribly sorry. I know Sam didn't mean to offend you." The detective turned to Sam. "Did you, Sam?"

"Mrs. Ransom. I'm trying to do my job here. I realize you're not in the best state of mind. We'll try to word things nicer." He had the kind of squashed-down face that unfortunately can turn the most benevolent smile into a smirk.

"My state of mind," Arliss murmured to a space above Mr. Wheelis, "is always impeccable."

"Yes, ma'am," said the Texan. "Don't you bother about Sam. He's just not too good at the courtesies. He'll do a bang-up job in tracing your missing daughter's whereabouts, you wait and see."

"What I have to know," Sam said, "is whether there was an elope-ment. That's the most usual cause, in a case like this. The telegrams you received from your daughter in San Francisco are the tip-off. See? Ten to one there's a boyfriend in it somewhere."

"I should not even dignify that with an answer, Mr. Wheelis," Arliss finally whispered. "But I will. No, sir."

"We can't work if we have one hand tied behind us, Mrs. Ransom," said Sam, unabashed. "Besides, what's wrong with a sweetheart, anyway? Even respectable Southern girls have them these days, I hear. It's nothing to be ashamed of."

"Mr. Wheelis—"

"Hush up now, Sam."

"I will," Sam replied. "Don't worry."

"We can put it down," Mr. Wheelis said to Arliss, "that there were no young men attending the—attending Miss Ransom in any way."

"There were plenty of young men who were mightily attracted to my daughter," Arliss contradicted. "They would have attended her if they could. She's the most beautiful girl in Bernice—in the whole county! Even the newspapers said so. But Sarah, I'm glad to say, is above all that. She won't waste herself."

"And the telegrams?" reminded Mr. Wheelis. "You received those two wires from your daughter—and then after that, not a word. I don't mean to be too bold, Mrs. Ransom, but that in itself—"

A silence dropped dead upon his remark.

"I should think it would be obvious to you," Arliss said coldly. "It is to me."

"Is it, ma'am?"

"Why, the telegrams were false! Sent to me to keep me off the scent. It's plain as the nose on your face."

"That's more or less what we felt, too, although in a somewhat different sense from what you mean." Mr Wheelis stared pensively at Arliss, his eyes holding a patience that suddenly made Viola cringe. He knows, she thought. They both do. "We'll pursue the kidnap angle, though."

"The kidnap angle," said Arliss regally, "is precisely what I think should be pursued. There can be no question but what that's what has happened."

"But the evidence——"

"There are more things in heaven and earth than are thought of by your philosophy." Arliss gazed at Mr. Wheelis intently, and Sam the Yankee scratched his nose. "You might give some thought, sir, to my ideas regarding those who might wish to defame my reputation. *That* is the kind of kidnap I would suggest."

She paused heavily. "Especially since there has been no demand for money."

"Well——"

"Oh, yes! I too am not totally a babe in the woods when it comes to the sins of the world. I have contemplated my terrible ordeal for several more hours than you, and I can say this: There are many jealous creatures on this globe, who would do anything to take certain others down a peg or two if they could. They will stop at nothing. Not even the ruin of a beautiful and innocent trusting young girl, a maiden untouched by any corruption, to achieve their ugly, vindictive ends. That is what I want your help on. You may scoff at any suggestion of a crime that does not include material gain, Mr. Wheelis. That is doubtless what you're used to. But you admit yourself there has been no effort to redeem the bank draft, no note in the mail calling for the family's lifeblood, no threats for what is termed 'filthy lucre.' Therefore, I believe there is only one answer that can fit the bill. And that is: character assassination."

"Well, ma'am," said the Texan. He glared stonily at his boot-tops, refusing to greet his colleague's leer. "We surely will investigate your ideas very thoroughly. It's just that, well, it would be unusual for folks to go to such lengths just for——and they would have to have your daughter's cooperation, or at least the facilities to keep her somewhere without a chance for escape. Do you have somebody particular in mind? I mean, you mentioned enemies——"

"I did not mention enemies." Arliss folded her hands. "My daughter, Mr.——Whatsis, could be secreted within a radius of five miles from this very spot, for all we know. At a ranchhouse, for instance.

There are a few of those around. Run by ranchers. Some of them young, and crudely bred. And perhaps eaten alive by a sense of grievance."

At this, Viola felt the blood drain from her face.

"There is a certain family, associated with us through business connections, who might feel I made myself a little too plain towards them a few years ago."

Suddenly William laughed. "Mother! You can't be implying you think *Grant* had anything to do with this." And Viola, on tenterhooks on the settee, breathed a silent rejoicing prayer that Mavis was safely in bed, and would have no more, not a jot more, to say about the situation. "I can't possibly countenance that, Mother," William said, still smiling. "Why, I was out there at the ranch just the other day to get Grant's signature on some papers."

"Keep your tongue still, young man. I am suggesting views to explore to this gentleman. You are being impudent."

"Why, I surely don't mean to be." He paused. "But I reckon I'd better say now that Grant Macafee is the last person you need to worry about. Why, heck. He's too serious."

"What is his name, this man you're talking about?" the Yankee broke in. He had suddenly taken on an air of craft that frightened Viola deeply.

"Ah—by 'serious,' do you mean that the fellow in question is an upright citizen or some such, Mr. Ransom?" the Texan intervened.

"That's one way of putting it. Yessir." William grinned. "Dry as a stick, old Grant. Foot, I went to college with him. Grade school too, for that matter. Presbyterian down to his eyeteeth."

They all turned to stare, Arliss included. He lifted his hand gently. "What I mean by serious, though, is that old Grant is just the proudest boy I think ever breathed air. That's what I meant." Then he reclined into his chair.

"Pride!" cried Arliss. "Sometimes, William, I have to wonder at your faculties." She tilted her head sublimely. "That, Mr.—Wheelis!

is the nub of it all. If misbegotten pride, pride with no rhyme or reason, is not a likely motive for this kind of crime, then I don't know what is. My son's simplicity can't seem to range past the missionary tracts. But mine does." As if the fire in the hearth had shriveled her listeners to their real dimensions, which the grandeur of her library had disguised, she said, "There is pride, and there is something else: and the something else, often called pride by mistake, is the proper estimate of a person's worth. That is an indisputable truth. There is only one thing to say about the person in question, and that is that his last name is Macafee."

"Still, Mother," William said quietly, "I have to tell you that you're being a little bit harsh on old Grant. Why, everybody in town thinks highly of him. Just like they did Archibald."

"Grant Macafee may be a different peck of greens from Archibald Macafee, but they both came from the same pot. Is this the best Yale University can do!"

William spread his hands high, and smiled.

"If you really have just cause, ma'am, to think that this Mr. Macafee had a part in Miss Ransom's disappearance—" Mr. Wheelis was trying not to sound dubious. Viola fastened all her will on the encouragement of that hope. But the Yankee shattered it with a single promise.

"We'll explore it, Mrs. Ransom. Count on that."

And Arliss condescended a nod.

"Mother, you can't think of siccing these nice gentlemen on poor old Grant! Not *truly*, now."

She did not reply.

"It's a wrong thing to do." William meditated on Arliss's set face. "You might be starting something there's no need to start. And who knows where it might end."

And thus it was, out of sheer self-protection, that Grant Macafee was goaded into marrying Sophie March.

The Seeds of War

The morning after the Pinkertons left the Ransom house that night in January 1922, they went out to Grant Macafee's ranch. Then, over the next few weeks, a series of advertisements appeared in the personal columns of newspapers across the United States. Thanks to Mavis, the scrapbook contains several of these ads: here, an example from Little Rock, Arkansas:

> Will those with designs to Ransom their eighteen-year-old goods in Central Texas please state their terms as soon as possible. The market is open, and negotiations are welcome. There will be no penalty for tardiness, so long as goods are in fine condition.

Arliss herself composed this cryptic opus. She also contrived several others, one of which the *Dallas Times Herald* carried for two months: "I will gladly Ransom the Lionhearted daughter if only the minstrel will come to sing his song beneath my window."

There was no doubt in Arliss's mind that she had managed to communicate her intent, suggest an amnesty for the criminal, and cloak the identity of both crime and victim in the pages of a journal published too close to Bernice for less convoluted means. The capital *R* in Ransom could be read as a misprint by the innocent. No one outside the Ransom household and the Pinkerton office, except for Grant Macafee, knew that Sarah was officially missing. And even Grant did not know for sure. From what the detectives reported later (Viola listening through the door) their evasions had been deft.

He must have assumed it was his affair with Sarah they wished to confirm. But his outrage that detectives were there at all would have been enough to seal our fates.

Especially mine.

It was after the *Dallas Times Herald* ad had run for three weeks that Sam, the Yankee Pinkerton, finally left the case. In the letter prompted by his complaint, the presiding officer said, "Our operative feels that he is too confined. With all respect for your desire for incognito, he begs that he be allowed to proceed with the methods originally outlined to you, which he has found profitable on past cases. We feel that his record justifies him in this request, and will wait for your decision in the matter." Arliss, up to this point, had restricted the detectives to Grant Macafee's harassment and the placement of newspaper ads. Her answer to the Pinkerton letter came immediately: "Fire your operative and replace him." But Sam's dismissal from the case had some side advantages. The Pinkertons (a second Texan now accompanied Mr. Wheelis when they called again in Bernice) were now freed to widen their scope. Sarah had then been missing for four and a half months. It was time to get down to business.

Arliss grudgingly agreed.

Mr. Wheelis asked for a scientific scrutiny of the letter from "Cousin Marion."

This had been an early request of Sam the Yankee. Mr. Wheelis now grew unequivocal. He told Arliss, in a courtly way, that Grant was spotless. Each of his moves was accounted for. He certainly could not be suspected of elopement or kidnap, engaged, as he now was, to another woman.

His new partner seconded him.

So it was that a famous graphologist, equipped with a trail of credentials won in criminal suits, traveled down on the train from Chicago to Bernice, and was made a guest of the Ransoms. Many were the forgers, the con men and counterfeiters, he had helped "put behind bars." Many were his mentions in tabloids and newspaper stories. When Viola described him, she said, "He looked just like a hoot owl, that writing man. He looked like a hoot owl about to eat up his mouse and spit out the bones." Perhaps a career in the witness box had given him this predatory air. But I suspect that Viola was influenced by the enormous pair of glasses, thick-lensed for close work, which enhanced his eyes. Little did anyone, least of all the graphologist, realize what a nemesis he was to prove.

The day the graphologist sat in the Ransom library to go over the evidence, even Arliss was visibly affected by a sense of anticipation. Her full cheeks sucked in. Her hands roamed the georgette of her lap. Her eyes shone brighter, as if touched by a mild fever. She seemed less all of a piece, autonomous, than usual. She did not really believe that on this, the first day, the expert would sift out the facts from his sieves of handwriting. It would take a long while, she insisted, for the idiosyncrasies of the criminal to show themselves, for the identity to be traced. But Mr. Wheelis and his partner betrayed their nerves, twitching a little. Only William stayed still, sprawling across the sofa next to his mother.

Viola, watching them all from the settee, ready to go fetch coffee, did not comprehend entirely the graphologist's function. He dawdled over his little microscope mirror. Arliss once again reassured the assembly, "I can't believe that thing is going to tell us who wrote that letter.

"Actually, I'm sure and convinced that it was done by Cousin Marion herself, in a lunatic trance. Or if not," she amended, "it will have been written so cleverly—I won't again say by who—that no microscope will ever be able to prove it." Nevertheless, her empiric faith remained greater than she declared. She gazed at the microscope as if at a Grail.

"It is I who will prove it," murmured the graphologist, shuffling through the pile of folded papers on the desk. Selecting one, he peered carefully at it, and then slid it under the optic tube.

Silence reigned.

"Can you tell offhand if that letter was written by a man or a woman?" William asked.

"Oh, yes." The expert's words sounded muffled by concentration.

"You can?" said Arliss sternly. "Why didn't you say so?"

"In a moment, please, Mrs. Ransom." The expert, without taking his eye from the lens, reached over to a pad and scribbled a note. "Unclosed lower case *a*—"

"Well? Which is it? A man, of course. What else?"

It was at this moment that the expert, finding his sight obscured, raised his head, pinched the glasses from his nose, took a handkerchief from his breast pocket, and wiped the lenses clean, and Viola knew him to be doom.

"It was written by a woman," he said pleasantly. "A young woman, I *should* say. She has attempted to change the slant of her script, but occasionally some letters are beyond her control. For instance, if you observe the *e* in 'invite' you will see that it is tilted a few degrees more to the right than the preceding *i*. The *e* is an excellent index, when the question of slant arises." He slipped the glasses back on, and pored over the letter.

"A—what?" Arliss gasped. William sat up on the sofa and patted her hand.

"An *e*," replied the oblivious graphologist. "It is a novice's work, of course. I should say this was the first time she had ever tried to forge anything. Very elementary, really—very little challenge. I expect Benjamin, in New Orleans, would have been equal to it, although I might have shown him some of the finer points. However, in a document like this one, finer points are more or less irrelevant. The mere fact that the writer has used such crude means to disguise the obvious· lets us know who she is. Forgery is a very complex art, very complex, and requires that one change the shape of every letter with a sure hand before it can be successful. For instance, if she had troubled to shift the curvature of the upper case *D*, and elongate the downstroke, it might have been a little more convincing, but not much." He glanced up, smiling, bemused. "I might remind you of the Seccles case, in Grand Rapids, and the shakey downstroke on the *K* of the false will that was the tell-tale, the tell-tale—hmph! Those uncertain strokes, even when the writer has altered the shape of the letter, are all the repudiation we need. Benjamin could have told you that. Nearer than Chicago, too. New Orleans is nearer, I mean."

"A young *woman*—who—?" Arliss panted.

"I don't know, however," the graphologist added, "if Benjamin could have detected this little point right away." He rifled through the sheaf of letters and papers, all of them specimens of other people's handwriting provided to him for comparison, and singled out a note-card, which Viola recognized as Arliss's stock for guest lists, the kind she supplied Sarah to use for her luncheons and teas. "This might have eluded Benjamin. But only at first study. The comparison between her ordinary way of inscribing a lower case *m*, for example, and the cunning—well, perhaps cunning is slightly too emphatic—in splitting the space between the forged *m*'s double curve—she noticed that, you see— Is there a train leaving town this evening, by the way?"

No one heard him.

It took him a brief moment to realize this.

In the ensuing flutter of motion and cries, Viola was given an instant of pure revelation before she had to race pell-mell to the kitchen for water, for brandy, and this was what she saw: that of all the people in the room, Arliss had demonstrated the most surprise. And that William revealed the least. His face was devoid of anything but a calm expectation fulfilled, and concern for his mother.

Arliss's surprise, in fact, was far and away the most powerful emotion. She sagged backwards from her rigid posture on the sofa, falling sideways, her mouth hanging in a skewed *O*, her facial muscles flexing involuntarily. Two bands of white marked her cheekbones. A white froth seeped around her lips. The lips grew purple, as did her cheeks, but the chin and middle forehead likewise were white.

Everyone surged around her except the graphologist, who blinked. Perhaps he was registering the paradox of the rational and the irrational which he had brought to bear on the Ransom family and himself.

The detectives, though at first engaging only mild surprise at the outcome of the graphologist's report, started slapping Arliss's wrists and arms. Mr. Wheelis turned to Viola as she ran for the door: "The shock!" By the time she returned with a water glass in one hand, brandy bottle in the other, he was yelling at William, "What's the doctor's number?" and then, without waiting to hear, he wrested the telephone from the desk and flipped the cradle up and down. "Central!" he roared, but the roar broke, and ended in a bleat. "Give me the doctor, quick! We should have arranged for this," he shouted at the graphologist over his shoulder. "You knew perfectly well— Doctor? Come to the Ransom house, as quick as you can. Mrs. Ransom has had a stroke."

On the word *stroke*, William paused in the effort to lift his mother straight.

The graphologist cleared his throat, and blinked again rapidly as if his eyelids had snagged on a cinder. The inane accusation had arrested him, or perhaps the preposterous notion that he had had a part in all this. He did not move at all.

And Viola, the water glass suspended in her hand and splattering its last drops on the Aubusson carpet, saw how Arliss's left eyelid flickered, flickered, and dragged downward as if melting, as did the left side of her face altogether.

Arliss's Synopsis of Life

There is no such thing as pure recontation. Every historian has a personal plan.

I know this to be true from the many hours I have spent poring over the tomes in Grandfather's library and contrasting the sometimes violent differences in the accounts of major events that I find there. No one, it seems, really agrees with another. Every writer views the past through his own chip of smoked glass.

Sometimes I wake in the night and lie under the satin sheets, listening to the soft breathing beside me, and wonder: where precisely *did* it all begin? Where in this smelting works of human folly was my future conceived? At what moment did they actually drop the spark in the crucible?

There is only one way to find out: track the lines back. Track them through the story; find the place wherein they must converge.

That way lies freedom for us all.

ON A day in June, a dry day following the dry spring, Viola climbed the stairs to Arliss's room.

She toted a silver tray, jamming it against her stomach for steadiness. Entering the wide hall, she crossed the foyer with its white panels, the loops of blue shadow across the bright parquetry. The leaded fanlight above the door caught the sun and prismed it — each cut glass a jewel. Pausing for a moment on the landing, she turned to see how the Venetian mirror above the credenza multiplied the jewels in turn, scattering them across the inlaid floor; they lay, mirages of brilliance, and as she stared she felt she was overlooking a gully full of wealth. Never had she envied the people she worked for, never coveted their vanities. But now she tried to imagine what it would be if the fractures of light were real, and she could scoop them up and let them trickle like rain through her fingers— diamonds loose as gravel, richness common enough to salt through her tough black hair. The dollops of summer light glittered more than Arliss's rings, which throughout illness remained on her stark hands, dimmed by smears of body oil, like mineral deposits embedded in bone. Shifting the heavy tray a little to one side of her hip, Viola sighed. The nurse kept insisting on using the Georgian silver for Arliss (for herself!) instead of plain tin; it weighed Viola down as much as the heat. That nurse was letting her post go to her head. Just a poor white girl from Bernice that William went to high school with is all she was. And Viola was forever to be hefting this silver platter up and down, her arms aching, working her legs to the tune of the nurse's wants.

Just as she was about to trudge on, she gave the litter of jewels a last look. Suddenly, in one area on the parquetry, they vanished, doused before her eyes. She glimpsed at the mirror, and saw the reason why. Mavis had surfaced there, staring out at her.

Viola swerved around to where she hunched, whey-faced and sulky, in the living room doorway. "You give me a spook, setting there in that mirror. It was like you swum out of the glass."

"Huh! I can't swim. You taking that tray up to Mama?"

"Yessum." Ever since that morning the previous January, Viola had minced words with Mavis.

"What is it? Can I see?" Mavis sidled into the foyer and up the stairs, shoving her nose over the tray's edge.

"Ain't nothing but some ice tea for Miss Arliss and the nurse, and some molasses cookies of Bessie's."

"I think Belinda's getting fat, working here. Wicky told me she used to be the littlest thing in school, but I noticed how she has to use another notch to buckle her nurse's belt now. There's a gray line, and the old hole is all frayed."

"Yessum. Well, I better get along now."

"Wait a minute." Mavis wedged herself against the tray.

"Don't you make me tote you up alongside this heavy old thing."

"I won't. I just want to talk for a minute." She pulled back, and squatted there on the tread. "I'm so bored I could cry. Nobody does anything around here anymore."

"Your mama's sick, that's why. You—seventeen years old! You got plenty of things you could be doing."

"Like what?"

"You got your embroidery that Miss Arliss started you on last spring. You got your scrap album. You got that puppy dog to play with."

"He's sick too. He's as sick as Mama, I think. Ezra told me he'll probably die from it."

"You better go tend to him, then, so he don't."

"Nothing *I* can do to help him."

"Listen here, child." Viola placed the tray on the tread above her, and massaged her arms. "I hear how you plagued Mr. William for that little dog, saying you don't got a thing in the world to love and see to. So now you got to tend to it, if it's hurt or sick. That's what we do, when things depend on us to live."

"Viola?" Mavis fluffed out the starched ruffles of her dress, and hooked her knees up under them. "What made Mama sick?"

"Doctor say a vein in her brain busted on her. You know that."

"It was really Sarah, wasn't it? Sarah being gone. I know what all those men from Dallas were doing here. Wicky said it was about business. Ha! Nobody tells me anything. And now I'll never get to San Francisco, or have a nice time."

Viola looked up the stairwell, fearful to catch the nurse eavesdropping. "That subject's done closed, Mr. William said, and your mama too. You just hush up about Miss Sarah."

"What were you doing here on the stairs when I came in?" Pensively Mavis ran her hand over the white flounces, batting them so they bounced.

"I was resting. Bessie's going to swat you good, mussing up her clean starch job with your dirty fingers."

"Funny place to rest. Were you thinking about Sarah?"

"Nome, I was not. You mind your own business now."

"I think about her almost all the time. Nobody asked me anything about her leaving, did they? But I knew things." She paused, and then declared, eyes widening, "I even decided to tell Grant Macafee, one time last spring. I was going to go out to his ranch. But then he married Sophie March, and we weren't invited to the wedding. So I didn't. It serves him right."

"How'd you plan on getting *out* to his ranch?" cried Viola, aghast.

"I was going to—hire a taxicab!" With relief, Viola saw that Mavis had invented this plan on the spur of the moment. "I would get the money from Wicky, and telephone the livery stable, and go out there and talk about Sarah. Grant would have listened." She was engrossed in her fantasy: the white-dressed schoolgirl, coming to arouse, to smooth things; the angel of mercy—who knew what Mavis pictured? "*Were* we invited to his wedding, Viola?"

"I can't figure you wasn't. Mrs. March sent the invitation, but I reckon folks here got too much to do." She gnawed her lower lip. "You don't go messing around with Mr. Grant and his new bride, now, honey," she said, loading her words with cautious tact; there was no telling just how much Mavis understood. "They want to be all by themselves; they don't want you to haunt them none. They been married no time at all! You just put on their shoes, and see what it feel like."

"Don't haunt them! You mean don't talk to anybody! Live here all alone and let the whole world alone."

"Just leave it be," said Viola.

"Wicky isn't letting them alone. I went into town with him the other day and saw him talking with Sophie outside Sopwith's."

"Why, what's wrong with that?"

"Oh—I don't know. It just reminded me of something. The way they stood. Something about Grant and Sarah." Before Viola could ask what, she said, "I want some ice tea, too. Give me some, Viola."

"You go ask Bessie."

Mavis's hand snaked out, and lifted one of the tall glasses from the tray.

"That ain't for you, child!"

"Belinda won't mind me having a sip. She likes me. She likes to talk. You know what she said?"

"What?" Mavis set the glass down, and Viola thought the nurse was getting no more than she deserved.

"She said she saw Grant and Sophie's wedding. Well—saw the ending of it, with them coming out the door, and people throwing rice on them. And the bridesmaids in lovely lovely pink dresses, with flowers. Not too many people came, though, Belinda said."

"Um, hmm. I got to go now, child, I got to get this tea up to your mama."

"I started to tell her who Grant really wanted to marry. I *wanted* to tell her."

"Oh, *child!*" This time the danger was so great Viola strained forward to seal Mavis's mouth. "You don't know *nothing*, you hear? You just imagining something. You just scatting round with what you think you know, what you think you see—you don't talk about it *no more.*"

"Oh, don't worry." Mavis tilted her injured expression sideways. "When she asked about Sarah, all I said was that she was in San Francisco, and we didn't know how she was getting along. I can keep a secret, Viola. Besides, it's my secret as much as anybody's. I was the one who found out, I wrote to—"

"You hear me now," Viola interrupted quickly. Once more she scanned upwards, and her satisfaction when she saw the empty hall was fleeting and harried. "When that nurse ask you about Miss Sarah, you don't tell her nothing. She just trying to shine you up, to find out what ain't her business. You hear?"

"How can you say that? She's my friend. She says she feels sorry for me, all alone with nothing to do, and she—"

"That's all I got to say. You don't make no trouble. You go be friends if you want to, but you hush up."

"I won't be friends with you," Mavis snapped. "That's for certain."

"All right by me. Now go along, and be friends to your pup dog, instead of letting him die all alone without no nursing."

"Good-bye!" Mavis humped up from the stair tread, staggering away. Viola sighed wearily and lifted the tray.

"OH, FINE. Tea—I'm so thirsty!" said the nurse from the chair beside the ducal bed where she sat reading. Viola could see her magazine, with a cover picture of a woman in crinolines giving a horseman a gold locket. "Are you thirsty, Mrs. Ransom?"

No answer came from the bed. The query was rhetorical; none was expected. Arliss lay propped up on lace pillows. Her eyes were open. The left eye drooped pathetically. Once in a while it winked. Her left cheek sank beneath it, a straggle of hair winding over the temple; the nurse often remarked how hard it was to keep her "looking nice," but only Viola detected Arliss's little static wince when she overheard it. The nurse chatted on as if Arliss had gone deaf.

Since the stroke overwhelmed her three months before, she had not spoken a word. Doctor Middleton had said her speech was impaired, but that she could speak if she tried. It was a question of desire. For now, nothing shook her from her listlessness. Arliss Ransom, who would not express, by look or gesture, anything she did not mean, lay transfixed in a parody of humor. Only Viola recognized the loss, the will and cynicism behind those eyes, and something else when they turned toward her: accusation.

"Put it there, Viola," said the nurse, pointing to the bedside table. "I'll give it to her in a minute. This *Saturday Evening Post* has some mighty strange stories in it sometimes, if you ask me. One here about a man who takes a balloon ride and goes all the way to Mars. I think the person wrote it must be crazy. What'd he eat all that time, is what I want to know." She sighed, picked up her glass, sparing the silver tray a glance before she drank, and smiled a little bucktoothed smile. "I was reading a story to Mrs. Ransom before you came in, it's a much better one. About this handsome young man who goes off to the war, fighting for the boys in gray, and his sweetheart, she has to toil on without him. That's it, on the cover. She seemed to like it, didn't you Mrs. Ransom?" She rummaged on the plate for a cookie, popping it into her mouth.

"Can I give Miss Arliss her tea, ma'am? I think she feeling thirsty." The vision of Arliss in her wreckage suddenly drove Viola with guilt. She was mourning, Viola knew—mourning over Sarah, whom she could not reach. The curtain at the window hung dense with shadow, the sunlight netted and turned back on itself. All through the house, a stuffy silence lay thick as dust.

"I usually do that." The nurse yawned, plucked the sprig of mint from the glass, and sipped her tea. She looked up at Viola. Something in her stance must have pricked her curiosity, for she peered wonderingly. "Well—I suppose it'd be all right."

Viola took up the glass, bending to Arliss. The mouth that could not be closed altogether twisted open a little more, and it seemed to Viola that Arliss was conveying an eloquence she had stifled for years, a need so much grander than thirst, which the sip of tea she offered would only symbolically appease. "Here, Miss Arliss," she muttered, slipping her arm around Arliss's neck. She raised her and held the glass to her seeking lips. "Have you some of this here cold tea. It's going to make you feel better." She tipped the glass, and the ice chinked against the crystal sides. "That's right," she murmured. "That's all right now."

Arliss's tongue, awry between the crooked lips, ran into the tea and then back inside her mouth. She took another sip, the slack left side of her mouth blowing outwards. Her eyes fixed on Viola's and did not stray, even when the glass accidentally nudged her chin; and suddenly Viola was visited with an absolute conviction: they apprehended one another.

Then, for a second, Arliss's left eye defied its valance of lid, widening.

"Ithe." The left eye winked violently. She gargled deep in her throat. "Ithe. I-i-icccce!" and she raised her good right hand, shoving the glass back at Viola's chest, and wheezed. The wheeze grew and grew. "Icccce!" she said again, and Viola realized she was laughing, proffering the key to the enigma of all that had happened, her paralysis, her mislaid daughter, her climb, her one-sided enmity with Archibald Macafee—even the detectives, even the bed she lay in. She forced it out, the magic word hissing on the dragging lip to share with Viola: a talisman, a good joke. "Iccce. Biola."

"Yessum," Viola croaked. "It's ice. That's what it is." She clutched the glass, spilling its contents on her bosom. "Just cold ice, for a hot old day." And then she, too, joined Arliss, breaking into cackles of laughter; and the amazed nurse stared goggle-eyed in her chair, before jumping up and racing down the hall, down the wide stairs, and into the gulch of diamonds to telephone Doctor Middleton that Mrs. Ransom had come out with something to say, after all.

Where Sarah Went

It was dusk, the close of the signal afternoon in which Arliss broke her long reverie, and confided her summary of cause and effect.

Everyone moved more briskly through the house. In the kitchen Bessie decided to stay up late, checking silverware for tarnish, going through the table linens, setting out extra bread to rise. "We all been living too dreary lately," she said to Viola. Mavis flittered about the living room, arranging flowers in the vases, convinced that now things would pick up and she would become the hub of a brand new social life. Doctor Middleton had come and gone. The nurse had dared to try a little lip rouge on herself, and gussied up her hair; over the dinner table she batted her eyes at William, but Viola saw with relief that he paid her only his customary compliments: a waggish remark about Florence Nightingale, a thank-you for his mother's progress. He seemed in fact less talkative than on other nights. Viola thought his mother must be on his mind. Back in the kitchen, Viola reminded Bessie that extra bread would be a waste, there wouldn't be any more people at breakfast than usual. But Bessie did not heed. On this night made celebratory, it was as if the drought had broken, or a joyous emergency been declared, which only food would stoke.

Viola left it to the nurse to discuss the words Arliss had spoken. Her own share in them was a solitary pleasure, a mystery inexplicable.

After dinner, she went out onto the back gallery, to sit awhile in the soft climbing darkness. A night bird chirped. Fireflies pulsed beyond her, little flickers of phosphorous; she remembered evenings when Sarah and William were small, jumping about the yard of the old frame house in Bernice and trapping them in Mason jars. That was before the ice money came. She swatted a june bug away from her ear. The jasmine was still in flower, and its pale dangling trumpets hung over the gallery roof, drafting a sweetness that stole down and faded on the twilight. The night loomed hollow, warm and vast. Stars constricted in the endless sky. A single square of gold fell against the dark lawn from an open window above her head, and she watched the gold shift when the breeze pulled the curtains, turning the patch of grass into a luminous emblem.

After a time she heard the squeak of the screen door to the kitchen. Someone slipped out onto the gallery. In the shimmering darkness she smelled cigar smoke, and knew who it was before she saw his form, milky and black, cutting the shimmer in two. He ignored the rustic chairs and instead stood for a moment looking at the light square on the grass, then dropped down on the edge and settled there. An owl called from the wood at the lawn's end. The tip of the cigar burned steadily.

"More hoot owls this summer than there used to be," he said.

"Seem like. Maybe they know the house done got quieter, maybe that's why."

"I reckon it's because of the heat. It keeps them restless."

"Shoot, it's always been hot here. Long before *you* was born to hear them hooty owls."

The easy silence surrounded them, counterpointed here and there with the whir of crickets and the owl's questioning note.

"Fine thing, Mother talking at last," said William after awhile.

"Mm-hmm."

"Been a day for messages."

"That's the truth."

"I got a message today." His voice was quiet, slumberous. "It came in the mail, down at the ice factory office."

"Hmph. I don't care nothing for that business."

"It wasn't business, exactly. I got it right before Belinda called to tell me about Mother speaking."

"Where'd it come from?"

She asked lazily, still drowsing in the slow cooling breeze; but something had invaded the air around her.

"From a town I never heard of. Chatham, Illinois."

"Where's that?"

"It's just some little town in the state of Illinois. On up north a stretch." He sent a curl of smoke from his nostrils, and tapped the cigar on the gallery boards. "There was a message in it for you, too."

"Me?" Now tension bound her. Watchful, guarded, she still was too discreet to turn her head to William and catch his eyes, striking against the gloom.

"She said," sighed William gently, "she said, 'Tell Viola everything went all right. Tell her it wasn't so hard, and I wasn't afraid. That I miss her and love her. Tell her thank you.'"

Viola said nothing. She sat motionless in the hush. The jasmine vine scented the air; the crickets burst shrilly across the garden. She could hear William's breath sing in and out, above his closed lips.

"So it's all right. You don't have to worry anymore," he murmured finally.

"Praise the Lord," she said, low.

"I've got the letter here." He rose from his elbows, one hand scrabbling in his shirt pocket. "Would you like to hear it?" He gave forth a ghostly chuckle. "Been such a to-do about letters in this house the last few months, I can't hardly believe this one's the real McCoy. However." A slim white rectangle emerged in his hand. He used it to wave away the same tenacious june bug. "It is."

"Uh-huh. I expect it would be." Viola stared out into the sky. After a long moment, she said, "I reckon we'd hear sooner. But it's hard for her, I expect, tending to what she's got to see to."

He unfolded the letter, tilting it towards the lamp of filtered gold on the grass.

"'Dear William,'" he began, and cleared his throat softly. "'I want to tell you where I am, because I need to ask for your help. It isn't for me, otherwise I would go my own way and keep silent. I know there's been a lot of worry by now.'" He paused, his voice abating, and raised his eyes briefly to the far corner of the house, the second floor, where no light shone from Arliss's window. Then he continued:

I saw an advertisement in a paper that Mother must have written, so I know she found out I wasn't at Cousin Marion's in San Francisco. She might know by now that I wrote the letter, too. That doesn't bother me. You'll understand.

I have had the child I was to have. I've given it to a kind lady I have boarded with for the past five months. I didn't want to leave it, but that is best, because I'm not able to look after it, and she has a husband who doesn't mind a new baby around the house. The child doesn't look like either its father or me—no Ransom showing, nor the other. What I want is for you to send some money, on a regular monthly basis, to this couple whose names I'll give you at the end of the letter. They'll bring it up for me. I can't come back home ever, as I'm sure you realize. I've gotten a job, and will give the people what I can. But they need more than I can contribute, so I ask you to please do this. I miss you all. Please don't tell Mother you've heard from me. She would only try to interfere and mess things up. And she would hate the way I've done them, and get into a tizzy. If she ever wants to know, you can tell her you are sure I am safe and well. Don't blame anybody about this either. He didn't want it this way. But I couldn't give in to all he wanted. So it was nobody's fault but my own.

One more thing. Tell Viola everything went all right. Tell her it wasn't so hard, and I wasn't afraid. That I miss her and love her. Tell her—

His voice, so remote as to meld with the darkness, lifted free for a second and rang with low certitude. "—thank you."

Viola waited. "She don't say if it a girl or a boy."

"Nome. Maybe she decided it doesn't matter. To us."

Almost dreamily, Viola asked, "What you going to do?"

"Why," William said, sounding vaguely surprised, "send the money, of course. Nobody else to help the poor little thing along. I can't have Sarah fretting her mind out about its welfare. We'll see it's taken care of." Then he hesitated, leaned back, and touched her hand. "You did the best you could, for all of us. Understand, I don't blame you one whit, doing what you did."

"Yes, sir."

"Out of love," he added. "That's the main thing." He squinted up at a cluster of stars above the black treetops. "Foot. All we can ever do in this life, is to leave each other alone."

"You ain't thinking of doing nothing else, then?"

His voice dropped to a level above a whisper, but so lenient that Viola could scarcely hear. "Nome."

Then, when the crickets had flared louder and subsided, he said, "Reckon old Grant would be better off never knowing, too."

"He don't," Viola answered firmly.

"I know it." William smiled, as if at a private thought.

"How?" It began to dawn on her, in a slow amazed circle of feeling, that William who sat beside her, for so many years her nominal son, the tertiary object of her devotion, after Sarah, after Arliss in her distant and close vitality, had now in the shimmering night and silence become someone else. Perhaps he had been someone else all along.

"I knew it was him," sighed William, "because who else could it be? Sarah had spent her whole childhood either hiding from him or staring at him like he was a damned soul she couldn't get enough of. Besides, he sure didn't keep coming here last summer because he liked my company."

"No, sir. That's the truth."

"Poor old Grant. The trouble with him is, he has no imagination." He brought out another cigar, long and thin, and scraped a match on the sole of his boot. "Or too much. I wonder sometimes."

"Maybe."

"Dry as a stick." He puffed the first gusts of smoke. "That's what I tried to tell those Pinkertons and Mother. You can't tamper in what's none of your business." He exhaled reflectively, and added, "Poor Sophie."

Viola said nothing.

"Besides," said William when the cigar had dropped its stubby ash, "Mavis told me." Viola flinched. "Why, you didn't expect her to keep a thing like that to herself, did you? And it was better, her telling me. That way she let off the steam."

"That nurse——" ventured Viola.

"She won't tell Belinda. If she says she will, she's just trying to get a rise out of you." He drew a long stream from the cigar. "Imagine that. Mother finally said something today. That's a step, at any rate. Ain't it, old lady?" He gave Viola's hand a little squeeze, where it rested on the boards, dark on dark.

"It sure is," she answered to her employer. "It sure enough is."

What Sarah Did Next

After that summer day of nouns in 1922, it was barely a fortnight before Arliss began to attempt predicates. One morning, in a limp late week of August, the nurse Belinda heard
the makings of a perfect sentence foundering from Arliss's throat. At
first she coaxed it along, crying aloud to Viola to come listen. But
when the sentence emerged at last, white and undefiled, it sent
Belinda pelting to her own room in tears.

"If you can dress your own hair like a small-town whore, you can
at least see to it mine doesn' look like a ras's nest." On the heels of
Belinda's flight, she continued, "Can't keep me looking nice, indeed!"

At that Viola hastened to the dressing table, grabbed up the silver-
backed brush and comb, and for the next hour brushed and combed
Arliss's steel gray hair, swirling it up into a knot at the back, massaging the grainy scalp, tucking the side curls into place, all the while
listening to Arliss jerk out articulate phrases: "Lip rouge! Cherry red.
She think I'm blind as well as deaf, that I can't see what she's trying to
do? Catch William! Imagine that cracker for a daughter-in-law!
There's life—me yet. *You* can tell me, Viola, if she tries—flighty
hussy. I saw look she gave him, when he came up say good morning.
She can walk. To Bernice. You go with William when he takes her
back to town. You watch, see to it he doesn't give more than wages. I
don't mean money. Tell him—no, I'll tell him. Now hightail it
downstairs, and get William come up here, so I show him I'm not
just bundle bones and rags. Thas better." She inspected the hand mirror, her left eye winking in burlesque.

As Viola passed Belinda's closed door, she could hear the sound of wails and sobbing, but her excitement was lessened by a sense of practical relief. William might be moved by compassion, but he wouldn't be tempted beyond his native inclinations. Viola had yet to see him stare hard at any woman. As for Mavis, she would probably interpret Belinda's loss as a personal act of spite; the social life she hoped for still remained a delusion.

Out in the stable garage in the scorching heat, she searched for William amidst the straw, the side-by-side loose boxes of horse flesh and Lincoln roadster. Arliss's Pierce Arrow stood disused and enormous beneath the shadow of a roof beam. William had mentioned putting it up on blocks. Recently Grant Macafee had purchased a Pierce Arrow, she had heard, for his wife Sophie to ride around town in.

William usually liked to go over his car at this time of day, checking the oil, rubbing away any specks of dirt. But he was nowhere available to her eye. She strained against the fickle rays of sunlight, swarmed with shadow and powder from the straw, and still could not see him. Then a movement shuttered the window of the Pierce Arrow. A white duck sleeve rose against the white glaze and glassy light, and Viola suddenly made him out, lolling at an angle against the driver's seat of his mother's car as if he was napping there. But his voice floated across the hay-matted floor and the dusty air to where she stood.

"You roving around in this weather for my sake?"

"Your mama want to talk to you," said Viola abruptly. "She's in a strong mood."

"Is she?" He lowered the window. The white sleeve draped across the green paintwork. He tapped his fingers idly on the side.

"What you doing, setting in that car?"

"It's hot out there, but hotter in here."

Viola did not see this as an answer. "You going to smother."

"Naw. Heat stroke, maybe. This big old car is like a steam bath. I was tempted when I got in to strip off my clothes."

"You gone crazy?"

"Foot, Viola." He smiled through the aperture, while the fingers drummed a rhythm: "Sweet Georgia Brown," a beat she recognized as the same dance tune he was forever playing these days, over and over on his gramaphone in the library after dinner. "I just wanted to sit some place and think to myself. That's all."

"How come in *there?*"

"There's no place more private than the inside of a Pierce Arrow. You ever noticed that?"

"Naw, sir, because I ain't never been inside one."

"Don't get scratchy on me. Just reckoned I'd give it a try."

"I raised you better than for you to keel over from craziness and the heat. Maybe you already *had* that heat stroke. Get on out of there and come up to your mama."

The white duck sleeve drew back into the interior where she could not see it. After an instant the car door swung open. William slid one leg, and then the other, over the running board and out onto the hay, but did not emerge completely.

"You better change your shirt and coat," Viola snapped. "You look a mess already, and only ten o'clock."

"Was it Belinda got her going?"

"Now, how come you to know that?"

"Poor Belinda. All she wants is to get on out of Bernice and move to a city where there's some excitement. I figured she could earn a higher salary by nursing Mother privately and then do something for herself."

"She don't behave like it," said Viola, giving him a sideways look.

They strolled together out of the stable and up the drive to the house. The post oaks veiled them with weak gauzy shade, no cooler than the gravel underfoot.

"Does she want me to take her on into town, or what?"

"She want me to go with you. Then she want you to drop Miss Belinda off at her folks' and hire somebody else, quick."

"I'll give her a little extra something. She's done a fine job."

"Your mama said——"

"Now, Viola. Never mind what she said." He laughed. "She probably wasn't talking about money."

"Hmph. No ladies ever come to this house painted up like the circus before."

"That's the fashion now. You forget how young Belinda is." William chuckled, his hand on the front door handle. "The ladies who come here have always been too well bred to be anything but pale as camellias. Don't worry, though. They will."

"I ain't seen Mrs. Macafee scrubbing her mouth with no lip rouge. She's just as young."

William turned. His eyes, so sleepy in crisis or amusement, meditated upon her with a studious intensity.

"Sophie March Macafee will be pale for the rest of her life," he said after a moment. "It's her nature, and it suits her." Then he smiled again. "Don't you start making mountains out of molehills about Belinda. *I* know how you tend to do. You reckon because you raised me that I'm going to get wild."

"Hmph!"

"We'd better go see Mother, she's probably writhing in the sheets by now."

"You go on in. I'm going around the back, I got to get her lunch tray ready before I can go to town."

"Leaving me to the lions, are you?"

"I done had mine, Mr. William." Viola snorted through her nose before paddling around the house to the kitchen door. She knew William would not fail to hear it.

AN HOUR later, she watched from the rumble seat of the roadster while the backs of William's and Belinda's heads performed a pantomime of chagrin and friendly consolation. The car's roar drowned out anything she might overhear. Belinda had descended the wide front steps with a face mottled red from insult and weeping. Her puffy eyes turned resentfully from William to Viola already waiting in the rumble seat. She refused help with the suitcase (now resting on Viola's knees) and stomped over the door sill and into the passenger's seat; William had had to take the suitcase from her by gentlemanly force. Now Viola could see him apologizing, and Belinda's handkerchief swiping occasionally at her eyes, but already she offered a profile which by the time they pulled onto Main Street had grown languid and forgiving. William kept his eyes always on the road. The car spun recklessly past the post office, leaving a newsboy and the shoeshine man grinning in admiration. Viola waved at the shoeshine man, her uncle on her father's side, and yelled, "We going to go see Miss Marianne before we get done in here," and then settled herself primly behind the suitcase once more.

They skidded to a stop outside Belinda's parents' house, on an unpaved street of chinaberry trees and bare yards. Carefully Belinda swung down from the passenger seat, demurely smoothed her skirt of wrinkles, and bent toward William at the steering wheel. "I just don't *understand* your mother, I'm sorry. We do not see eye to eye."

"She doesn't see eye to eye with a living soul, so don't let that worry you."

"Thank you for the present. That was real sweet of you."

"Don't mention it. I'm much obliged for all you've done."

"Shoot, that's all right."

Viola got down from the rumble seat, and stood the suitcase on the cracked dirt of the yard. As she scrambled back in, she saw that Belinda still lingered, biting her lower lip, on the rim of the fender. Restlessly she wrung the drying handkerchief between her hands. "I hope I can get a good reference from you, when I get to Dallas."

"That goes without saying," William replied. "You all right now? I'll come in and explain to your folks—"

"No," Belinda said hastily. "No, no. I told you, no need to do that.

Only—I hope y'all have a nice fall out there this fall. I hope y'all don't forget me anytime soon."

"Wouldn't dream of it."

"Well," she said at last, and grinned ruefully. "You tell your mama I hope she gets better quick. She was my first private patient. I don't hold a thing against her."

"I'll do that. Thank you."

"And tell Mavis I'll see her one of these days. Y'all take care now."

"You too," William said.

"Bye-bye, Viola," Belinda called in afterthought. "You be good."

"Bye," said Viola. "Wish you luck." And the car motor started once more, with Belinda still loitering under the chinaberry tree. William did not glance back.

When they reached the corner, Viola managed to screech a reminder. "You told me we could go by Miss Marianne's, remember? You can drop me off down at her house, if you want to see to some other kind of business."

"Nome, don't you fret," William turned his head and yelled into the wind. "We're going there right now."

They wheeled through the neighborhood of high front porches, then back across the courthouse square and down the main street to the East Side, passing a milk wagon blocking a side alley with its mule ducking low, an ice truck, several Model Ts, other cars, and pedestrians doing their late morning shopping. As they bumped over the railroad tracks, Viola thought she might be flung from the rumble seat and run over by the twelve-fifteen Santa Fe, William drove so fast.

"We should have brought Mother's Pierce Arrow in, to give you that ride you never had," William called out the window as they turned down a clay road of shanties and tin cans rusting in the ditch. "I'll think of it next time."

"Won't be no next time, you kill me this time," Viola warned, and then bit her tongue as they drew up outside the split palings of Miss Marianne's fence. Parked in front was a bottle-green Pierce Arrow.

Viola saw a jerk tighten through William's cheek as he saw it. "Look like Miss Marianne's got another caller," she muttered while he helped her down from the rumble seat.

"Uh-huh, sure does." He drew a deep breath and let it out. "What have you got in that little bag?" he asked casually.

"I'm bringing Miss Marianne some of Bessie's good cookies. She been sick with the gripes lately, I told you already. What's Mrs. Macafee doing here?"

"I imagine the same thing we are. She's got a right to come, too. Miss Marianne worked for her mother twenty years before she got laid up with that rheumatism."

"Huh! Think I lost my memory?" Viola blew out her cheeks, and scowled at the ground, feeling rebuked. The subject of Grant Macafee and anyone belonging to him made her uneasy. "Her mama, Mrs. March, ought to be the one."

"I didn't know there were any rules of precedence in seeing the folks you care about."

This was so harsh that she glanced up. "What's wrong with you?"

"Me? Why, not a thing. Howdy, Arnold," he called to the cowhand at the wheel of the Pierce Arrow who had chauffeured Sophie Macafee in from the country. "How's it going out at the ranch?"

"F-fine, Mr. Ransom. It's j-just fine. Couple c-calves got the b-b-black leg, can't complain, though." He grinned and spat a jaded wad of tobacco out the window.

"Drought giving you much trouble?"

"Well, it'd sure h-help if it rained."

"When's old Grant going to teach Miss Sophie to drive that thing herself? I'm sure he can't spare you every time she needs to come into town for a spool of thread."

"Haw, haw," Arnold sniggered, and tried to retort. "He's t-teaching her—teaching her al-l-long."

"He is, is he? Well, I bet you'll be glad to finally have your days uninterrupted by all these metropolitan joyrides."

"Ha ha!"

"Be seeing you, now," said William. He sounded so jaunty that Viola felt she must have imagined the spasm on his face before.

"You coming in?" said Viola incredulously, as they made their way up the yard, fording the tumble of squawking chickens that pecked at their shoes.

"Reckon I can pay my respects to Miss Marianne too, can't I?"

"You ain't bothered for two years!"

"Then I'm overdue." He smiled, taking the bag of cookies from her hand. "Poor old Granny, she probably thinks I've got stuck-up. Miss Marianne!" He strode onto the rotting porch. "We've come to wish you good afternoon!" The greeting thundered through the gloom of the house as he pushed open the screen door.

Inside the tiny room, Miss Marianne lay in a camp bed in the corner next to the iron stove. By her side a young woman dressed in a beige voile frock trimmed with lace sat glimmering in the half-light. Viola blinked to adjust her vision.

"Hello, Sophie. Hidy, Miss Marianne, how you doing these days?"

"I'm not too good, Mr. William, I thank you," Miss Marianne's reply creaked shallowly from her toothless mouth. "But I get by, sir, I get by. It's mighty nice of you to come see me."

"Not at all."

"Viola! Where you been lately? I been expecting *you* to come see me." Her fingers picked on a raveled square of the patchwork quilt.

"I can't jump on in here by myself, Miss Marianne. Mrs. Ransom, she's sick in her bed too."

"Is that a fact?" Miss Marianne swiveled her eyes towards Sophie in wonder. "How come you ain't told me, Miss Sophie?"

"Why, Auntie Marianne," Sophie murmured, "I told you about it months ago."

She sat, a being apart from the bed, from the corners of the room with their magazine illustrations pinned on the boards, apparently untouched by heat, illness, or thought. The dainty dress seemed something blown upon her by chance, like a sheet of newspaper blown down the sidewalk by the breeze. Her white brow and cheeks incandesced in the frail light from the grimy window.

"You did?"

"Yes." Sophie reached down and touched Miss Marianne's hand lightly. "I did." Her voice dropped into the stillness like a pebble.

There was about this poise, Viola observed, a faint resemblance to Sarah. But where Sarah's composure was made of health and fullness, Sophie's fragility reminded her of a bone china teacup found intact in the rubble after a tornado.

"I can't remember nothing these days," Miss Marianne grumbled. "How long she been sick, Viola?"

"I told you too, Miss Marianne. I told you three, four months back how Miss Arliss done had a stroke, and can't move a muscle from her head to her foot on her left side."

"Law, Viola, ain't that a shame. I got the arthuritis on my elbows now, can't hardly feed the chickens at all. I'm going to get up, make you-all a cup of coffee if you want it."

"Naw, you just lay there and rest awhile. We don't need no coffee."

"Miss Sophie, she brung me some fresh coffee. She brung me some nice ham, a keg of cornmeal, and two watermelons."

At that William suddenly sprang over to the bedside and thrust out the bag of cookies, flinging them on the quilt as clumsily as a half-grown boy. "Viola brought you some of Bessie's cookies," he cried, his voice cracking. Then he stepped backwards into the corner. "I don't know what kind, though."

"They're that pecan and butter kind you love so, Miss Marianne. They going to set real nice on your stomach."

"Why, that's mighty kind of you and Bessie. Yessum, I sure do appreciate you-all." Miss Marianne hooked her chin over the quilt's edge, peering down at the bag. "Look like there's a lot of them."

"Three dozen."

"My, I got to eat them up quick, before they go dry. You-all have you some cookies. Viola'll get out a plate."

"Thank you," said William, and at the same instant Sophie murmured, "No, thank you, Auntie."

In the awkward pause that followed, Viola saw Sophie lift her eyes and gaze straight to William.

He received her look as if stunned.

Viola's mouth opened. "I'm going to get the plate out," she cried. "They in that safe, Miss Marianne?"

"Yessum, that's where they're kept."

"Here you are, *cookies*!" Feverishly she poured the cookies onto the chipped plate. Her heart was hammering; heat coursed up her neck. "Take one!" She jammed the plate savagely at William's waist. He glanced vaguely down. "Go on, *have* you one," she ordered, wishing to slap him. His hand, straying over the plate as if it did not belong to him, finally picked a cookie. Then he dropped the cookie on the floor.

"Now look at that! You just a horror today. Must be that Belinda. Miss Arliss fired her. There was ructions this morning," she babbled to Sophie and Miss Marianne, trying to fill the pause. She stooped and grabbed the cookie from a crack in the boards. "Leave it there, it's going to bring the mice on Miss Marianne!" But Sophie just gazed at the small mesh purse in her lap. William stepped idly from foot to foot, unable to take his eyes off the bent head. Miss Marianne began to snore in thready gasps.

Viola tossed the cookie out the door for the chickens, and wheeled. "We better be getting along, I got to be back at the house for Miss Arliss's afternoon ice tea. And you still got to hire somebody to nurse her."

"That's true." William stared at her self-consciously and then looked at the floor. "I thought you wanted to spend some time here, though."

"Miss Marianne." Viola walked over to the bed and patted the knotty shoulder. The snores sputtered and ceased. "We got to get along now."

Slowly the old woman opened her eyes, veined like yellow agate. "Is that you, Viola? When you going to come see me? I been waiting for you to come see me."

"I just did this minute!"

Sophie did not lift her head.

"You come back, then. Come back before too long, before I'm gone."

"Yessum, I will."

"You too, Mr. William. Let me see you, hear?"

"Yes, Miss Marianne."

Sophie's cheeks were glowing pink. Her eyebrows flexed upwards only when William and Viola turned to the door. "Good-bye," she said, her sweet distinct voice rippling through the room.

"Good-bye, Sophie," said William. Viola waited for him to add a greeting to her husband to prove her intuition wrong. But then, as suddenly as he had given the cookies, he lurched out the doorway into the sunlight. His back stiffened when the hens clucked around him. Charging ahead of her to the car, he ignored Arnold in the Pierce Arrow, and climbed into the driver's seat without pausing to help Viola up in back.

They had rounded the courthouse square and were bearing down on the post office when William stuck his head out the window. "Doggone it, Viola, I nearly forgot to go to the doctor's. I'll run down the street and see if he's got somebody else to recommend for Mother."

"I'm waiting right here in this car. Too hot to take a step in town. You go on."

He parked the car next to the rutted alley opposite the jail. "I won't be long." He squinted down at her absently. "You sure you want to sit out in the sun?"

"Sun don't bother me, moving do."

She watched him amble up the sidewalk. His short body and legs seemed to grow longer as he receded, a trick caused by the heat waves rolling up from the brick-paved street. At this time of day, most people were home for lunch. Three old men played checkers on the courthouse steps; the shoeshine man peered from the portal of the Harrison Hotel. Otherwise the sidewalks and streets lay empty. "You sashaying mighty fancy in that car, Viola," the shoeshine man called. "Don't you ever want to walk like us plain old folks?" She grinned at him, defiantly proud. He shrugged and turned back into the Harrison's shadows. The hot tamale man, emerging from the alley where he had left his cart, picked up a few pebbles from the gravel at the curb and shied them down the slot between the post office and the hotel. A chorus of dog yelps broke out. The yelps changed to whining, and the whines died away in the distance. The hot tamale man wandered across the street with his head cocked up at the sky, disappearing into the drugstore. Gone in to beg a glass of ice water from the soda fountain, thought Viola. Presently someone came out of the post office door; Mrs. Sloane, the druggist's wife, in a print dress reaching down to her ankles, trudged down the steps, gaunt and brown. "Hidy, Mrs. Sloane," Viola called.

"Viola." Mrs. Sloane nodded severely, and made her way towards her husband's premises. Any minute now the hot tamale man would come flying out of the drugstore doorway, as soon as Mrs. Sloane found him leaning on Mr. Sloane's charity. He must have seen her go into the post office and timed it, Viola thought. She was watching the drugstore and calculating the precise second that this would occur when a clatter of boots on the post office steps distracted her. She turned just as the postmaster's son, Earl Ray Rutherford, stopped on the sidewalk beside the car.

"Viola!" His face was red, the little gold-rimmed spectacles lopsided on his nose. Viola rubbed her ear where he had shouted into it. "You here in town! Where is Mr. Ransom? This his car?"

"Yes, sir, it's his."

"I've got something here for him." He grabbed the belt of his pants and hitched it high. "I got here a telegram from the Western Union office inside. It's to Mr. William Ransom personal. Full day rates! All the way from up in Iowa somewhere. I reckon it must be pretty important. I was just about to go get the truck and drive it out to him."

"Well, he's right here in town. You want to give it to me, I'll hand it over to him when he comes back."

"He's got to sign for it."

"Uh-huh. Yes, sir." She could think of nothing to say to this. The boy stomped the sidewalk with his boots, reached into his breast pocket, and pulled out the yellow envelope.

"I better wait for him," he said. A sting along her nerves as she saw him produce the envelope from his pocket reminded her of another time, a similar gesture, enacted in the settling twilight of the Ransom gallery, and suddenly she pictured Sophie again, sitting beside Miss Marianne. Anxiety flooded her. She wished the boy would go away.

"You fixing to go get you some dinner?" she asked slyly.

"I was about to, when this telegram got here. My mama's got it ready on the stove."

"Uh-huh." Viola let the silence hang between them. The tamale man was back out on the street; she had missed his ejection. She kept her eyes trained away from the envelope: the vision uppermost in her mind was Sophie's pinkening forehead, a color like cochineal staining the smooth flesh, and William blundering out the door. The boy coughed beside her, shuffling his boots. She could smell the rancid white man's sweat from his body.

"Look here. You want to leave that thing with me, I'll see to it that Mr. Ransom gets it when he's through at the doctor. No telling how long he's going to be. He can go sign for it inside."

The boy hesitated. "I guess that'd be all right. You give it to him when he gets here?"

"He's just up Bois D'arc Street. I ain't going to run away."

"All right. Here it is, then. Just make sure he signs for it, though."

"I'll do that, yes, sir." She bobbed her head up and down. It was all she could do to keep from snatching the telegram as he waved it towards her.

Then she waited.

At last a figure turned the corner three blocks away. Against the haze of heat it could be anyone. But she recognized William; she could see the set of his shoulders, in the white duck coat. He strolled up to the car, and wordlessly she shoved the envelope at him.

"The doctor says he's got a nice farm lady he can—what's this?"

Viola gave him a prim look. "I don't know. That Rutherford boy done left it for you."

William fingered the paper. His eyes went dim and preoccupied. No change of expression marked him; he stood stone still, pincering the envelope.

"You got to sign for it inside there." Viola pointed to the post office steps. "Then let's get on home. I got a passel to do."

Tearing the envelope open in one clean rip, he read its contents.

"The boy say you got to sign. Mr. William—"

He looked up at her. His face revealed nothing; it was as if he held a newspaper. He looked very young.

"Mr. William—?"

"Sarah is dead," he said without inflection.

SOMETIMES WHEN I think back to that moment, I see Viola's life, with its solitude, marching straight from the peak of the terrible news to the present day in a straight line that no other events might ever divert again. There was no other way for her. Her home had vaporized, long before. Her old friends, her family members in Bernice, saw her as a defector, even in the midst of their knowing she had no other place to go. Her promise to Sarah rendered her into a fixed position of loyalty from which she could not swerve, no matter what might tempt her elsewhere. And after Sarah's death, the promise seemed to Viola more cast iron than ever. So if her choices later ground down upon me in a way no child on earth deserves, then it is not so surprising that she resolved to take that path. In her soul, I think she, too, longed to be free.

And there was William.

"The beloved is the guest of the heart," William read gravely. "Our loved ones are visitants of the mind and the flesh. We cherish them, and by our cherishing create their evanescence. We cannot get to know them, even if they are with us all our lives. And when they die before us, we realize how shortsighted was our love, how brief and chance-ridden our ardor, before they were served with extinction. Our desire to leave them to their own perfection is the curse, often misnamed neglect, of what in truth we saw to be a higher form of passion. And in the end, it is as if we dreamed them."

He ran his finger down the cleft of the book, and then entombed the sentences between the black leather covers. Lying back in the deep chair, he squinted at the library windows which stood open to the outside air. Mosquitoes sang in and out through the midnight breeze.

"Ahh," Viola sighed, after she was sure he had finished. She gazed down at the closed book in his hand, as if by staring at it hard enough she could excavate the meaning of what he had read, and refine it into words she could understand.

"That's for Sarah," he said. "I wrote it the other day, after—" His voice dropped.

"I cabled the coroner up there in that Iowa town today," he added. Viola's eyes were still damp with tears. "He's going to have her interred with a service in the Episcopal cemetery."

"You going up there?"

"What good would it do? Mother wouldn't accept any excuses I could give her for going away, you know that. And I can't tell her the truth now. It might kill her, too. Sarah's dead. It won't make any difference if I'm there to bury her or not."

Viola could not understand how he could bear to let Sarah sink down into the earth alone; she herself could not yet believe that Sarah was dead for good.

"That's what those words mean, that I wrote in here. We can't give up or say good-bye to what we left alone while it was with us." His eyes turned to the journal. Their rims were red. "You know what? Sometimes I think I started saying good-bye to Sarah the day she was born."

"Hmph! That's craziness talking."

"Still, it's a fact."

"You sound like you didn't even love her."

"Oh, I loved her," William murmured. "I love her."

"I ain't never," began Viola, her voice trembling, "said good-bye to that child. Not the day she left on the train. Not the day you got that telegram. Not ever."

William kept his eyes cast on the volume (the volume I now hold in my own hands, the diary he inscribed throughout his years at college, and which culminates in the entry he had just read aloud to Viola on the August midnight in 1922; I reread the words, deciphering, disinterring my grandfather's views of earthly love) and painstakingly tried to make himself clear to the only audience he had. "It's the same thing, Viola. That's what I mean. It comes to the same thing."

"How are we going to go on in this house like we done so far, knowing Miss Sarah's gone, and nobody else knowing? How am I going to look Miss Arliss in the face, or tell Bessie there ain't nothing wrong with me but the heat?"

"We'll manage," William encouraged. "We're both strong enough."

Now she asked the question she had held herself back from asking before, so frightened was she of the answer. "Did it hurt her much?"

"I can't lie to you," William muttered. "Spinal meningitis is not a peaceful disease. The doctor wired me the details. Apparently she'd been working as a waitress in a roadside café. A waitress!" He shook his head in wonder. "She was sick for two days. She went blind before—"

"*Never mind!* I don't want to hear no more."

"All right."

For a few minutes, neither of them spoke.

"May all her suffering be past now, dear Lord," Viola whispered presently.

"Even when we love, we can't take her suffering upon us." His voice surprised her, grinding hard against the late-hour silence.

"Mr. William, there's one thing we able to do. Please bring Miss Sarah's baby on down from that town in Illinois. Please bring Miss Sarah's child home where it belong. Bring it to *me*—"

"Hush, Viola." His whisper, so tired and troubled, fell commandingly on the sealed room. "Now isn't the time. Think about it. Think about Mother, and Grant."

"I don't give a hoot for that Mr.—"

"Think about it." He rubbed his eyelids, then the bridge of his nose with two fingers. "Maybe someday. Now hush. Hush." Then he murmured, "The child is better off where it is."

"Yes, sir."

For a little longer they sat in the lamplight, each perusing their own thoughts. She had begun to think that William was asleep, when he opened his eyes and flipped back the cover of the diary in his lap.

It was then that she perceived the fact: every page prior to the entry about Sarah's death, every scrawl depicting his youthful thoughts and experiences, had been blacked out. Only one page remained of his small regular script. Otherwise all was washed with ink, shrouded with blackest mourning.

"I've got to go to bed. All right, old lady?" Viola nodded, too beset to speak. She watched him get up and go to the big desk in the corner, unlock the lower left-hand drawer and drop the diary into it. He locked it again, pocketed the key, and walked to the table where the lamp pearled its light through a frosted glass shade.

"Good night," he said.

"Good night, Mr. William." As she stood, he reached for the switch and snuffed the glow. Together they moved in darkness to the doors, and then she stood watching him climb the stairs, slowly, like an athlete winded by a race.

What Happened When
Sophie Learned to Drive

"Ezra and I went into town for church last Sunday," Bessie said to Viola one morning during the autumn of 1922, "and what do we see? That Mrs. Macafee with her pretty little hands, setting behind the wheel of her automobile like the one Miss Arliss got. It look like she been swallowed up in it. She such a tiny little thing."

"Mm-mm!" said Viola, after a pause. "She sure is."

"It about scare me to death sometime, how folks drive them big automobiles around like they can keep them tame on the road." Bessie pounded a length of beef with a mallet, tenderizing it for chicken-fried steak. Her comments issued between blows. "That Mrs. Macafee, she was setting up there like that picture Miss Arliss has of the king of some land on the elephant, out in the hall. Except you can't hardly see nothing but just her hat and the tip of her eyes, bouncing along in the Baptist church lot. I believe she run over two chickens and a fire hydrant before Mr. Grant let her out in that thing by herself."

"You don't mean it."

"I tell you, girl." She slammed the mallet into the raw flank. "Going to be coloreds next, then they take them all to court and set them free with a slap on the hand for running down our children. Them white folk."

Pulling a bed jacket of Arliss's over the ironing board, Viola spat experimentally on the iron. "I reckon Mrs. Macafee would be mighty sorry if she ever done such a thing."

"Well, she may be different from the rest of them. I reckon she got no business out on the road, though." Bessie heaved the mallet high.

"This way she won't have to depend all the time on that Arnold what works for Mr. Grant to take her where she wants to go."

"Huh. I can't hardly blame her. You can't get one word from him, without it being covered in morning dew." Bessie threw back her head and laughed. "Law, girl! That man made up for the whole entire drought last summer when he opened his mouth to give the time of day. Rain? He's a *thunderstorm!*"

Viola snickered. "I reckon Mrs. Macafee need a new hat every time that Arnold drives her in for the groceries."

"That Mr. Grant now——" Bessie sank her voice to a marginal tenor. "He like to make any wife's life a misery, what with his do's and don'ts and long lean slitty eyes. I just hate to think what it'd be like, married to a man who don't appreciate a little fun."

"Or his food."

"Nome. That's true. Remember how he come here and you use to bring back his plate with the potatoes all raked up, but not a bite out of them?"

"That was just for awhile. There was that summer he come around every day, he ate it up then."

"Huh. It don't stick, though."

"No, it sure don't." Viola glanced down at the frilly jacket and decided to change the subject, a choice she had to reach more and more often these days, marooned as she was in her isolation of private knowledge. "You better get them tea cakes ready to haul up to Mrs. Arliss's room. She's having Mrs. Deloache over for coffee. The nurse say she want to inspect what you going to give them."

"Mrs. Deloache," said Bessie mockingly. "Miss Arliss never use to have to check my tea cakes. She knows they're better than anybody's in the county. How come she to start on me now?"

"I reckon it's the new nurse what really wants to. She thinks she cook better than you. I heard how she said so to Miss Arliss on

Tuesday. 'Dear,' she said, 'before you brung me out of retirement, I made the best devil food this side the Mississippi, and probably on that side too.'"

"Nasty old woman!"

"Don't worry. We know she's lying. Miss Arliss does too. She say, 'Not better than Bessie's, it weren't.' Makes me kind of miss that Belinda, though, sometimes." She exchanged the bed jacket for a pair of Mavis's camisoles, wondering on the tonic effect of Arliss's adversary relationships. To begin with, Arliss and Mrs. Joiner had gotten along easily.

"'I'm not your dear by a long shot.' That's what Miss Arliss say back to her. I declare that woman going to have Mrs. Arliss unwinding the knots in her tongue yet. She ain't never talked so plain, not even when she was well and kicking."

"THERE'S NO place more private than the inside of a Pierce Arrow," William had said.

Viola comprehended, during the fall of 1922, that meetings were taking place between William and Sophie on the back roads, and perhaps inside the Ransom grounds as well, in Sophie's car.

That William occasionally came home from an afternoon's "business" with a thoughtful dimness in his eye; that he spent long evenings alone in the library, no longer playing the gramophone, but absently turning the pages of unread books; that once or twice she found a dark hair woven into the shoulder of his coat on a morning after he had "attended a livestock auction"—these indicators were enough for her to rally the protective rationales. William had to stay close to home for his mother's sake. He had to forgo a young man's normal pleasures out of familial care. And even if it remained a sin that Sophie might, in her loneliness, find succor in William's arms, the presence of Grant on the earth meant to Viola an immediate revolt against all he stood for. He had breached himself with Sarah, had ruined Sarah's heart, lost her child, and brought her death. He got what he deserved.

She found a spice of irony as well, in the reversal of the situation: William and Sophie repeated what Grant and Sarah left off. In a narrow sense, I agree with her. But there was, of course, more to it than that.

It built my own fate, stone upon stone, as it went on.

What realms of tenderness my grandfather was capable of, I adduce from his dealings with me. What a conduit Sophie March Macafee must have been for that latent love: her pale lips, her frail bones and air of permanence. He could spend his passion safely with her. He would leave her perfection forever unblighted by so much as a kiss.

Or so he probably thought.

ON A certain day in winter, 1923, Viola was rubbing the claw feet of the drawing room furniture with beeswax when she overheard an argument in the dining room. The double doors stood open wide. From where she squatted, she could not see through them; but for most of the morning Mavis had sat at the dining room table, bringing her albums of memorabilia up to date. A pot of paste rested near her elbow, vulnerably uncapped (she had already upset it once, and Viola had had to clean the results with a rag). The table looked like a wasteland of old newspapers, pressed flowers, and records of Mavis's determined wistfulness. Letters she had written to sundry acquaintances and imaginary friends and never mailed lay strewn over the mahogany—"Dear Mrs. Harding, I wish I could accept your sweet invitation for tea at the White House, but as you know, Mother is not well, and it is so hard to get away"—and a stack of heavy-laced valentines with which she wished to weight the social consciences of family allies leaned nearby. The date was February the 13th. An ice storm had whipped over the Central Texas plains during the night, locking the trees and roads in sheaths of dazzling crystal. No one could leave the house under any pretense. So Mavis dedicated herself to snipping what family photographs remained unframed into suitable shapes for the album pages, and pasting the unmailed letters to New York debutantes and other celebrities opposite them, hoping this would achieve a symbiosis plausible both to the unwary guest who might peruse her handiwork, and to her own feeble imagination. Over the years she had become so adept in the art of deluding herself that, in an unreflective moment, she could open the pages and convince her eyes that these connections were a reality she had simply chosen to renounce.

The valentines were something else.

"I want you to please drive these into town for me," she said as Viola heard someone enter the dining room from the kitchen. "Tomorrow is Valentine's Day. The post office won't get them out in time if they don't get there today."

"Mavis honey, I can't——"

"Please, Wicky. It's so important that everybody gets them on the right day, otherwise I'll look like a fool."

A pensive silence, in which many things lay implicit, fell on her self-appraisal.

"*Wicky——*"

Viola heard the sound of scratching grate lightly. She expected William was frisking his scalp, as he did so often when confronted with the dilemma of Mavis.

"Honey," he said eventually, "I can't go anywhere in this weather. I think the block is cracked on my car, from the freeze."

"You can drive Mother's car."

"It's got low tires."

"You can pump them up."

"And a dead battery. Mavis, there's an ice storm out there."

"I know. So what?" Her voice struggled with petulance.

"I realize it's real important to you, honey. All these pretty cards, my, just look at them. Did you make these yourself?"

"No," said Mavis in a huff, "I bought them at the drugstore. You know I did, when you drove me into town yesterday."

"That's right, I remember. I just thought, since they're so pretty—I know how good you are with your hands."

"I did make *one*. This one. But you can see it didn't turn out near as nice."

"Why, it's perfectly lovely."

"No, it's not. That's why I bought the rest."

"I hope you're going to send it anyhow. Just look at those cute little elephants you've drawn—"

"They're cupids," Mavis corrected him flatly. For an instant no sound came through the double doors. Then William's apology collided with Mavis's hurt moan.

"I'm sorry, honey, they look just like—"

"Ohh! Now I can't send it at all, *elephants*—"

Viola left the rag on the floor by the claw feet, and scooted to a point where the dining room lay in full view.

"It's my fault, Mavis. I never have had an eye for art."

He stood beside her chair, clumsily patting her humped back. Mavis buried her face in her hands. "Everything in this house is just impossible! You can see for yourself how we used to have things. Parties! Just look at this album. Now I can't even make valentines, can't even mail them in time, oh, ohh—"

"Look here now. Things won't always be this way. We can't help it Mother is stuck to her bed. We just have to keep on as we go."

"Elephants!" Mavis perceived her leverage. "How could you, how *could* you call them—"

"I'm sorry, I said."

"You never would have said that if Sarah had made it."

There was a sudden silence.

"I can't drive into town today for you," William murmured after a moment. "I'm sorry, I wish I could. But it's the same everywhere. I sincerely doubt the postman'll be delivering anything in this weather. People will understand."

Mavis lifted her head. "I'll just look like a fool."

"Now, nobody would think such a thing."

"Yes, they will." Tediously she chanted, "They will. They will."

William sighed and dropped his hand.

"It was even different while Belinda was still here. Not like that Mrs. Joiner, all she ever thinks about are Mother's bedpans."

"Mavis. It's not nice to mention things like—"

"Bedpans!" Mavis exclaimed. "Nasty old—"

"Have some delicacy," William admonished, overcome for a moment. "You're a grown girl now."

Mavis gasped.

"I'm sorry," he said patiently. "When a girl is brought up to be a nice girl and keep company with nice people, she just doesn't bring such things into the conversation."

"You're my brother, though. I wouldn't say it aloud to anybody else."

"All right."

"Besides, how can I talk like a nice girl when I never have a chance to keep company with nice people? I don't get invitations to anything anymore."

"Well, they probably realize how things are, what with Mother sick and all."

"That wouldn't prevent them."

William could not contradict this patent fact.

"I just wish I had *something*—"

"One of these days," William promised helplessly, "something'll come along."

"Well, not if you do what you do."

"What do you mean?"

"Living like a hermit. You go out during the day, and stay home all night. How do you expect me to get invited anywhere that way?"

"I hadn't imagined that my habits had anything to do with your social life. But I suppose they do. I'm sorry, I guess I'm inconsiderate, I hadn't looked at it that way."

"See?" said Mavis with an edge of triumph. "You don't think."

"I try to, honey. I try to. I can't help the way I'm made."

"The only time we go anywhere is when you take me to town sometimes. Then it's just boring old offices, and buying things. We don't even go to church. You won't even take me to town some of the times I ask you. Look at last Tuesday——"

"I had an appointment," William murmured.

"What kind?"

"It was business. You wouldn't have enjoyed it."

"Huh! Business."

"Look here, honey. Show me some of these pretty cards. Who's this one to?"

"That's to Mrs. Deloache."

There was a pause. William bent over the card, frowning. A tentative surprise crept into his voice. "Uh-huh. It's very lovely. I'm sure Mrs. Deloache will be delighted to hear from you . . . being Mother's good friend and all——"

"I'm addressing it to the Governor too, on the envelope. I thought that might tickle him."

"Hm." Dubiously he asked, "What about this one with the little window and the violets?"

"That's to Dolly Renfrow. She married that German count. And this one, see that hand holding the inscription, like a calling card? I'm sending that to Mrs. Madison down in Austin. Remember when she and Mr. Madison came up for Mother's Christmas Ball that time?"

A ruminative sound, of William clearing his throat, stole to Viola across the loftiness of the drawing room spaces. "Are you going to send any to your girlfriends here in Bernice? I'm sure they'd be gratified to get some of these valentines. The girls your own age, I mean."

"One or two," said Mavis airily. "That's all I can spare. Here's one, though, I think it's just perfect. I picked it out especially."

Viola rested back on her heels, watching William as he studied the card. "What's that gewgaw he's holding in his hand?"

"That's Cupid with a little bundle of joy. See? It's like the bundle the stork holds. I added that myself."

"Why did you put it in?"

"Because," declared Mavis, cocking her head with condescension, "he's bringing a baby! I used India ink. Do you think it shows up all right?"

"Fine," William murmured. "Just fine. I spotted it right off."

"That's good. It turned out better than the other card I made."

"Who's it to?"

"To Grant and Sophie Macafee. It's a valentine for them and the baby they're going to have."

In the expressive silence that followed, Viola felt a chill creep up her spine. She clamped her teeth together.

"What's the matter, Wicky?" Mavis asked. "Don't you think they'll like it?"

"I'm not sure—I'm not sure—" He had gone white.

"Well, I'm going to send it anyhow." She turned away from him and picked up a stiff envelope. There was the saw of paper against doily-lace. "There, see? I'm sealing it, so you can't say you don't think they'll like it. It's too late."

"But honey," William stammered, "is it appropriate? I mean, I don't know if they'll appreciate a joke like that—"

"It's not a joke! Haven't you heard? I guess you haven't. Mrs. Sloane was talking about it at the drugstore yesterday with Mrs. Rutherford. They said Sophie's having a baby about six months from now. They said her mother had been in that morning to buy her some kind of medicine because she'd been sick, only she didn't realize what she was sick with, and it turned out Mrs. March had to explain to her. If you'd stayed in the drugstore with me, you could have heard it too. Anyhow, they haven't told people yet. So I thought this card would be a nice way of letting them know how sweet we all think it is."

He did not reply.

"Wicky?"

Viola crouched on the floor next to the enormous sofa. In her state she nearly missed William's response.

"No," he muttered absently. "No, I hadn't heard. Nobody told me."

The room seemed to crepitate with tiny noises, breathe with currents of air until now unnoticeable. They obscured Viola's hearing; it was hard to make out words and voices. Outside the drawn curtains, she could pick up the snap of ice cracking in the sunlight, the thaw dripping from the eaves.

"Just between you and me, I'm glad Sarah can't know about it. Wherever she is. It might bother her, don't you think it might, Wicky?"

"I—it—"

"Aren't you even listening? Nobody ever listens to me around here."

"I heard you, honey." His voice sounded faint, mingling with the icy air. "You have to remember, honey. I told you about that—that about Sarah and Grant. I told you that you misunderstood, that they were just good friends. I'm sure—" Suddenly he stood up straighter. His voice developed firmness. "I'm sure and certain that Sarah would be pleased as punch to hear how Grant and Sophie are going to have a—Mavis. Are you *sure* you heard right? Are you sure Mrs. Sloane and Mrs. Rutherford—you know what gossips they are. I don't want to malign their good names, but it could be a mis—"

"Wicky! I promise you. I swear!"

"Don't do that, honey, don't swear," William said tonelessly.

"It's not the same as cussing. Anyhow, there was no mistake about it. The doctor had ordered some medicine for her, and Mrs. Sloane said Mr. Sloane had only just then filled the prescription for Mrs. March to take out to Sophie."

"Um—"

"I would have thought you'd be happy for them. Your friend Grant."

"Oh. I am."

"Don't sound like it much. What's the matter with you? Honestly, these days you're just lost in a dream."

"Why, I'm just fine, honey. Just fine."

"So I want to make sure they get this valentine, I want to mail—"

"*No!*"

The stillness tautened. Viola saw William bend over the table, and heard a scrabbling, and once again the sound of paper under stress.

"*Wickyyy*—" Mavis's agonized cry filled the room. "What are you doing?"

"You can't send them that, I'm sorry, but you can't—" His gabble tore along Viola's nerves; his breath hurried.

"But Wicky—"

"I don't tell you many things you can't do. But they haven't announced it yet, it still could be a—God *almighty*, Mavis! I have to say it, you—" He gasped. His face had changed from white to crimson. He teetered above Mavis's chair. "They might misinterpret, think we're—they might—it's their private *business*! They—"

"Wicky! My card, my nice card," she moaned, rocking.

Viola heard a slam of fist on wood. She turned her head where she crouched, eyes widening, in time to see William stumble through the double doors, the torn envelope in his hand. He bowled through the drawing room towards the foyer, crashing into a small table. There lay in his blind face a concentration, as if the effort to take a definite stand had deprived his grosser faculties. He reached the front door. It opened and closed, admitting a gust of cold.

Viola stared. Then she looked back to the dining room.

Mavis huddled in the double doorway. Her jaw had dropped. When she focused on Viola, it hinged back into place; but instead of acknowledging her, she pursued the drama to its *finis*.

"Wicky!" She stretched her arms to the empty foyer, to the blank wall of the front door. "*What about my valentines?*"

How Mavis Started
Her Travels

Two or three days after the storm, the trees blackened with
saturation, the melted ice trickled down oak bark and the
slender magnolias. Spring eked in that March with Mavis's
woe its predominant theme. Her anger over William made everyone
downstairs uneasy. And the fact that William kept closer to the house
during the budding of the trees and creeping green of awakening
bulbs aggravated her mood. For weeks she refused to speak to him,
stalking out of rooms he had just entered, taking her meals in the
downstairs sitting room. Bessie called her a trial to Jesus. During the
weeks of chill following that Valentine's Day (the night of which
William had arrived at the kitchen door, fingers blue, a smile on his
lips that did not reach his eyes, and a sheepish apology for putting
everyone out over dinner), Mavis stationed her pile of valentines in
strategic places around the house, like the accusing remains of a murder victim. Once discovered in one spot, they moved on. Eventually
on a warm windy day William found them on the library desk where
he had sat down to do the accounts, and Viola, who was cleaning, saw
him throw them into the wastepaper basket with a gesture of harried
desperation. She picked up the wastebasket, took its contents to the
incinerator, and set them aflame. Then she returned to the library to
resume dusting the bookshelves. But as she passed the desk she gave
William a little pat on the back. He grinned and picked up his pen.
When Mavis peered around the door a few minutes later, glancing
expectantly at the desk, they both ignored her. The library door
slammed with the bluster of the defeated.

"Whew," said William in the reverent pause that followed. "That girl sure is hard on the woodwork."

Viola giggled.

A moment later a tap sounded on the door.

"Mrs. Ransom sent me down," Mrs. Joiner, the nurse, said when the door was opened, "to find out what that terrible noise was just then. It gave her a start."

"Why, please tell Mother I'm sorry about that. Nothing in the world but the spring wind, whisking through the house and shutting the doors."

"Maybe it would be better if people keep the doors closed from now on while this wind is up." Mrs. Joiner looked from William to Viola, seeing their merriment. She gazed suspiciously at the library window latch. "If people are going to be careless, I can't promise any kind of improvement in Mrs. Ransom's condition."

"Yes, ma'am," said William meekly. "I doubt it'll happen again. In my opinion, spring is definitely here to stay. What do you think, Viola?"

"I reckon it sure is, Mr. William."

"We'll watch the doors until the wind dies down, Mrs. Joiner."

Mrs. Joiner withdrew, closing the door pointedly. Viola and William broke into smothered laughter.

"I tell you, Viola," he said with tears in his eyes, "I'd just as soon turn Mavis loose like a monsoon in this house as long as I can get that woman's goat once or twice. However, it can't be the best thing for Mother's nerves, so I reckon we'll have to be satisfied with one time only." It was then that Viola realized how unique the sound of his laughter had become to her, and how she had missed it for the past six months. It occured to her that he had not spoken lightheartedly in a very long time. Now relief glinted in his eyes, a slackening of tension altered his mouth. She wondered if Sophie Macafee had ever heard him laugh. She wondered if the affair, so patently ended now, had not been harder on him than its worth justified. But most of all, she was glad to see him smile.

THE SPRING that year became famous in Viola's memories for several things.

It was the year that the azaleas, later to be a feature of the Ransom estate during my mother's day (I can see them now, as I look through the conservatory windows, wild and splayed, overpowering in their neglect, bleeding color across the shaggy lawns) were planted down the long drive from the house to the outside road. It was also a spring of silence. Not a whisper came from the Macafee ranch regarding Sophie Macafee's pregnancy. So extraordinary was this void, so baffling to the normal course of neighborly exchange, that it gave rise to rumor. No word traveled from the ranch to town about Sophie's child. No one could say if she throve or sickened with her condition. When Mrs. March was questioned, she lifted her brows and changed the subject; but she had always been known as an overly modest Baptist lady from Mississippi. When Arnold got asked during his trips into town for the groceries and supplies, he shrugged and stuttered out that he had not seen Mrs. Macafee lately, so he couldn't say. Sophie herself was not seen in Bernice, even attending church. Grant made himself conspicuous with absence. Because of this, people grew bothered. By the time Viola heard some real information concerning the coming Macafee heir, the child was due in four months, and Bernice had it that the mother was locked in her room out at the ranch—had been throughout the gestation—in a maddened state of mind. Also: that she was miserably unhappy with her marriage. Also: she lay at death's door—was too ill to carry the child—was too proud and vain to appear in town in the fullness of maternity, her figure destroyed, her beauty equivocated. Also: that she had taken on her husband's stern arrogance, and willfully abandoned her faith in God for putting such a burden upon her. In any case, she was unnatural.

It can be said that in most random rumors lie the seeds of truth. However, it does not do to generalize.

In late March, William decided that his mother was well enough for him to leave her for a short time in the care of Mrs. Joiner, and go to East Texas, where he owned a string of automobile dealerships that needed to be overseen. It was this which finally drew Mavis out of her pique.

"I can't stay here while you're gone," she announced, the first words she had spoken to William since Valentine's Day. "I keep telling you, I've got nothing to do. Mother won't even let me read to her these days. Not that I want to. She says she's too tired." What Arliss had really said was that Mavis's cranky voice tired her, and she'd rather read herself than listen to it.

"Honey, it won't be much fun. Just a warehouse full of Fords, nothing at all glamorous. These salesmen fellows and mechanics sometimes even use language that isn't fit for a young lady's ears, if there aren't any customers around. You don't want to—"

"I can stay in Marshall," Mavis said. "While you go out to the other little places."

"I don't know. I hear it's getting to be quite a railroad town now, infested with bad characters. I don't want anything to happen to you."

"I'll stay at the hotel, then. Only please, please don't leave me behind."

"Without a chaperone?"

"Wicky—" For the first time in her life, Mavis resorted to honesty to achieve her forlorn desires. "Look at me, Wicky. Now you tell me. Who'd want to hurt a girl like me?"

William was so touched by the truth of this, and what it meant for Mavis to admit it, that he gave in. That Mavis may not really have believed it, that her fantasy might have slipped for an instant, leaving her all too naked and ready to reclothe, was a possibility too ornate for his masculine sympathy.

"I'm sorry, Wicky, that I've given you so much trouble lately. I'm sorry that I was mad for so long. I really forgave you a long time ago. I should have told you."

"That's all right."

"I could see it got under your skin—me being mad and not speaking to you," she said with veiled satisfaction; and if she wished to ascribe William's late preoccupation to her own nuisance value, he did not contradict her. It was her dream of being beloved. "Now that I'm going to Marshall, I'll need some new clothes."

"Why, surely, Mavis. You go ahead. Now understand me, though—we won't be there for more than a couple of days."

"I've been thinking. Couldn't we just take a little detour for an extra day or two? I've always wanted to go to Tyler."

"Tyler? Not much to do there."

"Why, Wicky," Mavis rebuked, "don't you know that Tyler is just chock-full of interesting people? It's the center of the Confederacy for Texas! Why, during the Civil War it had its own platoon; it had plantations and everything. Mrs. Madison comes from there, her family's real old. I just thought maybe we could drop in—"

"Not on anybody's homes, Mavis."

"On the town! We could sightsee a little bit."

William considered the spark in Mavis's eye; he considered the fact that, while he was taking Yale for granted, Mavis never traversed beyond the outskirts of Bernice. Remorse and pity filled him. "All right. But only for a couple of days, mind."

"Oh, Wicky! That's grand. And you never know who we might meet."

"Probaby nothing but hotel clerks."

"That's all right."

"I'll go after Mother, then, and get her to let you go."

"Thank you, Wicky," said Mavis tenderly. "Thank you, thank you, thank you."

In the event, Arliss was by no means difficult to persuade, parting with Mavis's company with an ease that William did much to hide.

"Mother says you can go, Mavis, you've got her permission. She says to tell Viola to help you pack right away." He glanced toward Viola, where she sat mending some shirts, and she saw his dismay at his mother's callousness. The slow recovery from the stroke was more than ever diluting Arliss's sentiment. "I just hope that the trip will live up to your expectations," he said to Mavis; but she was already heading for the stairs.

So Viola spent the rest of the afternoon, with a sensation of déjà vu, helping the second Ransom daughter to pack for a journey. In the course of picking dresses and discarding them, frowning at her old underwear, toying with her toothbrush, Mavis said, "Wouldn't it be amazing if the same thing happened to me that happened to Sarah when she left home? Wouldn't it be amazing if I disappeared to some dark fate like she did?"

"What you talking about?" asked Viola, stung. But Mavis just blinked and rattled on.

"There's always the chance we might run into somebody we know, strolling around Tyler. We might even get invited to a party or two."

"Maybe so."

"You know what? I can't help feeling that this trip is going to be tremendous. I have a feeling, right here in my deepest heart"—Mavis thumped her skimpy chest—"that something is going to come of it. I think it's going to open up new horizons, just split my whole life wide open and let a new thing in. Did you ever have a feeling like that?"

"Nome. But I know about the town of Tyler, Miss Mavis. My own mama come from there."

"Not our part of Tyler! Anyhow, I just feel that something is just around the corner. It makes me shiver to think of it. I'm so glad," she sang, like a children's song, "so glad, so glad, that Wicky wants to escort me. Just imagine us! The two Ransoms out for the afternoon promenade, arm in arm. Do you think Wicky would take my arm? I hear Mrs. Madison even has a son and a daughter. We might even—I just can't wait. Here's this little coral brooch. Maybe it'll come in handy at last."

Viola saw it in Mavis's hand. She watched her hold it up to the light, examine it critically.

"It's not very dressy. I could use something finer. Maybe Mother'll loan me her amethyst. This will do for morning wear, though, do you think?"

Viola had to look away.

ON THE first of April, William and Mavis left on their small odyssey. Mavis had been packed for days, her valise and steamer trunk waiting in the foyer. She ran to the car ahead of William, who stayed behind and motioned to Viola that he wanted a word with her.

"If anything should arise while we're gone——" he began, and then lapsed, gnawing on his lower lip.

"Miss Arliss is doing real good. That nurse'll look after her, don't you worry none."

William stared out the open front door, into the middle distance of post oaks. "I have to tell you something, Viola," he said after a little. "There are more reasons than Mother as to why I've delayed this trip. I should have been there a month ago, come to that, they've already started building the new Longview shop without me. But——"

Patiently Viola folded her hands under her apron and waited for him to continue.

"I've sort of been expecting a message...." He sighed, and drifted into contemplation.

"Yes, sir?"

"Oh, well," he said finally. "Mavis looks like she's ready to toot the horn. I'd better get on. Never mind what I said, it doesn't matter."

"Yes, sir."

"You look out for everybody around here, you hear?"

"Yes, sir." She studied his resigned face. "It's only for a few days. Not even a week. Everything be taken care of."

"Uh-huh." A squirrel in the post oaks caught his attention.

"I know what you mean," Viola whispered; and it was at this, the whisper perhaps only half seized by his ear, that he started and turned to her.

"What's that? You know——"

"Never mind. I'm going to look after it all, Mr. William. I'm going to listen for anything you might want to hear." He gave her a curious gaze of penetration and futility.

"Mother, I mean," he said, his eyes fixed to hers. "I'm talking about Mother, of course."

"Yes, sir. I know it."

"Well——thank you."

"Bye, now, Mr. William." She watched him saunter down the front steps. At the car, he turned and waved. "Bye-bye, Miss Mavis, you have you a good time." Mavis offered a frenetic wave in answer. Viola shut the front door, and heard the car motor growl beyond the thick barrier of wood.

ON THE third day after their departure, Viola finally heard something concrete about Sophie Macafee.

Chance presented it. Or perhaps the point of this history is that nothing is ever really left to chance; the circumlocutions are too tight, coincidence too reliable. A chance is something I never had.

That morning Viola caught a ride into town with the doctor, after he finished his check on Arliss. She intended to go see Miss Marianne. In the back of her mind lay the possibility that she might be able to salvage some scrap of news regarding Miss Marianne's former charge; Mrs. March still visited the shack on the east side of Bernice, and there was always the chance that she had succumbed to confession there. Guarding her hopes, Viola armed herself with a cake and a sack of shelled pecans, and asked Dr. Middleton for a lift.

He dropped her off in the courthouse square. Resting awhile on the hardware store porch before walking across the railroad tracks, she stood in the shade among a cluster of other people, trading good mornings and catching up on her shoeshine uncle's gossip. There she heard how the sheriff had just arrested his own cousin for being drunk and disorderly, which could imperil his chances in the next election. No one, said her uncle, quoting two white customers he'd overheard, liked to think that a man with no family feeling was protecting the peace; it indicated a bent for corruption.

"He's a hard man, that sheriff," said Uncle Shine. "Mean as a snake. You hear what he done to that nigger boy what took Mrs. Sloane's washtub last year. Done whip him up good in the jail and sold him to the prison farm, down Huntsville. That boy couldn't hardly walk out the jailhouse to go. Lord knows what he liable to do to his own kin, if the judge don't took mercy. Whole town's fit to bust. They saying up at the courthouse, 'Ain't nothing sacred no more, the man's dangerous.' I heard that lawyer man, Mr. Buffert, he said to Mr. Deloache, 'He's nothing but a mad dog,' he said. 'Mad-dog sheriff—next thing you know he going to take money just to let folk off their crimes.'"

"He's just doing his job," Viola said. "You don't figure on white folk enough, that's all, Uncle. They have to do their job, they can't make the difference between kin and other kind of folk. It's called an exception."

"Shoot, Viola, you talk like Mr. Buffert. Exceptions! What you doing? Them white folk rub off on you what you work for out yonder? Sometimes it seem like you believe they're *your* family, you so particular to them all."

"I got to have a view. You just hush up, Uncle, until you know what you talking about."

Uncle Shine turned his head in disgust and hawked a gob of spittle on the street. "You go talk to Dandy, she's inside the store here now, come into town this morning. That nigger boy what got run up the prison farm be her auntie's boy. You just hear what she say."

"Dandy's here?"

"Back in the store there." He jerked his head over his shoulder.

"How did she come in?"

"That hand what works out at the ranch brung her. He's there too, buying up a bale of barbwire. I hear him asking Mr. Lanky for it." He grinned and ran a tongue over the nubs of his teeth.

"Hmph."

"Folk going to start calling you Miss Lord Jesus, the way you carry on these days."

Viola, who had been tempted to walk away, would not have thought of doing so now. "Reckon you better get on to church this Sunday, Uncle. You got the devil in you, saying such a thing." She took a few steps backwards to indicate her disdain, and sank into the deepest shadow on the porch to wait.

In a short time, Dandy came swaying out of the doorway of the hardware store, hoisting a bale of wire to her middle. She was followed by Arnold, whose hands swung limberly from his hips.

"Now listen, girl," Arnold said. "Y-you go back on to the car now. I'm g-going to have me a s-sip of something, before we drive back to the ranch. Do what I t-tell you, hear."

"Yes, sir," said Dandy. She was a woman broad as a hay barn, with a backside that looked waterborne, high and wide and firm; she hefted the huge wire roll lightly, and one could imagine that, behind her, she left a stately wake. (I myself met Dandy, when I was a child, on a day she came to visit Viola in the kitchen; she tossed my own minor immensities in the air, cooing, and winked at Viola. Her gold front teeth winked as well. It was the only time after infancy that I ever felt the miracle of weightlessness. "You make a fine little ham pie!" she told me.)

She was in no hurry to take the barbwire to the car. Her steps slowed at the porch's edge. She narrowed an eye at Arnold's rickety back, proceeding down the street toward a certain house where home-brewed beer could be bought on a hot day, even in a dry county. Then she dropped the wire unceremoniously on the porch boards,

116

where it bounced and quivered, and sat down on the bench to enjoy a little conversation.

Viola stepped out of the shadows.

"Hey, Dandy."

"Why, girl! How you making it? I ain't seen you in a cat's age." She chuckled. "Why, Viola, you getting to be fat like me these days." Slinging an arm like a haunch of venison at Viola's back, she squeezed her. (I remember the feel and texture of that arm, which I clung to as she threw me high toward the ceiling; the flesh sprang pleasantly against my clench, like soft warm rubber.)

"I'm making it, Dandy," said Viola.

"Shoo, don't tell me! You lazy, girl. They ain't running you off your feet over at Ransoms', just look at how fine you done grown. Some boy'll come pluck you soon. You getting ripe." She kneaded Viola's shoulders.

"How come you to come on in this morning?"

"That Arnold! He can't stand the idea he going to have to lift something extra. He brung me in to do his toting for him." She rolled her eyes. "Between you and me, I expect he just want a little fun. Ain't nobody laughed out at the ranch in awhile."

Viola reflected how this matched her own thoughts on William, a few weeks previous.

"What's happening out there?" she asked carelessly.

"Out the ranch? Why, nothing much." Dandy spotted another friend. "Hey there, Arthur," she shouted. "I hear the hotel done catched you again."

"Who told you that, Dandy?" a bald old man called from the far corner of the porch, where he stood swatting away the flies.

"Uncle Shine, he told me. You better watch out, boy. That sheriff'll get you good next time."

"Uh-uh!" mumbled the old man. "Uh-uh! They ain't going to catch me, Dandy. I ain't done nothing."

"Dandy." Viola lowered her voice. "I been waiting to ask you."

"Ask me what?"

"How's Mrs. Macafee? She getting through all right?"

As Dandy turned her full attention at her, Viola sighed and fanned her face languidly with a palm.

"Girl, I want to ask you something. How much you know about this child Mrs. Macafee's going to birth?"

Viola stared. "All I know is, Mrs. Macafee ain't come to town since she found out she's having one."

"That the truth?"

"You know me, girl."

"Well, I tell you this. There's something mighty strange going on about that child." Dandy paused, motioned to Viola, and pointed. Viola saw the Pierce Arrow parked under some cottonwoods on the edge of a lawn. Together they slipped off the porch and wandered towards it. "Mr. Macafee, he shut up tight as a trap, on the day Mrs. Macafee found out from her mama she's carrying," Dandy muttered. "That white girl didn't even recognize she was having a baby till then. Huh, I could have told her myself, I seen the way she was so sick in the morning. Evening, too."

Viola remembered Sarah's pale cheeks, two years before, with a stab.

"Thing is, there something peculiar about it all. You'd think Mr. Macafee's having a hissy fit, except he's different from any man I ever seen, white or colored. Ain't no nigger go so quiet when he hear his wife is having the first child. But then," said Dandy with venomous force, "it take a little something for a nigger to have a child. It take lying on his woman."

Viola gaped at Dandy in astonishment.

"I reckon maybe Mr. Macafee has him a miracle, he think he's so close to the Lord," Dandy said in the loaded quiet of the empty street. "I tell you this, girl. You ever hear of even a white man not having to get his babies on his wife with his own doodad? Because if you ain't, then praise Jesus. Mr. Macafee done joined the saints."

"How do you mean?" whispered Viola.

"How you think I mean? I been working out there for the entire time they been married. Mr. Macafee, he sleep every night of the year in his own room. Mrs. Macafee she sleep in the room what his daddy had, and if Mr. Macafee ever enter that door it going to be the day the moon drowns." She nodded cynically. "It's like Mary with the angel come to tell her."

"Shoo, Dandy. They're married, ain't they? You ain't hanging over their bed every minute."

"I know what I know. Don't I change their sheets?"

"Can't tell that way," muttered Viola.

"Then I ain't been a woman with three husbands, once even married in the church," Dandy retorted.

"What else you know?"

"That'd be telling, girl." She slewed an eye, heavy lidded, at Viola. "It was the first night Mrs. March say they going to have a new baby in the house," she whispered. "I hear Mr. Macafee through the door. He was telling something to Mrs. Macafee, real low so I couldn't understand it. But I hear her answer. 'No, Grant,' she say"—and Dandy mimicked the tight distressed tones of a calm woman—"'I can't explain it. I don't know.' Then Mr. Macafee, he don't say nothing else. I hear Mrs. Macafee crying. Then Mr. Macafee come out the door. He seen me and passed me right by. Mrs. Macafee, she was weeping real quiet like, she don't hardly make a sound." Dandy nodded once more, falling into thought.

"What happened then?"

"Nothing. Mr. Macafee just go on like he usually do, only he talk less. Mrs. Macafee, she take to her bed. She come out in the mornings, but she go back by dinnertime.

"Ain't nothing going to come of it," Dandy added. "They going to have their baby and act like it's just natural. Mrs. Macafee, she already asked her mama to buy her some material for the baby clothes. She's sewing little blankets. But I reckon, if they want it to seem like it's respectable, they be coming on into town and let folks see them. Mrs. Macafee needs to go to church like she use to. Then folks won't be talking so much. Oh, I know all the things they saying round town. It ain't none of it true. But Mr. Macafee, he don't hardly talk at all no more. He's gone so quiet, he just walk through the house like a statue moving."

Viola pondered, wondering how much to risk. But Dandy had not mentioned a candidate.

"How do you think she got that child?" she asked at last.

"Girl, that Mrs. Macafee, she's good as she can be. Ain't nobody in this town can throw a stone at her. That's what got me stumped." She said warningly, "Don't nobody know what I just told you. If folks get jumpy about the Macafees, it purely going to be the reason that they ain't show up in so long. But I say every time folks ask me, 'Shoo, they real private, Mr. and Mrs. Macafee. They like the country. That's all.' But Viola, you know what it means. It was when Mrs. Macafee learned to drive. But I can't to save my life figure on how and who. It don't make no sense."

"No."

"Don't you go telling Bessie what I told you. Mrs. Macafee a fine woman. I think she's the best woman I ever know, her heart made of gold. So I'm going to see to her, it don't matter what Mr. Macafee do or don't do."

"Don't you worry, Dandy," said Viola grimly. "I ain't telling nobody. Poor thing."

"Um-mm! It's a strange business all right. It sure is." They both gazed down at the fanning arcs of the brick pavement, laid so flat and precisely. The spring breeze scattered cottonwood fluff over the car hood. Dandy raked her stiff hand across the metal and brushed it away. "How's Miss Arliss these days?" she inquired.

"She's doing all right. She's perking up good. Got that Mrs. Joiner to fight with."

"She's a fighter, that Miss Arliss. I recollect when Mr. Archibald still alive, and she go after him all the time. Remember that, Viola?" She laughed.

"Lordy, I do."

"Mr. Grant ain't like his daddy."

"No. He sure ain't." Viola drew herself a little further inward. "That's the truth, now."

ONE WEEK later, Viola heard the sound of the car from where she stood in the pantry, the grating of its gears as it crunched to a stop in the drive. She rushed to the foyer. Mavis was already trudging through the door. She nodded dispiritedly to Viola before dragging up the staircase. William followed with the luggage.

"Hidy, old lady!" He set the valises down. "Everything doing all right here?"

"Yes, sir, Mr. William. Just fine." She smiled. "You-all have you a good time?"

"Well. We got a lot done."

"I saw Miss Mavis. She already went upstairs." She glanced towards the high well. "She looked mighty sorry to get home."

"Oh, I don't think that's the trouble somehow." He stood massaging the small of his back.

"You didn't have no arguing, did you?"

"Nome, we didn't. Nary a cross word passed between us." He grinned dryly. "It couldn't have, towards the last. She kept her mouth closed on me."

"Miss Mavis?"

"Yep. You would have been proud of us, we did you credit. Didn't have one fight the whole time."

"What you done to her?"

"I think she's a little peeved at the world, that's all. How's Mother?"

"She's doing good. She's sleeping right now."

"I'll wait a minute, then. What's the chances of a glass of ice tea around here?"

"You go sit down. I'll bring you one."

"Much obliged." William's eyes had grown milder in the short week he had been away. A tired opacity swam in them.

When Viola returned with the tea, he was in the library, sprawled in an easy chair.

"Viola," he said after draining the glass, "I've decided something."

"What's that?"

"I think it's time my sister got a chance to do some real traveling. See some scenery outside Texas, something—more stimulating. Unusual."

"Yes, sir?"

"Yes. Like Europe."

"You don't mean it."

"I do." He motioned to the settee. "Sit down."

She waited.

"I reckon," he said, staring at his lap, "I have never spent a more peevish week anywhere on this earth than I just did in East Texas." His hands fidgeted with a bunch of keys. "I shouldn't complain, it's not exactly polite. Mavis has her troubles, God knows. But do you know, it took all my endurance just to greet each morning without tearing out my hair—what there is left of it." He grinned once more.

"You still got your hair."

"I won't for long."

"Miss Mavis was disappointed."

"That is an understatement."

Viola stared at him in puzzlement.

"Miss Mavis was indeed disappointed. Although I don't comprehend how she could have expected anything else. I warned her." He rubbed the chair arm thoughtfully. "It could be that I'm just not compensating her enough for the way things are. But I don't know what else I could be doing."

"You want to talk about your trip?"

"I do not. And I advise you not to ask Mavis, either. There's nothing to describe that she found in the least desirable."

"You done tried," Viola said gently.

"Yes, I did that."

"You really going to send her to another country?"

"I think that if she had enough to do—sightseeing, new kinds of people—she might pull out of herself a bit. Give her a total change of scenery." He smirked. "Just getting her money transferred to pounds or francs would keep her busy for a whole day. What do you think?"

"Yes, sir," said Viola doubtfully.

"A challenge," William went on. "That's what she needs." His mouth curved. "So long as we can find the right set-up, of course—missionaries to China, or a two-year grand tour of Amazon headhunter country."

"You pulling my leg."

"Would I do that?" he said blandly. "Nome, anyhow—soon as I go and kiss Mother hello I'm going to bring it up."

"When you talking about for her to go?"

"We'll have to see. The best thing would be if we can find some nice friends who plan to go abroad. That'll take time, though. Can't be too good friends, they'd know right off what they're in for."

"Don't talk ugly."

"I'm not, I'm just teasing. Truly, though"—he leaned his head back on the chair and closed his eyes, "they'll have to be Christians."

"Mm-m!"

"How's Bernice been faring since I saw you last?"

"I went into town last week."

"You did?"

"Yes, sir," she murmured, and in the following silence, he opened his eyes and tilted forward. But he said nothing.

"Run into Dandy from the Macafee place."

"Uh-huh." The eyes, with their impenetrable sheen, reflected the plum-brown depths of the library walls. He did not leave her face. His hands rested, alert and still, on his white duck thighs.

"How's Dandy?"

"She's real busy these days, tending to Mrs. Macafee."

"That right?"

"Uh-huh." She watched him.

"She say it's mighty quiet out there. Mrs. Macafee keeps to her bed most of the time. Mr. Grant, he ain't in a talky mood either."

"She say why?"

"Naw, sir."

"Reckon they wouldn't want much ruckus, if Mrs. Macafee—did Dandy say she was poorly?"

"She ain't no more. She was at first. But that's the way it take a lot of ladies."

"Hm." A faint line appeared on his forehead. "I didn't know that. I mean if—" He cleared his throat. "She's healthy now? Not any danger of her losing it—or trouble of that sort?"

"No, sir, Dandy say she's sewing the baby clothes. She just like to keep private. She's carrying it fine, though." She turned away. "There ain't nothing much to do, except wait for her time."

"Don't suppose Dandy mentioned how Grant's health is, did she?"

"She say he just do what all he usually do. So I reckon he's getting on fine."

"Uh-huh." He began to clink his keys together. The line deepened. "Reckon they wouldn't want to be bothered by visitors," he said tentatively.

Viola did not answer.

"Thanks for the—" he began, and then faltered. "Thanks for looking after things here for me."

Viola gazed at him. "That's what I'm here for."

He ducked his head at her, embarrassed, and left the room.

AT DINNER, with the candle glow lustering her yellow skin, Mavis pecked at her food.

William appeared, as he ate the dishes he had requested—mashed yams, fried chicken, mustard greens, his father's favorite dinner—to be more relaxed. His brown eyes looked livelier, less reticent. It was awhile before Viola, serving the corn bread, realized what he was leading up to.

"What you don't seem to realize, Mavis," he said to the bent head opposite, "is that a trip to East Texas doesn't constitute 'the unusual.' You saw how it was. There's nothing of what you'd call romance to scrounge around for there. Of course, I'd say it was romantic, but then I like that kind of place. Red dirt. Pine woods. Wild animals lurking in the river bottoms. Lush growth everywhere. Dogwood and crape myrtle blooming in everybody's front yards. It was lovely," he said over his shoulder to Viola, "hot and muggy and the devil's paradise, but pretty as a picture."

"Yes, sir. I know it."

"Why, just the smells alone—that red clay mixed up with creosote, and simmering in the sun, and the flowers overlaying it."

"Ugh," said Mavis. "It made me sick to my stomach."

"Well, there you are. Can't please all the people all the time."

"It can get swallowed up in hell, for all I care."

"Now, Mavis. Don't use language like that."

"I don't care."

"I do."

She glowered at her plate.

"All those picturesque houses. Why, I know you liked them."

"Ours is better."

"Ours is newer. Not the same thing, not at all."

Mavis chewed a morsel of yam, and then had trouble pushing it down her throat.

"Maybe I ought to take you to West Texas," William mused. "Now there's where the wide open spaces really start. Flat as can be, stretching for hundreds and hundreds of miles. Tumbleweed, the wind scurrying around your head, throwing a little good Texas sand into your eyes. The mesa country—"

"No thank you!"

"Aw," William sighed, "you just don't have the love of your homeland that I do. That's the trouble."

"You actually love all this, don't you?"

"Honey, do you understand where you're living? If you did, then maybe you could get more out of it."

"What do you mean?"

"You come from here. It's where you were born. I take the view, moreover, that the particular place you come from is kind of special."

"Only to dogs." Mavis sniffed.

"It's a shame you feel that way. Let me tell you something. I've lived in another state in the course of my short lifetime—"

"No need to remind me!"

"No, now listen. It was a pretty place. Cold in the winter, but different. It gave me perspective. I think maybe your trouble is, you don't have any perspective. East Texas wasn't far enough for you to go."

Mavis eyed him sullenly.

"But be that as it may—"

Her interest dropped; she slammed her knife down on her plate.

"Bernice is where I learned more than any of the subjects they taught me in college. You see, this town is the equivocal part of Texas. It is the heartline where everything meets, and nothing conflicts. Brave tough cowboys, like they've got in West Texas. Old Southern traditions, a gracious code of life, from East Texas just next door to us. Dirt farmers, the true and forthright pioneers of this country. Oil drillers. Cotton industry. Why, when it comes to all the things that color the character of this state, you name it and we've got it. Right here in this little bitty town. We are a nexus, Mavis. Do you know what that is?"

"Don't want to know."

Viola listened; she had never seen Bernice the way William was describing it.

"It means a link, a point of connection."

"Nexus," Viola memorized in a whisper; but he heard her.

"That's right." He slapped his thigh. "Just like in a chain. Only in Bernice's case, it is the main link. And just think, Mavis. Your own daddy helped people like Governor Deloache put this town together. He helped perform the astonishing feat of making a place where it all ties up—everything this territory means, everything it stands for."

"A lot of hicks and dirt," Mavis said dismally.

"Look at that." William turned to Viola. "Only one generation, and they're already itching to get away."

Viola grinned from the shadows beyond the candle flames.

"Well," said William with comic torpor, "I guess there's no stopping a mule from going on to greener pastures. Reckon we better give them their head."

Mavis's head bobbed up. "What?"

"Yes," he said heavily, "send them on to wherever it is." He shrugged. "Can't keep them tied up to the harness these days."

"What are you talking about?" said Mavis, but with a quickening.

"Yep. Then when you mail me a postal card of the Eiffel Tower, or the Roman Coliseum, maybe you'll be nursing some little remembrance in the back of your mind. You'll say to yourself, 'Poor old William, back there in that sweet land of my youth, toiling away for my dreams—how I wish I could walk down the old road now, and catch a glimpse of the old homestead.' And you'll shed a little bitsy tear, just to think of it."

Mavis nearly upset the centerpiece of magnolia blossoms in her lunge over the table. "Do you mean it?" she cried.

127

"Heck, spoke to Mother just this afternoon. You'll be going to all those places soon."

"What?" she shouted. "When?"

"In a couple of months. Soon as we can get you a berth with some chaperones."

"Oh, Wicky! Wicky, Wicky——"

"Now don't get in a swivet," he said gently. "Look what you're doing to those flowers Viola arranged for our homecoming evening."

"Thank you, Viola," Mavis stammered. "Thank you—thank you—Wicky! I can't believe it! Oh!" She grabbed for William's hand, and the crystal bowl of magnolia overturned, flooding the table. Her face shone above the spreading pool. The huge creamy petals, thick as human skin, bruised against sharp crystal edges, releasing their musty spice into the air.

How an Heir Was Lost

Summer was here once more, smothering the road to Bernice in a pall of heat. Dust boiled up from the bed, mantling the bushes on either side. One day the skies blackened, and heavy drops flackered down, randomly at first, riddling the dusty leaves with glossy spots. Then the deluge began. Sheets of rain flailed the earth; the air hung so densely outside that it looked like an underwater scene in motion. As Viola worked her way through the house shutting windows, she got drenched to the skin. Mavis danced behind in her footsteps, electrified by the thunder and thrill of the torrents; she had spent two months trying to maintain a poise equal to her new status, but now all bounds were overthrown. "I love the rain. No drought this year! It's raining, It's pouring," she cried, until Viola longed to tell her to hush. Only when they passed Arliss's room did she hold herself in, tiptoeing abjectly by the door, for Arliss had lately been only too delighted to give Mavis an opportunity to travel. Mrs. Joiner had merely shaken her head and said a few things about foreigners.

"I'm a dyed-in-the-wool Texas woman myself. I know what's worth what. You won't catch me running around on camels and zebras. I hope you're going to take a first-aid kit with precautions in it. My uncle was a Methodist preacher, made a trip to the Holy Land once. Nearly died from dysentery, bless his heart. No, thank you."

Finally Viola made it to the third floor, where she discovered the last room, her own, to be running with water as if a bath had overflowed. Mavis, who was still trailing behind, stood in the door admiring the flooded bed quilt and the wreckage of Viola's Sunday dress laid out on a chair under the wide-open window.

"How come you live up here among all these empty rooms, and Bessie and Ezra live out in the cabin the other side of the stables?"

"Huh?" Viola twitched her lips at the mess on the floor, and began to staunch it with the rags she used for towels. "Miss Arliss put me up here when you-all moved house. You was just tiny then."

"Don't you ever get scared up here all by yourself?"

"Nome." Viola bent down on her hands and knees.

Mavis stepped over the threshold. "Not much in here, is there?"

"Don't need much."

"Viola, if you could have anything in the whole wide world, what would you want?"

"Shoo, child. I don't know." Viola wrung out the dress.

"I'd want—I'd want just what I'm getting. Plus something else. You know what it is?"

"Nome."

"I'd wish for the chance to stay over in Europe long enough to meet somebody special."

"How long would that take?"

"Don't know. Might take a day, might take a year." She skirted Viola's mopping, and walked over to the pine dresser, plucking up the palm leaf fan that leaned against the mirror and waving it in front of her face.

"Might get homesick, if you stay there a whole year."

"No I wouldn't. Not if I met somebody special."

Viola kept her head down; the last water soaked through the rag, and then she clambered to her feet and looked towards the dresser. Mavis stood hunched over it, busy, her shoulders folded forward. As Viola swung a few steps nearer she saw that the top drawer gaped open, revealing meager treasures: a green glass bottle with an agate stopper, a silk scarf handed down by Arliss, several photographs. One of them Mavis held in her hand. She raised it to the dim light at the window, where the rain strummed against the glass, crawling downwards in rivulets.

"What you doing?" Viola demanded.

"Do you suppose," Mavis said dreamily, "that that's what Sarah did? Found somebody special?"

"How come you to go looking in people's private property?"

"What?" The photograph, with its little cross of black taffeta pinned to one corner, caught the light as Mavis glanced up. "I'm not doing anything wrong, am I? I'm sorry, I didn't think you'd mind."

"Your mama done taught you to ask permission before you go through other folk's business. I told you the same, Miss Mavis."

"Who are all these people in the pictures?" Mavis lifted the deck of photographs from the drawer, her eyes rounded with sweet guile; her other hand fell to her side, still clutching the first photograph as if she had forgotten it.

"They my family. Other folk too."

"Who's this?" She selected a daguerreotype of a man with gray frizzled hair and a high collar.

"My granddaddy. He had that took after the time the slaves were set free. On Juneteenth."

"Was he one?"

"Why, yessum! What'd you think he was? All the people was back then. He come from Waco, he work for the family that had that house they call East Terrace, down near the river."

"How about her?" Mavis snatched another card from the stack, and thrust it high.

"My aunty Cloris, she is. You know that man that shine the shoes at the hotel? That's his mama."

"I thought his mama was Miss Marianne who used to work for the Marches."

"She's not his mama, she's Aunty Cloris's cousin. We kin to a lot of folk."

"You sure must be. Why, I had no idea. I thought when your mama and daddy and brothers and sisters all burned up in the fire, you were the only one left.

"I got other kin," Viola said shortly.

"But you came to live with us." Mavis blinked. "Why was that?"

"When somebody got to go out and work for a living, sometime they make their home there too." The old ragged gnawing of those first days of exile came back to her as she spoke: the loneliness, the nights spent shuddering and crying until dawn on the army cot in the Bois D'arc Street kitchen pantry, the firm, calm voices of her aunt and uncle as they instructed her: "Go on now. You can do it. You got to do it. You a big grown girl. Mrs. Ransom need a girl for some help, we hear. You go on and ask her. We love you, honey, but we just ain't got room to keep you here." And the set inevitability in her aunt's eyes as she patted her shoulder and sent her out the door. But then there had been the two children in the other house, waiting for her to pick them up, fill her empty arms with their warm bodies, and hold close, tight to her eleven-year-old chest where all the pain lived. Those children had been as eager to love her as she had been them. Of course, there had also been Mavis, the afterthought.

"So that shoeshine man is your cousin?"

"Nome. He's my uncle."

"How?"

"Aunty Cloris was my great-aunty—shoo, we can't hardly keep up with all the ways it hooks us together. I'm the one they come to, if they want to figure out who's kin to who."

"You keep it all in your head?"

Viola nodded. "Same as anybody does if they try. I've got the memory for my family. They know I'm real good at recollecting things." She eyed askance the one photograph, tucked half-concealed in the folds of Mavis's dress, that bore the black cross. As Mavis put the picture of Aunt Cloris back in the drawer she jerked her gaze away. "Reckon we better get on downstairs now. The rain ain't going to let up for awhile. I got to go get that washing in."

Unwillingly Mavis relinquished the card stack. Like an after-thought she dropped the single black-crossed one on top of the rest and gave it a sharp glance.

"You think that's what she did?"

"Who? Done what?"

"Sarah. You think she found somebody special and just decided to live another life and forget about us?"

"Law, child. How can I tell you?" Viola shrugged, keeping her eyes fixed on the door.

"It might explain things. . . ." Mavis touched the photograph one last time, and shut the drawer. "Well," she sighed as they plodded through the long hall of storerooms to the staircase, "maybe that's what will happen to me. And maybe you'll all forget me as easily as you've forgotten her."

To which Viola could not dare a reply.

BY THE following day the rain had ceased. The sky hung scrubbed and vacant. For the rest of the summer the heat filled it; on the days when Mavis's dressmaker came to complete the new wardrobe for Europe, she wore perspiration like crystal bead trim around the edges of her scraped-back hair. Often Viola would stop in the room where she worked and fan her for a few moments, to ease the heavy load of wool that swathed her knees: Mavis's future shipboard coat.

The dressmaker took a lively interest in Bernice news. She told Viola that the Renfrow family had gone to San Antonio for the wedding of their elder son, and Dolly Renfrow was to be maid of honor. Also, Grant Macafee had sent for a trained nurse to look after his wife during the last days of her confinement, and then dismissed her three weeks before the baby was due. No one could say why, least of all the nurse.

Viola pondered this.

She had had no opportunity of going into Bernice for several months, ever since Mavis began planning her travels. So far Mavis had filled three steamer trunks, and then emptied them again, asking Viola each time what would be suitable wear in the Champs-Élysées and the Tower of London. Viola stood patiently, nodding, while the names of unimaginable places whirled around her. Twice she attempted to ride with William to town, but Mavis stopped her at the door. No one wanted a tantrum this close to the departure date; for William had found the chaperones at last, a Dallas religious newspaper editor and his wife. They were scheduled to leave for New York on the first of October.

Throughout the deepening summer Arliss's health improved.

"I leave it to you, Viola," she said one afternoon in a speech cleared of debris, "to get that girl off. I shudder to think what I would have to put up with, if I wasn't a slave to my bed. It's almost a compensation for my paralysis to know I don't have the burden of it."

"It's all coming right along, Miss Arliss."

"On the other hand, it's not easy, lying around all day with nothing but my thoughts for company." Arliss smiled luxuriously at Mrs. Joiner.

"I do my dead level best, Mrs. Ransom." Mrs. Joiner took on an earnest manner, speaking slowly and carefully as she hooked a row of crochet stitches. "What else can I do for a lady born in a little old tiny tenant shack not ten miles from my own home in the cotton fields? Since you can't get up out of bed, it's my duty to bring the outside in."

"Very kind," Arliss nodded. "You are the soul of kindness, Etta May. It's a pity our social circles didn't ever throw us together before I had to hire you. I could have taken so much more pleasure from your long long descriptions. You seem such a part of those very cotton fields you pay tribute to."

"I never cared about such things like social circles. My parents and dear departed Mr. Joiner were very particular about the important things of life. Hard work, honest living, the Lord Jesus. Times was hard," she measured sweetly, "but we made do, and we thanked Jesus every night and day for our blessings."

"Such as they were."

"Why," cried Mrs. Joiner, "you should be thanking Him too. I did, when I came here. It was such a great change from holding our farm together with nothing but pure strength of will and the guidance from above. It's a positive vacation for me. Of course, you didn't have to make a change—not that much difference between taking your ease downstairs on a silk sofa and lying up here on a king's bed."

"Duke's," Arliss corrected. "But I believe a queen did sleep in it once."

"Nothing but strength of will, my good body that the Lord give me, and honest work. That's what kept that farm going after Mr. Joiner passed on."

"Not to mention the land bank. Very generous man, Governor Deloache. I'm proud to call him a friend, the way his bank acts as a charitable institution."

Mrs. Joiner smiled pensively. "Why, I'll have you know that it was my training as a nurse that my parents give me, to make sure I didn't wind up living off other people like a sinner, that provides my farm with its mortgage payments."

"I believe you raise peanuts out there now instead of cotton, don't you, Etta May?"

"Maize," Mrs. Joiner said shortly.

"Could have sworn you'd told me peanuts." Arliss mused. "Like that Nigra boy with the research up in Georgia, named after the president—what's his name? Carver."

"I don't rightly recall a president named Carver."

"George Washington Carver—he's in all the newspapers these days. You should read them once in awhile, so you can keep informed. It's been wise of you to take a few tips from a Nigra."

"Maize." Mrs. Joiner crocheted, smiling and flicking her gaze around the room. It landed on Viola, who observed the hard glassy brightness, sealing the eyeballs like lacquer.

"You know, Etta May, now that you mention it I must be one of the chief mainstays of your little patch—almost a majority stockholder. And what I advise is: follow the Nigra and stick to peanuts."

"I think it's just about time for your medicine," Mrs. Joiner said, arranging the crochet on her chair arm. "I noticed you had a new bedsore the last time you used the pan. Would you like me to get Viola here to put the ointment on it? Seeing as how you seem to prefer black hands to decent white ones."

"That would be mighty nice of Viola. I trusted her with my children, don't see why I can't trust her with my bedsores."

"The Lord blesses all kinds—money grubbers and harlots and nigger lovers alike." Mrs. Joiner measured a spoonful of brown fluid into a glass.

Viola felt the toxin stirring in her veins, but she was bolstered by a lifetime's habituation. "Here's the ointment, girl." Mrs. Joiner dropped a small bottle into her outstretched palm. "Just make sure you get it rubbed in good. Deep and hard, that's what Mrs. Ransom needs. Never mind what she says, I know what's the best thing for her."

Viola went to the bedside, and waited with her eyes downturned for Mrs. Joiner to help her heave Arliss on her side; behind the lowered lids she stared acid at the carpet.

"Etta May, I don't much like talk about nigger lovers and all when you're talking in front of them," said Arliss. "Viola's different, she understands. But a woman with any breeding at all knows not to do that—no point in hurting their feelings, they're not dumb animals. Please remember what I say in the future." She groaned as Mrs. Joiner grasped her shoulder for the push.

"I'll let the girl tend to the lower end. My training has prepared me for anything, but I think I can let somebody else do that job for once." Viola in turn strained against Arliss's rump. They had almost succeeded in overturning her when someone threw the bedroom door open. It hit the wall with a crash

"Mother!" yelled Mavis.

Arliss tottered and fell face down in the bed linens. Her nightgown had rucked up over her hips, its slippery satin bunched in a wad, exposing the oozing sore.

"What do you *want?*

The cry, gagged by sheets and pillows, was difficult to hear; but her right arm waved a frantic signal above her back.

"Mother!" Mavis cried again. She caught sight of the bedsore. "Oh! How awful! Mother, are you all right?"

Viola grabbed Arliss's head and turned it to one side for air. "Cover me up!" Arliss bleated. Tugging the nightgown over the wasted flesh, Viola pulled up the sheet. It was all she could do to stifle a smile. Mrs. Joiner stood to one side, taken aback, her soft doughy mouth folding in and out like an accordion.

"Mavis"—Arliss drew a breath and shrieked—"get out of my room."

"But I can't! I've just got to tell you!"

"Tell me what?" Arliss, in her humiliation, could not control her saliva; it frothed over her teeth and drained down the pillow case. "How dare you disturb me when I'm about to get treated? You—you—changeling!"

Mavis flushed. She had never got this charge directly to her face before. "I came to tell you important news," she wailed. "I just got the telephone call!"

"What call?"

"From the Macafee ranch! The call came to me personally. That girl that works for them telephoned me—me! I got it in the library."

"Since that's the only telephone in this house—" Arliss began crisply. "I'm getting a crick in my neck. Viola!"

"Yessum." Viola hurried to correct the angle; her hands trembled on the satin-clad shoulders.

"You don't understand! Sophie had Dandy telephone me. That's what Dandy said."

"For what, may I ask?"

"The baby got born last night. And Mother, the most terrible thing has happened."

"What was it? Boy or girl? If it looks like Grant, that's what's terrible."

"Dandy didn't say. Mother, it's just awful, it'll just break your heart!"

Viola clenched her hands beneath her apron, keeping her eyes glued to the floor.

"The baby had chest problems. Before they could even call the doctor or anything—and then they didn't, because it wasn't any use. Dandy helped it get born herself, and then—then—and it couldn't breathe, it couldn't get a breath. It's gone and died."

Everyone in the room paused.

Mavis looked at them, one by one. "Mrs. March wasn't there. Grant insisted, he had her go on all the way down to San Antonio to the Renfrow boy's wedding. The baby wasn't supposed to come for another two weeks or so. Sophie's all alone out there until her mother can get back. Grant won't let the doctor come now, Dandy says he's so cut up it's like he's gone crazy. The funeral's day after tomorrow. You wouldn't believe what he's planning, I can't believe it but Dandy told me—"

"You're going to die from no breath if you don't slow down," Arliss said calmly. But Mrs. Joiner had already begun to shake her head in commiseration.

"Dandy says Sophie managed to ask especially, in the middle of her trouble—she said, 'Telephone Miss Mavis Ransom and ask her to go to Bernice. Ask her to go to the Baptist church. Not the Presbyterian church, the Baptist. And to put flowers all around the altar. 'I want flowers in my church for my poor baby,' she said. 'I want Mavis Ransom to do it.' She asked for *me*, Mother. I didn't even get invited to their wedding! Isn't it the wonder of the world? I don't know what to think!"

"I suppose it's very sad. Poor little Sophie March." Arliss cogitated. "Grant's first-born, too. I suspect he is pretty outdone. Well— did Dandy mention if Grant was going to pay the florist, or are we?"

"How can you care about that?" cried Mavis. She turned to Viola. "Go out and get Ezra. Tell him to cut as many flowers all over the garden as he can get his hands on. I'll wire the Dallas florist and have them ship some wreaths down on the train for tomorrow. Meanwhile I'll take in the ones from here—get William for me, tell him it's urgent, he has to drive me to town."

"I suppose," Arliss said from the tangle in the bed, "that seeing as how we're partners, we can afford to offer a few blooms for the Macafee's dead child. It's a pity about the little thing."

"Go on, Viola! Are you ever going? Tell Ezra to get a move on. Great day in the morning!"

Viola lurched for the door. "When did it happen?" she heard Arliss ask as she left the room.

"This morning, early. Before dawn."

"It's a shame and a pity," cried Mrs. Joiner.

CLATTERING DOWN the stairs two at a time, Viola reached the foot and stumbled. The parquet spun beneath her in a pattern of golden squares. Her elbow was seized from behind. William stooped, pulling her back to her feet. He wore the bald round look of youth, and Viola, in a whirling vision of him that rose beyond her turmoil, mistook him for a William fifteen years gone: he was her boy, standing there.

"Where're you rushing off to in such a hurry?"

Then he saw the tears in her eyes. "Are you hurt, old lady?" The July dazzle wavered around them. The fanlight burned white hot on Viola's retina, with William's form black against it.

"No, sir!" she gasped.

"I believe you better sit down for a minute. Are you sure you didn't hurt yourself?"

"No, sir, I ain't——" Her eyes widened. He led her over to the hall chair used by some butler a century before in an English country house, and sat her on it, rubbing her shoulder.

"Could've sprained something, at least."

She nursed the breath that would make words. "Miss Mavis sent me down. She came up to Miss Arliss's room just now; she said 'Go find Ezra, go find William.'"

"What for?"

"She's got to get to town with flowers."

William laughed. "No need to snap your neck for it." Then he began to frown. "But that's not all—is it, Viola?"

"No, sir." Her mouth felt dry.

"Flowers—for what?" He was suddenly stern.

"She got a telephone call a few minutes back. From Dandy."

So quickly did his face lose color that he looked made of wax. "Flowers?" he whispered.

His mouth opened. It kept opening, larger than she could have thought possible, growing deep and black, a rictus too terrible for her to see. His head threw back on his shoulders, his eyes blind slits; he made no sound. The cords of his neck carved the flesh away, the silent howl drifting to the chasm of white fire above them, joining that arching place of light.

Then she was kneeling, holding his legs. "It's over," she whispered in little gasps, "it's done finished. Oh, child, oh child, come down, come down." She kneaded her fists against his legs, to wrest him from the abyss; throughout his suffering he became all the more terrible to regard, the face of the small boy she reared, collapsing into infancy and haggard old age, timeless. "Child," she begged, "child, come down to me."

He shuddered in her hands. Knees buckling, he slowly folded towards the floor. His shoulders heaved; but still no sound, not the dryest sob, cut the stillness. She held him, and pressed his face in her breasts. "All right now," she whispered. "All right now. Hush now. Uh-huh," she hummed, as the shudders broke in waves through him, "never you mind"; and it was her tears falling on his neck that made him lift and stare sightlessly at the ceiling, head twisted like an inquiring schoolboy.

"Ahhhh." He sighed. His hand crept to his eyes. He dug the knuckles into the lids.

"I don't want to hear about it," he whispered.

"Never you mind."

"She—she—" he faltered, still grinding the white sockets and the temples, where a vein throbbed with pale blue ephemerality.

"She's all right, she come through. It's only just the baby. She done asked Dandy to call." The wince, hidden by his fist, was visible when the vein jumped against the skin.

"No more," he whispered.

"Nawsuh. No more." She stroked the taut seersucker on his shoulder blades. "Can you get up now?"

"I think—I believe—" He staggered to his feet. A smile twisted strangely on his mouth.

"Miss Mavis, she's suppose to get Ezra to help her. Now you go on in the library. I'm going to get Ezra to drive her in, he knows how some."

"All right."

THE SUNLIGHT slanted through the oaks, laying dark bars across the gravel drive. Viola watched the Lincoln roadster shudder down the curve and towards the gate. Ezra had not yet mastered the clutch; twice he stalled the engine, revving it back with a roar, and each time the cargo in the rumble seat trembled and shed a cascade of crimson and purple petals. On the inside, Mavis sat banked in piles of roses, her yellow cheeks smooth and solemn, her eyes trained sedately ahead of her. Even when Ezra ground the gears she did not flinch.

Above her head hung an entire branch pruned from a bush, thorns and all; the spray just touched her temple, brushing a rose into her hair. She waited, aloof from the voluptuous mockery of roses. Her ugliness had grown maidenly, austere, endowed with a mission. She nodded once to Ezra when he apologized, and her hand gently teased the pendant flower aside. The tires launched ahead in a burst of dust. The next instant they were out of sight.

Viola lingered at the front door, feeling the four o'clock sun. What now, she thought. What can happen? What is one little death, after all? The fanlight loomed high behind her, like a crown over the door. Its panes lay flat and empty; there was nothing but the faint outline of the stair landing through them. One baby, born in the wrong. A small spasm caused her to close her eyes.

As she turned to go back into the house, she heard a whippoorwill ask its silly question, and then answer it, out in the woods.

IT WAS night, and still Mavis had not returned.

"You say Ezra drove her? Why not William?" Arliss asked, when Viola brought the dinner trays to the two combatants in the big bedroom upstairs.

"Mr. William got him a little touch of sickness. Just a little bug, he picked it up in town. He's going to feel better soon."

"A Nigra driving her all the way to town?" Mrs. Joiner said with sweet emphasis, and smiled over her dinner, the assiduous lips wrapping around her corn cob.

"Ezra has worked here for many years, Etta May. He and Bessie," Arliss intoned. "And now I've had William train him as a chauffeur. A step of progress—a new innovation, I'm proud to say. Perhaps you don't realize that I have quite a name around this county for them."

"Maybe they had a breakdown." The exigencies of a chicken breast absorbed Mrs. Joiner.

"Oh, I doubt it. I'm certain Mavis just ran into somebody in Bernice, maybe got asked to supper there."

"I've heard such terrible stories in my time," Mrs. Joiner said placidly, "just horrible things. It's always when folk least expected it, too. The temptation gets to be too much." She dissected a bone, and laid it on her tray beside the plate. "The world we live in!"

"Remember what I mentioned this afternoon, Etta May?"

"I believe I——"

"Just keep it in mind. That's all. Breeding will tell."

Viola refilled their tea glasses from the silver pitcher, keeping her eyes trained on the carpet.

"I hope William took his illness to bed. I don't want chance germs flying around the house infecting everybody."

"Yessum, he did. He's in there now."

"Glad to hear it." She fished in her glass with talons for the lemon and sucked on it greedily, leering at Mrs. Joiner. "Nice thing about being confined is, you can be yourself. Nobody of any account to shame with bad manners."

"You ready for your cherry pie? I'm going to go fetch it from Bessie, she'll take it out the oven nice and hot," Viola said. She refused to look at either woman.

"I think I'll skip the pie tonight. My appetite is getting daintier these days. But you go ahead, Etta May, if you feel your girth can stand it."

"I will have some, thanks all the same." Mrs. Joiner finished her chicken in the same way she measured her words, with regular soft bunchings of the lips.

"Just like flabby muscles working," muttered Arliss, but smiled playfully when Mrs. Joiner looked up.

THE HARSH electric light glared in the vault of the kitchen. The room always seemed to buzz at night, catching up the crickets and cicadas outside the screen door and blending in an undertone. Often Viola remarked to Bessie that the current might be leaking from the wires, tainting their every move. Tonight the hum droned in her ear, and the green paint gave the cabinets and walls a repellent aura. Her feet stuck to the linoleum; this was the hottest room in the house.

"How do you stand that noise?" she asked Bessie when she set the tray down on the sink counter.

"Don't hardly hear it no more, unless you make me." Bessie was kneading bread, her arms up to the elbows in white flour.

"One piece of pie, up there."

"Bet it's for the old sow."

"That's right."

"She going to have to wait," Bessie grunted. "I ain't leaving this dough." She flipped the mass over. "I done saved Ezra the turnip greens, some of that fatback and the pot liquor. He ain't come in yet."

"I know it."

Bessie turned a worried eye. "Where you suppose they be?"

Viola shrugged. "Mrs. Joiner said, 'Could've had them a break-down.'" She mimicked the nurse in a high drawl. "Girl, I'm too tired out to wonder."

"You sure in a persnickety mind this night, Viola."

"I just—land! Sometimes the way this house grows on my bones, I want to catch a train to Mexico."

"You mean them." Bessie glanced at the ceiling.

"Mm-m! I mean them."

"Well, when Miss Arliss gets good and well, she going to get rid of—"

"Girl. Ain't you figured the facts yet about Miss Arliss?" Viola crashed the plate of pie on the counter, and stood with her arms crossed in disgust.

"What you mean?"

"Ain't you figured out yet what that woman's doing? Or are you slow as Ezra?"

"Don't you bring that bile from up there down to my kitchen, Viola. We got to get along. What's been eating on you?" Bessie reared her head back, ready to defend her husband, narrowing her eyes.

"I'll tell you what been eating on me." Suddenly Viola felt so angry that her head ached. Somewhere a child, one year old now, was probably learning to walk, to talk among strangers. The crackle from the light irritated her to frenzy. "I'll tell you. In case you want to know. Miss Arliss she's talking good now, hear? She's talking just as good as she done long before she got her stroke. Well, don't you reckon she could walk just as good too? And turn herself over in that bed? And use the plumbing like the rest of us? She could. She can! But she won't. She won't get her girl ready for that trip, she makes me do it. She won't tend to her family what need her, she let that old devil come into this kitchen and run her fingers over the stove to see is it clean, and hound us and hound us—and you know why she do that, you know why she let all that happen? Because she likes it. Yes, ma'am, she likes it. She likes the wickedness. It don't matter to her who's wasting away where in this house. She'd rather have bed sores! Just as long as she can get that old hog to bow down, making her carry the slops! Her own shit. Rubbing that woman's face in it, laying up there like—" Viola stopped and knotted her jaw. Her face went stony, and Bessie was afraid. Viola saw the fear. "If you had you a child, would you send that child out into the cold, and nary a loving word from your mouth? If you had the blessings of God, and then took sick, would you come back from the dead just to rile a pitiful old hog of a white woman? If you able to walk again, be the Lord's kindness and a chance to redeem His love, would you play like you can't, just for the fun? I can't understand it," she cried, "I thought I could, I thought it's just white folk, making their own misery to the law we don't need, because we take care of our own. We take care of them the best way we can. I thought that's all it was." Her voice dwindled.

"But it ain't," she whispered. Grant's face hung in her mind, filling with emptiness, his eyes closed as he arched over Sarah. Then the eyes opened, and she saw the starved fury boring through the pupils. "It ain't. It ain't that. It's something else."

"Viola," Bessie said low. She stepped toward her, gingerly at first, and folded her arms around the trembling body. "Don't you mind now," she soothed. "Don't pay no mind. You can't let yourself care, that's all. You done caring too much—ain't we learned from the time we born we can't let ourselves care?"

"Yes," Viola whispered.

"If Miss Arliss can get well and walk, then she the one going to be mighty sorry she don't do it. She the one will pay the devil. Not you."

"You ain't understand," Viola mumbled in futility.

"Maybe I ain't." She hugged Viola and let her go. "Don't worry none. Ezra going to come home soon now, he going to be back before long."

"Uh-huh," Viola said abstractedly, taking up the plate of cherry pie; then she realized that Bessie was comforting herself. "They be here soon, girl," she assured in the tired voice. "They ain't had no accident."

"I know it." Bessie turned back to her bread dough. "Oh, yes, I know it certain." She thrust her fists in the mixture, steady and slow, to the pace of her worried thoughts.

IT WAS late. Viola dropped wearily onto her bed. The house rested all around her, its halls and caverns in semidarkness; only the kitchen lights still burned, and the sconces of the second-floor hall. She lay very still, slipping in and out of a doze. The walls between her and the half-empty storerooms echoed with creaks and silence. Once she came partially awake, imagining she heard a hollowness on the silence: a sound made of dream, a roaring kin to the surf in the conch that sat on top of her dresser, a souvenir brought to her once, long ago, by William, from Galveston on the Gulf. He was a little boy. His boy face smiled up at her in expectation, as she handled the flaring horn. Behind him Sarah danced in a pinafore, watching her delight. Then she fell into deep sleep once more. "Hold it up to your ear and hear the ocean," William said. "That's what it sounds like." And Sarah begged her to do it, plaits swinging in the motion of her head. "I hear it! I hear it," Viola told them, "That's the ocean inside, trapped in the heart—you brought me what I can't ever hear," and she smiled at them; "the shell recollects it and sings about it for good." "Yes," whispered William; "Yes," Sarah agreed, "it's for you because you can't go hear it for yourself." They listened, three ears pressed to the pink flange which glowed like a lamp. The sound of the surf breathed hollow, surrounding their tenderness. It grew and receded, a sound so remote and ineffable that nothing could change it. "I was worried. You come home at last," Sarah murmured in a contralto voice; above the ruffled pinafore her black eyes shone. "You been mighty long about it." Her little white legs kicked high, sideways. "You must be hungry if you didn't eat nothing in town before you got here." "I'm all right, child," Viola assured her; nothing could compete with this bliss. It was unlike Sarah to worry, Sarah who never thought of food. "You come in anyhow, come in and eat," Sarah urged with a grin; and then a door slammed behind her—"They'll wake up!" she warned. And Viola did, the kitchen door still slamming, reverberating through the open window by her head. The murmuring voices drifted up to her from the screen. But now she could not make out the words; only Bessie's low gruff pleasure came through a slur of sentences, their meaning unclear, and Ezra's higher-pitched easy replies.

Viola settled her head back on the pillow and shut her eyes. If she could recapture—but the dream failed, the sweetness lost, falling away. Ezra back and safe, for Bessie's peace of mind . . . the children evading her, growing up into creatures of dim intransigence . . . the shell squatting, quenched, on the dresser top. She could feel the chalkiness crumble between her hands, as she fumbled it to coax it back—and then she woke and sat bolt upright. There was a sound.

A sound, thin and shrill, sang through the floorboards to her room.

She blinked. She was not awake. But she felt the graininess of her eyes, and looked down at the rumpled quilt. No, not dreaming;

awake for certain. The sound swelled into a wail. It came from directly beneath her. It was unmistakable, a noise as unlike the roar of the sea as her own scarce breath.

Slipping off the bed, she paddled barefoot to the head of the stair. Someone had turned off the sconces. The piercing filament of sound traveled to her, carrying her back in time, and yet its impossibility transfixed her to the hanging dark, the chambered house: she was blank, groping for the dream, for sense. The wail died away, renewed. It compelled her out of the crystallized memories; it was immediate. She flew down the steps, searching in the gloom for a door, and at last found it. She flung it open.

Mavis stared out at her, blotting the light. A strange look of fright and stubbornness quivered on her features. She moved towards Viola; but the wail sharpened and jerked her back. She crouched over a pillow on the bed, and Viola saw the pillow squirm fitfully against its linen wrappings.

"I think he's hungry," Mavis whispered. "I tried to feed him, but I don't know what to do." She picked up a boat-shaped glass bottle from the bed, and fingered the rubber nipple.

Viola stood beside the bed. She was scooping up the bundle of wrappings, peering down at the contorted face; she was swaying to and fro, in wonder and bewilderment at the dream come alive; and a throaty sound rose instinctively from her. "Mmm-mmmm. Hush now, little baby," and she grabbed for the bottle in Mavis's hand, and touched it to the cheek on her breast. The tiny mouth found it, rooting on rubber; warm milk trickled out one side. The crying was gone.

She stared at the wizened face. The waxy coat of vernix clung to the hairs on his head. Under one fine lock she could see a smear of the mother's blood. He fell asleep quite quickly, milk bubbling a little on his lower lip. The lip curled, a scrap of mauve flesh, so insignificant as to stir Viola to the core.

At last she looked to Mavis.

"Will you show me—how to do it?" Her eyes, humble, met Viola's.

"Yessum," Viola whispered.

"Let me hold him. Please," Mavis implored, and that purpose which Viola saw in her face, earlier in the afternoon (could it still be the same day, the same year or century?) beatified her now. She held out her arms stiffly, like brackets, as if she could hold them that way forever. Her cheeks lay smooth and untroubled. Viola recognized the fecund gloss on her eyes, the inward-looking expectancy, even as she gazed at the baby sucking gently in his sleep.

"Bend your arms a little bit," Viola instructed in a whisper. "Make them like they nursing him."

Mavis did as she was told; her arms cradled in anticipation.

"Not too stiff and hard now, mind. He want to feel like he's lying on his mama."

She transferred the bundle to the outstretched arms. The baby shuddered and rolled his head, and then settled against them. Mavis fit herself around him. Her eyes did not leave his face.

How a Baby Was Found

Throughout the long night they sat there together, Mavis and Viola, keeping vigil.

"Where did you get this here?" Viola whispered, holding up the bottle while she waited for the milk to warm on the chafing dish stove she had brought up from the kitchen.

"I got it from the drugstore. After I found him, I knew he'd need something to eat. So I went and asked Mr. Sloane for a feeder. Mrs. Sloane filled it with milk. He wouldn't drink it, though, not until you gave it to him."

"That's because he's so new. He don't know how to eat. He's just a newborn thing."

"Is he?" Mavis peered with delighted interest at the little mouth, pursing and closing.

"Didn't Mrs. Sloane tell you that?" Viola gave Mavis a quick, sharp look.

"She didn't exactly see him. See, I left him in the car with Ezra."

"You what?" Viola, in her surprise, nearly let the milk boil. "You mean to say you left him with that Ezra? He don't know nothing."

"I—I wanted to keep him to myself."

"Miss Mavis. What in the world did Mrs. Sloane say when you came into the drugstore asking for a baby bottle?"

"She was kind of surprised." The house surrounded them with darkness and silence; Mavis's voice was husky. She unbunched one infant fist; the fingers spread like a sea anemone, then closed around her thumb.

"Uh-huh, I reckon! What did you tell her?"

"Oh, I told her I'd found a baby."

"Did you say where?"

Mavis lifted her head and gazed blandly at Viola. "I told her where. In the back pew of the Baptist church. I didn't even know he was there at first. I nearly missed him! Can you imagine? He would have been there still, right this minute, if I hadn't heard him crying just when I'd done the last roses."

"Ain't you wondered how he got there?"

"Oh, somebody broke in. The preacher found the choir door lock busted when he went in the back to look for some vases. He was pretty upset. Said it must be some more oil field people, tramps and such, like the ones that got in a few weeks ago. See, it was a Thursday today, the church wouldn't be opened again until Saturday. He might have died! Oh, how horrible!" And she squeezed him close, making him mew and squirm. Her head was propped on a pile of pillows; she stretched her legs in a luxury of relief. "But I found him. Didn't I, baby? I got you saved."

Viola did not know what to say. She poured the milk into the bottle, sorting in her mind through the minefield of possibilities. How much did Mavis realize? How much had she said to the people in town?

"What'd Mrs. Sloane tell you then, after you say where you found him?"

"Well, she figured out where he came from."

Viola froze in the middle of reattaching the teat.

"How's that?" she said.

"It seems a couple of those tramp people passed through here last month, a man and a woman. The woman was real big, Mrs. Sloane said—she was having a baby. They asked around Bernice for some food. They were very poor, come from the fields in Southeast Texas. Anyhow, she said she felt real sorry for them, because the woman looked so pinched up. She said it didn't look long before her time. They left town a couple of weeks ago. But Mrs. Sloane believes they must have come back—how else could it be?" Mavis added, with a trace of her old slyness, looking at Viola under her lids. "They would have had to give up their baby, see? Too poor to keep it. He's an orphan now. Anyhow, it doesn't matter, does it, Viola, where he came from. Whoever it was, they left him in the church on purpose. Just for somebody else to find. And I did, I found him. If I hadn't've come to the church—!"

Viola switched between the baby's face and Mavis's. He was so small; it was impossible to tell anything about him. Looks, resemblances, even the hair color was nondescript, a mousy shade that could belong to anyone. She fitted the nipple over the bottle mouth, and bent down, drawing it softly against his cheek where he nestled. "What you planning to do about this child?"

"What do you mean, 'do about' him?"

"You going to find him a home, or give him to the orphans' home up in Dallas, or what?"

"You know what I'm going to do with him, Viola," Mavis replied levelly.

Viola stared at her.

"It can't be, child. We can't do it. You don't know what all this means, you don't know what you taking on."

"If you mean Mother—"

"I ain't talking about your mama."

"Then it doesn't matter, then. Nothing on this earth will make the slightest bit of difference."

"Who all," Viola said ponderously, "know you have this baby?"

Mavis's eyes widened. She tightened her arm around the suckling form. "Mr. Sloane. Mrs. Sloane. The Baptist preacher." She paused. "Probably the whole town of Bernice by now." Her innocent defiance chimed too ready, too prepared. "Nobody's going to stop me. There's nobody that can complain."

"Have you asked yourself one question?" Viola went on doggedly. "Have you asked yourself 'Why?'"

Mavis dropped her eyes down.

The silence lengthened in the room. The churning sound of the insects rose and fell beyond the open window above the kitchen door. At last Mavis spoke.

" 'Why' has nothing to do with me." She knitted the edges of the baby's blanket together. "He's mine now," she whispered. "That was the way it was supposed to happen. That's all."

Slowly Viola walked to the rocker beside the window, and sat, staring out at the dark. There was nothing more to say.

SHE WOKE up, joints aching, in the rocker at first sunlight.

A breeze fluttered the curtains lightly towards her face. Her head felt heavy, fuddled in strands of dream. Outside she could hear birds' racket, and a distant cow lowing. She scrubbed her eyes, looking around. The bedroom was washed in the early colors: the shadows, mauve and rose, stillness everywhere, the ceiling rimmed and gilded. There on the bed lay the infant, a yellowish stream of excrement seeping out of his diaper onto the coverlet. Mavis was nowhere to be seen.

Viola heard voices in the hall and straightened up.

"Isn't it wonderful?" Mavis was saying with earnest ruthlessness. "Isn't it more wonderful than a trip to Europe, Wicky? Remember when you said, 'Something will come along'? And now it has!"

"I don't think — it wasn't quite necessarily what I —" William mumbled. "A baby, you say, honey?"

"Yes, a baby! Left in town by some tramp couple who couldn't take care of it."

"Now, hold on a minute." William began to come to. Viola could sense him, standing by the door, his face still swollen with sleep, the loss gaunt and still at the back of his eyes from the day before. She heard the early morning roughness in his voice: "Dragging me out of bed with hoboes —"

"I'm telling you! Come in here, see for yourself."

Viola gazed at the baby. In sleep he was whole, the face molded into smoothest petals, devoid of hunger, empty of feeling, like a cup waiting to be filled. She had forgotten the serenity of a sleeping newborn. He lay in perfect remoteness, his inner life as alien as a fish, swimming under the waters of distant worlds.

"Wait!" Mavis whispered. "I nearly forgot—you were sick yesterday. I don't want you to pass any germs on to him. Are you still—?"

"No, I don't believe so. . . ." He gathered focus. Viola could picture him beginning to put two and two together out in the hall. "I'm not sick now, honey," he murmured, and his voice was tinged with an aching discovery. "I'm just fine."

"Are you sure? I mean, Ezra had to drive me and all."

"Not sick. Not anymore." His tone lifted; now the wonder and misgiving rang like a bell.

"Shh! You might wake him. Well, if you're sure—"

William and Mavis appeared in the open doorway. They both looked strange, stepping into the sheltering light, into a new existence. Mavis held back for an instant, her face benign, rapt on the bundle of clothes. At first William did not follow her gaze. He glanced around the room, dazedly, in hesitant search.

"Where—" he whispered. Then he found Viola, and his stare locked on hers. He was a stunned man who awakes in a foreign room, to realize his past and future in a single query. She left his face and slowly turned to the bed. It was then, at the moment Mavis rushed to the bedside, hovering, that he dragged his eyes away from Viola and shifted them painfully to where she stood, and saw his son.

What Happened
at the Funeral

Much later in the morning, Viola made yet another of her innumerable journeys between the floors. She had carried orders of diapers sent from town to Mavis's room; she had carried boxes of baby garments up from the front door, where they were handed to her by the dry goods delivery boy. More things arrived from Sopwith's Department Store—rattles, a silver spoon, a porringer, a complete layette in embroidered batiste. The drive stretched through the trees, a viaduct of goods. Mavis had been on the telephone most of the morning, buying and buying. In between times she rocked her baby back to sleep, or tried to master the trick of burping him. At eleven o'clock the doorbell chimed yet again. Viola opened the door on a grim paradise: the front porch had become a raft of flowers, twisted into wreaths, bunched in funeral urns and towers of austere lilies. Hardly a brick showed beneath this floral monument, and she could not see the steps over them all. A man stood waiting beside the tallest lily mast. He wore greasy dungarees.

"Oh, Lordy."

"I brung these from the depot," the man said. "They come on the Dallas train awhile ago."

"What are they for?"

"Hell, I don't know. The order said 'Ransom' on it. The boss told me to bring them on out here in the truck. Y'all have to pay for the truck, he hired it out from under me."

"Don't know nothing about all this," Viola muttered. "Can you wait here a minute, please sir?"

"Wait here all day, excepting y'all have to pay me for it."

"Yes, sir." She puzzled as she crossed the foyer—had Mavis decided to celebrate? Then she remembered. These were the flowers from the Dallas florist, ordered the previous day to commemorate the baby's death. Viola stopped midway across the foyer, and leaned into the butler's hall chair to laugh, her amusement so deep and painful that she could not get up for a moment, even when the strange man peered around the threshold, frowning.

"What you doing there, girl?"

"I—I sorry, I just took a little dizzy, just a spell—I get that way sometime in here." She motioned to the spaces above her head.

"You better not be laughing at me," the man growled. "I ain't no fancy kind of flower wagon. Git on up and watch your step."

"Yes, sir."

"Where is the body these are meant for?" the man demanded.

"It—he—she's upstairs!" Viola gasped, and then caught his glaring eye and ducked her head meekly. "It's some kind of mistake. Them flowers all suppose to go to the Baptist church back in Bernice."

"How you know that? You ain't asked nobody yet."

"I can go get somebody for you."

"You do that." The man grimaced, and spat a jet of tobacco juice into a furled lily leaf.

"Mr. William! Can you come on down? Man here, wanting you."

William appeared on the landing. His step was jaunty, his expression suave and affable. "Hidy," he said to the truck driver. "What can I do for you?"

"It's them flowers Miss Mavis done ordered for the Baptist church," Viola whispered. "For the Macafee child."

"How's that?" He squinted at her, and then noticed the massy bower on the porch. "God Almighty!"

"Sure enough." Viola grinned.

"Ah—ahem! Yes," he said, surveying them gravely from the door frame, "thank you kindly for bringing them out. Much obliged to you. But they need to go to the Baptist church in Bernice. Just stop by the parsonage and the preacher'll let you in."

"I ain't hauling them back for nothing," the man replied.

"Course not, what an idea! Here——" William fumbled in his pocket, and brought out a bill. "This take care of it? I'll give you a hand putting them back on your truck."

"That Mr. Macafee's young'un, that who they're for?"

"That's right," William nodded, his face a picture of amiable reserve.

"I heard about that. Mighty sad. I worked for his daddy one time, doing some hay baling."

"Yes, mighty sad," said William.

"I'll probably see you there at the funeral," the man said from the cab, after the truck had been reloaded. "Whole town's turning out for it."

"Are they now?"

"Don't get funerals like that one any old day." He started the motor.

"Like what?" William asked in curiosity.

"Whole town's talking as how they're going high on the hog." He raced the engine. "So long," he called over his shoulder. William backed away, his head cocked at the man's remark.

"What's he talking about, you reckon?" asked Viola, when he entered the foyer. "What's he talking about, that funeral?"

"I can't tell you what I don't know." Then he smirked, and turned away. "Did you ever, Viola? Did you ever in your life see so many wreaths in one place? Mavis! That poor baby's going to think it was the botanical garden." And he climbed, chuckling, up the stairs, pausing once on the landing to intone, "In the midst of Death we are in Life." Then he disappeared around the corner.

I SAT, at the age of sixteen, in my special steel-reinforced chair in the conservatory, eating a tubful of cheese soufflé beneath the wisteria while Viola described my grandfather William's amusement.

" 'In the midst of Death we are in Life,' " she repeated. "That's what he say, there on the stairs. Then he climb on up to see the very same baby what the flowers come for." She laughed deeply, as she always did when she reached this part.

I considered, looking up through the wisteria leaves above my head. The conservatory plants filled the room with their heavy, scented moisture. "Sometimes I feel a bit like that myself," I said. "Death in the midst of life."

"Now, don't you start your moping. You a good, big, healthy girl. Don't you start that up, Victoria."

"I have not started anything. I was merely musing," I lied, and then took another scoop of soufflé. "I was wondering what he had in mind when he said that."

"It's just a story."

"But it happened! I can see it happening." I smiled. "It is as real as this spoon is to me. You have been telling me these stories all my life. That is why, when you reach the part where Grandfather turns on the stairs, I understand that he meant something more. Because that is the way it worked for him. And me — it is my way, too."

"All right, then." Viola pressed her lips together, wishing to change the subject. "Did I tell you what Dandy say, that time I seen her at the funeral — about how Mr. Grant carried on, and wouldn't let the coffin be open for the service — how he told Mrs. March when she come running back from San Antonio on the train that he don't want nobody looking down on his dead child? Won't even call in the undertaker. He took care of all the business himself."

I nodded. "Tell it again."

"Well, then . . . Mrs. March start wailing and hollering, blaming him because she say he made her go down to San Antonio in the first place, and now the baby come while she down there. She say, 'I'll never forgive him for it.'

"She took Miss Sophie back into town, to stay at her house till she get over the birth and losing her first-born child. Dandy went with them. But then, he come to the March house in Bernice, right before the funeral start. 'Sophie has to come to the funeral with me in the car,' he said. And Mrs. March, she's pushing at him, telling him to go away.

"But before she could do a thing, Miss Sophie come trailing down the stairs, dressed in a black dress, and a hat with a black veil hanging down, and she say, so quietly they can't hardly hear, where they all stand in the vestibule, 'I have to go, Mama.' She say, 'It's my duty to my husband and baby.' And without another word, she took Mr. Grant's arm. Dandy tried to stop her, too. Dandy's the one she made to help her dress. But she would not listen to Dandy. And she went on to the funeral with that devil man.

"Then they got to the cemetery." Viola paused, staring into the fountain pool as if it were a crystal, looking back on the past. "And the band was there, that he call up from Louisiana. And the whole town turn out, just like that delivery man said it would."

THE BAND arrived from Louisiana, from the town of Lafayette. They climbed down from the train that stood chuffing and wheezing beside the depot: five musicians, dressed in streaky black, with collarless white shirts buttoned high on their throats, their black skin shining with sweat in the late July sun. Viola witnessed their arrival herself, as she walked past the depot on her way to the cemetery. Ezra had driven her to town. Mavis and William both remained home, Mavis with Bessie to help her tend the baby.

The men looked around the platform, talking between themselves, and grinned audaciously at Viola when they noticed her picking her way across the tracks from the courthouse square. One of them lifted his trumpet high in the air. It scintillated in the sunlight, nickel silver.

"Hey there, pretty sister," he called.

Viola looked up.

"Where you high-stepping to so fast?"

She flung her head back proudly, ignoring him, turning her nose up. Who did he think he was?

"Whooee!" He tilted his head back and cried out. Then he whistled, nudging one of his companions. Viola watched him from the corner of her eye. "Them Texas gals look mighty fine to me!" he called. "Come on, pretty baby. Why don't you come on over here and give us a little bit of your time."

The man he nudged shook his head in disgust. He was short and squat, several years older than the trumpet player, and in one hand he clutched a trombone swathed in burlap flour sacking. He lacked the other's raffishness. A pair of spectacles, one hinge mended with twine, leaned on his nose. He stood, blinking and squinting at Viola, who had by now nearly gone past.

"Say there, sister," he called. Viola prepared to ignore him, too. But his voice held a slight, lost-sounding timbre. "Can you please tell us how to get to the First Baptist church in this town?"

She wheeled at an angle, and put her fists on her hips. "How come you wanting to know?"

"We got to get there quick as we can. There's a funeral at that church, we suppose to play it down to the graveyard."

"You what?"

"Yes, ma'am," he said with serious humility. Another one of the musicians, with a drum strapped to his back, idly shuffled a softshoe on the platform asphalt. "We got us this job, come up from Lafayette this very minute. You tell us how to get there?"

"Ain't no funeral, that I know of, except a poor little white baby. That can't be the one you mean."

"That's the one! That's the one!" The other four men nodded. The one with the trumpet slid his finger up and down his throat, still grinning as he eyed her.

"You going to play that funeral?" Viola asked slowly. The light beat down on the musicians, rendering them bizarre in their swallowtail coats and frayed pants. They might have sprung up from a vision, their incongruity in the Saturday-quiet Bernice like a Testament illustration. They were the black angels of Revelation, ready to blow Judgment Day.

"Yes, ma'am," rumbled the clarinet player, who stood behind the short trombonist. On the tracks the locomotive brakes squealed with release. "Reckon we going to be late, too, if you don't tell us how to find it."

"Aw, now, get back, Rondo. Don't go talking to her like that," scowled the trombonist over his glasses.

Viola assessed him, and then turned back to the clarinet player. "It's that way." She pointed toward the square. "You just walk on down there two blocks, past the hotel and the courthouse. You'll see it."

"Why, thank you kindly," the trombone player said. Then the man with the trumpet began to swagger towards her.

"What you doing tonight, with you fine proud legs?" he said.

"Hush you mouth, nigger!" Viola said coldly, and spun around and stalked away. She heard his admiring whistle, and then the sniggers of the other musicians as they taunted him, following her down the road.

But she looked back once, not heeding the lesson of Lot's wife. Her salty sweat trickled down between her breasts. She glanced over her shoulder at the cocky trumpet player, as he marched with a high-hipped swing beside his companions in the opposite direction. His elbows stuck out, his hands cradled the trumpet to his chest, where she could not see it flash anymore. The tall head was held high. His step was lively, next to the plod of the man with the trombone. A little shiver ran within her; she turned back to the road and snorted. No man in Bernice had ever chivied her so. She thought, "That boy's bold as Satan, and just as bad," and then she halted stock still, her hand curving over her mouth, and heard herself let forth a giggle.

THE CEMETERY was already crowded with people. Some sat under the elms, trying to cool themselves in the shade. Some of the women wore gingham sunbonnets; nearly everyone waved a palmetto fan. Most of them were Viola's friends. They had not, of course, joined the throng at the white Baptist church, but waited on the green paths for the graveside festivities. Now Viola learned what had coursed through Bernice like wildfire for the past two days: the funeral Grant Macafee had announced, to send his dead child to heaven, the invitation for which had been published in the Bernice newspaper, and which extended throughout the whole county, to include black and white, poor and rich, everyone who cared about sacramental occasions. Three tables, damask-shrouded, stood under a clump of elm and crape myrtle. On them perched vast silver punch bowls, and stacks of cups tottering from their own heights. When Viola stepped nearer, she saw platters piled with small iced cakes. By this time she was too dumbfounded to shake her head. "Where you been, girl?" someone cried, and she turned to see Uncle Shine standing behind her.

"What you gawking at?" he smiled. "Where's the rest of them Ransom folk?"

"Hidy, Uncle," she said cautiously. "I come in for them."

"Where they be? Ain't they going to give Mr. Macafee some respect in his sadness?" He sidled over to face her, sweeping his hand at the tables. "Lordy Lord, ain't that a sight! Best funeral this town ever seen. Plenty of folk from all over the county come in just to join the mourning. Poor poor child." He bent his head and sighed lugubriously. "We be sorry and sad to bury it this day."

He winked at Viola, licking his lips. "Looky there at that spread! Mr. Macafee's done Bernice proud. One whole table set aside just for the colored. You reckon he trying to grease that baby's way to heaven, Viola, giving us all a spread like that?"

"Don't rightly know, Uncle."

"Sure is something. I'm going to give Mr. Macafee my prayers for sure! Poor child. Poor dead thing, dead when it was born, the way I hear it. Mm-mm! I heard you got you-all a new baby out there at the Ransoms', Viola, when some folks from the oil fields left it in the white church."

"Yes, Uncle, that's the truth," Viola said, watching him from under her lashes.

"Miss Mavis and Miss Arliss, they going to take good care of it. Nome, I ain't chucking no bad word at any white folk this day. When a dead white baby be the cause of letting Mr. Macafee stick his hand in his pocket and fetch up kindness, I reckon that's the day to shout and praise the Lord. That the way with sorrow, Viola. It bring out the good in some folk. Miss Mavis, now, she's a good gal, taking in a poor baby when she don't even know his mama and daddy. I take back all I said to you that time I seen you last, about white folk. You hear me do it. But I say this to you"—he poked Viola's ribs, as a pair of little girls in tow-sack dresses wandered by and brushed against him—"this today, when the fine time come. I ain't going to be taking it back tomorrow, when everything the way it always be." He wheezed, poking her again. "Nome indeed, not tomorrow!" He rambled away, calling out to friends and relations in the pleasure of his joke.

Then Viola was left alone. She looked for a place where she could melt from public view, and slipped behind one of the elms' trunks, on the far side of the sumptuous picnic. Desperately she wished that she had not come, exposing herself to questions. The people around her chattered lazily on the grass about the Macafee death, compared to which that other event, Mavis's foundling, was secondary. Sooner or later, someone was bound to link coincidence. No one had any reason to suppose the baby's coffin, when it arrived, would be weighted with iron. The tree bole dug into her spine. If only she had known what to expect! A band from Louisiana, the petits fours and punch—what must Grant Macafee be thinking of? She huddled behind a screen of bridal wreath, praying that he would succeed.

Now strains of brass music began to stitch the summer afternoon. The cortege was winding up the road from the church, through the sun and smoky dust; they were playing "When the Saints." She could just make out the jangling tune. She pushed closer into the tree, afraid, struck with panic: in a short time, if she leaned around the trunk, she would see Grant Macafee himself, the face from her worst remembrances, the author of this fantasy of death. Nervous terror jolted through her; she craned her neck to reach a denser branch of leaves. But even here, she could no longer be safe. The leaves began to shiver. No breeze blew. Then an arm in a white sleeve appeared through the greenery. An eye, brown and lambent, half-masked by leaves, stared at her. The leaves rustled aside. With a startled edgy sigh Viola tipped forward into Dandy's shoulder.

"I seen you sneak back here awhile back," Dandy whispered. "I was laying out the last of the punch cups."

"Dandy! I like to dropped, when you done that."

"Huh! You better pull yourself together. The funeral's getting mighty close to the cemetery now."

"Why didn't you say hidy out there, if you saw me?"

Dandy regarded her with a blend of knowledge and cynicism. Viola shared her look. "Reckon you know the reason why." She smoothed her apron with small deliberate gestures. "Too many folks with their eyes wide open."

"I KNOW it, don't I know it!" Viola let out a little gasp.

Dandy peered at her meaningfully. "If this all do what Mr. Grant hope it going to do, then I say it's a miracle. Miss Sophie, she was so tore up with misery when she give me that baby to take away, I didn't know what to tell her. I been hoping you going to be here today."

"Shh." Viola stiffened. The music was now near enough to fill the air with din. The tones of brass instruments clashed on the heat, becoming part of it. Dolefully, a trumpet picked out the single notes of the opening bars of "His Eye Is on the Sparrow." Then the other horns joined in, moaning and wailing, and the people down at the cemetery gate droned in chorus the yearning words. Viola whispered, "I thought maybe Mr. Macafee was the one to put it in the church. Did you birth the baby yourself?"

"Surely I did. Who else was going to do it?"

"Then it's just you and me that know."

"That's right."

They stared at each other through the loose-patched shade. For a moment, neither spoke. The trumpet music mounted to the peak of the scale, shrilling out "on the sparrow," and then plummeted.

"It's because Mr. Macafee know it ain't his," Viola said.

"Yessum, why else?"

"Is Miss Sophie going to be all right?"

"I ain't to say. She the one asked me to telephone Miss Mavis. She reckon that was the best place. And the reason she done it at all was, she seen all of a sudden what was in Mr. Macafee's mind."

"How do you mean, what was in his mind?"

Dandy stared. "When I phone Miss Mavis, I told her the baby stopped breathing. Well, I said that for true in one way, Viola. That's what Mr. Macafee want to make it do. Stop breathing."

The chill started on Viola's arms. "Oh, my Lord God," she whispered.

"Miss Sophie was the one stopped him. She held that baby to her side, tight as she could. But we both saw how he saved it for later, just waiting his chance. Then she give me the baby, when he went out for a walk. She say, 'Dandy! Quick! Take my child, take him down to the Baptist church and put him in the pew. Break the door in if you have to. Then telephone Miss Mavis Ransom.' It the one time she stood up to him, and don't let him have his way. Why you reckon she chose Miss Mavis, Viola? Why you reckon she chose Ransoms?"

Viola gave her a long look, and then shook her head and dropped her eyes to the ground. This revelation of the depths Grant's humiliation and rage had sent him to was too dumbfounding for any other.

And then suddenly she saw him, sitting alone in the little parlor through the long night, his lean features rigid, while his wife, with whom he had never made love, gave birth in the next room to his oldest enemy's child. The enemy whose sister had taken all she wanted from him, and then shunned him and vanished. The enemy whose mother had spat on his family blood, and then hounded him with vengeance. And he—what had he done to deserve it? She saw all this. She felt sick.

"I thought about telling the sheriff on Mr. Macafee, the way he's carrying on," Dandy admitted. "Poor Miss Sophie! But then I thought, well, it's white folk business, it don't do nobody no good to get mixed up in their truck. Besides, who's going to believe a nigger woman round here? So I shut my mouth."

"You already mixed up in it. You birthed the baby. You helped save him."

"I know it."

"If you try to tell the sheriff things are different from what Mr. Grant say they are, why, he might get you blamed for the baby dying. And Miss Mavis liable to help Mr. Grant. She want to keep this child like I ain't never seen her keep nothing before. She going to go along with whatever Mr. Grant say." Viola sighed. "I remember once, she had a little puppy dog that she let die. I thought then, well, she won't never care for nothing. But I was wrong. She cares for this baby. She done gone crazy over him! Yes, girl, don't you get yourself in trouble trying to fix the wrong to right."

Dandy listened in mute balefulness.

"He's mean," Viola said. "He's a mean man. He'll do anything that suits him, if he think it's going to keep from dirtying his name or his righteousness. Righteousness! That's where that kind lands folk—next to an empty grave."

Dandy began to shake her head. "That's why Miss Sophie got herself another man. I seen what Mr. Macafee's like." She clutched her belly under the apron nervously. "You reckon he'd do that if I was to tell?"

"He will. It's best to keep shut."

"You afraid they might try to get you into trouble, with what you know?"

Viola hesitated, and then said quietly, "I helped them, didn't I? The Lord forgive me, for trying to make the best out of white folk's mess."

The music had drawn too near now, fulminating on the cemetery hush. Viola and Dandy leaned towards it, hearing the band strike into "On Jordan's Stormy Banks."

"I knows why Miss Sophie chose Ransoms," Dandy whispered. "Never mind about who I tell, I ain't telling nobody. Come on, Viola, we got to go."

"I can't look at that devil man." Viola cringed against the tree.

"Come on," Dandy urged, and lumbered around to the other side of the trunk. But her broad head reappeared, touching the bark. "Miss Sophie, she come to the funeral because Mr. Macafee promised her he let the baby alone if she come, he promise not to make ructions or try nothing. But she just about to die, Viola. Is that child doing all right? I got to tell Miss Sophie."

"He's fine, he's real good," Viola whispered. "You tell her don't worry. I'll help take good care of him." She paused, reaching out to grab Dandy's wrist. "Dandy! How much does Mr. Grant know about that baby's daddy?"

Dandy stared at her inscrutably. "The Lord know. All we can do is guess," she answered, and was gone.

The sound of the band swelled to a plangent fire in Viola's head; she could hear the crowd's staccato coughs, the scrape of boots on dry earth, as the pallbearers entered the Macafee plot. She shrank, wishing the tree could envelope her. And finally, unable to bear any more, she blanked her mind and jerked away from the bole, stepping out into the sunlight.

It was then that she realized how Grant had accomplished something the town had never before seen.

Not even on the fourth of July had Bernice County been so united; not on any other day in its history had the black and white population joined together, momentarily casteless, jammed shoulder to shoulder in purposeful intent. The realization trembled in her mind, lucid, absurd; it stayed, even as she peered over the heads to see Grant and his wife standing bowed at the graveside. It stoked somehow the stark black-suited figure's malevolence. "Killer. Murderer," she thought, and crept silently down from her vantage point, elbowing in among the solemn mourners, until she stood between Mrs. Sloane, whose stumpy little hat with its crown of artificial sweet peas jerked slightly, and Mavis's dressmaker, who gave Viola the nod of a stranger. Together they caught the dying moans of the band's penultimate tune. Then the Baptist preacher began to speak.

Viola stood on tiptoe in order to observe Grant in his hawk-faced posture of grief. But she only got a glimpse of him; someone's head intervened; a marble angel hid his profile. The shadow that she imagined climbing up from his old image was cancelled by bright July glare.

It was Sophie she saw.

The minister finished. The wide black hat, with its black drapery, lifted slowly to the light. Sophie stood rigid, one arm crooked in Grant's elbow. Some of the women around her were sobbing wetly into handkerchiefs. But the head under the hat stayed absolutely motionless, the porcelain face obscured.

The band members raised their instruments on high. Silver and gold played the sun rays into the crowd's eyes. When the song began, it was as a continuation of that play of light. "Sometimes I feel like a motherless child," the trumpet moaned. Viola scanned the musicians, looking for some remembered sensation, some glint of the outlandish feeling she had at the depot, fixing on the dark throbbing throat of the trumpet player; but that one flicker was gone. He had become something other than a man, other than an agitation within her: he was pure sorrowful music. Viola looked back to Sophie. As she did, the music rose in pitch: "Sometimes I feel like a motherless child," to the sweet high crest of lamentation. At that instant, Sophie, without a sway or tremor, pulled away from Grant's elbow, and crumpled to the earth.

The band stopped.

A paroxysm rolled through the crowd. Heads lifted, bodies pushed up onto toes.

Then came the voice. Harsh and hoarse, with the gravel of sleeplessness and hallucination rasping it, it came; and the whispers died on its bitter command. The hairs pricked up on Viola's neck. She backed away, until she stood again on the little rise under the crape myrtles, and saw Sophie's hat, lolling to one side, her spine supported by Grant's arms.

He was shadow itself. The darkness had absorbed and now underlay the skin, like smoke through a layer of wax. "Play to the finish!" he cried. "Play. It is God's will that her child is dead. Who are you to defy Him?" He stood, boosting Sophie's body upright, his elbows cocked like knives. The deep sockets of his eyes glistered with shards of light. The band raised their instruments to their lips. The drum started its monotonous hollow beat. "Sometimes I feel like a motherless child" quavered on the deadened air, a clean empty equation of music rising in a corona over the heads on the cemetery lawn.

"HE DONE drunk all his milk awhile ago, he's full as a tick. Brung up some gas, too."

Viola nodded, contemplating the little face. Bessie sat by the bassinet like a brooding tortoise. An aquatic light, wavery and green, filled Mavis's room.

"Where's Miss Mavis?"

"She in Miss Arliss's room. She went in there and ask me to stay with him till you got back. How was the funeral?"

"You ain't going to believe it," Viola sighed. "Ezra'll tell it to you."

"Well, I got to leave this child to you. I got to go fix their supper. He's real good, though. Never a sound, the whole time you gone."

"You the one who pulled the curtains?"

"Miss Mavis done it. She thinks a new baby ain't able to sleep unless the room's dark."

"She's got to learn sometime." Viola walked to the green drapes and let in the sunlight. "Reckon from now on, it's up to me to teach her."

Bessie nodded, rising from the creaking rocker. She lingered a moment, as if to confirm something to Viola—a decision, a vote of support. But Viola did not lift her gaze from the sleeper's face.

SHE WAS waiting for the baby to wake for his next meal when the screams from the bedroom at the far end of the corridor began.

No one had bothered to shut Arliss's door. She ran down the hall and pushed it open further, and stood stunned by what she saw: Mavis crouched over the huge bed like a cat, and Arliss levered up on one elbow, shaking a bony fist in her face. "You stupid half-wit! I'm telling you for the last time. Get it out of here! I'm warning you, get it out of here right now. Out! Out of this house. Riffraff! Trash! Poor white trash, I won't have it!"

"I won't do it. You don't have a choice," said Mavis. Suddenly Viola realized that it was Mavis who possessed more control, staring at her mother's braced body. "Oh, I know you hate me. I hate you too. That's the way it is, I know it. But I won't give him up. I love him, and there's nothing you can do about it."

"Stop! Stop!" shouted Mrs. Joiner. "Get back there!" She tried hopelessly to swing Arliss down from the buttressing elbow.

"You never wanted me. You hated me from the very start," said Mavis inexorably. "You had me, though. It's your fault that I look like this, nobody but yours. But I don't care anymore. Can you understand that? Calling me a—a changeling! I heard all the things you always said. I knew why you encouraged me to go to Europe where you wouldn't have to look at me. But I'm staying. You'll have to watch me doing what a true mother does for her child, loving my baby like a real mother loves. I know you don't comprehend it. Don't look if you don't want to."

"Not in my house!" roared Arliss. "That bastard won't live in this house. I told you yesterday, you had twenty-four hours to get rid of it—get rid of it!"

"No. I won't." Mavis stood up and folded her arms. Her face was set in the smooth strong purposeful look she wore in the Lincoln roadster, below a wand of roses. But her eyes burned intensely. Even as Viola watched, they reminded her of someone, and she realized that the resemblance had been vexing her memory for several days now: she had recognized it as Mavis sat rocking the baby, seen it surfacing and refining. "You only ever cared about yourself. Yourself and your plans for Sarah. Sarah! That's all I ever heard. But you let her get away, precious Sarah, and then you didn't even try to find her and bring her back. You didn't do to her what you've tried to do to me."

Arliss's eyes winced away from Mavis at the mention of the name; perhaps she too finally saw the resemblance. "I—I—" she stuttered, aghast, enraged. "How dare you," she groped. "I—how dare you—"

"Well, it's too late now," Mavis said. And Mrs. Joiner, noticing Viola for the first time, ran around the bed, seized her arm, and dragged her into the room.

"Back!" Mrs. Joiner yelled. "Get back down. Stop them, girl!" She thrust Viola forward.

"Because she's dead! Sarah's dead!"

The silence that fell after Mavis's cry was louder than the words themselves.

Arliss stared, jaw slack as a fish.

"Dead," Mavis whispered. Then, all of a sudden, she blanched. She gazed straight ahead, purpose collapsing, eyes contracting to beads. Slowly she turned. "Isn't she, Viola? Isn't she?" The whisper petered out, irretrievable. Upon her white face was scrawled her solitude, as it had been when she was small, a pitiful little girl committing acts of desolation. "The photograph with the black cross——" she attempted, but then backed away from the bed, knowing that remorse was not possible.

Viola observed her impassively.

"The baby——" She shuffled crabwise a few steps towards the door.

Arliss gaped. The hanging jaw, the tongue faltering blindly among the teeth, seemed to frighten Mavis to an intolerable crisis. She could not tear away. And then Mavis's sharp gasp broke the silence, and she wheeled and pelted out the door and down the corridor. At that instant the squall floated towards them, merging with Mavis's clattering footsteps.

Arliss muttered something. Her elbow slipped out from under her. She sprawled, fixed on Viola's stupefied expression. Once again her lips struggled to form some question.

Then Mrs. Joiner swooped down, voice ascending to a pinnacle. "I never! I never! Your whole family! Look at you, look at you! My Lord, it's a horror! My Lord, never in all my born days——" The scent of conquest made her shudder; she grabbed Arliss and heaved her up with one hand, imbued with maddened strength. "You sit up proper, you hear? You sit up on them pillows until I get the rag! My Lord, what a horror, my Lord, I'll never get over it."

Even as she yanked Arliss into place, she gabbled out a dirge of victory, unable to restrain herself: "Where's that rag? The shame of it! Here I couldn't even have children. You had children, look at you all!" Arliss drilled into Viola's eyes, oblivious to what was done to her. Mutely she stared, trying to wrest Viola from the stance of accusation. But this time there was no complicity; no word of alliance or solace arrived. The head sagged into the pillows, the eyes glassy. Arliss mumbled soundlessly.

"Here it is!" shrieked Mrs. Joiner, wringing the wet cloth and swacking it at Arliss's brow. "Look at me! Look at me now!" The rag rubbed at the heavy skin; she attacked the cheekbones as if to scour away some invisible scurf. But still Arliss strove over the hand, questing always for Viola's eyes.

"I said look at me!" Mrs. Joiner barked out, and jerked Arliss's jaw. "Not that nigger! Trash! Understand? All of you, trash!"

And Arliss left Viola then, and turned her eyes to look at Mrs. Joiner.

The only note that Viola heard when she bolted down the hall away from the quiet bedroom was the baby, repeating over and over his thin hungry complaint.

How Mavis Took the Helm

P riority: A history must recount facts.

Throughout this little family testament, I am trying to do the facts "justice." Facts are my chief purpose; for without them I will never be able to track my doom, or answer Viola's question.

Years ago, there was a saying my father used to use.

Whenever someone came to him with a piece of news—say, that Marco Polo discovered sphagetti in China, or that somebody's famous coon dog had pupped a litter of ten—he always stood with feet planted apart, thumbs hooked lightly in his belt, listening carefully. His head would draw further back, the better to admire the speaker and savor their communion; his cheek would swivel to profile, his eye gazing sidelong. Then he would pause. "Is that a fact?" he would exclaim. "Is that a fact?" confiding his awe and congratulations; and so sincerely he said it that the teller would nod enthusiastically and repeat himself, would see that look on my father's face, and go away pleased to the core, feeling that the news value had been enhanced to extraordinary scale.

Once, when I was five or so, I heard Viola tell him, "Victoria done read every single primer Mr. William give her. She read like a tornado, that child. She's so smart, you-all going to have to buy her a truckload just to keep her busy."

"Is that a fact?"

In the sweet amazement of these words, I chugged over to where he stood and nudged playfully against his thigh. "Daddy, am I a fact?" I said.

I watched his face change. The joy faded from it. An empty brooding look came over his eyes, as he peered down at me, and I felt a pang of anxiety. His hand settled on my head, lightly. One finger teased a curl over my neck. Such sadness! all compact, caught in a corner of his dissolving smile like water in a nook. He did not say anything, but after a moment, stooped and gave me a kiss. Then he walked away, preoccupied with heavy thoughts, and Viola gestured me to go to the kitchen. I think perhaps—yes, I think even then, at that perplexing, obscurely disappointing moment, that I vaguely began to guess at what I might be, what I might mean; but not for several years did my totality become clear to me as a function, a bale, in fact, of facts: the end result of a pattern of habits.

WHEN ARLISS suffered her second stroke, she did not die, but went on to "live" for eight more months, before finally succumbing to pneumonia. Then, as her obituary, preserved in Mavis's scrapbook, put it, "Mrs. Garner Ransom, widow of Garner Ransom, passed on yesterday, April 19th, at 4:35 p.m. in her home, from respiratory complications. Attending her were her nurse, Mrs. Etta May Joiner, and her physician, Dr. Middleton. The funeral will take place at 3:00 p.m. April 21st, at St. Stephen's Episcopal Church of Bernice. Mrs. Ransom is survived by her son, William Garner Ransom, and her daughters, Sarah Arlene Ransom and Mavis Jocetia Ransom." This is fact; yet the certainty that Arliss was already extinct inflates it to paradox.

The second stroke, of course, extinguished her. She never spoke nor moved again. It occurred the afternoon of her confrontation with Mavis and Mrs. Joiner; according to the doctor, the aneurysm burst while she was "lying peacefully in bed," getting a sponge bath from her attendant.

I understand from Viola that Mrs. Joiner was a model nurse during the months of Arliss's final imprisonment. But why should she have been otherwise? The battle was over. What had won it, vanquished Arliss forever, was nothing more nor less than the truth. But it is also true that Mrs. Joiner's conduct toward Viola, the only witness, changed remarkably after that climax. She ceased calling her "girl." She addressed her politely (eyes always a little unfocused, requests a little too sweetly framed, hands a little less firm than formerly when passing her a tray). With what meekness did she now change Arliss's gowns, sponge her brow, gaze averted; roll the inert body to one side in order to strip the urine-soaked sheets and replace them with clean ones. According to Viola, she never again gave anyone in the house a direct head-on look.

So Arliss expired, after eight long months of life as an effigy. And if her mind still roved among the dead and live survivors, if she still sought freedom in this most final jail, looking for a truth beyond the one that locked her there, who can ever say? Who can say if she attained it?

What is "fact" but a pushing-off place towards freedom?

ON THE day after the funeral, Viola was dusting Arliss's bed, thinking about the service in the cemetery. Mavis had refused to come; it was Viola who accompanied William in the hearse to the grave, ignoring people's stares as she stood one last time by Arliss's side. She mused on Mavis's reasons for staying home while trying to revive the latent gloss of old English wood (for throughout the past eight months she had not dared climb above Arliss's body to do ordinary cleaning). Her arms felt stiff at the joints from polishing. The fragrance of beeswax and lemon could not quite demolish the smell of death. She wiped a last film from the headboard, and paused to jerk the window sash open so the spring would flow into the room; there were months of invalid stench permeating the brocade wallpaper, and the last days' acrid reminder hung like a curtain against the fresh sluice of air. Suddenly the burr of the front doorbell made her drop her cloth with a start. She charged down the hall, halting at the top of the stairs to gather herself together.

A door opened in the passage behind her.

"Viola."

She turned. Mavis stood in a wedge of strong sunshine. Behind her Baby Boy was scooting across the carpet in the rinse of light, trying to catch up with his mother. He floundered halfway, his arms in a tangle around the overreaching knees, and hooted and chuckled at his sabotage. An embroidered dress dragged down over one pink fatty shoulder.

Mavis's face looked flushed. "It's for me, that caller. A lady, unless I'm very much mistaken. I've been expecting her. Would you please show her into the foyer—not the drawing room—and ask her to wait?" The flush deepened as her purposeful stare challenged Viola's good manners.

"Why, Miss Mavis, I can't ask no lady to stand waiting in the foyer!"

The bell jangled again. The lady was growing impatient.

"Just do what I ask you, please. I'll be right down in a minute, when I'm ready." She shut the door in Viola's face.

Mrs. Deloache's face, when Viola opened the front door, displayed only serenity.

"Good morning," she said in the faraway voice of cool fatigue. Although she was by now in her fifties, she still preserved the complexion of an eighteen-year-old, her most famous asset. "May I see Miss Mavis, please."

She stood a few steps back, on the porch. Beyond her in the drive was the black Packard, a uniformed chauffeur lounging against the hood. Lifting her hand, she languidly flicked her gloved fingers at him; he nodded and sat himself behind the wheel to wait. A web of chiffon floated about her on the breeze, and she seemed to sag within its inadequate support. Her hat, a tight cloche, weighted her head to one side like the heavy bud of a lily overbalancing its stem.

"Why, please come in, ma'am! Come right on into the foyer, I'll go call Miss Mavis now." Viola retreated behind the door to make room. Mrs. Deloache glided ahead. "Won't you please—sit down?" Viola said; and then the fullness of her predicament hit her. She hovered uncertainly over the butler's chair, arms extended in an apology which she could not explain.

Mrs. Deloache stared at her. After passing the merest glance at the closed double doors of the drawing room, she dipped into the chair, scarves settling. It was plain how amazed she felt by the way she arranged her hands in her lap, for, as a rule, she let them drip over the ends of chair arms like wet handkerchiefs. Viola knew what she must be thinking behind her carefully blinded face: Now that Arliss is dead, visitors are to be treated like deliveries; the Negroes get uppity, the place falls apart and manners crumble; all decency dies. More than the funeral or anything else, this brought home the gravity of change, and Viola felt its shame awaken her, on the silent scorn of the visitor. The Ransoms were coming down in the world.

She fled up the staircase and tapped on Mavis's door.

"I'm coming," called Mavis.

"Miss Mavis," whispered Viola urgently, cracking the door a fraction. She could not see within. "We just got to bring that lady into the drawing room. We just got to ask her to have some coffee and cake. Miss Arliss'd be turning in her grave by now."

"Viola." The voice was very near her ear, punctuated by little grunts of effort. The baby's coo sounded muffled. "Do what I say, or I'll be mighty provoked with you. I mean it, Viola. Go on back down. Don't offer anything." The door pushed shut.

"Your mama be the one provoked to high heaven, if she saw you now. I'm going to show her a proper seat this minute."

The door swung open. Mavis glared at her. In the black-clothed arms the baby wriggled and blinked. His embroidered dress was gone; now he wore a long white gown foaming with lace. A cap covered his round head, and he tugged at the ribbons tied under his chins, winding them about his fist and stuffing them in his mouth.

"We're ready," stated Mavis.

Viola widened her eyes. "Let me mind him for you while you go see to your company."

Mavis did not reply, but bundled the baby more firmly on her hip.

"You ain't taking him down?"

"He's dressed for it," Mavis snapped. "Viola, you better understand. I'm the mistress of the house now. Don't go contradicting what I decide anymore." Her face screwed with irritation; she looked, for all her regal imitation of Arliss, like a wizened dwarf kidnapping a crown prince from his christening.

Viola followed her as far as the landing. She saw Mavis stand above Mrs. Deloache, the baby writhing against her embrace. Mrs. Deloache tilted her head. "Hello, Mavis. Why—is this the baby I've heard so much about and never seen?"

Viola backed unnoticed to the top of the stairs.

"This is my son." Mavis's voice fell flat and cool. "My Baby Boy."

There was a pensive silence.

"My, what a precious," Mrs. Deloache said at last. "He's very big and healthy, isn't he? My, what an armful for you."

"Thank you."

The baby pronounced a syllable, as if in agreement, and then gurgled.

"I believe you must not have gotten my note," Mrs. Deloache ventured. "I wrote to you the day before yesterday, saying I had only just heard about your poor mother, and how I'd be coming out here to see you after the funeral. You know, dear, you have been very much on my mind, since . . . well, ever since her last illness."

Mavis said nothing, but grunted as if she was struggling with the baby, who would want to be let down onto the floor by now. "Why, can he crawl, dear?" Mrs. Deloache asked.

"Yes, he can if I let him."

"Why don't you call Viola, and she can take him back upstairs where he can play, while we have a little chat."

"I prefer to keep an eye on him myself." Mavis spoke in the same flat offhanded voice.

"I suppose you could let him play on the drawing room floor." Mrs. Deloache sounded dubious. "Anyhow. I never had any children myself. The Governor's boy by his first wife—he was already nearly grown when we married."

"You missed the best part, then," said Mavis with quiet warmth and pride.

"You aren't even sitting down! How do you manage to hold him so long?"

"I manage. I'm getting practice."

"Oh. Well. About the note I sent—you know, I've been thinking about you so much since your bereavement. Your dear mother was such a friend of mine. And I've grown very concerned at how you keep to yourself these days. Now you're the girl—*lady* of the house here. It doesn't seem right that we can't see more of you than we do." She spoke earnestly. "I can't tell you how much I admire you. Your fortitude and courage, facing life, and the way you've given this little child a home, and all—and, well, Mavis, I've come out here today to say I think it's time we brought you out into the light. Especially," her voice lowered, "since now your mother can't do it for us."

"That's very kind," Mavis said.

"Oh, not kind at all! Nothing less than your duty—and mine! It's a shame and a pity that things have been the way they've been while your mother was sick for so long. It hasn't been the least bit fair on us!" she drawled. "Not the least, to do without you. And I know that there may be—advice that you might need, oh, introductions and so forth—" Her voice meditated on these last possibilities. "You know," she murmured confidentially, "I hate to mention it, but when I arrived, the girl didn't even show me in. She had me sit out here as if I was, well—"

"I know. I told her to do it."

The silence lengthened. Not even the baby interrupted it.

"Oh," Mrs. Deloache said gently, "I see. You've had the drawing room closed off, perhaps, on account of—and of course, if you didn't get my note—I can't figure out why not, they're getting sloppy at that post office, I guess—why then, you couldn't have known who was here, could you? You must have thought I was just a—somebody." The speculations drifted away.

"Why, look there," Mrs. Deloache said uneasily. "He's gone right to sleep in your arms as we were talking."

"Yes."

"You want to take him upstairs? I'll open the drawing room myself."

"That's all right," Mavis replied "It won't be necessary."

"He would probably sleep better in his own bed. Such a load for your poor arms."

"It's not for long. I meant," Mavis said, with an edge of plaintive defiance, "that it wouldn't be necessary to open the drawing room."

"It—oh. Why is that, dear?"

For a full few seconds, Mavis did not reply. When she did at last, a world of bravery rang in her tone.

"It's too late."

"Too late? I didn't quite—"

"Too late for that."

Viola knew that by now Mrs. Deloache must be glancing from under lowered lids: had her mother's death addled her?

"You know, dear," Mrs. Deloache said firmly, "I think it's just wonderful the way I've heard you've devoted yourself to this orphan child's welfare. Spared yourself nothing, just as if you were his mother. And a child from nowhere. Only heaven can say what his parents were, and to leave him in a church pew. Well, Texas is full of such, I suppose, in the wildwoods or the—the Governor established three different State Homes during his term of office. So we think you're especially wonderful, not to have turned him over like most would do. But Mavis. Now, you know I was your mother's dearest friend. I'm saying this for your welfare. You must think of yourself, your position here. Live your own life. Mavis Ransom! Remember what you're due."

"Due?" said Mavis softly. "Due?"

"Well—yes. What we all owe you. Who you are." Mrs. Deloache sealed herself.

"Due?" came the slow voice, harshened now, tolling like a rusty bell.

"Honey," Mrs. Deloache said faintly, "if you had just gotten my note—"

"I did."

Viola felt her heart shrink within her.

When Mrs. Deloache spoke again, her tone had dwindled to the cold finality of the grave.

"Perhaps this was a bad day to come. I can see I am intruding."

"It was kind of you," Mavis said. "But too late."

"I'm afraid," Mrs. Deloache sighed, "that I do not know what you mean."

"I think you do," Mavis said, a note of fever rising against Mrs. Deloache's chill. "You know what I mean—too late. It is very kind and gracious of you, I'm sorry I can't return it. When I have wasted out the years of my youth in this house, wishing so desperately—no, never mind." She bit it off. "I haven't been of so much interest before. I appreciate the trouble you've gone to to show your interest now, Mrs. Deloache. But you know—being a changeling and all—I think you probably used to commiserate with my mother over her misfortune, didn't you? in the privacy of friendship?—anyhow, I now have better things to do. Now that I am, as you say, the mistress—the lady—of the house. My child, for one."

"Oh!" Mrs. Deloache gasped.

"Don't worry. I know you don't approve of a baby found in a church pew, and parents disappeared, roaming the earth on foot in their disgrace—if you only knew!" She paused an instant. "I haven't brought him into Bernice for people to see. I've had my reasons. You've just intimated one of them. He won't be afflicted with snubs. Not like—I'll see to that, anyhow. I know all too well what that is, and a bastard would get the same. So we'll keep to ourselves. I hope you don't think me too rude——"

"Rude!" gasped Mrs. Deloache.

"——but I believe that's the best thing for you, too. We're fine where we are. And at least for now, where he goes, I go."

"Good afternoon!" Mrs. Deloache whispered, and Viola could almost hear the sound of her scarves fluttering, winging her towards the door.

"You've still got my brother," Mavis called. "You've still got Wicky."

The door sneezed closed.

The dimness of the stair head engulfed Viola, as the sun slid behind a cloud. For a time she waited, her head empty and light with its sense gone.

Then the slow shuffling sound of Mavis climbing made her lean into the deepest shadows in the corner. When Mavis's crown appeared, rising above the treads, she licked her lips and closed her eyes. But Mavis did not pass on. Instead she neared Viola, hunching over her heavy burden, her face yellow and quick as flame. Viola opened her eyes again, and then they roved to the baby, pink and nestled——Mavis never was so pink, not even when she ate as an infant, not even when newborn.

"That's done," Mavis murmured. She stood as if there was nowhere else to go. But purpose tensed her skin with supple movement.

"Yessum," Viola agreed blankly. "It's done now."

"That takes care of his father and his mother, too," said Mavis with a dry twist in her voice. "No use leaving any loose ends, for the future to knot up. It couldn't be more settled now, not if the president had declared it."

How William Took a Trip

Baby Boy was building a tower of blocks on the downstairs sitting room floor. Up went the cubes of wood, each placed solidly on the last. Already Baby Boy got praised often for what came naturally to him: the precision with which he lined blocks together, or filled his spoon with mashed sweet potatoes, never dropping a morsel, or stepped through the woods by Viola's side, guiding each foot across tree roots and rabbit holes without stumbling. From the time he learned to walk, it had been obvious to everyone who saw him that he would not take a step wrong or make a mess of things. Even when roaming through the drawing room among Arliss's European porcelains and velvets, he could stop to examine a precious vase, content merely to peer. He never grabbed.

So when the sound jangled through the house, bursting the sitting room with its shrill chatter, and the blocks suddenly tumbled and bounced around him in an avalanche, Viola was surprised. He stared at her, eyes white around the iris. Then he bellowed, churning to her arms as if scalded. Before she could catch him his rare tears poured onto her apron and splashed into his open mouth.

"What's wrong with you?" Her eyes moved towards the door. Could she really have heard it?

"A crang! A crang!" He butted at her lap, face down.

"Lordy, honey, that's nothing but the old doorbell."

He raised his head and peeped, jaw still gaping. "Doorbell?"

"Yes, sir, that's all it is." She rubbed his teary cheek with her thumb pad. "Why, you've never even heard it! At least not—why, in more than two years. It's nothing to be afraid of. Just somebody come visiting."

"Somebody?" he faltered.

She pushed his hair back from his forehead, where it tended to fall in a little sheaf like his father's did, meanwhile straining her ear towards the open door. William came out of the library and greeted the caller. The low male voices knocked against the foyer vault, their edges lost to resonance; she could not tell who had rung the bell.

"Somebody," whispered Baby Boy.

"Yes, honey. Shh." She listened to the trenchant silence following the closing of the library door. The caller's voice had more pith than William's, a density that contrasted against his even tones.

Since the day Mavis renounced her old desires, there had been no caller to the house; nothing held Bernice to the two Ransom siblings anymore, or them to it, beyond a curiosity that by then had blurred like mist. They lived cut off from the civic pulse. Even William had found this fitting to his nature, and except for his forays out to the Ransom oil derricks, or to check on the Ford showrooms, he kept with ease to the grounds and stone protection of walls. Until now Viola had let herself forget the reason, lulled within the slow quiet days and nights of the woods and pastures surrounding them.

She knitted her hands together. Baby Boy, feeling them tremble, touched the left one as if to give back the fear they transmitted to him. "What's a body?" he asked.

"That's people. Shh." She shook her head.

More and more, over the last two years, William delegated his responsibilities to the lawyers. Whatever business he needed to conduct sat now on the library desk top, in a tidy system of folders and files. He had given up even the pretence of the office in town. The manipulation of money did not interest him. He tended to its duties in the mornings, bending over the desk in the late morning sun; but lately the hour when he rose from his chair to stretch had grown variable. He seemed to be chipping away at time itself by letting the work end earlier than it had the day before; but he apparently needed to convince himself and Viola that he was still working at the usual rate by insisting that his lunch be brought when he finished. Work done; time for lunch. The day before, he had eaten a sirloin steak, three baked potatoes, and half a pound of green beans at ten in the morning. The house suited him as world entire. When he occasionally made a trip away from home, he returned as quickly as possible, genial but silent, and went straight to the leather easy chair to pick up the book he had left butterflied on the arm, finding his place and resuming the very sentence he had abandoned three or five days before. Thus the library filled slowly with volumes of history and philosophy; thus he neglected the financial grind on his desk, sporting with time in order to sample centuries, places, the mental athletics of many people he would have avoided in the flesh.

As the absurd trembling left her hands, she pictured him in his library cloister, sitting in the desk chair, the faceless visitor residing in leather, folding words like notes and sending them across half a room. He could not be the person that she, for a terrified instant, imagined.

A little while later the library door opened again. The men were saying their farewells. Now she could make out a phrase: "On Monday at two o'clock, then," said the visitor with his decisive tone. The wide spaces burred William's reply down to a hollow sound of agreement.

As she passed the library on her way to take Baby Boy up for a nap, she saw William lounging in the leather easy chair. Beyond the window panes a redbud tree, blossoms long gone, bushed across his line of sight. But his eyes stared blankly. Not until Viola started walking up the stairs with the drowsy child in her arms did he call out.

"Where you going, old lady?"

She glanced back. He stood in the doorway, as sleepy seeming as his son, the lock of hair flipping over one eyebrow.

"Taking this one to bed."

He walked to the first tread of the stairs. "Is it that late already?"

"He fell nearly asleep while you had your caller."

William tipped his head, studying Baby Boy's face. "I was going to take him outside for a walk," he said absently.

"You got to wait now."

"Missed the one yesterday." His hand strayed near the gleaming hair, and then sank slowly to his side without a touch.

"You done missed it three days running."

"That right?" he murmured. "Hey, old lady. Do you reckon you could come into the library to see me when you've got him bedded down?" He smiled. "Seems like a coon's age since we had a talk. There's something I want to discuss with you."

"Discuss? What about?" She gave him a close look. "About that visitor, I imagine."

His eyes drifted away from hers. The smile grew private, secretive. "You're mighty sharp," he said, and then sauntered back into the library, threw himself in the easy chair, and picked up a book.

When Viola came back down the stairs, she closed the library door behind her. "Now, who you got coming out to see you this day? That baby and me nearly jumped out of our skin when the doorbell ring."

"It was a lawyer who came to see me." He snapped the book closed, but did not alter his position in the chair.

"One of your lawyer men?"

"This one's not mine."

"Who's he, then?"

"He's new. New in town." He stroked his thumb in a slow rotation on the book's cover. "He was hired by Grant Macafee."

Viola sucked a breath. She slewed her head to one side, an immediate response to the fear. Her eyes locked on him.

"Grant's been keeping him on retainer, apparently. You know what that is?" His tone was easy, fluid. "That means he pays him to wait for business. He said he's been hired for nearly three years now." He waited, letting the particular meaning of that time accrue in Viola's head, until he saw her face change.

"That's since—"

"That's right." He smiled. "But Grant's decided to use him at last."

"What for?"

"He sent him out here to ask me if I would dissolve our partnership."

Viola stood still. "When I hear that bell," she breathed, "and then that man's voice, I reckoned—" She stopped.

"It's taken him awhile. You reckon I ought to dump the ice business, Viola? Or give Grant a little bit of a fight?"

She stared in astonishment, until she saw he was teasing. "When are you going to do it?"

"The trouble is," he smiled, "it means having to drive all the way into Bernice. I'm too lazy for that."

"Monday. I hear that man say Monday," Viola calculated. Then she stared. "What do you mean, all the way to Bernice? You just come back from West Texas a month ago—that's a thousand miles!"

"Four hundred. Was it that short back? I must be losing my memory."

Viola reared her head and balled her hands into fists. "If it means getting shut of Mr. Grant—" She stopped.

William bent forward. "Yes?" he said, elbows resting on his knees.

"Now look here. I know how you don't care nothing about that ice business. That's something your daddy and Mr. Archibald got going. It ain't got nothing to do with you. It's just the chains that keep you bound to Mr. Grant."

"Is that all our chains consist of?" William murmured, and the private smile curved across his face as he turned to the window, looking at the sky.

"Child, you got to leave here and see him sooner or later. That's the only way you going to get shut of him: if you lay eyes on him yourself. That's why you ain't took no chances of running into him in town—I don't choose to say it, but you make me say it. He don't own you. You got to figure that out." She strode around the chair into his full view. "Lordy, Mr. William, I been just as scared of him! But I went to that funeral all the same."

"Scared?" The smile widened. "Scared. I guess it could have looked that way. I hadn't thought of it."

"If it ain't scared, then what is it?"

He dipped his chin into his collar, meeting her gaze. "You know what it is, Viola. Scared is just your way of putting it. Because there is no proper way to put it. Unless—dishonor." The smile stiffened, turning into gravity. "There are some things that can't be said. Time has taught me that. Did you know, time can teach anything?"

"You getting off the subject."

"No, I'm not. That's the point. I don't want to go to that office and see Grant—don't even want to close the partnership, come to that—because I can't see the top of the bubble yet."

"What bubble? What you talking about, you gone crazy?"

"That's what time is. A bubble. As clear as the soap bubble blown by a child. And we're trapped inside in a heap, and too blind to see out." He looked up at her. "I've been sitting in this house, still as I could sit, because I'm trying to learn what time can teach me. You can only begin to see through the clear walls of the bubble if you sit very still, like a mouse or a possum, and try to remember the part of your life that's going to come next."

"I can't figure what in the world you're saying! What's this got to do with Mr. Grant being a mean-eared hog that you're scared of facing?"

His eyelids drooped. "Maybe," he murmured, "maybe I just didn't want to leap into the change yet, that's all. Make something legal and final that has no business being settled that way. But of course, that's the way Grant would choose to do it. Maybe he thinks that's what will wind it up for him." He shrugged. Then he stood up and walked to the desk. On its top Viola could see a stack of papers in his close handwriting; she assumed they were notes on his visit with the lawyer. He picked them up, unlocked the lower left drawer, and put them neatly inside. Then he shut the drawer. "I've been listening to all you said," he assured Viola with his back to her. "You said what I needed to hear. Don't worry, it'll be all right on Monday."

He stood absorbed at the window, tracing the billow of a cloud, his arms folded. For awhile he allowed the cloud to engage him, the silence to swell in the room. Then the pale belly of cumulus slid across the sky, thinning and changing shape. He pointed to something the cloud's movement had revealed. "See that?"

"What?"

"That little bit of moon."

Sure enough, there was the transparent brooch, pocked and hazy, pinned to the blue: a moon at three quarters.

"You always use to show me that moon when you was still a young'un. 'Ain't that a miracle, Viola?' you'd holler. 'A moon shining in the daytime sky! How can the sun and moon be shining all at once?' you'd pester me. I didn't know what to tell you."

His arm came down and crossed the other one again. But he continued to stare at the milky repoussé of crater and shadow, as if he distinguished things she could not.

"Maybe you learned at that college how it can."

"It changes and changes, never the same two days in a row," he said. "But it always returns to what it was and will be. At least to our eyes. Over and over, a patch of the bubble showing at a time. What if we forgot what it looked like at the full? Wouldn't that be the terrible thing? To forget. . . . But then wouldn't it be the wonder of our lives, when we looked up one evening and saw the glory, a moon round as an orange, washing our faces with crimson light?"

Viola watched him, not replying. She had believed she did not understand him, but now, suddenly, she remembered the night after she thought William's child was dead, when she came into Mavis's room and saw Baby Boy lying on the pillow.

"I'll meet up with Grant on Monday and sign the papers," he sighed, his voice gentle. "He can keep the ice business, or sell it, whichever he prefers. My bet is, he'll keep it. He's paying me handsomely to buy it off me. And besides," he smiled, "it's appropriate that he should keep it. His own daddy's one lone risk—although it turned out to be so prosaic. Yes, I reckon that ice suits Grant. I wonder if there is any ice on the moon?"

"I can't imagine."

"Mmm. No, I suspect that the moon is iceless and waterless. Dry as a summer creek bed. That's what those astronomers say. Not a drop of moisture anywhere. There it sits, going around and around, coming full circle every time." Then he sighed, ambled over to the leather chair, and sat down with his feet propped on a footstool. "Not a thing a lawyer can do about it, even though he'd be tickled pink to have the power to call a halt."

"And you ain't scared no more?" Viola said, low and hesitant.

"Who knows what we're scared of? Who knows what we love most?" He stroked the calf binding of his book for a moment, and then dismissed her by opening it to the page he was reading when she came in.

"I RECKON your granddaddy was right about one or two things," Viola said to me in the gruff old age that finally caught up with her. "I reckon *that*, no matter how smarty you see yourself these days."

"What was he right about?"

She was very angry with me. Lately I had made the mistake of allowing some of my gathering ire to leach out into our conversations. It seemed the farther I advanced into my teens, the more difficulty I had containing it, seeing as I must contain so much else. I was sitting, as usual, in the conservatory in my special seat (the one that holds me now, built by a carpenter my father hired when he saw what was to be my destiny). The wisteria had lost its leaves. Around us the rank scents of flowers fogged the air: no sweetness, but their ordinary soil tang, with the earthiness of the African violets, the occasional whiffs of the plastic smell that some plants render, and the clay pots. Viola grunted, handed me a plate of sandwiches for my lunch, and stood above me like a Valkyrie next to the Ficus lyrata while I bit into one. "What was he right about?"

"That time he say that stuff about what all we can recollect. When he say if we stay put in one spot long enough, then it all going to come plain as plain. *You* maybe can't see it, even though you sit here in this house your life long. But I done got old now, and there ain't a thing I can't remember if I work my mind on it." She grinned triumphantly, as if she had just won a dispute that had taken up our time and energy for years.

"'Grant that in age I may not drift long years, my lyre forgot,'" I said.

"Why do you talk to me so sly?"

"That is from an ode by Horace. He remembered, too. I am sorry you could not tell by my expression that it was complimentary, not sly. I am aware that I have no expression much—other than when I smile."

"You're not smiling."

"Is there something funny to provoke it?"

"I tell you, Victoria. No matter what you say about your granddaddy, he was a wise man." In her anger she snatched up one of the Ficus lyrata leaves and stood massaging it, tearing at its broad shield with her thumb.

"Perhaps he was," I said pleasantly.

"There's nothing I don't see like it was a picture painting, setting on my mind's eye."

"There is one thing."

"And what might that be, Missy?"

"Whenever I have asked you about my grandmother, you do not seem to remember much. Perhaps you do recall her, as clearly as everything else. But perhaps you decided not to tell me."

Viola frowned. Already her eyes were glazing with evasion. But she met the challenge. "A body can't recollect what's hardly there in the first place. She ain't in this house long enough for notice. Besides, when Mr. William brung her on home, she was already sickly. It ain't up to me to mend what the good Lord done called for his own. And that sure ain't my fault."

"But what was she like?"

Viola parried the question with another memory. "Ask yourself what Mr. William like, once he come home from Bernice after signing away that ice house to Mr. Grant. Ask me then what he look like, seeing Mr. Grant face to face, with what that man schemed up like Satan's punishment, and maybe I'll tell you what got burned on my mind in fire. Then you can figure out what your grandmama was like, which was: nothing at all to match that stuff. What kind of girl you think he going to choose, after that meeting? Ask yourself!" she cried, and then stomped out of the conservatory on her flat feet, shoulders heaving.

I was by then no longer Viola's lamb, bursting with good juice.

THE MONDAY evening of the meeting with Grant, Viola heard the Lincoln roadster spin into the gravel of the drive. Shortly after, the front door squeaked on its hinges and she felt a draught as William secreted himself in his lair and closed the door behind him. She waited until Baby Boy was asleep, and then stole out of his nursery and down the stairs to the library door.

A slot of light was showing. She pushed the door slowly inwards. William sat, not slumped in the leather chair as she expected, but behind the desk, rifling through what looked to be official money papers with their stamps and seals and signatures. His shoulders rounded above the lamplight. The dead hearth was a scoop of black shadows in the mahogany wall, but he had balled up several papers and tossed them into the grate, where they burned with pale cold luminosity out of the darkness. As she pressed the door closed behind her, he turned. His face, parchment white, glowed with the same lambency, as if someone had crumpled it and then reset it on his neck.

She started to speak, then stopped. His mouth looked uneven, jagged, his lips without color: they might no longer be capable of forming an answer. He stared incuriously at her, like an amnesiac.

After a little time, he said, "I'll be going on upstairs to pack in awhile. You know, I can't figure out what I did with that docket—"

"Can you eat some supper? Some of that nice ham?"

"I'll have to write them to send another one, if I can't find it. Equipment for that new drilling operation. Could've sworn. . . ."

"Ice tea?" she hung back. "Let me bring you some ice tea from the kitchen."

"Huh?" He seemed to register for the first time that he was being addressed. "What was that?" he asked vacantly.

"Can I fetch you something to swallow? Mr. William. I ain't wanting to bother you, but—"

"Something—to swallow?" He tried to smile. "Oh. Well. I wouldn't mind a drop of bourbon, somehow."

"Yes, sir." Something was wrong, more wrong than she had anticipated. Her fear began to swell, like a small tumor below her heart. He bent over a stack held by a ribbon, trying to unknot the neat bow. His fingers jabbed under and over it, as if it were a Chinese puzzle, and they the blunted tools of a leper. "Dang thing. . . ." he mumbled.

"Let me do it." Viola stepped eagerly to the desk and pulled one loop. The ribbon fell apart.

He glanced up at her, dimly amazed, but his eyes dropped before they met hers. Immediately he began to sort through the documents, examining the rectangles of print.

She wanted to rest her hand on his arm. He was so engrossed in business that he seemed like a child playing pretend; only his white blank face stopped her, with its suggestion of deep damage. His lips moved meaninglessly over the papers, which he picked up and put back down at random. What had happened? She felt he was groping for something, and longed to find it for him. But after a moment he deserted the papers, and when the face tilted up to hers once again, it seemed as if the delirium, the illness, had already passed, leaving a mask without fluency, the unfocused smile of a cretin, directed just past her head.

"What did you say you're packing for?" she murmured.

"Huh?" The smile drifted. His forehead creased slightly.

"I'll go fetch that bourbon."

The hands slid off the papers, off the desk top into his lap. "That's all right. No need, no need at all."

"How come?"

Suddenly he rasped. "You know, it wasn't him so much, it was Sophie. To see her sitting there, with Grant and me both in the office, signing the papers—you know, Viola, I hadn't realized until today that that's never happened before. Do you know that not once—not even when we were—well, I never had been in Sophie's presence at the same time as her husband."

"What?" said Viola slowly.

Then she hissed, her head snapping back. "Miss Sophie was there?"

"It's not for me. It's for her sake I mind," he said, not hearing her.

"He dragged that poor woman into this? Not a dog would do that!"

He dropped his head between his palms. "He's gone about it smart, mind you. She was there, she had to be there, because he's buying out my partnership and then gifting it to her. He's made this meeting serve both cases. It's part of the deal. Part of my getting shut of him, as you put it." He shoved his chin deep into his chest, the hands cradling the moronic smile. "I'll never forget how she looked. Just like a doll that someone had propped in a chair. As if she'd endured such unspeakable—I don't even know if she heard what we were talking about. The signing and all. No one can say Grant isn't a prince of a fellow, and a dutiful spouse."

"He's a miserable hunk of hell," whispered Viola.

"It was what he said that was the worst."

Viola waited, unable to ask.

"Not that I didn't have it coming. That's what's worst about it. Oh, God!" he cried out, and then fell silent.

After a moment, she whispered, "What'd he say, Mr. William?"

"It was in front of that lawyer and his secretary that he said it." His voice was muffled behind his hands. "But they wouldn't have understood it. He knew that. He stared straight at me, with his eyes narrow as a snake's. Then he looked at her the same way. Then he turned back to me. 'I intend to see justice done,' he said. 'You know what that is, don't you, William Ransom? My wife does. I believe you're familiar with the behavior of prostitutes, aren't you, William? You know about their carryings on. Well, I think if more women were financially independent, they might not be tempted to damnation. Unless, of course, they've been born with it in them.' He was cool as a stone. 'My wife will always be free from sin now. You are making it possible, by signing your share of our business away, for her to be an independent woman. A sort of example for other philanthropists to follow. Besides, I've decided that ice is what Sophie needs. She has a streak of fever that needs something cold to leaven it.'"

William shook his head in his hands. "Then he said something more. 'It has come to me that this is a means of correcting many mistakes. My father made one once. We both know it only too well. It has cost me much foolishness, none of it—*none* of it—of my own volition. Ransomed indeed!' Then he kind of barked out a laugh. But he didn't sound amused. 'That's getting taken care of now. Some of it, anyhow. There will never be enough payment,' he said, 'to take care of it all. Remember that.' Then he said, 'It shouldn't take detectives for you to figure that out!' He was smiling. May I never live to see again such bitterness in a smile. Sophie just sat there, still as a dead thing. Her eyes were empty, Viola. They looked like they'd been stuck in a doll's face. Eyes made of glass. It was horrible." He shuddered.

The silence hung on the air.

"Oh, my Lord," Viola breathed.

William had lapsed into frigid whiteness.

"He ain't a hunk of hell. He's the devil."

Then, carefully she asked, "What'd he mean, 'There'll never be enough payment'? What'd he mean by that?"

But William did not answer.

"I'm going for that bourbon. I reckon you need it."

"No," he sighed. "No, I don't think so, old lady." His shoulders moved gingerly, as if with pain.

"What you going to do now?"

"I don't know." He seemed to have forgotten where he was. She glanced at the papers on his desk.

"That packing—" she ventured.

"Oh. Just a little trip. Thought I'd take—going to West Texas somewhere—"

"That'll be a mighty fine thing for you. You got some time on your hands." It was like encouraging Arliss to talk, after her first stroke. If his words were not aphasic, his mind seemed to be.

"I believe there are some fields," he began. Then his face cleared, as if reminded at last. "I've bought a couple new oil fields out there. That's why." His eyes flickered at her. "It went all right, Viola. Old Grant . . ." He went on after a pause. "Always the gentleman. You can always count on that. Which is—" This time he did not finish.

"And Miss Sophie?" Viola murmured, as if the name might implode.

"Ah. Fine. Fine." He nodded. "He was most correct. Most correct and proper." Then his face curled in and withered, as if the match had finally ignited; for a fleeting second, she could not decipher it. "Pillar of rectitude," he smiled, eyes gone to slits. "West Texas, now. I need to get on and pack."

"Yes, sir," whispered Viola.

By morning, without a word to Mavis or Baby Boy, he was gone.

"But didn't he say how long he'd be, at least?" Mavis asked several times during the first months of William's absence. "Seems like he could have said something. He's never pulled this before."

"Nome," Viola always replied, "he ain't mentioned it."

"Left us unprotected in this big place," Mavis said with her old petulance. "You'd think he'd consider. Suppose something happened to Baby Boy?"

"We got Ezra to drive if it does."

"Or if something happened to Wicky himself?" Mavis frowned, and then smiled fakely for Baby Boy's sake as he tugged at her skirt. "He could write, anyhow. What's to prevent him?" While she hoisted Baby Boy into his high chair, she said, "It's West Texas, remember. Deserts, fields, empty roads to nowhere. He could sit there for weeks with nobody to find him. Rattlers, sandstorms. Ugh! Yes, honeypie, big old snakes that bite—no, not fine boys like you, just mean people and rats and things."

"Snakes eat rats, Viola," Baby Boy said gravely.

"I'm disgusted with him, there's no excuse."

"Why, he has to see to business, Miss Mavis, and he been here so long—"

"Don't try to defend him. He always was your favorite, Viola. I swear, it's just like Sarah all over again."

"I always your favorite, Viola," Baby Boy said, and confidently fingered his spoon.

"Must be something in the blood of this family," Mavis grumbled. "Gypsies or something. Wanderlust, ragtag. Pure-dee lack of responsibility, I call it. It's pathetic. If I hadn't given up Europe when I did, Lord knows what I might have turned into." She patted Baby Boy's head and scowled, her yellow forehead rucked into its classic folds of resentment.

"I eat in the kitchen with Viola and Bessie," he told her.

"No, sugar lamb, see? This is the place you eat. At the great big dining table with Mama. This is our place, it's for us."

He surveyed the polished expanse and pursed his lips. "Bessie and Viola too," he said.

"No."

"How come?"

"Well, he probably going to be back before too long now," Viola said for the fiftieth time in five months. "Could be he reckoned a vacation's what he need."

"All the way to Mexico, knowing him."

"Mexico ain't so far. Not for white folk with a car. Now you sit still while I serve you some fried chicken. Bessie killed two this morning, one for soup and chicken salad."

"Please, Viola. Not the gory details, not at lunch, thank you."

BUT IT was another three months before Viola, late at night, was awakened by the throb of an engine, and slogged downstairs in her Mother Hubbard to meet a gust of April wind flinging back the front door.

Ezra, in all this time, had not yet oiled the disused hinges; they groaned as the wind swung the heavy wood and rushed past the oblong of darkness. Viola wrapped her nightdress tighter. Then she grappled at the light switch, and the hall sconces sprang on just as William appeared. He was sheltering an enormous bundle under one arm, walking it; it looked like a shrouded harp. But as he awkwardly guided it up the top porch steps, Viola saw that it walked itself: a man's raincoat stumbling into the pools of light.

"Why—" she exclaimed, whispering. "Child! Oh, child, good land, where you been all this time?" It was all she could think of to say. What surprised her most was how young he seemed, standing there with a pink gloss on his cheeks; even the tired lines drawing his mouth down looked familiar from long ago. Two, three years of slow mutation had been erased by the empty absent months. "I ain't seen you for—" But an earlier William was whom she meant.

"Can you give me a hand, old lady?" he said, grinning at her. His arm curved over his package. "She's a mite sick at the moment. We had a long drive today, she's not used to cars. Been seasick all the way from Alpine."

"Uhh," the raincoat moaned almost inaudibly. Viola stared at it, dumbfounded.

"If you could just help me get her up to my room—are there any sheets on the bed?"

"I been changing them once every two weeks. Didn't have no idea when you might decide to show. Eight months! More!"

"That'll do then. We'll get me settled later. Here, come take the other side."

Viola's eyes stretched wide. "Who is it?" she mouthed at him.

"Why—my wife."

"Your—what?"

"Come on, old lady. Let's get you up here." Viola started to answer as he propelled the sagging raincoat her way, propping her fists on her hips, and then realized that the old endearment had been addressed to the bundle. She skipped back a little from the raincoat. The night wind whirled through the open door, flipping the collar sideways to reveal a pasty brow, low and corrugated with distress, capped by a tousle of hair. But the sconces seemed to fight against wind and flowing darkness, and the impression was wrenched by elements she could not force into order. All she remembered later was the greasy pallor of the brow, that of a sick and sexless being, and the contradiction, almost like a pain, that she received a second later when William motioned her to grasp the left side: a warm slight body, swathed like the bones and feathers of a palpitating bird, with a convex belly jutting firm and smooth against her arm.

She jerked away as if burned. But her palm did not leave the frail elbow it supported.

"Mr. William!"

"Yes, ma'am." Intent on the first obstacle of the stair tread, he glanced towards her. Her awe, and other feelings, must have shown in her face, because his grew suddenly alert and reflective. "That's it, that's the way," he said over the hooded head, staring at Viola with raised brows.

Viola handled the elbow, a jointed flex of wire, up another step. Her eyes switched from William's to the disguised but unmistakable mound of pregnancy. "She's carrying," Viola whispered in embarrassment.

"Why, yes." She could hear his smile. They reached the landing. "You want to rest a minute, honey? Can you make it the rest of the way?" Viola gazed at the floor, still hitched to the stiff elbow. The girl—wife—had dug in.

"I can't see nothing." A breathy gasp filtered through the poplin. "Hep me, Willie." It sounded as if it came from somewhere above them all, dislocated in spirit. "Hep me," she repeated.

"All right there." Viola heard the ready tenderness in his answer as he eased the collar back off her brow, and saw the quick glitter of fever that obscured the color of eyes. She recognized William's remote gallantry: all the truth was told to her in one phrase.

"That better?"

"Yes. I think so."

"You still feeling like you want to—?"

"I kin wait for a bucket." She panted lightly.

"She's pretty far along," William told Viola. "The doctor out west said it looks like she might spring early. She's so young, you see."

They trudged the rest of the way to the second floor. "How far along?" Viola asked.

"Well—seven months, anyhow."

"That ain't so far."

"Well, she's busting with it already. And we know she can't be much more than that for sure." He grinned despite the limpness of his burden. "You've been saying to me all along, Baby Boy needs some playmates. I'll bet you thought I didn't hear you. We've fixed that, haven't we, honey?" His grin turned hapless. Viola padded along behind, waiting as the girl capsized at last onto the bedspread, where she lay unmoving, one nondescript strand of hair crossing the collar.

"I'll go fetch you a bucket," Viola whispered. William was already bowed and busy over the inert body, concealing it.

"Just leave it outside the door and go on to bed. I'll see you in the morning."

"Yes, sir."

"Hey — Viola." He came to the doorway. "Everything been all right while I was gone?"

"Yes, sir."

"Mavis and the boy, they doing well?"

"They just fine. Miss Mavis been missing you some, I ain't known what to tell her."

"No — trouble of any kind, from anybody in town, say?" His tone was cautious, too low to be heard from the bed.

"You expecting any kind of trouble?" In a flash, she was startled; the implication of things brewing, shadows forming beyond her line of sight. The light of the past few months shifted to an ominous new angle. "There ain't been nothing," she said slowly, and shivered. "That's finished now. Ain't that right, Mr. William?" Then, when he merely scratched his ear, she looked about her, at the window, at the scruffy pair of slippers peeping out from under the raincoat hem, at the staircase. "Yes, sir," she reassured firmly. The shapes lurking behind the trees outside dissolved to smoke. "It's all finished. You took it away and left it in West Texas. Everything going to be fine from now on." Then she smiled. "You got a child on the way." And he nodded, satisfied, and released her to go down to the back porch for the bucket, while he tucked the bedspread around his wife's round belly.

Viola turned for one more backwards glance, and perceived what could have been an optical illusion: the figure which she took to be short, shorter than William, under the raincoat had telescoped on the bed; the scruffed slipper points nearly touched the footboard, while the slightness she felt wrapped within poplin sprawled in an elongated S, knots and rope and bone under tarp, with the mysterious rise swelling up from the heap as the apex gathering it all together. For this reason she would never be sure of what the figure consisted, the length of leg, the turn of the breasts. She admitted to me, years later, one lasting image: how four weeks after that night, the hollow below the girl's throat pulsed in staccato as she bore the contractions throughout her long labor. But a hollow in a throat is an absence, an emptiness, and so can add nothing to me.

How Willie and
Bert Were Born

For nearly another month, as I calculate it (the data being sparse in Viola's reminiscences), the strange girl, William's wife, my grandmother, lived in his childhood bedroom.

She never left the bed. She spent her days in waiting, too ill to have much curiosity about the home she had come to. As for her own home, it remained nameless. The ceremony joining her to William was unexplained (justice of the peace, I wonder now, roused from a tedious afternoon? Some gray-board West Texas church set on the thousand-mile platter of land, with a turkey-necked preacher droning above their heads?); her presence recorded only as a vague biological shunt. When I was growing up, Father and Mother spoke of her as "Daddy William's wife," Viola of "your daddy's mama."

William, my grandfather, her husband, did not refer to her at all.

So she waited out the last month until the untimely birth would set her free, and among a household that kept to itself, she was the most isolated member.

William served her, changing her sheets, taking the trays from Viola's hands. Occasionally Viola heard her puny responses to his questions, there at the door. "Can you eat some of this soup Viola has brought you?" he would say. "We got to get some strength into you." Then, in a murmur, "Well, the baby needs it, sweetheart, even if you feel you can't."

"If you want me to, Willie," she sighed, "I'll try. But it just seems like it sticks in my craw, it won't go on down."

"I'll call the doctor again," he said anxiously, while Viola hesitated in the hall. For her the gestation was a prolonging of the arrival, a dream from which she could not pull herself. And that first amazement never subsided: craning around the door frame, she could still watch the hard hillock that dominated the bed, shifting and heaving with inner movement, and hid the rest of the girl's body by making a tent of the covers. How could it be? Where had it come from? Not from William, surely.

During the first week Mavis went in and out of the room. But then her visits stopped, and she saved her attentions for Baby Boy. Perhaps she was jealous of the coming child, who might divert William from the one she reared. Certainly by now the girl's accent had put her off: what common thing had William dragged into the house? And in other ways her feelings were made clear, to me, the collector of facts who has inherited the evidence. For now, all these years later, no photograph yellows in a frame. No image of the girl troubles Mavis's 1928 albums—not even an empty space where she should have been cornered with snapshot holders, bracketed by the clutter of our other, my other, lives.

When I used to ask Viola about her, her eyes would turn flinty with uninterest.

Viola did not give me so much as the rumor of a hair color to fill in the gaps. My grandmother's obscurity teased at my mind. Why had the family decided to forget her? Because she had done something wrong, looked strange somehow? The heap of odds and ends on the bed topped by a smooth mound tantalized me; it did not conform to a real person. The only clues offered were deduced ones. I gazed long at my grandfather, then at my father; then I noted what traits one had which the other lacked. Ah! She was tall and knobby; oho! her eyes tilted up at the outer corners, but rounded more towards the nose. Not until the day Viola challenged me to contrast her against other factors did I realize why she had been so neglected. I had focused on the wrong things, in thinking of her. I had focused on *her*.

Now she lay waiting, ill and heavy, in the mattress dented early by her husband. Her recent weight sank into the trough; she was all but swallowed up, as if a silent earthquake had split this altar of the house and tilted her in. But the belly rode above her, and her husband hovered over it, watching it squirm, placing his hand on the tightly packed flesh to feel the subterranean movements. "Kin I have a sip of water, Willie?"

His face, translated now to the youth Viola thought he had left behind, glowed with formal solicitude as he held the glass to her lips. He seemed preoccupied with his achievement: this child on the way, the batch of bones and spindles that was the wife the West Texas desert cast in front of him. He had salvaged her, from nowhere, got her with child; he could forget what his life had been for the past three years. But Viola remembered the question he asked her on that initial night. He had not really forgotten. Perhaps he believed that this girl, this child, would help him "get shut of Grant Macafee at last."

On the afternoon the girl went into labor, William attended her. Viola, after a glance at the pinched-up eyelids, the jumping hollow of her throat, ran down to telephone the doctor; William did not leave her side. The doctor arrived just in time to deliver the child. Then the truth swamped them. For the girl, so anonymous all along, so indeterminate, had done something extraordinary. The boy infant inched out of her, greeted by her moans: my father. William watched while he got born, gaze fixed and stunned on the rubbery limbs. He watched Viola bathe him, as the doctor tried to birth the placenta. But no one in the room was prepared for the tiny pair of feet that flopped out in place of the afterbirth they expected. The mother wailed, mingling her cry with her already-born son, as she shoved to force the legs and rump of the second child. He came flying; got stuck at the shoulders; and Doctor Middleton, in agitation, screwed him the rest of the way. Before his head emerged, they could see it was another boy. The glistening blood filled his eye sockets, glued his hair down. He in turn received his bath, but the blood did not stop. At last, when the mother was drained, she collapsed, too spent to ask what had happened to her, her face turning white and then yellowing into the pillow.

"Twins!" William muttered over and over. "Twins, by God!" He shook Doctor Middleton by the shoulder, thumping Viola's back as she balanced the two babies in the crooks of her arms. But by the time he turned back to his wife, she had already performed her last act: to lick her parched lips and close her eyes. Doctor Middleton could not staunch the blood, or retrieve the broken pieces of placenta, before she slipped away, back into unremarkability, effaced by the vital presences she had carried into the house.

"But what was her name, Viola?" I used to ask. "What was she like?"

Viola would settle back in her rocking chair in the kitchen, folding her lips in a seam. This being when I was still childish, she forgave me the curiosity, and what I was to become in all my meanings.

"He call her honey. He call her old lady. He bury her Mrs. William Harris Ransom on the stone."

Then she would pick and choose among the words to describe that first night's advent, the erratic memory that was my grandmother. A shimmer from the eyes, a lock of colorless hair: such details as she could spare to a weekend guest, a visitant who did not count.

And of course she could not count: what did she have to do with the real core of the Ransom lives, here in Bernice—the true contract, the only relationship that could have any significance for them?

But they did not count on me.

Of Baby Boy and
His Brothers

Bessie knocked her knuckles on the underside of the table, watching Viola and Ezra eat lunch. The sound drummed evenly on the kitchen air against the syncopation of rain. Outside the oaks and lawn trembled with motion. As Viola stabbed a hunk of meat with her fork, she ran her other hand around the back of her collar, pressing in the light sweat. The winter of 1934 was a soft one; blue skies had blessed Christmas a week before. The rain started after New Year's, thumping and irregular, big drops that had continued to fall for two days. Viola listened to the sound of Bessie's hand as she chewed her bite. "What you trying to do, give us music to eat by?" she said when she swallowed.

Bessie stopped abruptly. "I'm just wondering how long that rain's going to last." She leaned over the table to check their plates. "You want more?" she asked Ezra.

He shook his head. "I got to get that new car clean for tomorrow. Don't seem like it'll do no good if the rain keep up. Just splat all my hard work away."

"If Miss Mavis want it clean for Dallas, then you've got to scrub it anyhow," Viola said, and Bessie, her finger scraping the pie plate for a lick of apricot, snorted derisively.

"It ain't even been drove yet. How much scrubbing she need?"

"The first time she going to leave this house in nine years?" Viola said. "Girl! It's got to be clean enough to eat off the bumper."

"She order it new just for this trip." Ezra was still amazed by the fact. "This trip and the other. Just so she can ride in style."

"That old stable going be full of cars before too long," Bessie exclaimed in disgust. "Miss Arliss's is still there, them two of Mr. William's, now this thing Miss Mavis done bought."

"She ain't bought it," Viola said, "she just staked it. Lordy, Bessie, she owns it already, seeing how she owns half the Ford store in the first place."

"That how it works?" Bessie asked with interest. "She don't have to pay?"

"If Miss Mavis have the world set up the way she believes it ought to be, she ain't going to pay for nothing." Viola smiled grimly. "'I'll take some of this and some of that. Send the bill to my brother.' I heard her on that telephone night and day for nine years now. 'Send it out express,' she says. 'Tell your boy to bring it around the back way.'"

"Mmm-mm!" Bessie nodded.

"The only time she's ever going to set her foot in that new car," Viola told Ezra, who gazed in rapture at her scowl, "is to go to Dallas this time, and then take Baby Boy for his first day at that school. Then it's going to sit there and get moldy, just like Miss Arliss's done."

"Some folk," Bessie muttered. "Dandy says Miss Sophie still got the same car—that Price Arrow, like Miss Arliss's—what Mr. Grant give her when she got marry." She thought a minute, her finger rimming the pie plate. "Ain't going to make her no difference no more, anyhow," she reflected, "that her husband's so stingy with all his money, from what I hear."

"What's that?" Viola lifted her head. She had heard nothing about Sophie in several years.

"Why, ain't I told you?" Bessie slanted her gaze solemnly. "I thought I told you last Sunday, when I met up with Dandy at the church."

"You told me," Ezra said.

"You the one then. Well—don't know how I ain't told Viola, it's such a piece of news."

"What *is* it?" said Viola sternly.

"Miss Sophie left the ranch the day before last Sunday, and hauled off to Arizona to some kind of fancy playtime place. And Dandy say, she ain't coming back."

"She what?"

Bessie nodded her head quickly as Viola's jaw dropped. "She took the money she got from the ice house. She been stashing it back in the bank for a heap of time now. You know Mr. Grant give her that ice house? Seem like nobody in the whole town knew it, it was a secret between her and Mr. Grant and some snaky old lawyer they got in Bernice. Whew! what folk don't know! And here we reckoned this was a place where everybody's in on everybody else's business." Bessie sneered into space. "Took her five or six years to save up what she figured she need. That's the reason why." She jabbed her elbow toward the electric refrigerator in the corner, its top-heavy motor thrumming. "It's only poor folk what still use an ice box these days. Mr. Grant he don't give her nothing he able to turn a dollar on. He ain't no fool. But anyhow, she caught the train on Saturday for a little rest in Arizona. But she ain't planning to come back. She leave him, Viola. She leave him to Dandy and that Arnold, what can't talk without spitting like a faucet. And I sure guess why. You know what she done? She ain't gone alone. Nome! She took her mama with her!"

There was a pause. "Did Dandy say what Mr. Grant's going to do about it?" asked Viola, low.

"Naw. She ain't said nothing. Ain't had the time, I reckon yet."

"Uh-huh." A slight dizziness made Viola rest her forehead, for an instant, on her hand; she seemed to feel the earth turn beneath her, as William claimed it did, turning and returning like the moon and stars on their abstract axes.

"I'M GOING to want you to get Baby Boy ready by eight tomorrow morning. You know how he likes to hang back in bed. Can't really wake up, sweet thing, before seven-thirty has struck already. But he'll need to be bathed and dressed by then. That cowlick: wet it down and try to get it to stay down, otherwise I guess I can hide it under his sailor cap." Mavis stood a few degrees in profile before the pier glass of the ducal bedroom, fastening her coat experimentally down the front. It was the same coat the dressmaker sewed on, wool heaped over her knees, that hot summer before Mavis was to go to Europe. Nine years old, like Baby Boy. Fur decorated the collar, the last touch of the seamstress, created on the eve of the discovery in the church. Viola remembered how she savored her gossip, and the distant smile tendered at the funeral. But the coat had spent the ensuing years stored in a wardrobe. Mavis emanated a smell of camphor as she angled this way and that for the glass.

"Fashions won't have changed that much," she said with decision. She fluffed the collar towards her throat, and then touched her ears, from which depended her mother's diamonds, refracting the cool afternoon with a wink of fire. They swayed against the neck too short for them, and Mavis leaned mawkishly to one side, testing the effect. "The stores in Dallas'll have everything we need for his school clothes. Still, I could try Sanger's, I guess, if all else fails, for the things I want myself. A new dress to take him to the school in. I'll be meeting the headmaster to have a little chat about Baby Boy's diet and so forth. Imagine—military school already! I just hope they don't turn him into a little soldier. If Wicky hadn't been so sure this was the best thing—"

"I'll have him spick and span," Viola promised. "He'll be ready before eight."

"I still can't get over what Wicky said about his name. Said we should change it. 'You don't think we're sending him someplace where boys are brought up so badly they tease a friend on account of his name, do you?' I said to him. 'Because if we are, then we can just cancel. I won't have a hair on his head altered, well, maybe tame that cowlick, but his own name? What's wrong with calling him Baby Boy, I'd like to know? The school must be full of barbarians.' He said to me, 'No, just natural boys, Mavis,' and gave me that long-suffering smile. 'Suppose you let him pick out a name for himself? One that he wouldn't mind being called by in a classroom full of boys, or by a cadet officer mustering the roll? Put yourself in his place.' Well, I've been doing that for nine years—look what I've sacrificed, and gladly, just to do so." She arranged the coat placket; the earrings trembled, making her look like a yellow tree toad struck with dew. "I suppose it could sound odd, if people took it at face value. I've been saying it so long, it's a string of letters that means something else entirely to me. Is that how the name sounds to you, Viola? Someone we know and love, even manly?"

"I ain't never put my mind to it before," Viola admitted, thinking about the child himself, and Mavis's softening stare into the mirror as she nurtured the syllables.

"He can do as he likes once he gets there," Mavis sighed. "But he'll always be Baby Boy to me. How does this coat look, do you think?"

"It look just fine."

"You'd better go round him up for me, I want to have a little talk with him this afternoon. About Dallas tomorrow. Not the school yet."

"I believe he's out in the stable, pestering Ezra over that car."

"Oh, no. In this rain? He'll catch a cold before we can even use it!"

"I'll go out yonder and holler at him."

"Not too much, Viola," Mavis chided, her mirror self congesting into a look of wan love. "Not too much, too loud. I'd hate for him to get unhappy this close to the hour." Her eyes welled with crystal self-pity, matching the diamonds' spark.

WILLIAM RETURNED from wherever he went, and launched the twins on their primers in the downstairs sitting room. Viola could hear Bert shouting to Willie Junior through the door as she went downstairs, "That's a *B*, you stupid!" and Willie Junior's slow easy reply, "Well, I don't know everything," and then his abashed laugh before his brother's aggression. Bert was a fireball. The whole house, once so quiet, racketed these days with noise from triple pairs of feet, all clattering in different rhythm. Above the drum of rain, Viola could tell Bert was up to mischief as usual. "You think that one's an *S*? That shows what you think. That's not even a letter at all, that's nothing but a double comma!"

"What's a comma?" Willie Junior asked humbly.

"A comma is a thing you use for a sentence. One of those hook lines Daddy showed us yesterday. A double comma is for two sentences at once." He snickered as Viola moved away. "Naw, stupid, it's an *S* after all, you'll never learn anything. You're not even my twin, did you know that? You were foaled."

"What's 'foaled'?"

Sooner or later, Viola thought, walking through the foyer, Willie Junior would learn not to ask questions, with a brother like Bert.

She passed the library, where William sat at his desk, rapt over a paper in his hand. Of his three sons, only Baby Boy resembled him, wearing often the generous smile William kept for those he loved. The other two were reflections she knew nothing about. But in Baby Boy the self-confidence had not yet eroded, and perhaps never would. His mother's gathered stillness, her mindless poise, had permuted to a suspension that he used for private thought and ends. And ultimately, although both William and Sophie were so visible in his face and stance, the echo he sounded loudest in Viola's mind was that of his aunt Sarah.

William looked up as she peered in the doorway. He flattened the paper between his hands. "Everybody buzzing with the trip tomorrow?"

"Miss Mavis surely is. I'm just on my way to get Baby Boy from the stable. He sure loves that new car, can't see enough of it."

"Something I've been wanting to say to you." He nodded towards the leather chair, for her to sit down, and rubbed his hands together through the onionskin paper, crackling it.

"Yes, sir?" There was always an absent space now at the end of his phrases when he spoke to her, a tenuous breath of what had once been caress. Not since the night his wife climbed the stairs to his room had he called her "old lady." He sat waiting, fulsome, mature, growing a little stout above his belt. His passivity had become set, the sadness hardened to a regular manner, without much depth. Still, she could sense the withdrawn meditations that had always moved her without her knowing their language or syntax, lurking behind the eyes' surface.

"It's nothing much," he continued, "really just a sort of 'thank you,' more than anything else."

"Thank you, Mr. William?"

He waved the flimsy paper in the air, in easy negation. "Well, don't want to get too formal about it. It's just that, well, you know, you've done a lot for us in the past few years."

Viola poked her chin forward, frowning. "I ain't done nothing I ain't choose to," she said dryly.

"I know that." At once he was discomfited. "Don't want to sound as if I'm pensioning you off or something. But you could have had a different life, all this time. You could have—I feel like we've perhaps been selfish, taken you for granted, enclosed you—" His eyes slipped away from her frown. "It's just that you've done an awful lot for us, Viola. For me. Shoot, you've been central to my life ever since I could remember. My rudder." He smiled apologetically. "I know there's no real need to say these things, it's probably—offensive. But seems like it's about time they were acknowledged, that's all. Considering what you've done for—for my mother, for Mavis and me. And now for my boys."

Viola felt appalled. He was suggesting, by even mentioning gratitude, that things could have been otherwise.

"I've gotten to know you—some," he murmured. "The sole person on earth I can say that about. You're the only human being I feel I haven't dreamed." He looked down at the sheet of paper in his lap.

For an instant she assumed he was embarrassed. But his face looked inward. "I just want to say I love you."

The anger, peaked to indignation and a strange sense of her separate self, slipped away. "Well," she mumbled, "that's why I'm here still."

"What I'm also saying," he said, now looking directly at her, "is that I can see that's what you're becoming for my children, too. And I'm glad about it. Especially," he leaned forward, "especially for Baby Boy." Then he rested back, fingering the edge of onionskin. Viola saw suddenly that it was a letter, written in a dense flowery hand. "Now that he's going away to school, you see, he—well, I'm glad he'll always have you to come home to. When I consider how he came into the world in the first place—"

"He's a fine fine boy," Viola said with pride.

"He could have ended up in a mess," William said flatly. "Anywhere."

"Naw, sir," Viola whispered. "Somebody seen to that."

William's mouth hardened. "Be that how it may. . . . It's funny, isn't it, about that boy? Does he ever remind you of anybody?"

"Yes, sir. He do."

He glanced swiftly. "You mean his parents?"

"Oh, there's plenty of mama and daddy in him. But that ain't who I mean."

"Sarah," William murmured, hardly a breath.

"Mr. William," Viola was smiling now, "that boy's a real nexus."

William gazed at her slowly, his face caught in surprise. Then he grinned. "Why, Viola, you never cease to amaze me, you know that? That's exactly the word for it, that's exactly what he is!"

"I've seen it for quite awhile."

"You know," he mused, "it relieves me, in some ways, that he's been out of the public eye all his life. That particular quality wasn't so apparent when he was a tiny baby. But now . . . I'm not so sure I would want to have it observed." He looked carefully at her.

She fidgeted with her apron. "That school a long ways from here, ain't it?"

"Why, yes, it is. Down near Kerrville, in the Hill Country."

Viola nodded.

"Very different landscape from here, down Kerrville way," he continued. "Seems like we got every kind of geography in the world nearly, right here in Texas. And all boys come to that time in life when they want to explore." He rumpled the letter. "Oh, yes, I don't say Mavis wasn't wise, when she took to privacy the way she did, even if her motives weren't the purest. But we're not the only people in the world. He'll find boys to befriend, areas of human education we haven't been equipped to give him."

"Yes, sir." But still a sadness gripped her, thinking of Baby Boy in several stages of his brief years. Suddenly she returned to a decision she had already discarded. "Mr. William? I just now hear some news I reckon you might want to know."

His eyes looked slick and dark. "You did?"

"It's about Miss Sophie."

The letter rustled against his thigh as he shifted position in the chair. His eyes did not move, but she saw them change, narrow; and she realized that they filled already with a gentle irony.

She glanced down at the letter, its unfamiliar script dashed thickly across the page. Carefully lifting it up, he wrung it in one quick motion between his wide hands, took the wick it made, and coiled it in the ashtray. The files on the desk slid aside as he fumbled for a match. Striking it on his boot sole, he set the letter alight.

"You know, Viola," he said, watching it burn, "I considered as late as this morning just keeping Baby Boy here for a year or two more. Of course I'd already committed myself to sending him to that school. But this morning, after I got the mail, I thought: Well, what if I changed my mind? Just for a year or two? Mavis would be tickled to death, she's been so loath to let him go, and really, there was no need yet, after all. I went out for a long walk, thinking it over. He's very young, he could stand hanging around here. I could hire a real tutor, someone who could come out to this house, maybe live in. Teach him what he needs to know." The paper suddenly flamed up high, its inked letters standing out for a second against the blackening twists: Then it disintegrated, soft gray ash, a whiff of searing smoke, thin as the scent of some herb. He smiled. "But then I thought, well, what's done is done. We won't meddle. Burned bridges, all that stuff. And besides, when I considered it carefully, I saw that school was the best thing. For him, I mean. Now that some things are—changed." He mashed the ash to dust with his forefinger. "It's never been my policy to rock any boats. Not if I could help it."

Viola stared at him throughout this confession as if he had lost his wits: what could he be dreaming of, to consider such a thing? And then, suddenly, she realized her nine-year misapprehension. William had never known the true mechanics of Baby Boy's rescue. He must believe it was Grant that ordered the infant into the church pew, not Sophie at all! He did not know what Grant had intended, he sat to this day unaware of that murderous desire. As the revision clicked into place, she saw a new picture, blatant in its import: it was Grant he had spared all these years, Grant's feelings he would protect through his own sense of guilt. Grant, whose wife had now left him. This sequestering in stone of the misbegotten child was not out of fear—or at least not the fear she herself had always brooded on. William's dishonor, his debt, was something apart.

The other factor—the resemblance, so obvious to her, the portrait Baby Boy made of his mother and father—would have been accessible to anyone in town. William had prevented Sophie's exposure by sealing their son in the house's fortress: in the moment of a single candid smile, Baby Boy would have ruined his mother's virtue forever.

And now William waited, that guileless smile on his face, for her response.

"He going to go on, then," she said, struggling against her stupe-faction.

"Oh, yes, ma'am. This time tomorrow we'll see him all spiffed up in his new uniform. Can't imagine what he'll look like, can you? Seeing Dallas for the first time, too. He's been asking me lately why he couldn't even go into Bernice. Why, he'll come back tomorrow night with eyes as big as saucers. Street cars, the Texaco building, all the people on the sidewalks. Stores, trains. An entire city."

"I reckon so," murmured Viola.

THE FOLLOWING night, when William escorted Mavis through the front door after the ride back from Dallas, Viola again saw his repli-cation, the small boy fixed on inner discoveries, stumbling in his wake like a luminous shadow.

She heard the door from the twins' room, where she was putting them to bed, and rushed down the stairs. William stalked inside, rain beading the gray wool of his overcoat, his arms stacked with boxes. The fanlight above him was milky pale. "Viola!" Mavis called out, laughing as if she were returning from a journey of months. Then she shook her hat off into her hand to reveal a transformation sharper than laughter: she had had her hair cut and marcelled in some Dallas beauty parlor during the course of the day.

"My land, Miss Mavis, what you done to yourself?" The diamond earrings spangled below the terraced hair, bouncing on the lobes like prisms below a lampshade. Mavis's face creased with joy.

"Oh, the day we've had! I'm simply worn out, you never in your life saw such a crowd! Oh, and that man in the boys' department at Sanger's, so rude, I had to simply make him show me. You know, Viola, it was as if I'd been going out of this house every day for the past nine years! And lunch, we had it in the Adolphus Hotel, I'll have to tell you. William, do something with all those packages. No, don't dump them on the floor, for heaven sakes—"

"What do you think of my sister?" William yelled, smacking Viola on the back with his hand heel. "Can you imagine she's the same person?" He swiveled to observe Mavis, his smile fond, as if straightening her lopsided spine, buoying up her tired pleasure. Viola felt their excitement. She did not immediately focus on their companion, and when she finally did, it was as an awareness of something that seemed to float in behind them out of the sloppy weather. Then she looked. Looked again. And suddenly her heart constricted.

She hastened headlong to him, but halted before she could sweep him up against her the way she had done for nine years.

"Why, honey," she said tentatively. "How's my big boy doing?"

He wore a remote expression she had never seen before. Abruptly she squatted, Mavis and William silently looking on, and laid her hands on his shoulders. The brown cheeks were pale with fatigue, the left one ironed into creases where he had rested heavily on a fold of material; and his square forehead kindled pink below the forelock. But it was his eyes which moved her, caused her to kneel in front of him. They were not big as saucers. Rather they looked clouded, a part of the rainy evening, and stared at her, too full for speech: a disorientation drowned the trust she had always read there. "Viola," he said uncertainly. He looked away, at the foyer dancing with yellow light, at his father and Mavis. Viola saw he had suffered some jolt.

"What'd you think of the city?"

"The city?" He groped for his most recent memories, frowning slightly. "Oh. Dallas."

"You chase them big old street cars?" she teased. "You see some big tall buildings, and all the folks in the stores?"

For a moment he did not reply. Her arm wrapped around him, closing him limp to her side. "Oh, yes. We saw all that."

"You ain't never seen nothing like that before," she prompted, to bring back the boy who roamed through the house and woods so easily, touching physical objects and people with fealty and respect.

"No, I haven't." He stared at her. "It's good to be home, though," and she could sense the doubt. But at last he hugged her back. Then a yawn overtook him.

Mavis and William burst into laughter, and Mavis's exclamations continued where they had left off. "That girl in the beauty parlor, she kept trying to convince me I should have a hair dye done! I had no idea that Dallas had grown so—" But Viola remained clasped to Baby Boy, holding him as if she snared some ebbing sweetness.

"Your mama sure look different," she whispered, tugging the moist hair on his temple. "My, just in one day, see what a day can do?"

He nodded.

"It come on you quick, sometime," she murmured. "Baby, I know. It come on you quick, like lightning, some things in this world." She was trying to articulate her own impressions, pour them on him at that moment: the vision of him stepping into the foyer, the child she had helped raise, two lives, three lives repeating in his familiar body. Until now she had not understood.

He nodded again. "I fell asleep on the way home. Uncle Wicky had to wake me up. And I didn't know where I was." Gravely he turned the thought over in his mind. "Isn't that strange? I couldn't figure out what I was doing in the car, or where we were. It was someplace new. All I know is this house, and I didn't even recognize it, coming at us out of the dark."

"But you ain't never had it happen that way before, driving up to it in a car at night. No wonder!"

"Baby Boy?" Mavis called. "Would you like a bite of supper now, honey?"

"I'm not hungry, thanks, Mama," he said.

"Viola, you've got to let him away from you sometime," Mavis cried brightly, turning it into a joke. "He's just come back, he's not going anywhere soon."

Viola released the stocky shoulders and stood up. But she could not force a smile towards William or Mavis, radiant in the lamplight, replete with what they had accomplished. She smoothed Baby Boy's hair, still riven with that sudden revelatory love; and then she turned and strode down the hall to the kitchen. "Bessie fixed something hot for you-all," she said without looking back. "I'll tell her to set it out in the dining room."

"Thank you. As for you, fellow, if you don't want to eat, you go on upstairs and get ready for bed. You must be about to drop."

She heard his quiet answer, heard the scraping of his feet on the parquet. And though she was already pushing on the kitchen door, she went with him, an unseen guardian climbing, climbing up the stairs to his room.

An hour later she bent in that room to say good night.

The nightlight suffused the corner beside his bed with rose, its color bringing back to her those days early in the century: the shaded bloom of kerosene, the two heads sleeping in the droning summer heat. At first, when she entered, he was a dark splotch on the pillow. But she saw his chest rising and falling beneath the cover, and then the fluid gleam as he stared at her out of the dusk. The glow plated the bed rails, and on the chair beside the bed rested an alien white pyramid, all surface and edges.

"You still awake?"

"Yes." His eyes flickered under their stiff lashes when she stooped over.

"Reckon you all right." But it was as if the contours of his face had, in one day, firmed into a will apart from her. She was reminded of Sarah's strength, foreseeing unknown destinations. When he spoke, his voice overflowed and spilled on the room's soft silence.

"It was a grand day, Viola." Then she knew he had been scanning a panorama in his memory, of women in high heels, shop clerks, clothes racked under wide mirrors, restaurant meals. People, cramming the streets, bustling past him. People everywhere. This is what he had discovered. Not just the same old set of three black faces; he did not need to tell her. She knew.

"How much longer now until I'm supposed to go off to school?" His voice was alert, restive.

"About two weeks, I believe."

He sighed. The light struck on his iris like a film as he switched a wary look towards the boxes on the chair.

"I guess—" She started to say something about his new uniform, but felt the phrase stifle in her throat. "How about we go for a nice walk tomorrow, down in the woods?"

"Mama won't like it, if it's still raining." He offered it as an apology.

"I bet it going to quit by then."

"Maybe so." He slung an arm outside the covers. "Maybe we can go hunt up that squirrel's hole, you know, the oak down by the pond."

"That sound nice. Maybe we wake that old squirrel up from his winter sleep."

"He's not asleep. He's just snuggled up in there, living off the pecans and acorns he got last fall." His tone had grown desultory. "You told me yourself that's what they do. Remember?"

"Why, I forgot."

"There's probably a lot you've taught me that you've forgotten," he smiled drowsily. "I depend on you to keep up with the squirrels and things when I'm gone. Don't let anybody come shooting them, or anything."

"Nobody don't come in here."

"They might some day. There's always a first time. And the twins, they might." Then he paused. "Do you suppose that now I've traveled to Dallas, I could go into Bernice with Unca Wicky someday?"

Viola looked at him.

"Wouldn't hurt, would it? We could take the twins with us." The arm slithered up to his head, scratching his scalp in a gesture so like his father's that Viola jerked involuntarily. "They'd like to see a town. Bert would go just crazy to race around the streets and the stores and stuff. Can't you just see him, with Willie bobbing along behind?" He pondered. "It's strange that we never have gone in before. I didn't see it, but I do now. Other people don't live the way we do. I always thought, well, that's the way things were supposed to be like. I never thought one way or another about it. Not until—not even when we were in Dallas today, Viola. Heck fire, it doesn't even seem like it was today. Seems like a long time ago already. But not until"—he yawned—"we were already back. And I woke up, and saw . . ." His voice lapsed into the pillow, nearly asleep.

"Just like lightning all of a sudden," he said, blurring with the darkness. "Like you said. Those white columns. Never noticed before how they shine."

"CRASH! CRASHITY crash!" shouted Bert, whacking his drumsticks on the side of the toy drum. "Tootle toot! Come on, Willie, do what I tell you. You're supposed to be the horn."

"I don't know how to be a horn," Willie Junior said mildly.

"Put your hands up like this, dummy, the way Viola showed us the horn man plays. Hurry up, we're the band. Crash, crash!" The drumsticks spattered a tattoo on the metal face as he marched in a circle around the drawing room floor. "Catch up with me! This is a parade."

"Wish I never showed you how that man play the horn," grumbled Viola through the dining room doors, as she set the table for Baby Boy's eleventh birthday dinner. "Nothing but band, band, band, all the livelong morning."

"Not like that!" Bert roared, suddenly in the throes of his quick temper. "You don't know how to do anything. I told you how to do it! If you can't understand, then just go away."

Viola heard the sound of a slap, and careened through the double doors in time to see Willie Junior press a hand to his cheek. But he gazed blankly ahead, ignoring his brother; the stunned look in his eyes already transposing to that caution she knew so well.

"Bert!" she cried. "You come here, you!"

"*No!*" He scampered away from her reaching arm, the strapped drum jogging on his chest.

"You're going to get it!" But before she could go after him, he whirled and lunged straight into an end table. The crash jarred ghostly sounds from the grand piano in the corner. A few shards of color, curved as blades, littered the Persian rug by a splintered table leg.

Willie Junior stood aghast, his face opening up again like a flower. One burning cheek was turned to Viola as he stared at his twin, while the plaintive piano sounds faded away.

"That's your grandmama Arliss's favorite vase," Viola said quietly. "It come all the way from Germany." She regarded Bert, flinching above the wreckage. Everything about him looked belligerent, the squared shoulders, the drum askew around his neck, the bunched mouth.

"You go up to your room. You set there till I fetch your daddy to tan your hide."

"He wouldn't do what I said!" Bert threw back his head and spat at her, still transfixed with rage. "He was balking me!"

A voice floated down the staircase. "What is all this racket down here? I swear I cannot endure another minute of those bangs and hollers. If you boys want to play, then play outside."

Neither Bert nor Willie moved. Viola stepped deliberately to the foyer.

"An accident in here, Miss Mavis."

"Oh, no." The voice drew closer as Mavis descended and stood in the doorway. "Oh, no!" she wailed at the scattered pieces of porcelain. "Not that one. That's Mother's Meissen, I can't believe it!" Behind her, Baby Boy looked away, after one glimpse of his brothers, and slipped to the foyer's far side while Mavis quivered with thwarted grief, rinsing her hands over and over before her skimpy breasts. "You—you—you're a pair of seven-year-old demons, that's what you are! A pair of horrible half-breeds!" Her face contorted; she wheeled on Viola. "Why didn't you prevent it?"

"Why, Miss Mavis, I was in there getting the dinner table ready—"

"That's not enough!"

"We're not seven. We're eight!" All three of them turned in surprise.

"Well, if you can remember his birthday"—Bert pointed to Baby Boy, sitting in the butler's chair of the foyer—"you can remember ours."

"Don't you say a word to me!" Mavis blurted. "You have a whipping long overdue for your impudence!"

"You called us half-breeds." He narrowed his eyes.

"Go on! Get out of here! Viola——"

But Viola had already snagged him by the nape and steered him toward the staircase.

As they passed Baby Boy in his chair, Bert threw him a curious look. It contained an amalgam: anger, defiance. But most of all, it implored. A fraction of a second was all it took; but during that time, Viola saw Baby Boy meet the look, and his small nod in Bert's retreating direction.

"Don't you reckon nothing or nobody's going to save you this time," Viola muttered to him as they trudged up the stairs. "Not even that soft-hearted boy. You wasted one sweet heart that loves you, you hit your own twin brother. You got to learn somehow." When they reached the landing, she gave his arched back a shove. "Now run on up to your room and stay there." He did not look back at her, but stomped the rest of the way down the long hall.

WHEN VIOLA returned to the foyer, Mavis was agitating above Baby Boy's head. "Oh, the ugly things! You can't remember, honey, but when you were just a little baby, you used to toddle through that room and study that vase, just stand there quiet and sweet as could be, studying it so close! I suppose you liked the pictures on it——"

"I remember," Baby Boy said. "It was the pictures I liked."

"Oh, honey!" Mavis swayed over him mournfully. "See? It was your favorite, too. I could just kill them, something so precious. Oh, I know what it meant to you!"

"It doesn't matter, Mama," he soothed. He was not watching Mavis at all, but staring through the double doors to where Willie

Junior slumped in misery. He stared intently, his expression gentle and empty, as if willing Willie Junior to look up at him. "It was just made of clay. You could get another one."

"Never!" Mavis declaimed. "It was irreplaceable."

"Don't get too upset," he murmured. "If I could, I'd find you another one. But you know, Mama, it wasn't really Willie's fault. I'll bet it wasn't, was it, Viola?"

Mavis turned, tearfully questioning, to Viola.

"Nome," Viola whispers, shaking her head.

"Well, I'm sorry. But they're a pair! They do everything together."

"Bert eggs him on," Baby Boy corrected her. "And Bert doesn't really mean any harm, either. He's just—jumbled up sometimes. There's a boy at school like him. Bull Talbot. I met him when I first got there, he gets into a lot of trouble." Baby Boy paused. "He got me into trouble once. The same way. Talked me into sneaking out the window right before roll call. There were some pecans on this tree outside, see. I wouldn't have done it by myself, but he was so excited about those pecans. And then I was the one got punished. But I did it." He paused once more, thinking, as if something had just come clear to him. "I did it. It was only right, if I did it."

"Why, Baby! You never told me about that." Mavis pulled back, stung and marveling.

"It was—it was kind of private. During the first semester. They're real strict about stuff like that at school, Mama."

"I hope not about a boyish prank. I mean, well, I know you meant no harm. Now did you? Just some old pecans!"

Baby Boy sighed. "You see, those are the rules. That's how they do things, Mama, I knew that." He subsided, rubbing a mosquito bite on his leg. "I don't think I can explain it to you right."

"What is there to explain? Some boy named Bull, for heaven sakes."

"But it was right," Baby Boy repeated quietly.

Viola glanced to Willie Junior's head, lifted and listening. His hand massaged the reddened cheek, dropped to his side.

"Anyhow," Baby Boy went on, "some people are just made that way. They don't mean to be bad."

"They've got to learn!" Mavis sniffed. "Bert's got to learn. Hasn't he, Viola?"

"He got to learn to obey," Viola said slowly, looking from Willie Junior to Baby Boy and back.

"So you see? I'm going straight in to Wicky. I'm surprised he hasn't taken his nose out of his book, hearing all this commotion, frankly. Just oblivious, as usual. Y'all just continue with your business. Baby Boy, this is your day, honey, I don't want it spoiled by ugliness. You find something nice to do while I talk to Uncle Wicky." She humped to the library door. "This time maybe we can get a little peace." She turned the knob.

Viola watched Baby Boy. But he leaned back with his lids closed, brooding in that still place somewhere within him. She passed out of the foyer and through the drawing room, sparing a sorrowful glance for Willie Junior. But it was wasted; he too had retreated again, lying on the sofa, face ground into the velvet cushions.

The flowers, already arranged, filled the centerpiece in a star-shaped mass: August blossoms, daylilies, roses, gladiolas. She lined knives and forks on the cloth. The twins were not the playmates William had envisioned. If anything, they served to make Baby Boy stand apart, and he, in turn, had a name for them, which he applied whenever they came shooting into his room to grab his toys. "Wilbert! Now if you want to play with this, ask me instead of snatching it away. Listen, Wilbert, don't tear that book, just sit and turn the pages." He never, never grew angry or impatient; in that he was like his father. Sophie too, for all she knew. But he was also something more. Like one of the daylilies, dusted with golden pollen at its heart, belling out serenely, then furling at sundown into a tight-ended fuse, the gold shaken onto the damask cloth below, but some of it hidden, secreted still.

She sighed, switching the placement of a salad fork. The twins were no longer "Wilbert." But he was right, he had something there. For they struck her, in some ways, as the two hinged pieces of a whole object, two halves of a peach. No. Not that. They wound and raveled with each other. It seemed funny that she had never realized how influenced the family was by Baby Boy's simplicity: all the household regarded them that way. Every null space within the one was filled by the other, every cry had its resonating echo. Bert blustered where Willie Junior shirked; Willie Junior proffered the politeness for both. She had watched them play together often enough, when they believed no one overheard: in the treehouse above the kitchen window, for instance. And then, although they looked nothing alike, it sometimes sounded as if they spoke with one single voice, quarreling, agreeing, conspiring through the long afternoon, among the thick clusters of pecan leaves. When had she sensed things changing to a point where the isolation was broken, the tidy cell breached, so that Bert could fling that wrenched, rebellious wish at the boy sitting so apart in the butler's chair?

She stepped to the sideboard for the plates. Suddenly she stopped still. A low noise came from the drawing room, a sibilance interweaving on the air. She listened.

"But he didn't mean to," someone whispered. "I don't care."

"I know he didn't. You can't let him bully you, though. If you just, I don't know, tell him in a big strong voice——"

"It doesn't matter." The whisper mixed with the jingle of insects through the open windows. "Will Aunt Mavis let him come down for dinner?"

"It's Uncle Wicky. I think he will."

"Will he tan his hide, like Viola said?"

"Have you ever seen him spank any of us? Naw. He'll just give him a talking to."

The insects slid up the scale, crescendoing in the heat.

"Baby Boy?"

"Yes?"

"What's a half-breed?"

There came a scuffling noise, of shoes on parquet. Viola heard him settle into the velvet sofa beside his brother.

"It's like when you take two different kinds of corn and blend their seeds. We studied it in school, in science class. You take their tassels, see, and—and then you rub them together or something, and then it makes new kinds of seeds from the two you had before. And then when you plant them and they sprout, you get a brand-new kind of corn. A better kind, called a high breed."

"Better?"

His voice drifted above a whisper, in easy solace. "Yes, better. That's why they do it. That's a half-breed, mixing two old useless kinds of corn to make a better kind."

"Are Bert and me, are we—?"

"There are two of you, you see. Half and half. But two new kinds, that's what she meant. Higher."

"She said 'horrible.'" The whisper quailed. "I don't understand, that part about the corn."

"All you have to understand is that it's better. That's all. Don't pay any attention to the other. Mama was just real mad."

"Are you going to tell Bert about the half-breeds?" He sniffed. "I think he might understand it better if you tell him. He got mad about it."

"Sure. I'll tell him."

Viola glided silently around the table, laying the plates while waiting to hear if there was more; her smile contracted with a mysterious pang, as she pictured a field of corn in Baby Boy's eye, stalks dipping under the breeze, bearing ears of yellow splendor.

"Do you really know a boy named Bull?" Willie Junior's whisper was admiring.

"Sure."

"That's a funny name. Bull."

The lazy thoughtful murmur came like a breath. "No more funny than Baby Boy."

THE SUN was directly above the earth. Mavis squinted as Viola spooned rice on her plate. The diamond earrings were augmented by an emerald necklace which Viola had not seen in thirteen years, and saw last on Arliss's firm neck in 1922, above a green evening gown. But Mavis plucked at the stones, as if chafed by their luxury. Her print dress was too tight under the arms; she felt out of sorts because of Bert's presence at the table, disrupting the reverence of the day. He should have been punished; her protests showed in her every move. Once she glanced up to the birthday boy, pleating her lips in a querulous smile when he asked for a double helping of fried chicken.

"I had Bessie cook your favorites," she said wistfully.

"Thank you, Mama." He beamed at the laden plate. "I've missed Bessie's cooking as much as just about anything while I was at school."

"Well! Maybe we can bribe a conductor on the train once in awhile to take you a special dinner, when you go back in September."

"How would you like that, Boy?" joked William. "Your own personal meal delivered to your dormitory. Wouldn't your friends be full of envy?"

"They'd never let me live it down." But Mavis knit her brow, and then they realized she was serious.

"Aww, Mama," said Baby Boy softly.

"Not a thing the matter with it," she reproved, hurt.

"I—well, thank you, Mama. But it would be like singling me out from the other fellows. Their parents don't do things like that. They'd call me a—they'd say you were spoiling me."

"Hmph. Only because their parents don't care, don't miss their children, or aren't used to giving them treats."

"I'll bet he considers coming home the biggest treat he could possibly get. Don't you, Boy?"

"Yes, Uncle Wicky," Baby Boy answered, and then, looking at Mavis's crushed expression, "That's the truth!"

"You get to see us then, too," Willie Junior said shyly.

But Bert said nothing at all.

Viola leaned back against the sideboard, watching him as they ate. The image of ripening corn kept returning to her mind. But how did it equate with this sullen silence, with the screwed corners of his mouth? He looked like a stranger child, suspicious at the hosts' table, an orphan at a Sunday feast. But Baby Boy, the nominal orphan, sat relaxed in pride of place, at home, raising a drumstick to bite. His eyes met Bert's. Bert instantly glowered down at his untasted food.

"I wouldn't mind it," Baby Boy said, "if Bert and Willie Junior were allowed sometime to come down and see me. That would be a treat, all right."

Bert's hand froze where it had been fingering his knife.

"Why, Baby! What about your own mama visiting you? You haven't asked me."

"But I thought you didn't like to come. You always stay home, Mama." He sighed, yet he was watching Bert from the angle of his eye. "Of course I want you to come. But see, Bert and Willie, they're boys, too. They might like to see the football field and all the fellows in uniform during parade drill, and the rifle range, and all that stuff. You know, boys' stuff. Do you think they could sometime, Uncle Wicky? They could come on the train, even. Or you and Mama could drive them down."

"They'd have to do something to deserve it," Mavis began, but William interrupted her.

"That's not such a bad notion." He set his hands palm down on the snowy cloth. "Sure wouldn't do any harm."

Mavis fidgeted with temperament. "You can just imagine how they'd behave, Wicky, no thank you. Careering through the hotel,

smashing who knows what, making an embarrassment of themselves—"

"Now, Mavis. You know you don't mean that, honey."

"Can't see you heaving out of your chair and a history book long
enough to spend a few days in the Hill Country."

"Well." He scrutinized her, the heavy face firming for a moment. "I
guess we all can make a sacrifice, every once in awhile."

She flapped her fingers at her brow. "Oh, let's just—drop the subject!" With a visible effort, she strained for a grin, and turned to
Baby Boy. "We'll talk about such things later, sweetie pie."

"I remember a time when I took you to a hotel in East Texas."
William lounged back in his chair, cracking his knuckles. "You recall
that? All the dogwood and azaleas rioting through Tyler on the way?
Just devoted to trying to catch your fancy."

"Wicky!" Her voice sharpened.

"I tell you what," he said, folding his arms behind his head. "Why
don't we mull it over?" He winked casually at Baby Boy. Bert peered
under his eyebrows. "All the time in the world, September is still
three weeks away."

"I've got a better idea," Baby Boy said slowly. "Why don't we all go
into Bernice tomorrow? That way the twins can see what it's like, the
streets and all, the stores, the houses. They could even see the hotel.
If Bernice has got a hotel."

The hush that followed seemed palpable.

"Of course it's got a hotel," Mavis snapped; and then mashed her
hand to her mouth. "I'm sorry, sweetie, I didn't mean to say that."
She turned flustered and angry to William. "Now just see? See what's
happening?"

"Far be it from me to perturb things, Mavis."

"Mama?" Baby Boy said. "We could go to Bernice. Why not?"

The two adults suddenly seemed to pull away from the boys, like
creatures caught apart, out of their habitats. William sat still in his
chair. Mavis laced her hands together, glaring sternly at the ceiling.

"It's the town closest to us," said Baby Boy, with the bewildered reasonableness of someone who knew he had stumbled on a barrier that did not belong there. He turned to Viola. She could tell, by his steady frown, that she presented the same mystery. "You've always kept us out here. Why, even though I've been to Dallas and to Kerrville and everywhere else, you've never taken us into Bernice." His voice caught. "I don't mean to be impudent, I really don't. But I'd like to see Bernice, and the twins, it would do them good. They could learn how to behave." He halted, pondering his elders, kneading his thighs between his fingers. "Bert could—if he could maybe meet some other people, there must be boys in Bernice—in town— it's only three miles away, no reason they couldn't have friends to play with. Mama?"

Mavis's head jerked swiftly, uncontrollably. The diamonds jigged under her shingled hair.

"It's less than three miles, Boy," William said; "it's only a couple, and getting nearer all the time."

"What?" whispered Mavis, twisting toward him.

"That's right, honey," he said gently. "It's grown a bit lately. The new iron works, a hat factory, an expansion at the chili cannery. All kinds of progress. Some new people, too."

She sighed.

"But we"—he turned unseeing at the three boys, eyes dimmed and lightless—"we don't really go in there. Why, I hardly do myself, not in a long time, gave up the business I had there except for the Ford dealership. It runs itself."

"But why?" asked Baby Boy carefully. "Why, sir?"

"We have nothing to do with those people," Mavis prompted. "Your grandfather helped found the town, and then, well, you just have to take our word for it."

"But Bessie goes in. Ezra goes in all the time, Bessie at least once a month, to church. And Viola"—Baby Boy turned to look at her, in his stare a new examinatory light—"you go in sometimes. I can remember, once a long time ago when I was little, you went to a funeral, somebody named Miss Marianne. You told me about it. And I always thought everybody in Bernice must be like you, must be— colored." He stopped, and then went on, as if the ripple traveling through the adults was nothing but a wave of the summer heat. "I thought everybody in the world was. Except for us here. Ransoms. Even when I went to Dallas that time. Because the delivery boy from Sopwith's is and the boy from the grocery store, and the hardware store. And then, when I went to Dallas and to school—you see, Bert, you see, Willie," he turned to them earnestly, "that's what you probably don't realize. There are all kinds of people everywhere. White ones and colored ones and lots of others, too. Like the pictures in the books—"

Mavis gasped. "Wicky!"

Then Viola saw the way William's auburn brown eyes had flattened in his head. But a slow strange curl began on his lips.

"No, son. You're right. There are all kinds of people in the world." He smiled oddly. "I never thought. It never occurred to me before." He looked at each of the three faces before him, the twins' open mouths, the astounded innocence.

"No, Wicky! No! You will not, you will not. Not to prove a point, I don't care how big it's grown, how many new people. You know—"

Bert burst from his chair like a projectile. "I know why you don't want us to go. You'll stop us. You won't let us. I heard the reason. Because we're half-breeds!" He thrashed about, battering the air. "Half-breeds, me and Willie! You don't want the people in the town to see!"

William's face decayed suddenly. His mouth went sodden with shock.

"I was good and mad!" Mavis railed. "You caused that mischief, you broke Mother's vase, Baby Boy's favorite!"

"You called them what?" William's voice dropped to steely quiet.

"They know perfectly well I didn't mean it!"

"Mavis," William whispered as if to himself. "Mavis." He shook his head.

"But that's all right," Willie Junior said shyly, and for the first time they noticed him. He leaned over the table edge. "Baby Boy explained what it meant."

William stared at Baby Boy. The brown boyish cheeks flushed scarlet. "You did? Did you explain?"

"Yes, sir."

"It means we're better," Willie Junior confided. "We're two new high kinds from the old useless ones. Like what they do with corn."

Baby Boy was squirming on his seat. Bert poised like an avenger. "New kinds?" he choked. "High?"

"He was going to explain it to you, too," Willie Junior said, swiveling to him. "As soon as he got the chance."

Baby Boy ducked further, skin blazing. But on William's bleakness a grin was forming.

"Oh, Wicky!" bleated Mavis.

"Boys." He sprawled back in his chair. "Boys." The grin widened; he surveyed the expectant attention written on their faces. "I believe that tomorrow morning we will pile into my old car. Or my sister's recent one. And then we will drive down the road. And when we reach Bernice, I'll take you all into the drugstore belonging to Mr. Andy Sloane, and there I will buy you each a hot fudge sundae and a soda water of your choice."

Mavis throttled a moan, her hands flung high.

"Honey," he said and, reaching out, lowered the arm nearest him. "Honey."

"What?"

"It'll be all right."

The boys goggled. A dreariness overtook Mavis, her forehead crumpling. She lolled to one side of her chair back, meeting no one's eyes.

"Don't you see? It's time. It's been long enough now." Behind his back, Viola began to work furiously, grabbing cake forks from the drawer. But the chink of silverware made him pivot. "Viola. Don't you agree?"

"Ain't none of my say." The forks were sheaved in her fist like tridents.

"Well. I think so." He raised a hand to scratch his scalp. "Don't know why I didn't see it before. I guess I've imagined these hoodlums would stay babies for an eternity or two." He grinned at the blank faces, then stabbed his forefinger at Bert. "You just sit right back down." Without a ghost of expression, Bert sank into his chair. "But they sure aren't babies anymore. They have to occupy space like all the rest of us. Collide with the population."

Mavis sniffed.

"Everything grows. Everything expands, even water," he said elliptically.

How the Young
Ransoms Met Bernice

The next morning the car bumped and skidded down the road towards Bernice. Bert exclaimed at every new sight, crashing into Viola in the back seat in his attempts to view from all the windows simultaneously. Willie Junior, however, remained silent, his lashes brushing the glass in concentration, and pressed his nose to the pane until a smear like a snail track lay across it. They passed one landmark after another, the examples of which the twins had seen only in books: railroad trestles, mules and wagons, the county reservoir with a fisherman standing in a boat among the bulrushes, a livestock truck porting a lone cow, a string of tenant houses at the ends of the corn rows. But when they stalled the car to watch a train barrel past, far across the pastures, Bert fell speechless. A remote thunder pounded on their ears, loose and regular as a pulse. "A train," Bert breathed, after it was gone, "I've seen a real train at last."

Viola ruminated. It all looked different to her. The landscape she had known all her life, switching across the windshield in the pitiless sunshine, had changed—even the light looked different. Gone were the cool skirts of shade under the oaks that she was now accustomed to, the stillness beneath the hum of insects, the leaves trembling on a breeze so slowly she could count each fanning flicker. The long quiet stroll through the woods, the bridal wreath clipped back in a wall. The jasmine around the back gallery. She lowered her lids against that brunt of glare, until she could only see the fields stretching towards the horizon, plowed with streaks of cotton. Such a huge sky! Each tank glinted below it, a puddle of mercury motionless in its cup of trampled mud. Did she remember that tin sign on the road's shoulder? Clabber Girl Baking Powder, with a girl in a sunbonnet. She must—it hung at a slant on its post, scabbed by the weather; but for the life of her she had no recollection of it, it could have grown there during the past months, patches and all. Had she forgotten what the rest of the world looked like? Even the messages and news she had received over the last few years from family members seemed like daydreams, unconnected with flesh and blood: Bessie's word of mouth. Had her kin been living all this time under that white hot ball, sharing these sights? And the billboard, "Tex-Rite Hats, Inc., Men's Headgear for Every Occasion," was like another harbinger of change, conferring information she had no means to decipher.

She huddled back into the leather seat, suddenly afraid.

Bert jumped up. "Ah!" he yelled, pointing wildly. "Do you *see* that gray deer, setting so still like he's paralyzed?"

A straggle of houses appeared around the bend. They were new, their yards scrubbed bare or just sprouting, the white or green painted clapboards hazy behind screened breezeways. In front of one of them knelt a concrete deer. By another, a woman hung washing, popping sheets straight before she pegged them. William slowed down. The yard after the fifth house revealed a giant crape myrtle flowering over a broken path of stones. The path led to a gray house face, a porch buckling on one side: Viola at last recognized the house of the postmaster.

"Why," she said in astonishment, "that's Mr. Rutherford's house."

"Uh-huh," William said. "We're in the outskirts of Bernice."

"Oh, my Lordy Lord." Viola closed her eyes.

"How long has it been since you've come to town, anyway?"

"I don't know. Law, a long time."

"I hadn't realized that," he said softly. "Can't figure why, though."

He brought the car almost to a stop for an instant, with Bert thumping against Viola's legs.

"Yep, old Army Rutherford's not a rural dweller any longer. The town has spread. His boy's due out of the penitentiary next year. Remember when I told you Earl Ray Rutherford had been sent to Huntsville for mail fraud?"

"I done lost count," Viola murmured. "I recollect when you told me, but it seem like just the day before yesterday."

"Nearly finished serving his time now." William gunned the car.

"I feel like I died," Viola whispered, but William heard her.

"It's just change, that's all. Just a sample of what time can do."

"Oh, *look!*" Bert shrieked. "Did you ever—"

The water tower rose before them, a canister on stilts above the housetops and the roof of the high school. It was the tallest thing in town, usurping a wedge of the naked sky, its catwalk circling it like a belt. Around the silver tub appeared broad letters painted in black: ERNI, and, disappearing on the far curve, the arched bow of the C.

"It's bigger than I ever imagined a thing," Bert stammered. "Willie, do you see that thing?"

"Yes," said Willie Junior. "I see it, Bert."

"What is it? A machine?"

"It's a giant cistern, son. Whole town takes their baths from that, when the reservoir gets too low during the summer."

"They climb up there and go swimming?" Bert breathed.

A smile crossed William's face.

"Could we do it? Daddy? Could we crawl up that ladder today?"

"You'd fall and split your head like a watermelon."

Viola sighed. "That ain't what they do, child."

"BERNI," Bert read. His eyes were glued to the spire far above his head. Now the wide yards spread out on either side, striped with shadows, planted with trees and shrubs and houses.

"This is Bois D'arc Street, boys," said William. "I was born on this street."

They wheeled towards the corner to the courthouse square. Viola felt a tightening in her throat. A Grecian Revival mansion stood beyond a tended garden, pillars smooth and creamy; next to that a sloping brick and stone bungalow. Next to that was the wooden house built in the shotgun style, with two fake marble planters, chipped now and overgrown with weeds, squatting beneath the steps, and the single cottonwood tree.

"Down there's Governor's Drive, where the Deloaches live. Or the son Henry, anyhow, with his stepmother. The Governor passed away some time back." William gestured down a street of green tranquillity. "We won't pay them a visit today. The son got married a few years ago. He took over his father's bank."

Viola realized he was speaking to her. It was as if he told her a folk tale, of characters he had read. She shook her head, tears stinging her eyes, and looked backwards out the rear window at the ruined pedestal of a planter, bought with Arliss's hoarded egg money, and once crowded with geraniums.

"The road's changed, I didn't even notice it! See? It's not dirt anymore, it's brick! And some black stuff, further up."

"Asphalt, Bert," William murmured. "Easier upkeep. That's the courthouse square. And there's the courthouse."

"Oh," said Willie Junior. "It has a clock in the—the—that hat part."

"Yep. Never kept the right time in living memory."

"There's a man sitting out front on a chair! A giant!"

"That's a bronze statue, Bert. That's Governor Deloache."

"What's the book he's reading?"

"A list of the county founders. Why, your own great-grandfather's name is scribbled on it. Alongside a heap of others," William said wryly, guiding the car to a parking place against the curb. Viola looked up and saw the spacious post office steps rising above her.

"They put that statue up to him when Bernice was still nothing but a spot on the map. Civic pride, plus some contributions from the pertinent parties. Why, when I was still a boy, my daddy used to bring me down here and boost me onto the Governor's lap. I would sit on the crook of those open pages, feeling the raised letters through my short pants, then I would look out over the entire city—the jail, the hotel, a few nice houses—and feel like the king of the mountain." He chuckled. "I'll never forget the start I got once, when I spun around and saw who the man was. Recognized him, you understand, for the first time. The Governor, a person I knew perfectly well. But made all out of metal. I could hear the hollow ring when I drummed my heels on his knees. Like to scared me to death."

The boys stared about them, climbing out of the car. But Viola, shading her eyes with her hand, looked at William. She had not heard him this talkative in more than a dozen years.

"Just as if he'd somehow died and turned to mineral. And then suddenly I heard him wish Daddy good evening. His voice sent chills up my arms. I looked up in terror from the statue, and there he comes, strolling down the sidewalk, a sliver of moon hanging in the sky over his head." He paused. "I imagined the statue had spoken." The three boys had already run to the courthouse lawn. Viola saw Baby Boy reach out and tentatively stroke the statue's bronze thigh. "It was a curious moment," William said. "A mockingbird, I remember, suddenly flittered up from a branch. That one right there, in the old elm, see? It went winging away in the moon's direction. I leaped down off the statue and grabbed Daddy's hand. Once the Governor had passed on by, I broke away and ran. I couldn't wait to get home to you. I was all the way to Bois D'arc Street before I remembered that we didn't live there anymore."

Bert raced across the crimped yellow grass and tugged at his elbow.

"Daddy, look! There's Sopwith's store!" His voice lurched. "And there's two—no, three—*ladies* coming out the door."

"Yes, son, so there is." William turned and gazed at the facade.

"Hidy, Mrs. Burly. Howdydo, Mrs. Briscoe." He nodded politely at the third lady, who stood squinting at him in doubt: someone he did not know.

Mrs. Burly was the first to hobble across the street.

"Why, William Ransom! Do my eyes deceive me, or is it really you? I declare. It is! I must have gone and contracted heat stroke, to witness this vision."

"How are you, Mrs. Burly? Yes, ma'am, thought I'd ramble into town this morning and take my boys on a sightseeing tour."

"If this isn't just the most gladsome day!" Her voice faltered like a jerky violin. "Mary Sue Farmington! Elva Briscoe! Come see what the cat dragged in." Leaning forward, beaming upon him, she tilted her cheek for his kiss. "My very own star pupil, left my classroom nearly eighteen years ago to go to Yale University. I can hardly believe it."

The other two women sauntered up, their court heels smacking through the tarry asphalt. "Good morning, William Ransom," said Mrs. Briscoe. "Haven't seen nor heard from you in this long while."

"That's so," he replied, ducking his head, suddenly bashful. "Good to see you now, though. And Mr. Briscoe, how is he?"

"Oh, we're just fine, William, except for the rheumatics. Both of us is got them. We all've been at Sopwith's, to select some new dishware for the church. You know we built us a fellowship hall."

"Is that right?"

"This past spring, it was."

"That's mighty fine," William said gravely, as the other two boys wandered around the car nearby, circling it, touching the fenders for assurance and casting the ladies sidelong glances.

"Come over here and meet these folks," William called to them.

Baby Boy stepped up, steady and solemn; Willie Junior trailed a few paces behind in an agony.

"I heard you had you some twins," Mrs. Briscoe said.

"Yes, indeed, about time you graced us with their acquaintance," cried Mrs. Burly, clacking her dentures. "My stars, aren't they big, though. Nearly grown!"

William introduced them one by one.

"This is Mrs. Otis Farmington, moved here from Maypearl," Mrs. Burly said. "She and her husband are our new church members. Her husband's with Tex-Rite Hats."

"I'm so very pleased to meet you," William smiled, and bowed to the unknown lady. She was much younger than her companions, hardly more than a girl, and she shone out very pink and blond against their elderly gray coloring. Her matron's status she wore as if it were a hand-me-down suit which she was struggling to make fit, but was still too plump and unformed to cram herself into its dignified lines. Her adolescence seemed very close behind her.

The three boys repeated William's formula parrot-fashion, with Willie Junior managing to get as far as "Pleased," in a strangled whisper.

"I'm so pleased to meet you, too!" cried Mrs. Farmington eagerly. She pumped each of their hands up and down with violence. "Aren't you all so big and grown! I should just love to have you all over to my new house for lemonade sometime."

The twins pulled back in alarm, and Viola herded them behind her. Baby Boy remained by William's side. Before five seconds had passed Bert was already making his escape, roaming towards the entrance of the hotel. "Bert! You get on back here until we say," called Viola.

"Can this be the—is this here Mavis's boy? The child himself?" Mrs. Burly wondered. "Why, it must be! Why—"

And then she stopped suddenly, her faded eyes riveted on Baby Boy, the gray irises clear as jelly jars. "Oh!" she cried, breaking off in a fit of coughing.

William patted her arm while the ladies fluttered over her. When she had struggled back to self-command, she looked back at Baby Boy, her tone pitched low and emphatic. "Why, what a fine boy you have there, William. I'm eighty-two years old, and have taught heaven only knows how many classrooms full of fine children in my time. But I'd like to say I've never seen one quite as fine as you." She studied Baby Boy intently. "Except maybe once upon a time, long long ago, when I taught your—uncle." The sharp stare turned back to William. Baby Boy blushed, and murmured his thanks. A few more passersby strolled down the sidewalk behind him: a pair of businessmen in suspenders, out for coffee, a woman pushing a little girl in patent leather shoes along.

"I taught your mama, too." Her lips pinched together. The gray eyes, bright as a bird's, brushed Viola with a cold impassive glance.

"Oh, how is Mavis doing?" gasped Mrs. Briscoe. "My, it's been such a long while. I hope she's full of health?"

"Yes, ma'am, thank you."

"And I knew your grandmother well," Mrs. Burly continued, eyes piercing each boy in turn. "She was a purely magnificent woman. Much too exuberant for the likes of us poor Berniceans. Larger than life, Arliss Ransom. An edifice."

Willie Junior nudged his forehead into the small of Viola's back. Bert started edging away again. But Baby Boy stood his ground, while the other ladies' sheer dresses swished on the breeze.

"Where are you going to school, young man, may I inquire?"

"I go to the military academy out of Kerrville, ma'am," he replied, "Sauter Military."

The eyes appraised him up and down. They were knowing, guessing everything, pondering the iniquities of a classroom delinquent, accepting as a truth of the earth plaits dipped in the inkwell, commandeering through the wooden lid the horned toad mesmerized inside the desk. "Very fine indeed. I hear they teach well there."

"Why, Mrs. Burly, surely no better than you taught here in your day!" cried Mrs. Briscoe.

"My day's past, Elva." She stretched her lips into a puckery smile. "Just like my husband and my cannas, withered away in the last drought. But my memory for children never withers. Not even at my age." She paused over Bert's head. Willie Junior was not visible, except for the toes of his shoes under Viola's skirt. "I have imprinted on my mind the likeness of every child ever passed through my hands. Or my paddle," she said proudly. "Never forget a face between the ages of ten to fifteen."

"You're a remarkable lady, Mrs. Burly," said William. "It's an honor to have been one of them."

"I'm not surprised you haven't brought these young'uns in, though. Brought them up to the simple country life, nothing more commendable. It's an example to us, in this age of gross materialism. Why, I bet you've tutored them yourself, with your wonderful education."

"Much obliged to you, Mrs. Burly. You know, that's just what I've done." William's voice sounded a trifle strained.

"Thought so!" She grinned in triumph. "More power to you, in this day and age. They've doubtless benefited. I must tell you I'm very fond of you, William Ransom, you always did me proud. It's a pleasure to see you again." She stepped up closer, peering into his face. Then she held her palsied knuckles to his cheek, and stroked against it. "Three fine boys. You're doing all right."

"Thank you, ma'am."

"Mrs. Burly? If you'll excuse us, I don't want to spoil the reunion, but I've got to feed my chickens," Mrs. Briscoe cried to William.

"In a minute, Elva." She pressed on William's face, her bright eyes rheumy with nostalgia.

"By the way," said Mrs. Briscoe, "did we tell you even who Mrs. Farmington is?"

"Why, bet we didn't!" chirped Mrs. Burly.

"Yes, ma'am, from Maypearl, Mr. Farmington with the hat people." William smiled again at the pink-faced young girl, who smiled broadly back.

"Why, that's not all. There's lots of new folk here in Bernice these days, but Mary Sue Farmington is no stranger. Not only is she the best solo soprano the Baptist church ever had, she's even kin, in a way!"

"Why, is that right?" William offered Mrs. Farmington a polite gaze. "Kin to who?"

"Grant Macafee on his mother's side. Her mother was his mother's first cousin. She's Grant's second cousin once removed! Would that be right, Mary Sue?"

"That's right," Mrs. Farmington nodded, touching her blond hair where it crisped above her dress collar.

"Isn't that nice. Old Grant. Mighty nice."

"We haven't seen much of him since we moved here. We're just getting settled in these last few months. But it's good to be in a new place where your family's known to others."

"Uh-huh. Well, you be sure and look him up, I'm sure he'll be tickled."

"Oh, my, yes." But a quaver of doubt made her lift her eyes to the sky; then she smiled at William, refitting the youthful confidence.

"We will. It's just that I'm sure he's often so busy, out at his ranch and all, and then we're Baptist and he's Presbyterian. And we're just kind of gradually getting to know him on a personal basis, you see, because *we're* so busy——"

"Oh, yes. Yes, I can imagine."

"We plan to spend a lot more time with him soon, though, since he's now on his own. I guess you know about his separation." She glanced reverently down for a moment. "And he doesn't have the ice business anymore to——but wait a minute!" Her blue eyes blinked and widened. "Ransom! William Ransom! Are you the same Ransom family that had the ice business with the Macafees? The RanMac Chill Company?"

"Yes. That's us," said William shortly, glancing down at the curb.

"Oh, but this is wonderful! His old partners. Oh, but you must know Grant very well, then!"

"They grew up together," said Mrs. Burly gently, half-smiling toward William. "They went all through school together, and then college."

"Oh, yes. That's right! I'd heard Cousin Grant went off to Yale University, way up north. Well, my! Isn't this a coincidence, meeting you here, Mr. Ransom?"

"Ah—certainly. Yes, it is."

"Well, I just can't wait to go out and visit Grant now. Wait till I tell him! My goodness." She smiled with a proud pleasure. Viola saw William's lips press closed.

"Well, I have to be going, I'm afraid my hens just won't wait. It surely was precious to see you again, William."

"And you, Mrs. Briscoe. You be sure and give my regards to Mr. Briscoe."

"Bye-bye, nice to meet you," Mrs. Farmington said.

"Much obliged." He dragged his eyes back to her blue ones, and bowed slightly.

"Mrs. Burly? Can I walk you home, ma'am?"

But Mrs. Burly took William's hand between her two, massaging it with the gnarly fingers, and then reached up and forced his gaze to meet hers. "You've done real well. The right thing. You remember I said that." Her eyes fixed into his. "Take good care of your sons," she said, as if drilling William on a vital point in a history lesson. "Take good good care. They're all in your keeping." Then she let go his hand, and, bending, he kissed her once more on the cheek.

"I'm coming, Elva." She turned to go.

He stood, motionless, thoughtful, and watched her walk up the street. He waited while she, Mrs. Farmington, and Mrs. Briscoe rounded the corner, and then glanced to his eldest son, an inscrutable look in his eyes.

247

"Well, now. Who's ready for a little something to wet our whistles?"

"We are!" Bert jumped forward, and Baby Boy licked his lips. Willie Junior finally emerged from behind Viola.

"Let's mosey on over to the drugstore, then. Viola?" He paused. "May we bring you anything, ma'am?"

"Isn't she coming with us?" Bert cried, already tugging away. But then Baby Boy gave him a tiny shake of the head. Bert frowned, bewildered.

"You have to come," said Willie Junior desperately. "I need you."

"There may be more people in there he has to meet," Bert explained.

"You all go on." Viola slipped her skirt from under his grasp. "I got to see some folks at the hardware store. I'll meet you back here at the car."

William nodded. From a distance a sudden shriek tore through the air, and instantly the boys were diverted, listening: "Hot tamaleeeees!," it came. "Hot tamaleeeees!"

"I ain't going to say no to an ice cream cone," Viola muttered in William's ear, and then, without a backwards glance, straightened her waist and marched to the far end of the square, towards the wooden porch with its deep cool awning shadows and the group of loiterers she had not greeted in a lifetime. Catching sight of Uncle Shine's head, the bald spot on top like oiled ebony in the yards of distance, she quickened her steps, shoes clicking on the hot tar. As she drew nearer, Uncle Shine's head jerked up, his brow rumpling in the glare; he was forming a shout. A man in a seersucker suit overtook and passed her, obscuring her view for an instant; she caught a swift glimpse of his face: nose jutting, mouth like a slice, eye sockets thumbed out of thin skin. He loomed too tall for her to crane around his stiff, narrow back; that pale crescent of jaw severe as if cut from shell. First she hurried. Then she stopped. Uncle Shine's cry reached her: "Viola! Well, I be danged—" But she stood paralyzed in the middle of the street. The man winched his head around in profile then, darting a glance at the hardware porch to check the shouter. And she saw, heart ratcheting on her ribs, that he was a total stranger.

How William
Erected the Stone

The day Viola walked me all the way to the gates to see it, it was still legible. Only on the uninscribed base had the moss encroached, felting it with green, the plaque of growth lending it an ancient air. Viola told me how it had come to be there while I spelled out the letters with a finger, scraping away the ragged stars of lichen in their deepest grooves. Even broken, it loomed much taller than I. The top was jagged like a decaying tooth. Two fissures split the crown to a point midway through the lettering. Possibly by now the inscription is completely obscured; possibly it has been transmuted by those who pass it to a talismanic symbol, placed there by the Indians or Spanish—a milestone of sacred significance; or perhaps a battle marker, which would be more appropriate. Certainly my grandfather's impulse has long ago been perverted by the erosion of weather and events. I was not more than seven when Viola showed the stone to me. Already its purpose had been lost, and I stood on legs aching from the long unaccustomed walk while she repeated its history.

"He got it made when Baby Boy been gone to that school for four whole years," she said. "By then, the folks from town, new folks, mostly, that didn't know no better, they was wandering into the property, come hunting the rabbit and squirrel and quail, and he reckoned it was time to make it plain what he like and what he don't. He called it a"—she dug in her mind, and returned with the cache— "a catalyst."

"What did he like?" I was puffing less from the hike than from the discovery. A crunching sound neared us on the road, and soon a car drove past, tires sizzling on the asphalt. For now this was actually no longer a road; it was a street we stood next to; our gates with their branchy awnings of post oak opened onto the vista of a Bernice city block at the edge of town. A couple stared out of the car windows at us. I saw their white faces flash past. Then the car picked up speed and disappeared. I was too young yet to feel gratitude to the deep-set drive, the hedge of azaleas that partially concealed us. I shoved my head around a tangle to watch the tail end of the car before it was gone.

"I believe it say right there what he willing to put up with," Viola said. "He had it carved in that rock. And that rock come from all the way down in the Hill Country, it don't come from around here."

Carefully I read out loud: " 'This is the ho . . . ansom Family.' " The center words lay on a large chip half-buried in weeds by the stone's root. " 'We welcome all visi . . . ould stroll through these woods. Avail yourselves of what . . . eautiful, but please leave your arms . . . ome, that no creature may come to harm. Please preserve our privacy as your gift to us. The Ransoms' hospitality ends at the cattle guard. You are requested to leave at sunset. Trespassers during the night will be prosecuted. Signed, William Garner Ransom. Anno Domini 1937.' "

I had to scratch a mosaic of lichen off his perfectly rendered signature.

I turned and gazed upwards at Viola.

"I ain't never hear it out through to the end since the day he hired the tombstone man in town to put it up here," she said. "Took him three helpers and a bunch of pulleys before they heft it right. But he read it to me in his library before he got it carved. He wanted to see if it sound good. Funny thing to my mind, how all the people took the words and stuck to them."

"But why did he have it done?"

"Law, child, I told you already: the new folk from town. Bernice grow real big in those times, just like a gravy stain spreading out towards this property. You see now how it is." She jabbed her thumb behind her at the big suburban houses across the street. "We don't have us no callers all the while Baby Boy was still tiny. Then he went to school, and just like he was worrying before he go, the strangers started pouring in with guns and picnics. These woods started looking like a mattress full of bedbugs. Made Miss Mavis mad! She was like to bust. Scared her more than made her mad, too.

"She go white and run into the house, the first time she saw some man with his wife and children out by the little pond with a big sack of groceries setting there by their side. 'Wicky!' she screeched out, like a chicken snake was after her egg, and she busted into that library faster than a rainstorm. He had to go settle it with those folk right then." She thought back, blinking her eyes in the sun, the whites discolored and webbed with red veins. I swatted at a swarm of gnats. "Trash, is what I reckon they was," and she snorted. "Trespassing on good folk's land. But he figured out the way he want it, and then he drove to Bernice with the twins rassling in the back seat, and ordered up that rock. More than a sign, he say. 'It's got to be better than a piece of wood.' Something to declare his wish for all Texas to read until the Judgment Day."

"Why doesn't he take care of it now? Why doesn't he get it cleaned and fixed?"

"Seem like it's doing just what he want it to do," she said, and considered for a moment. "I always reckon he meant that stone for somebody in particular." We sauntered past a copse of mesquite, seeming incongruous amidst the leafier trees; beyond a mass of azaleas stood a lone cactus in a clearing of harsh rusty grass.

"Uh-huh," she mused, "like it's a letter he want to send, but he wrote it on a rock like it was meant for just anybody. His Declaration of Independence." She paused. "Only that one person ain't never read it, not the livelong years between then and now, I don't reckon."

"Who? Who was it for?" I swung her hand in mine.

She looked down at me and licked her lips. "Some hunters don't kill in the woods," she said.

"What do you mean, Viola?"

She did not answer.

"HOW YOU could do such a—a tacky thing, I'll never know," Mavis cried. "Not to mention the sneakiness, keeping it such a deep dark secret, and then telling me after it was too late. A declaration of love and welcome for every piece of riffraff that takes a mind to invade us."

"Why, honey, it's meant to be a warning to leave us alone, too. There's no need to be so high-strung about it."

"Stop acting like an old maid, you mean. Just a glib and thoughtless brother, you are to me." She lay back stiffly on the chaise lounge and closed her eyes. "If anybody had ever predicted how you'd turn out when I was eight years old and worshiped you, I'd have slapped their cheeks."

"Mavis, the question of your marriage prospects never entered my head. That's just unfair. And besides—"

"Besides what?"

"Why, I think you're probably the only person in the county who sees yourself that way. Most folk in Bernice regard you as heroic."

"Just why would they do that?" The loops of jasmine dangling above her head seemed to Viola, shelling peas in the last chair on the back gallery, to confute her sarcasm, waving in the light May breeze, a curtain of flowers conferring their sweet scent against the air.

"Why," said William, "taking in orphans, I suppose."

"That old story! I bet I have Mrs. Deloache to thank as the author of that," Mavis sneered.

"She's not in a position to author any opinions these days. Poor lady."

"Yes, you told me about her failing mind. But you and I know perfectly well such a comment is not referring to orphans."

"Now don't jump to—"

"Oh, hush, Wicky. I don't care." She gripped her lower lip between her teeth. "I don't understand," she said, voice beginning to tremble, "why you have to force me into a situation I have avoided for very good reasons for the past thirteen years. That's what you've done, Wicky."

"I've what, honey?"

"That awful monument. How could you? How could you issue an invitation for the entire county to come and satisfy their curiosity? How could you expose me so?" Tears started to well up from behind the tight-shut eyelids.

"Oh, now, Mavis." His dismay spread across his face. He reached out to pat Mavis's hand.

"Any Tom, Dick, and Harry who's heard of the crazy cripple living the life of a nun in the Ransom house, telling their children, 'Let's go out there and take a peek, we might catch sight of her if we're lucky!' and hauling their wives and floozies and who knows what, stomping through the grounds our own daddy established, for my humiliation—" The fingers laced and unlaced on the breast of her dress.

"Honey," William said.

"I'm sick and tired of hearing you urge me to come with you into town. And now my boy's growing up, now he's getting so big, and he's been my only comfort, and before I know it, you'll be telling me, 'Well, it's time Baby Boy went off to college. I think Yale is the best place for him to go.' Yale! Thousands of miles away amongst a bunch of Yankees! And what good did it do you, I'd like to ask?"

"Now, I don't necessarily recommend Yale."

But Mavis lay very still.

The bridal wreath bushes shuddered at the far end of the lawn. Bert whooped and appeared briefly as an arm and a leg through the leaves. William lighted a cigar.

"That child's coming home tomorrow," Viola said. She waited a moment, folding the newspaper of black-eyed pea pods into a package in her lap. "You ain't going to meet him with a heart full of misery over nothing."

"Nothing!" grunted Mavis. But she opened her eyes and sat up. "I don't know about this train arrangement. I think I preferred it when you used to drive down to Kerrville for him, Wicky."

"He's able to take care of himself now, honey."

"All that way, and only thirteen. It makes me anxious."

"He'll be just fine, you'll see."

"Well, I hope you intend to be in plenty of time to meet the train. Make it a half hour early, at least, would you do that for me?"

"Yes, all right."

"Or even an hour."

William sighed.

"There's still one thing I can't comprehend," she said. "You still haven't explained to me how in the world we'd know if somebody did come trespassing after sundown. Cowering in the woods, turning our land into a Lovers' Lane, or worse. How would we know, what could we do to stop them?"

"The gates are locked by Ezra every single night."

"Gates! Every gate is made to climb, every fence is for shinnying over."

"What are you expecting, honey?" he asked mildly. "Pirates and cutthroats? This is Bernice, Texas."

"Peeping Toms," Mavis muttered. "Viola, have you told Bessie to make that lemon chiffon pie for tomorrow? Baby Boy just loves it."

"I told her."

"Well, I've decided something." Mavis paused. Her shoulders stooped forward; she stared obliquely at William until she snagged his eye. "I'm going in with you tomorrow to the depot."

William's jaw went slack; Viola's own surprise sent the newspaper package tumbling onto the gallery floor.

"That way I'll at least know we won't be late," said Mavis, and neatened her skirt sedately. But Viola saw the fingers' tremor.

A roar burst up from the earth, and all three staggered to their feet in startlement. Mavis screamed.

"I got you!" Bert yelled. "I got you good!" He laughed and laughed, the sudden "Arrrrgh!" he had shouted from beneath the gallery still resounding on the air, like a materialization of Mavis's fears.

THE NEXT day, the twins leaped through the open car doors, while Mavis fumbled into the front seat. They had shot up in the past year, Viola thought; they were a head taller, and their outgrown clothes filled a closet on the third floor. Bert called out to William, brushing past Viola in the front doorway, "Can we go to Sloane's for a soda, Daddy?" and the effect upon Mavis was immediately visible.

"Just hold your horses," William answered. He loped to the driver's door. "Bunch of sweet-toothed boogers. We'll see you in awhile, Viola."

"Yes, sir." Mavis stared fixedly ahead while William started the ignition, and Viola was reminded of the day she rode beside Ezra, the car full of thick flowers, that one rose spray garlanding her hair. That face had grown strained in the years since, as if a hand had tooled the yellow kid; two deep lines indented from the spur of her nose to the corners of her mouth. But she sat erect, the anticipation of her posture as rigid as iron.

"See you later, Viola," Bert shouted through the window.

"See you later," echoed Willie Junior.

The expedition, Mavis's emergence into her own country, had begun.

Of Mavis's Party

Over the next three years, Mavis came into her own.

The trip to the depot signaled the beginning of every social flowering Mavis had ever dreamed of when she was a lonely young girl, counting her miseries. For after picking Baby Boy up from his train, the party went on to Sopwith's to shop for the twins; and while there the Ransoms met up with several people of good family who exclaimed loudly and with ostentatious pleasure at the sight of Mavis; and the next thing she knew, she was invited to an anniversary tea for Mr. and Mrs. Gosford. After that the invitations started pouring in. Soon she had been overtaken by her own position in Bernice society. And her spirit, so long iced over, thawed into a public softness.

Mavis, at last, had everything she wanted. She was happy.

"Now, if we're going to do this thing, we're going to do it right." She looked brightly around the circle. "And since it's your party too, I want you all to help me."

"What do you want us to do?" asked Bert. "We sure can't help out by cooking the cakes and stuff!"

"Why not?" Mavis's tone was sly. "I think it'd be just lovely, you and Willie Junior batting around that kitchen and turning out a few dozen cookies." She turned to Viola. "You suppose Bessie can spare a couple of extra aprons?"

"Why, yessum." Viola winked.

"See there?"

Bert flushed. "I'd just as soon skip the darn party, then, if it's all the same to you." His fists jammed in the pockets of his school uniform pants; he scowled toward Willie Junior. "I'm not some sissy."

"Look at that, Viola! Home one whole hour from military school, and already playing the general."

"Mm-mm!"

"I could try to make the cookies, if Bessie would show me how," Willie Junior offered.

"You what?"

"Now, Bert, you know perfectly well I was teasing the both of you. I have no intention of you getting under Bessie's feet. Hush up, or you can just go right back to Kerrville and spend Christmas in the dormitory."

"Don't forget they've turned the heat off for the holidays." Baby Boy grinned.

"Rather be on the football field anyhow," Bert muttered.

"Hush, I said. Let's hear a little Christmas spirit around here. Now, here's what I want you all to do: there's a heap of mistletoe growing out in the woods. I want you to get some garden shears and gather it, and then help Ezra cut holly. Only bunches with red berries, mind, we need the color. Then we'll bring in ladders, and you can put clusters over the doors. I'll do the mantelpieces myself. That's not so hard, is it?"

"I don't mind climbing trees," Bert conceded.

"That'll be the fun part. Hanging the bunches'll be trickier. But I'll show you where."

"Now who's the general?"

"Why, Bert Ransom. I am." Mavis smiled.

"You know what mistletoe is for, don't you, Bert?" Baby Boy nudged him. "If a girl is caught standing under it, you have to kiss her."

"Nawww!" Bert scrubbed his lips in disgust.

"Are there girls coming, Aunty?" Willie Junior asked, his brows pulled together.

"Why, what do you think accounts for half the world's population, but girls? I declare, just because you live in a football squad and all-man rifle range most of the year round, doesn't mean you're going to live there your whole life through!" She twitched her skirt hem. "I've invited many old friends to this party, and some new ones. Most of the ladies in my Literary Club are coming and bringing their children, not to mention a great many people who have been so kind as to come in from out of town." Her eyes roamed the ceiling, as if seeing lighted chandeliers. "Not like my mother's time, when folks came for weekends and stayed the month, or attended the balls all the way from Austin, I'll admit. It's been too long since this house saw a proper party. But the Christmas of 1939 is going to be different. We're going to make up for things. Aren't we, Viola?"

"Yessum, indeed."

Mavis regally folded her hands. The soft December light touched glimmers in her hair, its dullness crimped with a powdery sheen. She would not be standing on the stairs and yearning over the balustrade for this party.

"I'll just eat the food, thank you," said Bert.

"You are not to make pigs of yourselves. I expect you to be ready to take plates to some of the ladies. This is a training exercise. Now, there will be plenty of Bernice boys here for you to play with. Some of the friends you made last summer, and the two Summerall boys you saw at Thanksgiving. Although those two are a little wild." She tapped a finger on her cheek. "I expect you-all to keep your guests in hand, and conduct yourselves like gentlemen. You are the Ransoms, remember."

"It'll be all right, Mama," Baby Boy promised.

"I spoke with Dolly Renfrow yesterday, she's bringing her nieces from Waco. One of them is your age, Baby Boy. You make her feel at home. And the ladies from my church committee, they're bringing all their older family members. It's not quite an open house I have in mind, but we will be entertaining people a little outside our social circle."

Now that there is one, thought Viola.

"You know those cream horns I had Bessie prepare for the bridge tea last week? Well, they were such a success, I'm having her do them again. Imagine! Who'd have thought I'd ever learn to play bridge? And here I am winning all the time—as if I'd been doing it all my life, instead of just a year and a half." She smiled complacently. "Oh, my, there's the telephone. Baby Boy, you answer it, it might be about the poinsettias. Now, you twins get a good night's sleep. The party's only two days away."

"I'll go help Bessie with dinner."

"That's fine." Mavis's face mellowed as the twins dashed up the stairs to wash their hands. "A party," she said. "A party at last. Viola, you know what? I'm not even in a dither." And she lined her lips together like a discreet bride, eyes wide and candid, holding herself in readiness for the consummation.

"VIOLA," SAID Baby Boy thoughtfully, "have you ever seen Mama as happy as she is now?"

"No, sir." She moved back to his suitcase, bent over it. "No, I never seen your mama so happy. Not in all her born days."

"Not even as a little child?"

Viola lifted a jacket and shook it. "She was no kind of happy child, your mama. She wasn't full of the devil like that Bert, nor sweet and shy like—she always seem tore into, somehow, when she was little. But she didn't come to grips with it. Lord, when she was a tiny thing, I reckon I hadn't never seen no child so whiney and so warty, with misery like it was her born nature. But that was due to a lot of reasons."

"I know."

She glanced at him, and picked up a hanger. The flag of hair on his brow nearly shaded his eyes' gleam. The head sat solidly on the short neck, yet there was a fineness there, too, a modeled articulation to the ears; and the hollow at his clavicle belied what would be coarse.

It was the closed-off quality, even as he spoke to her, that brought Sarah back. "Over dinner was when it hit me most," he said. "It's like she's let a part of herself glue together. I listened to her while she planned the party, but it was at dinner when I saw, you know, for the first time, she doesn't have a piece of her missing, lost somewhere."

"That's so."

"Even when I was a baby—or a young boy—" He smiled at her. "I know. I'm still a young boy. But I caught on, even then, that somewhere inside she was always strung real tight. Like trying to make do. It didn't make me love her less. But it made me feel like maybe her loving me wasn't the right fit for that missing piece." He paused. "Shoot. I can't describe it right."

"Never you mind, honey," Viola said quietly. "It ain't like that no more."

"I hadn't really thought about it until this year. One night at school when the lights were out I lay there, picturing how she used to be, and then how she was this last Thanksgiving. And I realized."

Viola put some underwear in the dresser drawer.

"Are you glad?"

She looked up, startled.

"You mean about your mama?"

He stared at her.

"I reckon I'm glad. But to tell the truth, I ain't put a lot of stock in some things for a long time."

"What do you mean?"

She shrugged, unwilling to tell him that she did not, and had not ever, really trusted Mavis's character change. "I'm glad. I'm glad for the whole passel, except for all this extra work I ain't use to doing no more." Then she laughed, to keep him from plumbing what else she would not say.

But he said, "It's us, me and the twins. We're your stock."

"Now, you just don't go laying your high talk on me, child. It's enough trouble just raising you, you think you ain't wore me out yet?

Hmph!" She whipped out some pajamas, and glanced cautiously at him.

"I'll watch out, then," he smiled. "Reckon that's why you insisted on unloading my suitcase yourself, when I told you I would do it. My, what are you going to do? You going to beat us over the head?"

"Sass," Viola muttered.

"Say, Viola." He watched her snap the suitcase closed. "Have you ever heard of a man called Adolf Hitler?"

"What you make me out as? I ain't ignorant. I listen to the radio, Bessie and me in the kitchen."

"It's a funny thing." His eyes were nearly shut, tilted up at the ceiling. "You know what?"

"What?"

"I asked Uncle Wicky in the car today what he thought of Hitler. Because of the the war in Spain. I asked him what he thought of the rumors we've been hearing about Hitler's plans to take over the world."

"Don't know much about that."

"Well, the word is, see, he's out to monopolize Europe. I have a friend at school, Bull Talbot, whose brother went over to Spain to fight in the Lincoln Brigade and came back home wounded. And he told Bull and me what Hitler's doing. Bull wants to quit school and go fight in Spain too. Because his brother says that's the place we have to stop Hitler before he gets any more out of hand."

"What did your uncle Wicky say?"

The mouth composed itself, forming the answer with careful judgment. "He didn't."

"Didn't hear you, you mean?"

"He didn't answer. He heard me. See, that's just it. He just didn't say a thing. I said to him, 'It sounds like the most evil thing I ever heard of.' I hadn't ever really thought about evil, either, until this year. It was just a word, like we hear in chapel at school. But when I understood what Hitler was proposing to do, it came to me suddenly, clear as clear. 'This is evil. This is what it means.' He stared at her. "It's there, staring us in the face. And nobody doing durn all about it."

A moth flapped against the lamp shade.

"Folks don't believe what they don't want to believe," Viola said, low.

"But Viola. When I asked Uncle Wicky about it—do you know what happened?"

She looked away.

"His face just kind of went—deaf. It just kind of caved in for a minute, like his bones had gone soft underneath. Then he wet his lips. His hands were shaking, Viola. He ignored me. And the next thing I knew, he was pointing something out to the twins in the back seat, pointing through the windshield." Still the depth of his voice did not fail. He confronted the memory, the new man's tone measuring it out piece by piece.

"I want to go to Spain too," he said. "I want to fight."

"What? Shoo, you hush up!"

"I want to stop it. People here are going to let it happen, because they don't believe it. But I'd be willing to die if it meant stopping that kind of evil."

"That just ain't—" She felt her heart go cold.

"Do you think Uncle Wicky just doesn't understand about evil?"

She knotted her hands above her apron. "What do you think, if that's how he does?"

The silence lengthened. "Ahhh," he sighed. "I see."

Then he said, "But how could he know? He's never seen a war or anything. He never goes outside this house, except into Bernice, and there's nowhere more peaceful than Bernice."

"Oh, child," was all she could answer. "Oh, child."

BY NINE the next morning, the twins were thrashing through the tree branches, snapping off the clumps of mistletoe. Viola watched from the back door. "Don't you let me catch you eating them berries! They're poison."

"I just wanted to see what they taste like."

"Well, you let them alone. And get yourself further back on that limb."

"Aw, all right."

The ground below was scattered with silvery green. Baby Boy circled under the trees, gathering it into a bushel basket. "We're going to have a powerful lot of kissing going on, if you pick much more of this."

"Don't worry!" Bert hollered. "You'll be the one to get it, just the way you want to."

The kitchen door banged open behind Viola. "I've made the most terrible miscalculation," Mavis panted. "The party's tomorrow, and we're short some things." Her breath hung on the air, scarving her with mist. She watched another shower of moonstone berries. "Don't you make such a mess of the lawn, before people can see how nice it's kept." She turned back to Viola. "It's not just the food. Do you realize I have invited one hundred and forty-three people to this thing? I didn't realize it myself until Ima Littlefield telephoned me a few minutes ago to say her Planeau cousins are in town, and she wanted to know if she could bring them with her, too. Viola! What am I going to do?"

"Why, Miss Mavis, all we got to do is get some more things from town. Bessie and me won't have no trouble fixing plenty to spare."

"But the eggnog! Wicky's already got the bourbon in, and what if they don't have more cream?"

"Those Littlefields are Church of Christ, every last one." Viola wrapped her arms around herself against the chill. "They don't touch a sip of liquor, them folk."

"Oh, my heavenly days, that's the truth. Well, fruit punch for them, that's solved—but Ezra just brought the tree in through the front door, and it's the biggest we've ever had. Fourteen feet high. You know what that means, don't you?"

"Nome."

"We don't have enough ornaments! It'll just be a disgrace."

"They got plenty decorations at the dimestore, Miss Mavis."

"Do they? Oh! well. Baby Boy! Drop that basket and come over here a minute, sugar pie."

"Yes, ma'am?"

Mavis watched him walk across the sharp grass, his boots leaving ovals on the frost.

"Why, it's always a miracle to me how much you grow in just a month. You'll be taller than Uncle Wicky soon. Now, here's what I want you to do. Go ask Uncle Wicky for the car keys, I can't disturb him for an errand while he's busy with his letters. Then you drive to the dimestore, and buy as many Christmas balls and tinsel as you can find. Uncle Wicky'll give you some money, we don't have an account there. You use your good taste, though. Do you feel you can manage the road in this weather?"

"Oh, yes, ma'am." His grin kindled, even in the wintry sunlight.

A thought seemed to grab Mavis. Suddenly her cheeks reddened; she gasped. "Oh! Actually—"

Baby Boy waited. She stared at him. "Why, of course," she said. "Why not?"

Viola and Baby Boy watched, mystified.

"Come on, honey, let's go find Uncle Wicky." She grabbed his hand, churning him through the door.

Fifteen minutes later, Bessie and Viola were icing cupcakes when they heard the blat of a horn in the drive.

"We got us some early visitors," Bessie said grimly. But the horn droned on and on, a chain of squalls, and they looked at one another, knives frozen in midair.

"Somebody done lost their marbles."

"They best quit before Mr. William calls the sheriff."

But when Viola strode to the foyer, Mavis and William were standing in the door, their faces shining in strange delight. Then

Viola heard the car motor. Pushing over William's shoulder, she looked out. A sports roadster with tires like white-rimmed doughnuts chugged by the steps, making a circle around the center of the drive. Around and around, wheels grabbing the gravel; Viola got a glimpse of the driver as the red paintwork flashed in the sun.

"Viola! Look at this!" He tooted the horn energetically. The car spun like a carousel horse, bridled in silver and chrome. When it came around again, he yelled, "Did you ever? It's my Christmas present!" He waved above the wheel, his hand a banner behind glass. It was as if his glee spilled through the car, through the air, and touched them with liquid sparks. The bare gray limbs above the drive were stern, eternal, spitting the blue sky; the car slipped below them like a creature from another world.

"We gave it to him early," Mavis said, never taking her eyes off him. He gave a final wave and turned the car down the long ribbon, pressing for town. A bend hid him from view, but they still could hear the horn, the pitch retarding and dwindling until it was as moderate as a lawyer's, floating back to them above the treetops on stillness.

"Looks like we're going to have a party, all right, old lady," William murmured, and clasped Viola's shoulder. "Your boy's grown up."

"NOW YOU roll these sand tarts in powdered sugar, while I arrange the pecans. Oh, Bessie, if you could have seen that boy!" said Mavis.

"I hear him, all right," Bessie grimaced.

"Wasn't he a sight, Viola? Showing off to beat the band."

"Yessum, he sure was."

"Pity he didn't make it home for lunch. I expect he's eaten a sandwich in town—if he remembered!—and now he's racing around on the back roads. At least I can count on him not to go too fast, he's so fine and full of common sense. I wouldn't want those ornaments broken. Has Ezra finished clipping the holly yet?"

"Nome, he still out in the front, doing it now." Viola's fingers whitened with sugar as she dredged the crescents deep in the tray.

"That drawing room might have to wait until morning, at the rate we're going. Who's that knocking on the back door? Ezra? Open it and tell him to bring the holly through the front."

The sugar left smudges like snow on the knob. Viola cracked the door open, unwilling to let the warmth escape. But the old man's face on the other side was doughy with more than cold. He scraped his boots together on the boards, short legged, his overalls washed thin and pale, bagging around the shanks. The folds of his dewlaps bristled with week-old beard. He did not speak, although he wrung his nose, and she heard a wet sound. But something about the way he stared at her stopped her from asking what he wanted. The hand dropped, scrabbled uneasily at his jacket pocket, jerked and quivered to his side.

At first she did not see Ezra, crouching on the gallery like a dark shadow, just beyond the white man. His eyes bugged and blinked at her, and he seemed to be gnawing on a gob of food.

"Viola?" Mavis asked from the kitchen table.

"There's a man here." Viola flicked back to the old man's face. His stare unnerved her.

"Can I help you?" But still the man was silent. The pinched, snotty nostrils contracted.

"I brung him back here," Ezra cranked out suddenly. "He came while I was cutting the bushes."

"Mister? You step inside here," Viola said in a dim voice.

"Viola! What in the world?" Mavis jumped up from the table, out of patience. "Don't ask just anybody into the house like that," she hissed, bustling to the door. "Is there something we can do for you? If it's my brother you want, I'll send the girl for him." She took a closer look at the man, and her tone flattened with doubt. "Viola, you go get Wicky."

"Are you Miss Ransom?"

The man spoke from his throat, stopping Mavis in midstep.

"Why, yes, I am." She edged slowly back to the sill. "Were you looking for me?"

"Yes, ma'am." He coughed. The raley rasp seemed to punctuate something in his mind. "This here boy," he said, and poked a shaky finger toward Ezra. "This here boy done said how you'd be the one to tell."

"Tell me what?" She folded her arms. When the man hesitated, she glared over his shoulder. "Tell me what, Ezra?"

But Ezra shrank into the gallery pillar, plastering himself like a swatted fly.

"What I done found," the man said. His eyes glistened like blisters.

"Well?"

"I come here first," the man explained. "Got the name from the autymobile registration. I ciphered some about going on in to the sheriff, by rights he was the one to tell. I had to drive my old truck, hit's still got the feed in the back, but he's setting on top of that. Hit won't hurt nothing." His cough rattled in his throat. "Nope. Jest maize. Won't hurt nothing."

"Won't hurt—" Mavis repeated uncertainly, staring at him in fascination.

"I still can't figure how it come to be in my henhouse. Not a mark on him, neither. Just laying there like he gone to sleep. But I seen quick enough he weren't asleep. That there autymobile, it was stuck out behind the henhouse, which is the reason I didn't spot it first off when I come in from the field." He halted, brooding for the space of a second. "Then I seen the henhouse door was open, well—"

"What?" Mavis whispered, and shook her head as if to clear her ears.

"I'm right sorry, ma'am. Hit done nearly keel me over." He bowed his head, fingers trembling and fumbling at his eyes.

"What?"

But Viola saw, the smoky dusk of the henhouse, the roosts scabbed over with chickenshit, and the rustle of feathers, the soft bawking as the birds complained around the intruder. The grid of shadows slanted across one pale cheek, as if penned there, under the chickenwire wall; a straw slipped through the forelock; and the down settling, even as the farmer stood with his jaw slack, onto the camelhair coat, drifting and settling like motes in a dream, silent as snow.

"What?" Mavis whispered once more; her head wagged back and forth. Then the crooked shoulders rared high. She turned and without another word ran through the house—up the hall, into the foyer, her crabbed gait making no sound. Viola followed silently, just behind her as she wrenched the front door handle. Then they were outside, Mavis stumbling ahead towards the ancient pickup parked in the drive. Before Viola could stop her, she had grasped the high tailgate and looked inside, and thrown her head backwards in a scream. It was Viola who unthinkingly reached out and caught her before she fell.

"WHAT?" I demanded of Viola in a litany. "What made him die? What caused him to go to the henhouse in the first place?"

"You just hush right now. I'll get around to telling you, you bide your time." She toed the gallery floor to send the rocker rolling back and forth. It made a sound on the autumn air, regular and bumpy, the way I imagined a slow train would sound. A sharp pleasant scent came to us on the breeze from the front lawns, where the garden boy was burning leaves.

"Your great-aunt Mavis, she was the one took it real bad," Viola continued. "You never known nothing like how she took it." When I heard this, I instantly thought of medicine, the spoon rammed down my throat by my mother, to minister to my "condition."

"How did Mavis take it?"

"Shoo, child, you seen your great-aunt Mavis all your whole life long. You seen how she wanders around the house, the times she'll even come out her room, and how she eats her dinner setting there at the table with your granddaddy and your mama and daddy and you, and she just muss the food around some, and won't say a word."

"That is because she is senile," I said. "Mother says so."

"That's because she been that way the last twenty years!" Viola retorted. "Nigh on, anyhow."

"She hasn't spoken in all that time?"

"Nome, she ain't. She can't."

"Why not?"

"Because of what she did the day after Baby Boy died."

"What? What did she do?"

Viola pursed her lips and scowled. "She got up from her bed where the doctor put her after he gave her medicine to make her black out, and she went and done something terrible."

"But what was it?"

Viola would not answer.

"Is that what made her shrivel up, and her hump grow larger?" I tried a different tack.

"It's what make her die right there. Her hump ain't grown, it's just because she hunkers down under her bones, so she won't have to look at nothing."

"Why does she not want to look?"

"Because she don't understand what she's looking at no more, that's why."

"Can she not use her mind to understand?"

"I'n going to tell you. I'm going to tell you all about it by and by. Just wait."

"But Baby Boy——"

Viola clamped her lips together.

"Did they ever find out how he died?" I pursued. "Try to remember, Viola, please."

"I recollect all right," she said crisply. "I'm just not in a mind to hamstring it out, like I done some other memories. It ain't what I choose to linger on when I lay down at night to sleep." She shook her head. "We can't all just up and go like Miss Mavis, even when we want to do it."

"Oh."

"It liked to made me move back to Bernice," she muttered, and closed her eyes. "All those years, sweating for this family, and then it come to me. It come to me how somewhere along the line I done lost my faith in the Lord God Almighty. I ain't never know it happened, it was just creeping up on me slow, over all those years, when I listen to your granddaddy do his talking about how time pass and all. Seem like I let his talk take the place of the Lord God Almighty inside me. But it was that child dying that made me see. Then I seen what a sinner and fool I been."

She stopped rocking and talking. I waited beside her, shifting my eleven-year-old weight in the chair and hearing it groan in the slats beneath me. A few brown leaves spiraled from a branch to the ground. Then a few more, and then three, one by one, as if singled out deliberately by the breeze.

"When I seen how my Mr. William grew up," Viola murmured, and the rocking chair resumed its steady roll, "under my own hand, from a child to a man, and what kind of man he grew up to be, then I must have done it. He was always thinking. Seem like nothing touch him from the outside much. It seem a peaceful and safe way to be. He's a good man. He don't do much with hisself. Just read them books, and think. After that time that baby got killed—"

"He was killed, then? He didn't just die?"

"—got killed," she mumbled on, ignoring my interruption, "he commenced to doing it again. Don't go into town. Don't pay no mind for a long time to the twins, I'm the one got to tend to them, never mind how I feel. But then I seen how he come to be the Lord God Almighty to me, to me, Viola, how he was the first baby I raised, and sweet and good as the Lord's own son. Then I seen my sin. Because he can't get rid of the devil. I got peaceful. I thought his goodness done won out after all that time. It was so many years. But even if I took him to be like Jesus, he can't get rid of the devil. I raised him, and he was a version of the Lord God. But the devil, he the Lord God's enemy."

She fell silent again. But I saw the devil behind her closed eyelids: lurking as shapes under the cemetery trees, or the oaks out in the woods, or goaded by a stone monument: always reminding her that he was still there, still waiting his chance. "There will never be enough payment. Remember that."

The devil, renumerating iniquities—the lost lover, the spoiled marriage, the shame on his name, the chancre, and the Ransoms who drove his torment and punishment—smarting when they broke free of him, pricked when he heard a rumor or chanced to focus on a boy that bore too close a resemblance to his first mistake, Sarah, the reason for his fall from grace. This was the version she was giving me, this was my legacy.

She had never before told me about Baby Boy's death.

I glanced down at my body, catching my breath with the effort to bend my neck so far forward. The seat squeaked in protest underneath me. I felt my heart thud hard, deep inside my chest.

"I tell you the story, lamb," Viola said. I looked at her; she was staring, and must have witnessed that furtive survey. Her voice warmed and caressed me, trying to make up for it, laboring under the delusion that I was in pain. "I tell you the rest. I reckon I got old enough to recollect it without it break my heart. If you be wanting to hear."

"Yes, thank you."

"Well, the farmer, he have Baby Boy's poor body laying in the back of his truck, on top of a mess of cow feed. It lay there in the grain, and that grain look like a golden bed holding him in his sleep, or like a big cloud of gold shook down from the sunset. But his eyes lay wide open." She shook her head and smiled. "Wide open, but easy. They ain't scared or popping out of his head like I'm so scared of seeing. And I helped Ezra and the farmer carry him off the truck, while Mr. William just stood there like he been turned to stone.

"The twins, they come romping downstairs where they been playing in the playroom." She sighed.

"I hollered at them. I was wailing so loud it must have been hard to make out what I said. Seem like the wailing and the moaning stuffed my mouth. But I hollered at them, like I ain't never hollered before. Or since. 'Get on in! Get on back in. Go back and hide your face. This is your brother what's dead!'"

The silence sank between us.

I saw the picture. The desolation, even now, reverberated on a winter sky. There she stood, face cast wildly to the two boys, and in her arms, sagging with his head lolled on her belly, the son; his eyes fixed incuriously on a patch of gravel in the middle distance. And the twins, poised in the act of advancing, staring at the picture. Bert stuck out a foot, pulling it back in. Both of them locked onto the scene, incomprehension making their faces blank as eggs. And then the color in Willie Junior's face drained away, as if a plug had been pulled; and the farmer and Ezra, frozen in the act of stooping to pick up the legs, to hoist him like a broken wheelbarrow, or a bag of cotton bolls filled and heavy with harvest. And Viola lifted her long throat in despair, wailing to the two innocents, seeing their innocence change and permute as she cried out. Then Willie Junior turned and fled, his fist crammed in his mouth, back through the door. But Bert still lingered. "Get out! Do what I tell you!" Viola screamed, and he wheeled, stumbling in the wake of his brother, but his head craned around over one shoulder, his staring eyes glued to the eyes that did not look in his direction but looked, placidly and without question, at the patch of gravel, examined with no movement the panorama of rocks and dust and pebbles; and the eyes were unwinking, peaceful, and slowly turning a milky color.

"The twins went inside the house," Viola said. "They stayed up in their room for the rest of the time we was bringing him in. And we carry that child up the stair, we carry him and lay him down to sleep in his own bed. And the farmer stand there and shiver. But he ain't say nothing. He ain't say nothing else. He just look at that child, laying there so peaceful, and shake his head like it was some kind of puzzle he can't reckon out. Then I tuck that child in bed. I pull up the cover, and tuck him in, like I done the whole time he was a little baby boy, and I put him down to sleep in the evening. Only I can't make my hands pull the cover up over his face, I can't close his poor eyes and cover up that face like the way you suppose to do, when a soul's died and gone to the Lord. I can't do that. I ain't got the strength." She paused, and I saw her bunch her apron in her fingers, and pluck it.

"And William?" I asked softly.

"We stood there awhile, looking at that child. Ezra squat at the foot of the bed, too scared to groan. We left Bessie to tend to Miss Mavis. I didn't know what they was doing in the drawing room, and for a while it plumb left my mind. All I seen was my boy. But then I come to. I caught a look at Ezra, and I recollected." She sighed, rocking gently back and forth. "'Go down, Ezra,' I say. 'Go down to Bessie, see if she need some help with Miss Mavis.' Then I say, 'You tell her, use the telephone and call up the doctor.' He went on out. And the farmer shuffle around on his feet, turning his back on the child laying there. Then he start towards the door. But before he go through it, he say one last word. 'Reckon I got to speak with the sheriff now, girl. Reckon I got to tell him what I done found.' And I say to him, 'No you don't. You ain't got no call to go back to Bernice and tell him. You let Mr. William do the telling, and they'll find you when they need you.'

"He looked at me like he can't figure it. 'It's my bounden duty, girl,' he say. But, 'It's Ransom business,' I say. 'You know that when you brung him home.' He scratched around on his pocket with his old hands, like he trying to scratch an itch. 'I'll wait, then,' he said. 'You be sure and tell Mr. Ransom. Tell him I'll go on back to my farm and wait to hear from him.' 'I'll do that,' I say. But it was hard to keep my mind on it. That child lay there, calm and sweet like he have a dream wisping through his head, and he ain't going to move his eye until it pass on through and finish. But that dream last all eternity.

"I ain't even hear the farmer go out, and climb down the stair." She raised the hand that had crushed her apron, and wiped her round black cheek. But there was no moisture to wipe away. "After while, I seen how the dark done come," she said. The failing twilight took the huskiness from her voice and left it deep again. I watched the rectangle of window in Baby Boy's room turn green and then indigo. I watched her walk to the bedside table, her mouth twitching with control, and touch the switch to the rosy nightlight. The color steeped his skin, which had now gone almost transparent, with a life-like blush.

"I turn away then," she said. "It's too much like he just sinking under that dream, just about to rouse and stir in a minute. I can't look no more."

I saw her descend the stairs, treading down the shallow steps. She did not stop when she reached the foyer. She did not choose left or right, but kept walking through the dark well, under the vaulted ceiling, and the fanlight pierced with stars, until she came to the front door. It was still open. The farmer had not closed it behind him. But she could see the drive, and the ancient truck was gone.

The drive was not, however, vacant.

Someone stood on the gravel. His form blotted the hollow darkness. No detail could she see, except the paler darkness of his white shirt; there was no moon to flare on that paleness and bring it up to her eye. The back of his head could have been a boulder set on a monument, so immobile it was; and the cold windless night spread out before him, in a vast bowl of empty space.

She began to walk again. Her feet crunched into gravel as she stepped off the porch. But she did not speak until she stood before his face.

His eyes probed out beyond the treetops and stars into nothing.

"What are you going to do?" she said.

And as she repeated the words to me, I heard the cold winter night, the implacable command grinding them from her mouth.

"He's dead," she said. "That child is dead. What are you going to do?"

Still he said nothing, the nothing his eyes sought on the blue-black depths.

"You took him into town, where them people seen him, and seen who and what he be. That ain't enough. You kept taking him in, laying him like Isaac on the mountainside to be blood and sacrifice. You showed his face and body—you, who done stepped off the path of righteousness and give the weapon to your enemy, by making that face and body in your image, and the image of your enemy's own wife. You know that man have the devil in his soul and breath, and covet your sister, and be the cause of her dying in the wilderness," and her words carved into the still night, cold as chisels, striking the words into the cold windless air, "dying alone in the wilderness because of his own child, what he made her bear in sorrow and a strange land. Then you fall off the path of righteousness to that devil's very arm. And you're to blame. You ain't done nothing to clear the sin and the shame away. And you took the blessed fruit, that come into the world from your sin, and you feed it and nurse it to your bosom. Then you took it to Bernice where the folk put their eye on it, on that poor baby what know nothing but love and kindness and the pureness in his heart. But that ain't enough." She paused for a breath, the words still knifing evenly on the air before his motionless face. "That ain't enough. You took him to the lap of your enemy, and you say, 'We are safe. We are safe from you, because we are good and turn the other cheek.' And you put up that stone in the drive, and say, 'Welcome. We are ready to welcome you, devil. Because we are good. Look what the stone say. It say, 'We are good and share it all, come take it.' And now"—she stopped and filled her lungs with the chill oxygen and the frosty starlight, but she did not require much—"now he's done it."

The eyes did not flicker from the void. They stared, gleamless, matte and empty, and all she could see was the blurred paleness of his square face, dug with two pits under the brow.

"What are you going to do?" The question echoed over the years, the times she had asked it and repeated it now condensing together, culminating, until time and the words were packed tight into one hard missile, a chisel of steel.

"What are you going to do *now*?"

His lips looked laid together, what she could see of them, like slabs of stone. They did not stir.

But suddenly the words crumbled, the void echoing them as they crumbled and broke on the sob rising in her throat. And a distant roar began and grew in the void beyond. On that last ragged ringing demand, a double shaft of light lanced the blackness under the trees, stabbing, then wavering to one side. Then it roared closer, closer, picking out the man set like a pillar and throwing his features into sharp white relief, and the other beam blinding Viola as she turned, holding her hand to her eyes. The sound surged, pressing against her ears. She could see the pebbles at her feet splash with light, develop shadows like rims of black velvet. Then the sound cut abruptly away, leaving a ticking on the night. But the headlamps stayed bright, pinning her into place on the white gravel, bleaching William and outlining him in heatless fire.

It was the doctor's car.

"THE DOCTOR, he stay out here most of that night," Viola said.

I gingerly moved my position in the chair, to ease the cramps in my thighs. A fresh breeze brought the smell of burning leaves again. Somewhere out in the afternoon woods, an owl hooted.

"He stay to see to Miss Mavis. What he had to do about that child, he done mighty quick. But Mr. William just go with him in the house, then stay in the library and lock the door. When the doctor finish with Baby Boy, he go to the door and he knock on it. Then Mr. William, he let him in, and left the door open. I stood outside it. I heard what that doctor say."

"What did he say?"

"Say, that boy must have died from heart failure. Was no sign of a hurt, or a wound. Say, it must be the drinking."

"What drinking?"

"There was a smell of bourbon whiskey on his tongue, the doctor say."

"Whiskey?" I sat up, the chair shuddering under me. "Did Baby Boy drink?"

She sent me a look. "Nome," she said, "nome, lamb child, he don't drink."

"Then how did whiskey get on his tongue?"

She folded her hands and stopped rocking. Behind us in the kitchen, I heard Bessie turn the radio on: a commercial, a jingle for Spearmint gum.

"He was a fine one, my baby," she said slowly. "If somebody waved him down from another car, real friendly—like they want to say good morning to him—likely he stop. And if they say, 'Have a sip of this whiskey, have a Christmas sip for company's sake,' and he so full of gladness and grown up because he got his very own new car, driving it on the country road, and safe in the loving and the kindness of his mama and daddy and his Viola," her voice scraped, "then he most likely say, 'Why, much obliged.' And he done take a swig. Then maybe he say, 'Thank you kindly, sir. My name's Baby Boy Ransom. Who may you be?'" She stopped. The toe shoved out, hooking on the boards.

"Then maybe that stranger he say, 'Why, I'll be! I'm an old friend of your family. It's a pleasure to meet you. Now, you go ahead and drink that up. Yes, drink it right down. Don't stop. It's Christmas. Just pour it straight down your throat.' It happened real fast, the doctor say. He said to Mr. William, it was heart failure, alcohol poisoning, come on sudden from fooling around drinking the liquor too quick. He say Baby Boy was just young, he was just trying to experiment, and ain't known how to drink right, he ain't got the knack and he probably threwed that whiskey in a big fast slug down his gullet and then it stop his heart."

"If that were true," I said, the logic clicking away in my brain with the precision of eleven years, "where was the bottle? Was it in the henhouse with him?"

Viola narrowed her eyes, assessing. "Why," she said, "you be pretty smart, lamb child. That's what you be."

"Well? Was it?"

"All the time that doctor talk," she said, ignoring me once again, "Mr. William just listen. I seen him through the doorway. He just set there, listening, and letting his eyes play around the room and look anywhere but at that doctor standing there. Once or twice he'd grunt, or give a wheeze. It ain't easy to say what he was thinking. If he was thinking at all.

"Finally the doctor say, he reckon that farmer picked the bottle up and kept it, to keep him warm on the cold nights. Because he was just a dirt cotton farmer, he ain't got no money to buy high-class bourbon whiskey. At least, that's how the doctor figured. He say, 'William, I believe you-all had a big case of bourbon in for the party tomorrow, isn't that so?' And Mr. William, he kind of blink his eye. Then he nod yes. And the doctor, he nod back."

Viola went silent. Then she turned slowly, and stared at me.

"And then the doctor say, 'William, I'd better go on and call the sheriff now. I have to report this to the county.'"

I waited, while Viola reflected on the memory of that late-night conference.

"Then Mr. William spoke up at last," she said eventually. "He say, 'Byram,'—that's the doctor's name, old Doctor Middleton. He say, 'Byram. You have to report to the county, for a case of heart failure?'"

"And the doctor, he say, 'Why—yes. I believe I better.' And Mr. William say, 'Byram, do me a favor.

"'Our boy died today. I'd rather it not be a case of public interest. This tragedy is ours, it's no concern of the sheriff. If he died of heart failure, then you go on and report that to the records at the courthouse. But I've got no use for the sheriff and I don't much like the man. I prefer we keep our own to our own. It's our grief and burden to bear.' And he look that Doctor Middleton straight in the eye. 'You know better than anyone how much tragedy we've had in this family,' he say. 'Can you understand my feelings?'

"And after while, the doctor nod real slow. 'Sorry about the boy, William,' he say. 'I'll see that it's just a county death certificate. There's no call to make it public tragedy, and let the buzzards in. Not with Mavis in the state she's in. I understand.' Then he say, 'It's not really a case for the sheriff anyhow. Just a formality.'"

I sat very still in the chair. From around the corner of the house we could hear the garden boy whistle a tune off key, and the sound of his rake dragging through the dead leaves.

"Then I seen how Mr. William plan to go," Viola said.

"Yes?" I whispered, after the bars of the tune had run through all their stanzas, and become another tune and a third altogether.

"I stood out in that foyer, and my teeth just clenched at my tongue trying to make it tame. Because I seen what he plan to do. He give me the answer to what I ask, out in the drive before the doctor drove up it. And I bit that tongue, to hold it still, keep it ahalt from yelling, 'Oh, Lord, Lord, why have you forsaken me?'"

"He was going to see to Grant himself," I whispered. The tune flagged and shredded into the autumn hush. The radio suddenly blared out a dance song. "He was going to take revenge in private."

"Oh, child," she said, and settled her head tiredly into the niche of the pad. Her hands fell against her skirt. "He ain't plan on doing nothing at all. Just nothing at all." She pressed her lips closed. Then she opened them slightly.

"Nothing at all.

"And that was just what he did. Nothing." She looked at me, her old yellow eyes with the red scrollwork of veins. "Now you tell me why," she said quietly.

BOOK TWO

My Life

"Tell me why," she said to me.

I WAS born on October 17th, 1947. Two years before my birth, the United States razed two cities in Japan with a new kind of bomb, and changed the pattern of history. Several years before that, Hitler did indeed try to take over the world in a frenzy surpassing Baby Boy's expectations, congregating the populations of several ethnic groups in camps and beginning their extermination. In the years following my birth, new nations were established and set at war with unprecedented rapidity. Large groups of people were compelled to reappraise the old definitions of freedom, loyalties, honor, and truth. The world was a giant vat of fermentation, death, change, new life, ideas, and allegiances, just as it had always been and always will be. With more efficient methods at its disposal, of course, for disposal of itself.

How did this affect me?

It was all a myth. All legend.

To me, and to those who surrounded me in this house set in a wood, it was hearsay.

But there was the stone planted at the mouth of the gates.

My grandfather's interest in history did not extend to the second half of the twentieth century. Nor indeed to any events that took place on the other side of that broken molar, his engraved and permanent salutation.

My interest in history did. But within very finite limits. From the earliest moments outside the cradle, from the season in which I began to disentangle the sounds that issued forth when adults worked their mouths, and measure them into words, so that their meanings became, in a sense, fuel, informing my tissues, saturating my brain and organs with feelings and reasons and life itself: then I began to grow interested in history. For history was what I heard, every day: vivid as the color of the sky over my head, rich as the odors of milk and my own excrement and the breakfast bacon; sharp as the dawn screech of my grandfather's peacock, when it perched on the gallery roof outside my bedroom window, thrusting high its serpentine little blue head, and I looked out to see it swoop down, down off the roof onto the lawn below in an iridescent flash of color, the grass beginning to seep with emerald as the sunrise flowed over it.

But the history I heard was a history of the stone walls of the house. And how those walls had come to be built. And the people who had died within them, or still lived within them. It was the lifeblood Viola shared with me day after day, year after year, superseding the novels I read, or the Gibbon and *Walton's Lives* and mathematics my grandfather fed me; for I, like the three boys preceding me in that house discomposed by childhoods, was a home-taught child. The history was, in fact, my memory, as real as anything I experienced first hand. It filled me as surely as the dinner did, fleshing me out in a slow round ball. But the stories—the memories—were more real to me than the people who surrounded me, and who had devised the history in the first place.

With one exception. I must remember to cite the exception.

Viola was real to me.

There was no break in continuity with Viola. She was time personified, living and breathing, as she had all through the decades of Ransom lives she related to me in a long unending stream.

For my first eleven years I could have said, in all honesty, quoting my grandfather's phrase, "Viola. You are the only human being I feel I have not dreamed."

DURING THIS time, I was aware that two people loved me.

My mother usually stayed in bed until ten or so. My father, if he had not drunk too much the night before, might have already dressed and gone into town to eat breakfast with some of his cronies at the Harrison Hotel coffee shop. If he had drunk too much (which was the case on four days out of seven), he would be found snoring haphazardly on the drawing room sofa, his shoes still on.

So I ate breakfast with Viola, in the cheerful warmth of the kitchen, while Bessie thumped about and set the bread to rise.

Over eggs and bacon, biscuits and fruit, she would unwind a reference from her spool, and start clacking away like a spinning jenny. But it was bound to be something innocuous, as long as we were in the kitchen where Bessie could overhear. She waited until we had finished the meal before she would take my hand and lead me to the little sitting room, "to set and allow our stomach to quit steaming," and there in the green calm, to touch on more salient and secret points of the morning's anecdotes. Such as: the carnal knowledge between Sarah Ransom and Grant Macafee. Or the illicit meetings William (Grandfather?) had contrived for himself and Sophie. Or the miracle of the orphan child, and his true lineage.

After an hour, she would stop unwinding and ask me certain questions. Had I remembered to brush my teeth? Had I washed thoroughly that morning in all the crevices and hard-to-reach places? As if recovering a dutiful normality, she went over my toilette, and then said, "Well, it's just about time now for your lesson with your granddaddy. You go on and knock on the library door, we ain't finished yet, but I tell you some more come dinner time." And she would shoo me up from the sofa and give my buttocks a tap, as if springing the balloon from its moorings.

Out in the hallway, the morning sounds of the house crepitated distantly through stone. The garden boy swept the front porch bricks, whistling tatters of Elvis Presley songs. I caught a glimpse of his head through the sidelights, and heard the whisk of the broom straws. The chink of crockery sounded from the kitchen. My father's snores bubbled in and out, remote as an Eastern tide, from the double doors. As I rolled on past the Venetian mirror, a shadowy phantom surfaced and followed me like a playful whale.

There was no need to wait for an invitation to open the library door. Chances were my grandfather did not hear the knock, engrossed in deader voices. As the door swung wide, he glanced up from his book, his face inquiring.

I always sat at his feet.

He always seemed to me, tucked in that leather throne, like a pensive statue, a man turned momentarily to bronze, and the book in his hand a ledger of historical sums. For a space, it was as if he could not retrieve the present, as though he were still submerged in centuries or philosophies separated from this moment by uncharted seas. The book he was holding prickled my mind with curiosity. Could those pages carry him away so completely, and make it so hard for him to navigate back to my world?

I thought, He is dreaming me as well. The way I dream him as he is now.

But then he closed the book on his forefinger, went to his desk for a bookmark, and stepped over to the built-in bookcase on the wall.

"Well, Victoria." His eyes roamed over the bindings, hovering on a title, rejecting it with a blink. "I believe you're due for some English literature today. Let's see." He sorted through the stocks of cloth and leather. "A little Dickens. That's what's on the curriculum. *Bleak House*. Yes. And the legal reforms. Of course"—he fumbled through the pages, licking his finger—"I don't take to novels much myself, as a rule, but you have to get a good dose of literature." He pressed a leaf flat, running his fingers down the lines, then ambled back to the leather chair and sat down, with *Bleak House* balanced on his knees like a navy cruiser. I craned sideways as far as I could manage under the circumstances to read the title myself before he sank back into the flux of a different century. I sat patiently on the rug until he came back from his journey.

"Well," he said, the eyes drifting from the window until they rested on my head. "Yes. Well, Victoria. Here we go." He cleared his throat and began reading.

We would sit that way until noontime. His voice murmured on the air, and I listened to him spin the story of nineteenth-century trial and errors, much as I listened to Viola rehash the twentieth. When the grandfather clock grated its cogs and struck out the twelve leaden notes, he would hand me the book, Cicero or Dickens or *The Anatomy of Melancholy*, and smile again before I left. Sometimes, while I was still small enough, he would gesture to me to sit down on his lap, and then he would administer those impartial pats to my shoulders. As I neared puberty, the lap became impossible. There was no spoken agreement that this was now so, merely my sensibility that he grunted deeply when I climbed onto his knees, and that the chair creaked. So I remained standing, while he patted the forepart of my arm.

It did not occur to me for a long long time, the significance of his pats. It did not occur to me that this was perhaps a deviation from what Viola told me. When she told me what he had read to her in his journal, I did not immediately think of his soft hand delivering the touch. His love seemed something to be taken for granted. It was everything my parents' love (or what they offered as love, the pity, the wince as the medicine went down) was not. Once only I had, in my innocence, tried to draw near my father: the time I had sidled up to him and asked him, "Am I a fact?" I did not forget his response. But Grandfather offered something different. The love he extended to me was what he seemed ready to confer on everyone: a splendid transcendent algebra, a good will removed from greed, or demands, or joy or pain.

From the realms of his books, he lifted his head, and bestowed the smile like a balm of disinterest.

So I did not, for a long time, examine the meaning behind those dry dim pats.

But later I did. And when I did, his eyes came back to me, brown and gleamless, in the shadow of the chair wing. And I said to myself (for although it was before his death, I was already eleven; and so there was no one left to confide in), "Perhaps, just perhaps—he has already found me imperfect enough. To touch me would mar nothing that mattered. I am, for him, safe."

From Viola, I could depend on the attention, the possessiveness and greed, that no one else paid out to me. She wrapped my life round with it. I was her last child. So if I could not discern the people in her stories through the faces of my family, it failed to matter.

Until one autumn afternoon in 1958, a month after my eleventh birthday.

We sat on the gallery. The breeze was crisp and thin as wine. A curl of invisible woodsmoke, scorching leaves, gave the air an added pungency, like a mulled spice. The rocking chair rolled on the boards. Out in the woods, an owl burbled his question, the resinous sound blending with the rocker's beat, like a bow lifted and sawing one operatic remark. Then silence before Viola resumed; the muffled quiet.

"Then I seen how Mr. William plan to go," she said.

Somewhere a whistled tune curled on the breeze. I heard the rake drag across the grass, skewering leaves in a mat.

"Yes?" I breathed.

A blue mist hung over the treetops on the far end of the lawn.

"He give me the answer," she said. "Out in the drive before the doctor drove up it. And I bit that tongue, to hold it still, to keep it ahalt from yelling, 'Oh, Lord, Lord, why have you forsaken me?' "

"He was going to see to Grant himself," I whispered, homing in on the crux of the story, endorsing the dream William in his crisis, the William that would finally take action, go seek his enemy at last, the William who had turned the other cheek once too often, until now the destruction was more than a slap, or a just reward for his crime. No longer vindictive glances. No longer the veiled threat. But tangible, the sacrifice, the murder of his son. Now he would rise up, and go to his enemy, and smite him down. "He was going to take his revenge in private," I whispered.

"Oh, child," she said to me. And for a moment, I saw him sunk in the leather chair: the gentleman scholar, the "old useless one." His brown eyes followed the lines of German philosophy, tracking the verb in a stalking motion. But that grandfather blurred and vaporized, and instead I saw the man, still young and vigorous, standing in the firelight of the library, saying to the doctor, "I prefer to keep our own to our own." He would plan his revenge, keep it a secret. He must nurture his fury until it burst the seams, and yet still guide it, steer it to business. He must quench it with blood. Eye and tooth, he must seek Grant Macafee out.

"Oh, child," she said to me, while the two visions rose and faded on the emptiness of her voice.

The words fell dull, hollow, and I watched her hands flop against the skirt of her dress. "He ain't planning on doing anything at all," she murmured. "Just nothing at all." The lips pressed closed.

"Oh," was all I could say, as the visions collapsed, leaving the void as the void truly is. "Ah," I whispered, even as the sting of Baby Boy's death went numb with the deadness of her tone. I had ached as she ached; I had felt that death through her. That was its meaning to me.

And now she was meaning: It is all fruitless, all dream. There is no meaning.

Or so I thought she was saying.

Then she looked at me.

I saw the eyes, their tiredness, their disgust, which overrode whatever she had gained from telling me the story: love, a reliving, an entertainment for a lonely child, a sense of fealty. The disgust accused the house, the lawn, and me, of a breakdown of nerve, a failure of strength and moral certitude, that subsumed all history.

It made of her love a mockery.

She said to me, "Now you tell me why. You be the one hear it all, by and by." And the eyes looked at me, as if seeing me clearly for the first time. And something, something after all besides disgust, flickered in them: a flash of pure perception.

"And when you done heard it all, got it all saved up in you, got Mr. Grant and your granddaddy and your aunt Mavis and Ezra and that poor sweet child, and all the rest—"

"And you," I whispered.

The eyes never left my face, bathing its globes and nooks with that perception. They searched me over, ticking off the layers of fat, the cells and stuffing, while she pondered on her creation. For she had invented me, she saw now. I watched it dawning on her. She had made me what I was: a repository of all the events left behind her and relived, an archive of her own acts and feelings; the wrenching deaths; the question to William. In that instant she neither loved nor hated me; in that instant borne of her defeat, she merely pointed her arrow and sent it in.

I saw what I was, for the first time; the message that those eyes relayed. My purpose, or lack of it. I saw the direction her love had taken, through the eleven years of my life, as surely as the arrow hit home.

"When you got it all pinched up and tucked inside you," she murmured, "the way the entire town of Bernice ain't never had a chance to have it—then, child." The last spark of perception struck and flared. "Then you come to me. You come to Viola."

I steadied myself, a solid block against the chill. I knew now. And in that instant, all the connections were joined at last, all the people of her stories sprung up, fleshed skeletons, and lived and walked and ate beside me. The past meshed with the present.

"And you tell me why."

So the relevance of global history slipped away.

I could not tell her why. It was not time. I did not know, nor do I yet. I only knew that now, all of a sudden, the world had gained a sense it lacked before. If the sense was colder, more comfortless, than life had offered up until that moment—if it meant that, indeed, there was to be no love for me from anyone, not Viola, not the dream-and-flesh grandfather who unequivocably dispensed his acceptance, well then. It did not matter.

For people were now real.

There were no more dreams. Just the truth of the flesh, pulsing away in the dormant bodies. And truth can be a solace. There is consolation in knowing your own function, in discovering what you really are.

And the further thing you are to become.

The Courtship of
Willie and Bert

The morning after Baby Boy died was a terrible day of reckoning, for it was the day that the old Mavis awoke from her fifteen years of deceptive milky-hued slumber, to stride forth and wreak a terrible vengeance upon the world for her lost self and child.

That dawn she rose with the sun. Most of the household were still closed off behind their doors, sleepless, trying to recover from the blow of the night before. Bessie had left Mavis's bedside in the early hours to catch some rest in the downstairs sitting room, rather than out in her own little house with her husband, so that she could be on hand should she be needed. No one, while he or she stood watch over the dead, was standing guard over the living. So no one knew it when Mavis scrambled up from her sheets and marched downstairs and out of the house to storm Ezra and Bessie's door, wake Ezra, and demand that he drive her immediately into Bernice .

He probably protested. Seeing her standing there in her nightgown, disheveled, gibbering, commanding, maddened, he probably raised some timid objections—perhaps suggesting that they delay long enough for both of them to dress. Or perhaps he merely gulped and obeyed, realizing that there would be little use in arguing. We will never know for sure. Whatever the case, he left the house and grounds in Mavis's company without saying good-bye to his wife or explaining where they were going, and the next time he was seen, he was slumped dispiritedly behind the wheel of Mavis's car, parked at the curb beside the courthouse, while Mavis clawed her hump-

292

backed way up the lawn's steep bank and onto the stone base of Governor Deloache's statue.

By that time, no doubt, he had given up trying to stop her.

I can see the scene now. In the early morning stillness of the wintry hour, she clambered up the legs of the bronze statesman, elbows and knees scissoring sharply as she gained a purchase on his book-filled lap. Her hair stuck out in tufts from her scalp; her nightgown rucked up over her scrawny thighs. A small crowd of people gathered at the statue's foot to watch. Some recognized her and called out. "Miss Ransom, are you all right? Can we help you, Miss Ransom?" But most stood silently, curiously waiting, perplexed by yet another eccentric disgorged from the land of the wealthy, and when at last she had achieved her goal and stood upright upon the summit of her alp, only one person had gone to fetch the sheriff.

She planted one bare foot on each of the book's open leaves, straddling the bronze spine. Then, rearing to her full height, she stretched out fists to the sky, and screamed and screamed.

Mutters and murmurs flowed through the crowd; it was obvious to everyone that Mavis Ransom had lost her mind. After several minutes of this, the sheriff appeared in the distance down the street, accompanied by the courthouse janitor who had gone to his home. Mavis, from her lofty post, saw him coming. With a banshee shriek she gestured wildly to the onlookers and then turned around and climbed even higher, cursing all the while, in an effort to perch like a bird of prey on the tip-top of the Governor's head.

She never made it.

The sheriff drew nigh. From her purchase on the Governor's shoulders, Mavis observed him approach. Hastily she attempted to mount all the way, but her bony limbs skidded over the frosted metallic surface of dome, and as she hoisted upward, rump thrust out, she lost balance and fell the ten feet or so to the concrete base below, landing on her head.

The sheriff shouldered outside the people who crowded around her body. "Get back. Let me see to her." Everyone withdrew to give her air. But before the sheriff could so much as kneel, Mavis opened her eyes and sat up.

"Unh," she said. "Gah."

Then she crawled a few inches, rose to her feet, and staggered towards the car, resisting all hands that tried to hold her back, including Ezra's. "Get in," she snapped at him, pointing to the driver's seat. When he mutely opened the door for her instead, she just shoved him away and motioned to the wheel. Her head lolled to one side, it was noticed, and she reached up and touched her temple several times, wincing. "Miss Ransom, now, please let me take you home," the sheriff said. "Come on, now. I'm going to call Dr. Middleton, you need to maybe lie down and rest, ma'am." But she would not stop.

Ezra got into the driver's seat and turned the ignition. The last thing the onlookers and the sheriff saw was the car pulling away from the curb and heading down the street towards the Corsicana highway that led past the Macafee ranch. The next thing they knew was the information about the wreck found in the ditch by the deputy that the sheriff had telephoned to waylay them. The car had overturned on the icy pavement at the curve by Lake Bernice, and come to rest upside down, like a big june bug, next to a stubbled cornfield. Mavis was thrown end over end behind the wheel, her hands locked onto it in almost a death grip (although she was merely unconscious), her forehead crammed against the windshield, and a double knot big as a split peach at her temple. Ezra, on the passenger's side, was dead.

IN THE years following Baby Boy's and Ezra's deaths, Willie Junior and Bert grew to manhood.

No one ever left the Ransom house anymore, except the new gardener who drove the cars, Bessie, and the twins. After the deaths, the twins returned to military school in Kerrville. They came back to the house for part of the summers, and for July and August they were sent to a summer camp in the Hill Country. There they rode horses, swam in the Guadalupe River, ate chuck wagon meals, and generally grew strong.

They came home at Thanksgiving, Christmas, and Easter. But home was a shadowy place for two thriving boys, with Mavis creeping through the rooms like a ghost, and a father lost to scholarlship. It became Viola's task to force a lilt of gaiety in her voice when they stepped through the front door. But she could not change what they had seen: the truck stalled on the drive, the young man's limp body and open eyes. She could not erase that moment; she could not suck the words she had cried back into her lungs. She could not call Ezra back, either.

Even in the act of hugging and exclaiming, she would sense the crippled quality of their return; she would enfold them in her arms, and feel the jumpy heartbeats as they glanced around the familiar vault, the butler's chair, the fanlight. By the next morning they would be asking the new gardener to drive them to Bernice, and she would see the relief rinse their faces as they opened the car door and dove in beside him and made their escape to a world she had almost forgotten existed.

THE TWINS graduated from Sauter Military Academy, neither with honors. Bert had scraped by in brilliant starts and lazy fits. Willie Junior made steady C grades. William contended that they were too young for the war which was eating away the youth of America. Presumably his money and position made the Bernice Draft Board agree. So they enrolled in the University of Texas, and by the spring semester of their sophomore year, were flunking out in a haggard way.

But they both met a girl there.

Her name was Anabelle Lacey. She came from Galveston. Her family was an old one which had done well in its time, but by the war years had "decayed." Her father, a shipping firm president, failed to adjust to the war boom that should have increased his holdings, missed some important bids, and lost the firm to one of his competitors. Or so she always claimed, insisting that he had been too much the gentleman to "scramble around like a shark in a bloodbath," and take advantage of "the poor boys gone overseas to defend their country." Her version was vague and illogical when she spoke of her father's bankruptcy, frequently alluding to "carpetbaggers at a nigger auction" and other dark forces that had nipped her debutante season in the bud before she could even order her white evening gown. She would complain about the ruthlessness of businessmen, and occasionally have a fit of weeping at the moment she laughed most delightfully her silver girlish laugh, there in the front seat of the twins' blue Mercury, as they all three whizzed down Nineteenth Street in Austin on their way to a barbecue joint.

"I could have gone to New York! I could have been in London by now, getting presented at the Court of St. James's and the Silver Rose Ball. And where am I?" she would say, the tears like dew on the full rose cheeks, the laugh beginning to tinkle in her throat. "Stuck between a scaredy cat and an old reprobate. You're a rascal, Bert, just look at the way you took that corner! Scoundrel! Stuck between the two of you, in your old blue jalopy, in nasty old Austin, Texas! Well, all I can say is, Daddy didn't intend it this way. If he hadn't been such a gentleman, I would be where I'm supposed to be!" Then she would reach out and snag both their elbows, Bert's cocked over the steering wheel, and Willie Junior's trembling on her other side. And she would squeeze them in her white hands, in an excess of forgiveness for taking her to eat barbecue. "I guess I'm cursed to be a coed."

Willie Junior absorbed every word she spoke, cupping it in his brain to taste, meanwhile only smiling a timid smile. And he pondered those words, late at night in his fraternity-house bed. But Bert merely spun the car around another corner, and let out a whoop.

"You be glad you've got what it takes to charm two good boys like my brother and me into your power!" he'd yell. "With every Pi Phi on campus just begging for us, you're the one we want."

"You horrible critter! If that's your opinion, I don't want a thing to do with you. Willie can take me to the dance on Saturday, can't you, Willie? You just get yourself a Pi Phi, Bert, that's all you're good for. The Kappas wouldn't have you on a silver platter!"

"Anabelle Lacey! The most beautiful girl on campus. We'll fight duels, won't we, Willie? Just for the privilege of falling dead at your feet. 'Oh, Anabelle, Oh, Anabelle; Oh, have you seen Anabelle; Oh, Anabelle the Tattoo'ed Lady,'" he sang. "When are you going to decide which one you want?" And Willie Junior said nothing, but watched the blush progress down her perfect neck, and slip under her twin-set collar like a pink inflammation. He would imagine it reaching her breasts. But he never tried to touch her.

Then something occurred to change things. It was at a sorority dance, late in the evening. The lights had been extinguished, all but one chandelier hung with crepe paper, and as the band started to play "Good-night, Ladies," Willie Junior stood alone near the edge of the dance floor. Bert was nowhere in sight. Willie Junior assumed that he had stolen out beyond the terrace with a couple of Dekes, to drink from a bourbon bottle. At this point, he himself had no use for liquor; his head was too weak. He and Bert had both escorted Anabelle to the dance, making a sensation among the more conventional students.

It was a spring night. Midterm exams were over, everyone was celebrating. Willie Junior's fate already lay inscribed on his grade reports, and he knew he would not be returning in the fall. Perhaps Bert could talk his way back into academe. But the sweet spring air pouring through the French doors of the sorority-house ballroom filled Willie Junior with forebodings of nostalgia, lost chances, remembered idylls, a feckless life to come. Once he left here—And it stirred something else within. The scent of new-mown grass, fresh under the quarter moon, the smell of the cedar trees fringing the terrace, combined to evoke a memory he had suppressed throughout the college years, and release a niggling ache there.

What was he going to do? What would he do with himself in the stone house at the edge of Bernice? How would he fill the years of adulthood that stretched before him? He stuck his hands in his pocket, gazing through the French doors at the terrace beyond. Bert was no doubt crouched in the shrubbery, working on a pocket flask of bourbon; he would always be successful and erratic, he would invent his plans as he went along. Look at the way he had whirled Anabelle across the floor earlier in the evening, dumbfounding everyone with his flair; and Anabelle giggling and squealing in his arms, alarmed by her own delight. She did enjoy the scandal the three of them provoked. He knew that. She loved the way she could fold herself so safely between the Ransom boys as they strolled out of the English Department building, and know that her reputation was not really in danger, as she teased and flirted and cajoled; for the balance protected them all—it was the secret of twinship.

Now that would fall apart. There would be no more curiosity as to when she would finally choose Bert and leave Willie Junior behind. And he did not begrudge his brother even this, for his malaise was so fundamental that hope never entered his head. In all the world, no examples rose up to suggest a method for life. Bernice waited. The woods waited around the stone house, cloaked in their Christmas dusk. Nothing imposed, not the minutes ticking away under the quarter moon, nor the music reaching an end, nor Anabelle's protracted stay in the powder room, as couples clung and revolved.

But then she was there, yanking at his jacket sleeve.

"Willie!"

He looked at her. The bright eyes filmed over as she switched them away, glancing around the room in the midnight shadows. Her hand twitched on his arm. A thought occurred to him: had she got sick in the powder room? Somebody had spiked the fruit punch halfway through the dance. And she had been gone a long time. Come to think of it, a very long time.

"Are you all right, Anabelle?"

"No! Yes. Willie," She was still whispering, her mouth scarcely moving; the lips looked full, swollen, under the smeary purple lipstick. "Willie, take me for a walk."

"Don't you want to go on upstairs?" he said. "You look kind of—"

"Walk! Please, Willie. No, not that way." She dragged him away from the French doors. "Out the front."

So he took her arm, and they nosed across the floor of dancers and into the vestibule. He reached for the handle to the front door.

"Here, let's just stay right here," she said. Her smile seemed tense, hooked across her jaw. Her eyes were welling up at the lower lids, and a dewdrop lay captured in the lashes, beading the black mascara. He would never forget how she looked at that moment. "This is just fine. This place is just fine." Her face, convulsing slightly as another couple made their way past to the door and went out, nevertheless achieved a strange repose. She met his stare. She saw his wonder, no doubt. "I want to tell you something," she whispered.

"What? Is anything the matter?"

"Well, I guess that depends on you."

"Why," he said, "why, Anabelle," uncertain what was expected of him. For once he did not feel the parched hopelessness her nearness usually evoked, for he had been too overwhelmed by the malaise to feel much of anything. "What depends on me?"

"Well—it's not customary to leave it up to the girl." Her eyes flicked across his face, around the paneling, through the ballroom door and back. "You should be the one, the way it's supposed to happen."

"Honey, what do you mean? I'm sorry," he said awkwardly. "I can't quite catch your drift." He rubbed his chin, sensing that he was failing her at a crucial juncture.

"Willie Ransom, do you want to marry me or not?" she demanded suddenly.

He gaped. She looked confidently back. In the ballroom, they could hear chairs sliding over the floor, the band packing up their instruments, people saying good night. Her eyes grew peaceful, stayed on his own. When that happened he felt the old disturbance spring up, and he stuttered, "Marry—marry!"

"Yes," she whispered.

"Marry you!"

"You heard me."

Only one thing floated up to the top.

"But—what about Bert?"

"Bert?" She blinked at him, and then turned away with a jerk of her shoulders. "What in the world does Bert have to do with it?" Then she drifted toward him, softly, the anger dissolving. "What would I want with a rascal like your twin brother? That dirty dog, no telling what he'd try to make a girl do. Trying to sugar his way—" She mashed a finger to the corner of her lips. A tiny frown dented her forehead, but she drew the finger away, and the smudge of purple lipstick was gone. "You're the quiet one, you're the one I want," she whispered. "Haven't you figured that out yet at all, Willie Ransom?"

"Why, no, I . . ."

"You would never try to—to force anything on a girl she didn't want, would you?"

"No," he breathed. "No, I wouldn't do that."

"See?" She laid her hand on his cheek, and then dropped it quickly as a couple passed, laughing, to the front door. "I know perfectly well what's good for me."

"You'd—you'll really marry me? You really would marry me?"

"Well, naturally."

"I've flunked out of school, Anabelle," he said, moved by a compulsion to make everything clear. "I won't be able to get back in."

"So what?"

"I won't have any kind of profession, it'll just be living in the house at Bernice, working for my family businesses—"

300

"Or traveling," she said. "We could always travel."

"Yes," he said doubtfully, too amazed to contemplate what she had obviously already thought through. "But I've flunked out, I—"

"I don't care. So have I, for that matter. All that silly trigonometry and biology and English and Government—you think I've been spending any time worrying my head about such piddle? That's not what life is for. Why are we talking about it, anyhow?"

"Marrying—" But then she took his hand, and laid it like a book on her open palm.

"When?" he said.

"That's better." Then she giggled. The repose in her face drew her smile peacefully together; her features suddenly seemed to relax and fit. "That's more like it." Then, as his hand slowly stirred to life on hers, she lifted it and draped it across her shoulder blades. He clasped her, hesitant, too frightened to crush her, and she lifted her cheek towards his mouth. "Are we engaged?" she whispered.

"Oh—yes."

"Then as to when—the sooner the better." She sighed with satisfaction.

"The sooner the better," he echoed, and the truth stung him when he lowered his lips to kiss the rose cheek. Not until then did it penetrate. He felt the creamy skin brush, tingle; he saw her eyes wide and fixed on the ceiling, intent, blameless, blank; he registered the sudden painful surge under his belt. And the awareness of joy, mingling as it hit him with an awareness of his own ignorance, and most of all, the distant reverberation, like an aftershock of the quake, a faint echoing doom as the malaise cleared away.

The Expatriate

They married in Galveston that June. Anabelle's aunt and uncle had to plan the wedding; her father was too ill to preside. Bert, of course, was best man. Willie Junior remembered, years later, the way Bert had kissed the bride after the ceremony — darting at her lips, and then staring into her face intently. He glanced towards the groom, as if to counsel him on some matter; and then turned back to Anabelle. "Well, now you're in the family. I'll be seeing you." Then he suddenly grabbed her hand, stuck it in Willie Junior's, and said, "You take good care of Daddy, I'm off to Europe this afternoon. Have fun in New York." Then he left, not even staying for the reception. Willie Junior thought, "Uh-oh," because Anabelle, as he put it so long afterwards, "had a look on her face like she'd been poleaxed." But she did not say a word. Together they watched him go from the church, at once adrift and uncertain; they could scarcely look at one another. They honeymooned in New York as planned; Willie Junior's imagination had not anticipated farther countries. Then they returned to Bernice, and there Anabelle, in a moment of pique, scolded her new husband for his brother's bravado.

"There was nothing stopping us from doing the same," she cried. "And now he's gone and done it ahead of us. Well, I hope he gets mixed up with some nasty Paris woman, and gets his comeuppance."

"What do you mean?" Willie Junior marveled. "A Paris woman . . . comeuppance?"

But she fell silent, and then took up her buff to polish her nails. Another day she said, "You know, Willie, I just love this house. It's furnished in the most wonderful antiques, and it's so private and cool and all. And your daddy is the sweetest old thing—hardly ever says boo to a goose, just locks himself away in that library, reading his books and planning more oil wells. He's a fine man, I just knew he would be when you told me about him."

"I'm glad you're so fond of him, honey," Willie Junior said.

"But there's one little teeny thing that bothers me about living here."

"There is?" By now Willie Junior had discovered his ignorance. They had been married for three months. Already Anabelle basked in the plans for the future: the parties she would have, the friends she was already making among Bernice society, the sorority sisters she lured up from Austin on weekends, to parade her married spectacle before; the occasional trips to Galveston to see her invalid father (the bankruptcy had finished him by then; he was destined not to last out the year). But one certain aspect of the marriage perturbed Willie Junior. It had to do (as he delicately hinted years later to me, plucking up his modesty and tossing it aside when the whiskey went down) with the ducal bed in the room upstairs which now ensconced their conjugality. No, there was no clarity there. There was only tentativeness, and pert indignation. And lately something else: repulse.

"There is, honey?" he asked, as she balked with coy eye whisks from revealing her mind. For there was certainly something bothering him.

"Well, sugar pie. You know I want to ask a few people out here for a dinner party next week."

"I thought you already had."

"Yes, I already have. I sent out the invitations yesterday. But there's a little problem."

"What's that?"

She looked at him sideways out of her green eyes. "Guess," she murmured.

"Is it the furniture in the drawing room? I know you wanted something more modern. Well, honey, I'll just be glad to speak to Daddy, I know he won't mind in the—"

"Not that. Besides, I've come to realize just how lovely and valuable that old furniture is. Genuine Empire, Dolly Renfrow told me—really, your grandmother had very fine taste. No, Willie, guess again."

"I don't guess I can."

"Oh, you're so mean and horrible. Are you going to make me say it?"

"I don't mean to let you down—"

"It's your Aunt Mavis," she hissed. "I mean, the poor old thing just sits all the time. Have you seen the way she eats? Spinach hanging off her lip, that glassy look in her eye. Sugar pie—don't you think it might be a good thing—a better thing for her, far better than piddling around this house and sagging like a lump of flour—if you just whispered a word in your daddy's ear that she might be happier in a home?"

Willie Junior did not reply at first. When he did, the answer seemed to clog his vocal cords. "I don't think Daddy would hear of that, honey. I mean, she's his sister. He takes care of her. She's family."

"But you never know when she's going to decide to creep up behind you through a door, or stack her roast beef into a tower and then flip it down with her knife. She just flips! And there the roast beef lies, smack dab on the tablecloth. Don't you think it's awful?"

"Maybe," Willie Junior pondered, "we could get Viola to take her her dinner on a tray the night of the party."

"But a home would be so—" She did not finish, but bit her lips.

"A tray would solve things, wouldn't it, darling?"

"I suppose so. For this one anyhow."

So Mavis was relegated to her room on the nights my mother entertained, and this was made policy. My mother was no longer humiliated in front of her friends. But any other innovations she had intended—the plans to travel, the villa she envisioned on the Riviera

—shrivelled and died, reduced to ashes. For by the June of her first anniversary, two things had happened. Bert came back from Europe, and found a bachelor-sized house in Bernice. And Anabelle, to her chagrin, discovered she was pregnant. She could not understand how it was so, she told my father; she could not comprehend how it had come to be, considering that he was formally denied entrance to what she had believed was the proper chamber. She had not realized that his "knocking at the door," as she put it to him—the only congress she permitted—could have the same results that the painful part did. But it did. And I was born the following October.

My Condition

Victoria Grace Ransom. She named me the first because I was to be her little princess. The Grace was for counterpoise.

It was during my fourth year that I contracted the measles which affected my hypothalmus gland.

The chances of a cute snub-nosed Vicky, doing cartwheels on the football field with her cheerleader skirt twirling around her thighs, even then did not desert her. She could not relinquish me to a career less sublime than her own; and day after day, as she watched me bloat and smile, she would remark to Viola, "I believe Victoria's just having a growing spurt. Maybe we need to get her on a diet, quit feeding her so much starch." When the measles had struck, I was so sick she had taken me to the hospital. There Doctor Middleton had seen me through the worst, and told her what he feared. The fever had been remarkably virulent. There were possibilities of brain damage. "Encephalitis," he said. In his experience, he had never encountered such a bad case; and his gentle warnings as to "glandular reactions" reduced my mother to tears. But she forbore taking them to heart. I got well again; I watched her gravely from the crib in the hospital, and apparently my stare was alert enough to prompt relieved congratulations from the nurses and Doctor Middleton himself.

But the secondary complications gradually began to appear.

There was the day she tried to squeeze me into a smocked dress I had worn before the measles attack.

"I simply can't believe how much this child is filling out," she complained to Viola. "Would you look at this! Her arm's as fat as butter."

I stood beside her chair in the nursery. A toy dog crouched at my feet; it must have been soon after the return from the hospital, for I remember looking at the pink fluff of the dog, balding where I had sucked it, and trying to recall how he came to be one-eyed. We had been parted so long by the half-sleep of fever that he was a stranger, his battered spots a new territory. Mother hauled me back as I stooped to grab him.

"No, Victoria, we've got to get you presentable before you go playing with your toys." She held out the creamy material and slipped it over my crown, blinding me in a gauzy curtain. "I can hardly get this neck down over your head!" she chided. "It's unbuttoned, too. Viola, has Bessie been washing this dress in hot water for it to have shrunk so much?"

"Nome," Viola's voice came to me, faceless and noncommittal. The neck of the dress cut into my forehead, but Mother strained at it, trying to force me through. I was in a mad impatience; I wanted the dog.

"There!" she cried, and I popped out the hole like a cork. Sunlight, the furniture of the room solidifying like a stage set; and Viola's face blooming up above me, imponderable and dark.

"Brand new as well," Mother grumbled, "I bought it right before she got sick. Well, I never heard of sickness making a child fatter, you'd think she would have wasted away some. Most be the hospital food. . . . Never mind," she said, establishing the refrain that was to echo through the next few years. "She'll thin down in the gawky stage, before she gets to be a teenager. They always do."

But I recall the incident more because of what followed.

"Now this is just ridiculous," Mother clucked. "Her arm will not—I can't seem to get it through the sleeve! Viola, maybe you can—never mind. I'll just—keep—working at it—"

I yelped. Layers of flesh rucked under the sleeve band; it was like a ring of iron, and Mother jammed my arm inside, and let it hurt. I forgot the dog.

"My goodness!" she cried. Now she sounded more bewildered than unhappy. "Oh, my goodness, Victoria. What have you done?"

But the pain subsided. I looked up at her, eased and curious, and saw her recoil from me as if I had lisped an improper word. She was gazing at the offending arm, at the dress sleeve. Her eyes were slitted like a cat's. Turning my head, I glimpsed the tear, the Viyella frayed in a long rip to the shoulder.

"Oh!" she said. "The material's clean gone. It can't even be mended, except to patch it."

And she peered at me, aghast, while I shrugged the dress up, freeing the tight skin from its shackles, and scooped the dog off the floor.

"Paddy," I said, remembering his name at last. But Mother merely stared. The lines in her chin deepened.

OVER THE next few months it grew plain that diet was not going to help.

"Whatever is the matter with her?"

Mother's question sounded as if spoken by someone else. The clinic room was pale green. They had perched me on a high table top, and the brown linoleum seemed far away. They grunted, and thumped my knees with a rubber hammer. The stethoscope was icy, laid against my chest; it had by then a familiar feel, roving over the pudgy breasts and halting at a tender cavity. Next would come the prick in my finger, the blood siphoned through a glass straw; perhaps some shots. Then a treat to atone. This was the Ochsner Clinic in New Orleans. Baltimore had preceded it, and before that, the Mayo Brothers, Dallas and Baylor Memorial, and several experts in New York City. Mother's restless heels clicked to the desk and back, as the doctor nudged the glands under my jaw, frowning.

"Measles," he said. "Mmm-hmm."

"Sixty pounds in one year," my mother whispered, and the whisper came from far away, hardened with subtle urgency.

Their tones vibrated on my ears. They took on a flavor of despair that comforted me. It was what I heard at home, the keynote to my days. I sat passively while the doctor prodded and squeezed, the pink dog Paddy waiting by my side.

"Nothing." It thrummed from the doctor's throat, merging with the fluorescent light, the steel and chrome. ". . . careful eating habits . . . at this point in time, nothing . . ."

"And not even——" Mother's voice tensed. "They told me back at——"

I stroked the pink fur, and pushed the eye button around on its loose thread.

IT MUST have been soon after that that the stories began.

Long afternoons, playing with my toys on the back gallery. The pangs as my stomach seethed; the odor of fresh-baked biscuits eddying through the kitchen screens; a swat as I reached to seize the forbidden food, and the reproofs: "You know you ain't suppose to touch them biscuits. Your mama done have my hide, she catch you eating on them. Now here's one, just one, now; you go on out, I send Viola to keep you company. I ain't tell your mama this time."

Back into the stupefying heat, where Paddy dragged limply across the grass. A lone twitter from the mimosas over the lawn: I must not venture that far. The biscuit crumbling on my tongue in sweet buttery fragments. But no jam. Then looking up, to see the rocking chair rolling back and forth, and the old woman herself eternal as stone, her head rested on the pad. At no one moment did the rich dark voice begin; it seemed to have always been moving through the heat and the sunlight. And when night descended, it would still be there, the murmur flowing through dreams.

There came a year when my mother gave up the battle. By the time I was seven years old, I too was sent into seclusion, eating every meal except dinner in the kitchen. I did not mind. I was spared the sight of her puckered chin and tight lips, as I ladled gravy over my vegetables. During dinner I was still expected to sit with the adults, and throughout the ordeal my mother would loll in a kind of trance, her eyes unseeing even when they skimmed my plate. There must have been a great deal she inured herself to at the dinner hour: Mavis dabbling with her spoon, my hunger, my father's drinking. The poignant stab of his gaze as she rose. Grandfather's silence. Gradually I watched her vivacity dry up. She would sit mute; fret with her necklace; her eyes would go opaque, the unhappiness showing only when she had to wipe Mavis's mess off the gropey mouth.

But there were still her parties, when she would incandesce and laugh her nervous gay laugh; the coffees and teas, the gossip among the powdered women who came to call; the banter at dinner parties, traveling up the stairs to the landing where I hung back in the gloom and listened. She welled up then, as if only society could slake that drought and refill her. And she was charming. I eavesdropped on the parties, singling out her laughter, dredging her jokes up from the merge of voices. I learned to divine her accent, no matter how soft and low. It fascinated me to hear her, to mark the change that came over her as she served drinks or dealt cards on a winter's afternoon. She was the one element that did not feature in Viola's tales: the sole person without a history. I drank her in, the way my father's hungry, wistful stare tried to do as she left the dinner table, and he clutched his whiskey glass instead. She excited my curiosity. How could someone so beautiful exist? How could such a fairy princess have come to live in the white stone Ransom house? And I knew, before I was very old, that she was more painfully baffled than I.

When I was a child, I did not always notice the seams in life. It was only many years later that I realized the fact that her retreat from us coincided with my father's alcoholism. But I knew even then, at the ages of seven, eight, that I was not the only reason for my parents' sadness.

When Father took to the bottle, I was still small enough for him to kneel to cuddle me in his arms. I remember the earliest taste of his breath as he kissed me, mumbled on the taut cushions of neck, the chubby pads of wrists, and stared benignly into my eyes. He would exhale a sigh of endearments, calling me his little raisin bun, clumsily gathering me to his chest, and his breath tickled my nose with mint. Later it was to be fumes; the cuddles ceased, the sighs grew maudlin; but the failure I represented was only a part of a lifetime's melancholy, the inevitable bequest of Baby Boy's death, his wife's rebuffs, the motherless house and isolation. To discriminate among his weaknesses would be foolish. For him I was merely a proof of ongoing feebleness, and not something to drown. Moroseness wore him down; the piquancy of Anabelle's beauty taunted him; but it required a disaster to incite the drunkard.

Uncle Bert

"Ain't she the juicy thing!" Dandy cried in the kitchen, while Viola pushed me forward and stood beaming. "I declare I ain't never seen such a little hamsteak, I eat you up!"

"You'll be eating a passle if you do."

"I mean! Let me get aholt of you." She plunged down upon me like a falling tower, and hefted me and threw me high, chuckling through her wide open mouth, from which gold winked. I was a morsel, a feathery bit of meringue, and in an instant would be swallowed down, eclipsed into nothing. I felt my head graze the light fixture. Then suddenly I swooped to earth and was set lightly on my feet. Her massive arms shook. She stood big as a mountain, the grin splitting the bottom half of her face like a dark watermelon with golden seeds.

"Yessum, I need you to come out to my house, I'll feed you some cooking you ain't never have. That old Bessie," she teased, and raised a fist like a squash at Bessie's smile, "she ain't been doing you justice."

"Reckon that's all she need to grind her down to skin and bone," Viola sniffed. "Mr. Macafee's ranch."

At that age I had not yet discerned the fabric of the histories. They swarmed around me as resonances, dark sound and bright image touching points in the brain like electrical charges. Sarah sweeping out the stable in a flurry of straw; Grant fixing her with somber contemplation while the dancers careened under the Christmas lights. The creatures of fable, gifted by Viola's tongue with speech. Here was a name I knew well. Macafee.

"Now you got no call to go spitting out that way. How come you

312

to act like that in front of this sweet child?" Dandy tossed her head, her tone booming with covert warning.

"Ain't a thing I can't say in front of Victoria Grace. She's heard of Grant Macafee by now."

Dandy turned and leaned down to me. "You got to watch that Viola! You got to watch out, what she say." She stuck a finger in my ribs. "You going to go on about the old times, you best tell this little chitlin a good story. Not some truck about how things use to be."

Bessie cleared her throat, bent over the counter, chopping something green.

"Oh, I see now," Viola bit off, and sent Bessie a narrow glare.

"You listen to me, child," Dandy puffed, squatting down beside the table, leering into my eyes. "I work for Mr. Grant Macafee, out on his ranch. Done worked for that fine upstanding man a mess of year, can't hardly count them up, I'm so old now. He's one of the best men ever drew breath in Bernice, Texas—you ask any fool in town. Good Christian man, ain't never tell a lie or cheat a soul. He had trouble from time to time. We all had us some trouble. That what come from getting born, Lord know."

"I tend to my business, Dandy." Viola's voice slid like a blade between us. "You tend to yours."

"Land, girl! Seems like it about time you tend to your *kind* for a change."

"Dandy," I said, "Viola is kind."

"Why," Dandy goggled, "why, child! I ain't never said—"

"She tends to kindness, I mean."

Dandy's grin turned wry. She reached out and screwed the huge finger into my cheek. "Miss Victoria," she declared, "ain't nobody kinder to her white folk than your old Viola. She be the queen."

"She tells good stories," I persisted.

"Mmm-mm! I imagine. Come on here to me." She gripped my shoulders and pulled me towards her. "Viola, she the colored queen of this county. Shoot, I reckon I'm the only person in Texas has the gumption to sass Viola. Ain't a soul don't look up at her, and say, 'There go Miss Viola Lewis, proud and proper, fanciest colored woman Bernice ever seen.' She just full of her place, old Viola. I only sass her because somebody's got to—I been at it a long time, long before you born, or your daddy neither. There's got to be somebody with a devil streak, or else she get too set in her ways."

"The devil recognize the devil," said Viola.

"I was named after a queen," I said.

"Why, you don't mean it! Who that be?"

"Queen Victoria of England."

"What'd she do, then, when she was queen?"

"I am not too sure," I mused. "But Grandfather told me she shut herself up for a long time after her husband died. She would not for anything come out of her castle and meet her people face to face."

"Oh, I believe I hear about her." Dandy raised her Mason jar and gurgled the iced tea down. "Mr. Macafee done told me and Randall that story once back last year. He was talking about how some folks have to act like royalty, like that queen who shut herself away inside her house."

"I thought Mr. Macafee don't say nothing much to you nor nobody," Viola said dryly.

"He got talkier the last few years," Dandy replied. "He work less and talk more, here lately. You'd be mighty surprised, Viola, if you hear him go on nowadays."

"No, thank you."

"He's getting to treat me like family now, after all those years," Dandy said. "Well, nearly, anyhow. He likes him a bit of company. Mr. and Mrs. Farmington and their boy Randall, they done kneaded him a little softer. Mr. Macafee ain't had no real kin after his daddy died way back yonder in 1919. But now he's got to know his own first cousin and her husband and boy so well, he's a real family man again. I hear how he plan on leaving Randall the ranch and the money and all in his will. He treats him just like his own boy."

"Huh!" Viola said, glowering with familiar scorn. "The day he gets soft and leaves his self-righteousness behind'll be the day you shinny past Saint Peter at the pearly gate."

"You best watch out, I'm going to take this here little old bag of beans home with me after all," Dandy chuckled, and gave me a suffocating squeeze. "Then where you be?"

"Still loaded down," Viola said cryptically.

"That's just how you made, Viola."

"That's how I'm made, and that's how I stay made."

"Whoo-eee!" Dandy quivered like a custard. "Hey then. I hear some other kind of news last week I plan on asking you."

"What's that?"

Dandy released me from her embrace. I rolled over to Viola to cement my loyalties.

"I hear how Mr. Bert Ransom coming on back to Bernice at last, after he done spent the Lord knows how many years across the ocean in Europe."

"That's the truth. You done hear right," Viola said. Her hand settled on my crown.

"He ain't been back in how long?"

Bessie flung the answer over her shoulder. "Not since awhile after that there child was born."

"Why, you don't mean it! How old are you, Miss Victoria?"

"Seven. I'll be eight in October."

"Shoo! You sure is smart for seven, and that's a fact. Randall be going on nine soon, but you smart as him!" She fanned herself. "So you ain't never seen you own uncle yet!"

"I did as a baby, I think."

"How come he to stay away that long?" She lounged back on the creaking chair. I could not stop admiring her; the difference between her and Viola was more than mere vastness.

"Reckon he found it livelier over there," Viola said carefully. "He always was a lively boy. He like to travel."

"Ain't Texas got enough good times for him?" Dandy grinned and winked at me.

"Once he come home the first time, he bought him a house. You know his house in town?"

"Yessum, I know it. I recollect the last time he was here, when he got it. Everybody in Bernice know that house, because of all the high living and the parties and the girls from Dallas and Austin he brung to it on the weekend." She snorted. "How come him to reckon he has to go all the way across the ocean to find fun that he can get right here?"

"He wanted to see the world," Viola said.

"He want to see more than just the world! We know what that boy wanting to see. Yessum. Maybe you-all Ransom folk just a little too proper for Mr. Bert." Her fist thumped against the bouncing thigh. "He's a scamp!" she hooted.

"He's a disgrace, what he does," Bessie said from the sink.

"Reckon maybe his twin brother has something to do with him traveling so long?"

"What do you mean, Dandy?" Viola looked askance at the sliding eyes and pursed lips.

"Maybe his twin brother got something he wants and can't get."

"You right about that," Viola said smoothly. "He's got Victoria here."

"Uh-huh!" Dandy said, and paused heavily. "Well, my cousin Rochine, she takes care of that old house he got fixed up so nice in Bernice. Rochine, she go in there once a month and clean it for him. She's done it through all these years, rain and shine, keeping it nice for the day he come back. The same white woman's underpants she found in the bed sheet, she got all folded in the drawer waiting for him to give them back to the owner." She raised her eyebrows archly. "The same liquor bottles he left on the buffet, half-full of liquor like he left them, just setting ready for him to pour out and finish them off."

"*She's* the one told you he's on his way back, then," Viola said, and I could feel her hand go slack, as if relieved of something. The fingers slipped gently down my hair.

"She the one. Ain't nobody else, like maybe some *white* woman, if that what you mean." Dandy eyed Viola brightly for a second. "She hear the message through the bank man, when she stop by for her pay. And it go: Air out the house and do it good. Mr. Bert's coming home, he wants it ready."

"Reckon word'll get spread all over Bernice, if that Rochine got hold of it."

"Naw," Dandy said airily. "She only told family. It mean she's got a job working for Mr. Bert regular, after he comes off the airplane."

"You'll spread it around for her."

"Why, Viola! Only folk I mentioned it to be Mr. Macafee. And Mrs. Farmington, when she brung Randall out to the ranch for a visit."

"You told her?" Viola said; and I was astonished to feel her hand tighten on my neck, tense as it had been before.

"She was glad to hear it, too. She perk up and laughed when I told her Mr. Bert's on his way. She be mighty fond of Mr. Bert, when he a young boy at college, and that year he spent here before he run off again. Shoo, Viola, it don't make no difference anyhow. Whole town know before long. He be back himself to show it. Since when you get so huffy about folk telling news?"

"I know you. Your tongue is loose as your leg use to be." But this was mysteriously evasive, I sensed; her reply had nothing to do with the hidden fingers digging below my locks, torturing the skin there. "Ransom business is our private property, it ain't up to all Bernice to figure on."

"Well, I say this to you, Viola." Dandy blew keenly, and shrugged. "You changed so much in the last few year, I don't hardly know you no more. You a grudgey old woman now. You ain't like you use to be."

"I seen a heap of sadness *you* never saw, while you been out at the Macafee ranch," Viola said. Her voice was cool. But a tinge of acid came out with the name. "You're one of the Macafees now, Dandy. You the one done changed."

Dandy stood up. The polished floorboards creaked beneath her. She swayed majestically towards the kitchen door, her wide face full of dismay and incredulity. As her hand reached the knob, she gave the three of us one last survey; her jaw clenched tightly, the ball-bearing eyes rolled over us, and her forehead remained smooth as the flat of a shovel. "Mm-mm. You got bit a long while ago, and the poison still working in you. But that was old time. Time change us all. It makes me sorry how it changed you. I be seeing you around, maybe. But I ain't catching that bus out here no more. It ain't worth the trouble."

After the screen door slammed behind her, Bessie turned around and stared at Viola, her eyes filled with outraged reproach.

"As for you," retorted Viola to her, "some folk need to watch how much they talk around here."

There was no installment of the history that afternoon. Instead, we arranged ourselves in the playroom on the second floor, Viola on the divan, and I ostensibly engaged with a dollhouse. But instead I listened to Viola's shallow breath, the sunlit silence, and pondered on Dandy's visit.

At last Viola stirred. "Poison!"

"What?" I said.

"Poison! What she say, that Dandy. Poison, huh!" She knotted her hands in her apron. "Those Macafees, they the ones who know about poison."

"What is poison, Viola?"

"Stuff to make you sick and die, that's what."

I puzzled this out.

"The devil know about poison."

"Does the devil use it?"

318

"Indeed he do." She sounded blighted; the hands fidgeted. "He use it all right. Him and his whiskey bottles."

After a moment, she said, "Ain't nobody cunning like the devil. He look like a clean, fine, upstanding man. He's real good at fooling who he need to fool. He lives like a Christian. Oh, yeah! Don't ever lie. Not so folk hear him at it. Nome, he's too cunning. But then he snake round in the dark, and he wait in the trees, spying to see who's ready. And he reckon ain't nobody the wiser. He chip away and chip away, make folks afraid their whole lives through. But nobody can point the finger. If one little soul of goodness makes him mad, with their decent ways and their clean mind—then he don't never let go. He plagues them until he's got them in his box. And he march off, and carry their souls away."

"Does he have a name? I mean, besides just 'the devil'?"

Her eyes narrowed. "You find out in good time."

"But how does he plague people?"

She licked her dry lips. "He makes sure they live unnatural. He scares them until they spend their whole life hiding away from the evil touch, trying to hang on to their goodness. Just because they rile him once upon a time. Then, when they old, and they look back, what do they see?" She drew in a little tremulous gasp. "Nothing but waste. Because the devil done eat up their years. They ain't done nothing to stop him."

"You have seen people he did that to?"

She did not reply, but sat there like an effigy, motionless and inward.

Then, shortly, she said with abrupt venom, "That Mrs. Farmington. Huh. Well, I'm glad Dandy ain't coming here no more. I'm glad she going to stay away."

"What do you mean?"

"'She perked up and laughed,'" she mocked. "'She be mighty fond of Mr. Bert, when he was a young boy at college.' Well, *that's* the truth! Oh, yes! That boy grew up handsome, all right. But he ain't got no devil in him. That ain't *his* trouble."

"What is his trouble?"

"He always sunk so low in this house, he need to push out and shake up some life. Ain't got no mama, except me. Bert, he was scared of what he couldn't have. Not what *Dandy* means. Dandy look at a sweet flower, the sweetest flower in the garden, and she say, 'That flower blooms so nice because it's fed on cow dooky.'"

"What can Bert not have, that he is scared of?"

"He might have wanted it once upon a time, but not no more."

"What? What did he want?"

She scowled. "He done lost the older brother he look up to. Lost that good child before he could grow to a man. I saw how that clutch Bert hard in the darkness. Then, when he was in college— just after he come out—it was women. Oh, Dandy don't tell a lie there. He messed round with *more women*! Living wild, throwing the liquor parties, till the sheriff got mean about it. And then you got born to your daddy and mama. And I saw—" she sighed. "I saw what Bert want. I saw it pass through his head, sure as it was painted on his face."

"What?"

"You."

I sat, flabbergasted.

"He looked at you, baby. Your mama and daddy showed him their fine new child. And he shrunk up inside."

"He *did*?" I whispered.

"He don't have no pretty lady that comes respectable like your mama, and no fine baby to love and raise. If he did"—she paused, "maybe it would soothe him down. But he run away. He hightailed it off. And he ain't come back for six whole years."

"But he is coming back now," I murmured. "Grandfather said at the dinner table, 'Bert will be home next week, he is taking a plane from Paris.'" The news that I had been wanted that badly by someone made me giddy.

"Yessum. He's coming." She stared at her shoes.

"Mother's face went funny. Like this." I puckered my chin in imitation, and lidded my eyes.

"She's fond of her brother-in-law!" Viola said sternly. "They been friendly since the college down in Austin. She be glad to see him. For the right and *proper* reason, not for any of that wicked hogwash *Dandy* try to claim! Your mama is pure as snow. Don't you forget it."

I waited.

"Not like some others."

"Others?"

Viola scowled. "If some *woman,* what's already going on forty, and ain't got nothing better to do—if some woman like that saw him and his high ways and good spirit, could be she'd want to dig her teeth in his neck. Just like a old hound dog, when it find the coon. She'd want to hang on for blood."

I shivered, terrified. "Did some woman do that? Try to bite his neck?"

"It's the other real true reason your Uncle Bert left Bernice like he done." She rinsed her hands, over and over in her lap. "A woman who's *respectable.* Already has her a child of her own. Has her a good husband! But she can't keep off the fresh meat what's alive and kicking. Not her. She want that throat."

"Oh!" I clapped a hand over my mouth.

"Just gnawing and gnawing."

Suddenly the longing to see my dear uncle Bert, torn away from me because of such danger, grew unbearable. He loved me!

"She's the devil's own blood kin. And now she and the devil have got real close. Dandy said so! They in each other's bosoms. And one thing you can say about the devil is," she sucked a breath, "he don't ever get tired."

"Or old?"

But she said nothing more.

SEVERAL MORNINGS later, on the second floor, I found a door ajar, and went through it.

I was immersed in a game of pretend at the time: I was invisible. And if I was invisible, my body was also changed: light as down, able to float up the staircase, glide down the hall, ignore the sound of feet, the thighs pumping on the stairs, the longer and longer time it took me to climb them. Such a child would Uncle Bert be glad to love when he got home, such a weightless child as I had been when a baby. With single-minded airiness I scouted past the linen closet where Viola was counting sheets, past the upstairs bathroom door, where the shower was running, to the far end of the hall. There I found the door. It gaped a little. I tested my state by trying to waft through the crack without pushing it wider. There was no idea in my mind beyond the game.

Then I looked about, and saw where the chase had led.

The door was to Mother's bedroom.

Mother had said long ago that her "boudoir" was a sacred zone. It was the one place she could find privacy, where people could not intrude and make her nervous. No one had ever seen her in the act of getting dressed, or caught her in her negligee. Each morning she emerged, her face creamed and painted; but if even Father knocked on the closed door while she created herself, he would be ordered away.

I stood on the verge of the Aubusson carpet. A scent of mimosa, so thick it could have been wrung from the air, came from the hangings and walls: Mother's smell. The ducal bed was curtained with brocade. A row of electric bulbs above the dressing table cast a blond light in one corner, and sifted the mirror with false dawn. Nowhere else in the house had these eternal shadows, this climate, this chilly luxury. The dressing table, its vestal lamps burning, stood crammed with glass and crystal jars, gleaming bottles. Satin cushions lay strewn on every piece of furniture: the chairs, the chaise lounge. Viola told me Mother had revamped the furnishings since Arliss's time. But the the bed, of course, was permanent, monstrous with prestige, looming in the central space. On its other side sat an armchair. The bed posts nearly hid it; but it commanded a fine view of the dresser mirror. The mirror enlarged the whole wall it fronted, and when I looked into it I saw the crystal vials and bottles range back, back into murky caverns, an evening scene twinkling with stars.

I paused by the dressing table. A little ballerina stood against the mirror on one porcelain toe, poised forever in an act of grace. Her skirt was made of stiffened net, her arms formed an arc, and I could not resist touching her uplifted breast. One vial sat unstoppered near her curved foot. I raised it to my nose and sniffed, watching its counterpart fly up through the cavern like foxfire. Mimosa. My fingers clenched: it was as if I held Mother's essence in one hand. So this was where she borrowed the sweetness that surrounded her.

I set the bottle back down, and then wandered across the carpet to the bed. A small pressure told me how soft it was, slick with satin, webbed with lace. I dared not muss it. Instead I crept to the armchair and sat down. I must have sat for some time, when suddenly the wedge of light by the door widened and then vanished. I heard a rustling sound. Mother had come in from the hall. She made her way to the dressing table, arraying herself on the stool. Her body was wrapped in a velvet robe—it must have been her shower I heard, splashing behind the bathroom door. She untied the sash, and slipped the bathrobe from her shoulders. Beneath it was a slip, filmy and tucked with lace. I could see her brassiere through the material. Only half her face showed in the mirror. The other half was eclipsed, and I could just discern an eyebrow and cheekbone in the fuzzy light. For a few moments she leaned forward, probing the mirror's deeps. Then she selected something from the tools and vials on the dresser top. She gazed into the mirror again, fondling her chin. I saw her frown, musing on it; then her right arm rose, doubled by reflection, and steel tweezers glittered in her hand.

"Now I wonder if that's just another length of the same hair I keep plucking out, or if it's a new one growing in the old one's place? I swear I get the root. Such a pesky——" And she jabbed the tweezers at her chin, and jerked.

Who could have guessed at such a flaw, the coarse hair sprouting from the cream? Did she not realize I was there? But I was invisible: of course! the game came back to me.

I was afraid.

A sound forced through my throat.

"Oh!" She cried out, turning so swiftly that she dropped the rouge pot. "Oh!"

I could say nothing.

"Victoria?" Her wide eyes seemed to entreat, to regard me with cautious alarm. "What are you doing, sitting in that chair?"

"I was just——"

She stared at me. She did not expect me to finish my excuse. The bathrobe stayed sloped below her shoulders. A dusty yellow suffused her face, from the frail light of the mirror. The frown had disappeared, leaving her dim and alert, like a bird listening for a worm in the ground. Then, softly, "How long you been sitting there, honey?"

"I don't know."

"Oh." She ran a finger under her slip strap. Her face grew meditative. She seemed unaware of her dishabille, the transparent silk, the tweezers glittering on the glass top. "Well, you certainly gave me a surprise. I had no idea you were there."

"I'm sorry," I mumbled.

The stare continued, pensive; for once she did not deflect from what she saw. She roved over my legs and trunk and head, her head tilted to one side. She was actually looking at me. Presently she took her eyes away, and bent to pick up the rouge pot from the floor. One leg slid out of the bathrobe: a stocking top was revealed, clasped by a garter. "Next time, call out to me or something. I nearly had heart failure when I heard you."

"Yes, ma'am."

Then, amazingly, she turned back to me, and smiled.

"I slept so late this morning I don't even know what time it is. You must have already had your lesson with your granddaddy."

"Yes."

"What was it?"

"Arithmetic."

"I always hated arithmetic myself." She swiveled to the mirror, dipped her finger in crimson, and buffed more rouge on her cheeks. "My worst subject at school. I was just terrible. Are you any good at it?"

At first I was too struck with wonder to answer. Was she really talking to me like this?

"Grandfather says I am."

"Don't know how I got such a smart daughter. The brains must come through one of your granddaddies. Your daddy and me aren't too brainy, that's for sure." She sounded smug.

I could not reply. The sensation of unreality stopped me.

"Wish I hadn't slept so late," she went on, now tipping a wand of mascara to her lashes. "It's my insomnia. I get it real often these days. Every time we have an evening out somewhere, I come home and can't sleep a wink until four or five in the morning."

"Viola told me you can't sleep," I said.

"That Viola. She knows about everything in this house. Thank goodness she's here. I couldn't have inherited better help with my marriage—a true, old-style mammy. Don't know what I'd do without her." Her lips stretched into an oval; she blinked at the wand's touch. "I tell you, it relieves me of a lot of worry."

There was nothing to say.

Presently she set the mascara down, and flapped a powder puff in the air. Clouds drifted through the light. "What do you think about your uncle Bert coming home at last? Has anyone told you he's traveling back to us?"

"Yes, ma'am." Perhaps she had not realized that I listened to the adult conversations at the dinner table.

"Well, you're in for a real surprise. There's nobody quite like your uncle Bert. Dashing! That's the word." She smiled to herself, a deep, private smile. She looked different all of a sudden, which made me glad. "And now he's been gone so long, living in France and Italy and England, no telling what all he found to do with himself over there. Didn't write much. I believe he spent a whole year in Spain. That old scoundrel," she cried, and then narrowed at the mirror and unclipped her lipstick. "He'll be full of beans. Living the gay life, going to the bull fights. Betting on them, if I know him. Fighting the bulls *himself*, I'll bet you a nickel. Acting like some playboy, as if he didn't come from little old Bernice, Texas, at all. That man—" She sighed happily, and drew the cupid's bow with the lip brush. "Wouldn't be surprised if he's learned a foreign language. Just to order his drinks, of course." She jerked out a tissue and blotted her lips. The stare she gave the mirror was long and pondering. Her lids drooped over the green eyes. "Wonder what he'll make of us all," she murmured.

I summoned the courage to ask the burning question. "Mother? Will I get to meet Uncle Bert?"

"Why, of—" Suddenly the eyes stirred in the mirror. Her arms went limp. Then, slowly, her head turned, until she was staring straight at me. "Well, Victoria. Of course you will. I guess." The gaze moved, perturbed now. She took hold of the bathrobe's lapels and shrugged the garment on, cloaking her shoulders. She knotted the sash tight. "Ahhh, Victoria," she whispered. Her voice carried the sadness across the room. It settled, tangible as fog. "You'll be meeting him," she said, and her eyes skated above my head, looking through me. "Maybe not right at first. You'll be in bed when he gets here, his plane's scheduled real late. Then the drive from Love Field. Yes. But later on, after awhile—when I've prepared—" She strained a brightness. "I've known your uncle Bert since I was in college. Used to ride around with him and your daddy, they were both courting me some. Once, at a dance—" But she did not finish. For an instant the sentence hung on the stuffy air.

"I was considered a very pretty girl back then, if you would believe it."

"Yes, I believe it. You are beautiful now, Mother."

She flushed, and bit her lips. "You see, Victoria——" Then she said, "Thank you. Thank you, honey. I'm glad you think so." Then she added, "It's funny. Sometimes I forget how young you still are. I mean, with your——and all. But you're really just a young child. Just a little girl."

"Nearly eight," I said.

"Yes. Nearly eight." She stood up from the stool. "Now you have to run along and play. Or get Bessie to fix your lunch, it must be time. I've got to get dressed now. I know you'll find something to do."

"Yes, ma'am." I sidled off the chair.

"And Victoria——" She skewed her face slightly, not meeting my eyes. "Next time, don't just barge into my room, okay? If I'm not in. Or give the door a knock, if it's closed."

EVERY EVENING while Viola served dessert, Mother and Grandfather discussed the various projects they had undertaken together to improve the estate grounds. They had already built two more arched bridges over the lakes, under which white and black swans lazed and swam; a pavilion with a lattice roof for a grape arbor; and an orangerie based on the one at Hampton Court Palace in England that they planned to fill with miniature blood orange trees from Seville. Every day the carpentry shop Grandfather had had added to the old stable building hummed with new activity. It was full of power tools: drills hung on the walls, band saws and sanders and table saws that Grandfather had once demonstrated to me while the workers were eating their lunches outside, a huge buzz saw for milling planks right here on the property, which left a smoke of sawdust pluming above its teeth, erased by speed, when Grandfather switched it on. Together he and Mother had made many imaginative leaps of faith, including an aviary for hummingbirds, which unfortunately did not work; the hummingbirds had died, their heads knocked against the glass when they tried to escape, and wound up in a litter of green and crimson. Tonight it was the formal rose garden. "Daddy Will, I just don't know about those Flames of Araby. I've been turning it over in my mind, and I've come to think they would clash with the American Beauties. What do you think?"

"Why, Anabelle, I don't know. I kind of like those two colors together. But I reckon you should decide."

"It's your project too."

Father sat silently twirling the wine in his glass.

"Now, I depend on you to advise me. What do you think of the idea of some Earl of Rochesters instead?"

But once Grandfather had made his contributions, he would sit back in his chair and let his last words hang on the air. His eyes would grow smoky and blank, his lips seal together. His preoccupation excluded us altogether. After this happened we would not hear him utter another sound until morning.

I tried to imagine what he was seeing in his mind's eye, as he sat there transfixed, his shoulders squared back against the chair, his eyes as still as if they were balls set in wax. To me he was in his most interesting state. As the reverie deepened, and his face reached a stage of imponderability, Grandfather showed no vital signs, not so much as a muscular twitch. But somewhere under the tablecloth's folds, life was stirring; and suddenly a cigar levered upward, like a cannon aiming. Then it flipped backwards into the unseen: Grandfather had it in his lap. But his face did not reveal the feat. He continued to stare at his sublime visions, eyes motionless, brow reposed. I heard the crunch of dry tobacco mashing, and now the left hand performed, darting quickly up from the depths and snatching the silver lighter beside his dessert plate. The right hand came looming into the light, planting the cigar exactly in the middle of Grandfather's lips. Thus grafted, the cigar hung down like a spear; the lighter rode through the air. A blue flame blossomed. The flame touched the cigar end; Grandfather's lips convulsed; he sucked three times, hard and quickly, amidst wreaths of stinking smoke. Not once did he blink. I had watched this skill every night since I had been allowed to join the adults at dinner, and he had never faltered yet. The greatest wonder lay in his ability to unite flame with tip, unerringly, while seeming to live in a trance, elsewhere.

As a rule, once the cigar was lit, my mother would cough discreetly and rise to excuse herself. Viola would then come forward and seize Mavis's elbow to guide her away. But this night Mother lingered; the cigar was eventually doused in lemon mousse (I preferred it when we had baked Alaska, and I could watch the charred log float in the ice cream puddles), and still she stayed. She too pursued her own thoughts, sipping at her coffee like a finch. Eventually she spoke: "Well, the plane'll be landing in another hour now. We can expect him to be here in two, I imagine."

"Less, knowing him," Father said. "He'll rent a car and drive like a bat out of hell, now that he's on Texas roads."

I jerked up. I had not realized that tonight was the night of Uncle Bert's return.

"But the luggage might take awhile." She glanced submissively at Father, smiling a hesitant smile.

"He won't have much luggage. That old Bert boy—"

Grandfather abruptly came to life.

"What about Bert?" he asked. I had never seen his after-dinner reverie broken.

"We were just talking about his plane, Daddy."

"Oh. I see." His hands, attached now to the rest of him, lightly gripped the table's edge. "Do you know, Willie, I plumb forgot it was tonight."

"Yes, sir."

"He's due from New York in another hour, Daddy Will. Now won't you be tickled to see him after all this time? That old rascal!" Mother's gaiety had a brittle edge. "I hardly know what I'm going to say to him. You think maybe I should scold him a little for deserting us all so long?"

"Well, that's up to you," said Grandfather.

"Why, I—" She paused. "Maybe you can knock some sense into him, now he'll be back. I declare, it would be a mighty fine howdydo if he just stayed long enough to kiss us all hello and then took off again. It's about time that rascal settled down, maybe made a *home* for himself. Don't you think so?"

"I couldn't venture to say," said Grandfather gently. "If that's what Bert would like to do, though. I suspect you and Willie Junior might know best, you seem to understand him more."

"Understand Bert? Why, Daddy Will," she giggled, "that's like saying a mortal human can understand a tiger."

"Hm. A tiger." Grandfather began to muse. Then abruptly he smiled. "It'll be especially good for Victoria. To have her uncle back at last. Won't it, honey?"

Suddenly everyone looked at me.

"I reckon Bert will have a high old time, playing with you," Grandfather beamed mildly. "Chasing around the back yard like he used to do when he was a boy. Remember what you and him would get up to, Willie Junior? Those tree houses, and the games of Indian—why, Victoria and Bert will hit it off right away. Don't you let him throw you down and tickle you!"

"Where is Viola, anyway?" Mother fretted. "It's so late, way past Victoria's bedtime! I wish she would—"

"I'll warn him about the tickling," Grandfather assured me. "I'll just let him tie you up and do it a little bit."

I shrank back in my chair, thrilled, and Grandfather winked.

"There she comes!" Mother cried. "Thank goodness! Viola! Can you please rush this child right off to bed, she's practically nodding off in her chair."

Grandfather turned to my mother. "Why, is she?" Viola beckoned to me from the doorway, and slowly I clambered out of my chair and went to her.

"Good night, Victoria. Sleep tight, now." Mother waved, and then the hand touched her hair.

"Good night, honey," Grandfather called softly. It was the first and only time he was conscious enough to wish me good night, through all the years of memory.

AS VIOLA buttoned my pajama top, I said, "Did you know Uncle Bert comes back tonight?"

"Um-hm. I sure do."

What would he be like in the flesh? Would he look just like my father? Would he embrace me? Would he still feel as drawn to me as I was to him, now that I was no longer a "sweet baby girl"? Possibilities unfolded, one by one, in an expanding array, gradually illuminated brighter by my hope. Grandfather and Viola had both suggested it: the chance of joy. An uncle to love. The hero. Who might interest himself in me, play with me, *see* me; it was something so remote from my ordinary life that his image swam before me like a magic lamp. If I asked Viola another question—if I breathed his name—it might ruin the magic. But somewhere out there he was advancing towards the house, approaching through the sky across the darkness, and when he came at last through the front door, it would happen— it could happen—that he would open his mouth and ask for me by name.

When Viola left, I slipped under the coverlet, reached up, and switched off the night-light.

A long time passed. Slowly my eyes adjusted; a halo bloomed around the drapes' aperture, and the density took shape, moving when I looked in different directions. The dark had a life of its own, shifting like fluid. Across the room I could see black blots: the dresser, the closet door standing ajar. Soon the room might flood with dazzling light, and the beloved would stride to my side. "Victoria," he would say. "Victoria Grace." He would—but I could not form what he would do next. Time bundled together, strung out within the bed's chamber. The absence of Viola's voice made a hollow on the night; a new myth took its place, wordless, soundless, molding on the substanceless waters.

Then suddenly the silence was broken. A peal of music showered through the house.

I struggled up from the pillows and ran to my door, opened it. The sconces bathed the hall with soft gold.

"Why, it is!" Mother cried out, distance muffling her. "It's that old scoundrel himself. Let me look at you!"

I heard a mesh of male voices, low and indistinguishable. Viola's joined the jumble, rebounding in a slurry of exclamations. Then the confusion crested. Someone shouted something: a jovial retort; I could make nothing out. Listlessly I sank against the doorframe. The night seemed to creep up on my back, sliding over my head. To go into the lighted hall was forbidden, more so tonight than at any cocktail party or dinner. The sounds of reunion began to die away. Despair tore me. I would not hear him speak. My knees sagged, I crouched beside the door, half in darkness and half in light.

Then suddenly, at the instant the voices were fading, one bass lifted above the hush in a whoop.

"But where is my little Victoria? Victoria Grace?"

The cry rang unmistakable, tolling gold.

I bowled through the hall to the stairs. Wheezing for breath, I ran down the first flight to the landing. They were moving into the drawing room, nearly out of earshot. Mother, Father, and Grandfather had already disappeared beyond the double doorway. One lone figure, caught in the act of passage, still stood in the foyer. He heard me. His tall, dark head swiveled. The handsome face, so like and unlike my father's, lifted, and he peered up the the stairs. Our eyes met. He drew a breath, a quick, sharp gasp. Then, just as his heavy brows relaxed and he started to speak, Mother called.

"Bert? Come in here, you monster!"

She was laughing.

I turned and pounded up the stairs as fast as I could go.

I AWOKE the next morning before dawn.

Through the drapes seeped the early light, gilding furniture and blazing the closet. The anticipation waited at the back of my mind like a gift. I watched the dresser slowly lose its fire and grow opaque, and all round, through the bedroom door, I could feel the sleeping house, the mute dream kindle and subside as the morning slipped forward. Somewhere down the hall Uncle Bert was drowsing. Soon he would rise, would amble out of his room (which room? Viola had not said) and want a bath. He would wash the residue of other places from his body, dash the water in his eyes, and then go downstairs to drink his coffee. But not yet. It was still too early yet.

I whiled away the next hour in the conservatory, plucking dead leaves from the plants. The windows received the full sun here; it was hot as August. At one end the marble nymphs Mother had ordered from Italy sported in rigid abandon, circling the fountain pool. I trudged among them, inhaling the scent of wet loam and humus, the sultry sour orchids, the gardenias' sweet musk. On one stone wall grew a vine with stalks as thick as wrists, trailing in cascades. Mother called this room her "bower." She would lower her lashes and glimpse at Father as she said it, daring him, I suppose, to challenge her impersonation of an English duchess. But he would never have done so. Perhaps now Uncle Bert would mock her, and laugh at her self-consciousness. I remembered the whoop I had heard the night before, boisterous, healthy, denying that shadows could exist. I had just sat down to review that golden note, that look, when a swish sounded at the threshold, and Mother came in. She saw me too. She gave me an enameled smile which did not reach her eyes. "Victoria. You in here."

"Yes, ma'am."

"Well, don't dabble your hand in that pool. I've just had those lily pads arranged to exact perfection. I don't want you mussing them around."

"Yes, ma'am."

She went to the white wrought-iron table by the chaise lounge, and picked up her little watering can. The early sun drifted on her hair; her ruby taffeta dress incandesced behind stem and foliage, like a tropical bloom. Silver secateurs dangled from the dress belt, glinting with clinical threat. I watched her spill a few droplets on the African violets, brow frowning and intent.

"Isn't Uncle Bert going to get up soon?"

"Is he what? Victoria, who knows what that rascal—" Suddenly she snapped to attention. "Now, how should I know? His comings and goings—I believe he should be up by now, if he hasn't developed the worst habits. You may as well know what a reprobate he is, if I haven't told you already. But I'm not exactly sitting beside his bed, taking his pulse and bringing him breakfast, am I?" Her shoulders sloped. She banged the full watering can against the rack.

"But shouldn't someone wake him up?"

She sighed, exasperated. "If his girl—what's her name? Rochine —doesn't do it, we'll just have to count on the birdies, won't we? Or the Bernice lunchtime traffic! I suppose *European* travelers have to sleep *off* their trips, *I* wouldn't really know."

"Rochine? But she is the one who cleans his house in town."

"Well, of course she is."

"He did not sleep here last night?"

She wheeled on me, the watering can forgotten. "Honestly, Victoria, sometimes you are the most aggravating—I just told you he left here and slept in his own house on Collins Street, didn't I? Just took off and left! Wouldn't stay in this house for a *mint* of money, nor for love either! Oh, no, not his family home!" Her green eyes narrowed. She no longer saw me; she was staring at the vine. "Has to have his own bed, his own territory. Even one *night*—"

I huddled on the ledge, surprised.

"But he will come here today," I said. "He will be coming out to see us today."

"If he can make time!"

"He will come. He will make time."

"Ha! You don't know him. Scamping around, calling up all his trouble-making friends. 'Pull on your boots! This old son's back in town!' I'll tell you who hasn't changed! Not one jot, not one—no, sir!"

"He *must* come."

But the chorus was dying in my throat.

"Leaving people in the lurch. Having his fun, then—faithless! Hmph! We'll have to see, won't we?" She grabbed a sprig of brown fern and crumbled it fiercely between her fingers. Then, without a backwards glance, she left. I heard her heels clip on the parquet down the hall. "Viola! Bessie! Meet me in the kitchen at once, I want to talk to you both."

The kitchen door slammed.

For a long time I sat there by the fountain pool.

The anticipation, so cherished at dawn, had grown stale. It now hardened to a porous shell, hard as Mother's voice. Minutes, hours would pass; night would come. Viola would tuck me into bed, sit down beside me, and tell more family history. The words would snug around me, penetrate inside, and then I would slip through them and under them to the dark waters. Tomorrow Uncle Bert would visit. Or perhaps tonight—yes, surely tonight, I knew that—but once more be deflected from me. And if Mother could not have her way, she would see that I did not have mine either.

A distant sound jangled through the interior wall. At first I did not notice it much. But then I sat up, alert. The telephone was ringing in the library. Suddenly the heat stirred and changed, the sunlight spangled the leaves with fire. He was coming! He was coming after all! Mother was wrong. I knew him. I felt I had known him always, through Viola's stories. I was the baby girl he had loved and coveted. The ringing stopped. He was coming for lunch; he was phoning to say he had just woken up, and would be home soon. And sure enough, I heard the library door swing open, and Grandfather's slow gentle step pass down the hall to the kitchen, to tell them to set another place.

VIOLA CRANED around the conservatory, standing in a patch of sunlight, shading her gaze.

"Victoria."

"Yes?"

There seemed something peculiar about her gait. Then I saw that she was limping, not with one foot only, but with both, stumping across the room to the pool. Her eyes looked stern, sunk in the sockets. Her hand rose, spread in a claw.

"The devil's come."

"What?"

"The devil's come. He took his time, and he come. He turned the knife. He's come to kill the children, he waits till they ready, and he strikes them down!"

"What has happened?" I asked.

Her shaking lips worked to and fro on her teeth. And then, suddenly, I heard other noises. The roar of a car motor came through the window. A scream, swelling up from the rear of the house, squirted in shrill jerks through the downstairs hall. Someone sobbed, wailed, sobbed. Then the wails climbed, the sobs replaced by steady gasps, drawing nearer. The peal of the doorbell shivered through in silvery counterpoint.

UNCLE BERT'S murder became notorious throughout the state of Texas.

No one was apprehended. I have before me now the report, taken from the *Bernice Sun*, September 19, 1956, stating that he had expired from two wounds in the abdomen, and loss of blood. The instrument used was a poker, brass, part of a hearth set customarily kept under the mantel of his den fireplace. It gored the stomach, then was retrieved by the assailant (the iron barb on the end furthering the wound as it withdrew) and forced again into the victim, this time disemboweling him.

There were no signs of a struggle. The coroner noted that the deceased was sitting in a chair near the fireplace. He was asleep when death took place, apparently around 2:00 A.M. An empty bottle of vodka stood on a table next to him, and one glass, partially full. He had drunk enough to succumb to unconsciousness. Presumably the murderer found him in this helpless state, and killed him. Motive was unknown; possibly he had stirred or mumbled when the presumed burglar made entry, although no property was found to be missing. Plainly the killer had snatched the closest weapon at hand, and used it (this classic blunt instrument!) not to strike the victim's skull, as would have been logical, but to stab. The glass of one window had been broken, but broken outward, scattering fragments onto the lawn below.

Dandy's niece, Rochine Rogers, was minutely questioned. She had let herself onto the premises at eleven-thirty on the morning after the murder, and found Uncle Bert where he sat. Then she had run screaming into Collins Street. No one had seen any prowlers. The block had been asleep. Rochine Rogers admitted to the police that she had been "grateful to hear Mr. Ransom come back to Bernice," because it meant more regular employment for her, and steady money for her family.

I was too young to comprehend many of the details surrounding Uncle Bert's death. For me, the impression of softly babbling fountain water amplifies always to include another music, the quarter tones of Mother's wails. All else is blurred, obscure; and I have depended on the years since, and Viola's grim evocation, to order it on these pages. For of course, once the police had driven back to the station, once the hush had fallen once more on this house, then Uncle Bert's murder joined our Archive.

And it came as no surprise to me that Viola could assemble what the police failed to find.

Oral history is all very well, but I am grateful that grief prompted my mother to preserve the printed word. Here, on the yellowed foolscap, dry among the bones, lie scraps of flesh and color. Viola dwelled on the supernatural aspects of Uncle Bert's demise, ranting about devil women with bloodied teeth. Thus she conveyed to me her belief: Uncle Bert had been murdered thanks to a Macafee lady's malice.

There was no question. Pattern follows pattern, and some memories are long. The Ransoms' fates had been laid out on the loom for four decades. There would be no variance now.

In vain the police tried to track down the killer. But I did not question the police's bafflement, for my own life was a mystery, a dead end. If I knew the truth from Viola, she and I also knew that it could not be shared. It had somehow become arcane, beyond the reach of human interference.

FALL, I remember, came early that year. By mid-October the leaves were spinning from the boughs, and the sharp woodsmoke veiled the afternoons. Viola and I went for walks among the musty aisles of oak. We seldom spoke until we had left the house far behind. Then she would motion for us to sit down on a mat of leaves, and the voice would strum on the silence.

Through her long recitals, I would hear the memory of Mother's sobs. She did not come back from Bert's death with ease. I had seen those shoulders heave up and down, the bowed head buried in her hands, her back turned to me. A marveling would come over me then, that Mother had so much grief to spare. Where did those funds of lamentation come from? What energy, besides the banked-up gaiety and the party laughter, was stored within her body? I still recall her face when she stepped through the front door after the funeral, the pale cheeks, the dark smudges under her eyes. She walked up the stairs like a somnambulist, clutching a handkerchief in her hands; her black dress moved from side to side with each lifted foot. Then she disappeared beyond the landing, and it was as if the upper gloom had snuffed her out. She stayed in her room for two days, alone, refusing to eat.

Grandfather, also, disappeared into his library. He remained there for nearly a week.

When Mother came out, she wore the full quota of makeup, her hair was curled and neat. But at dinner one month later, when Grandfather once more brought up the subject of the rose garden, Mother gave him a vacant glance, and mashed her napkin to her mouth. Her green eyes filled with tears. I never again saw him make such an effort toward lightness.

Father stopped talking altogether.

As fall wore on into winter, I spent more and more time at Viola's side. Something within, a growing hope, had been so thoroughly cauterized by the September murder that all I cared to do was to listen to the past.

I plowed through a geography lesson, and outlined the coast of California with my finger. I was secretly tracking Sarah's journey, wandering along the railroad routes of the early 1920s, sucking my tongue with satisfaction when I reached San Francisco. In arithmetic I secretly bought and sold blocks of ice instead of apple bushels. I read "The Highwayman" and saw Grant Macafee, gaunt in the shadows, listening to the lovers and plotting revenge. The images were no longer isolated flares. The stories began to connect.

Grandfather alone, once he reemerged from the library, seemed unchanged by Uncle Bert's dying, practicing the acceptance, the submission to fate, that was his born nature. If he had ever overheard Viola's stories, he might have been uncomfortable. If he had seen the new concentration with which I listened to her, he might have asked her to keep silent. But he would have blocked off the only pleasure I had.

At mealtime I would listen and watch other things. Viola stood against the sideboard, serving us stuffed squash, ham, okra, and rolls. Mother dawdled with her wine. Mavis spat out her masticated food. And Father now drank whiskey.

On the winter evening I saw him drain an entire decanter in forty-five minutes, I knew that he was different.

Thus I entered into the time of ciphering.

For the next four years, I would eat with them, observe them, ponder their walls and barriers, see my father's wistful appeal when Mother rose from her seat, watch Grandfather shorten his conversation, meal by meal, and slip into catatonia, the trick with the cigar, the pallor on Mother's face as she passed from us through the smoky reek, and try to join these people, these facades, with the characters that filled my days. Then came the autumn day, when I was eleven, and understood at last why I had been told their stories.

N*yla*

On a spring afternoon in 1961, I sat in the kitchen with Viola, watching Bessie drop cookies on a sheet. A bridge party was going on in the drawing room. Occasionally the laughter would flutter through walls, or a conversation wind around the dining room door.

"You can only eat twelve of them cookies, gal. The rest be for you mama's company." I complained until Bessie cured me with leftover luncheon food. Then Viola, creaking in the old rocker, cocked her head towards a loud shriek of mirth, and frowned at the closed door.

"You reckon that party's pretty lively, child? Did you hear your mama make her joke?"

I shrugged. My mouth was stuffed with biscuit. "Not a funny one."

"What's that you say?"

I glanced at the counter, where Bessie's gray wool trembled on her head; she was subject to palsy nowadays, and had grown slightly deaf.

I raised my voice. "Mama's joke was not a funny one. She told a lady she must have the only true blue heart in the room, because her partner had all the red ones."

"I ain't figured that out," Bessie grumbled.

"They were playing bridge. Bidding hearts—you know, trumps and things."

"You talking some kind of French talk, Victoria?"

"Never mind."

"I reckon your mama's joke went over right good," Viola said, and arched her eyebrows. "And you peeking in, you saw who she made it to."

"I did." I picked up a third biscuit, and bit.

Viola squinted darkly. "Yessum." She hitched her buttocks backwards in the rocker. "Mrs. Farmington, that's who."

I said nothing.

"Them ladies all whickered fit to bust." Viola shot me a trenchant glare. "Seem like it's the time the lion done lay down by the calf. But if the calf knew what the lion eat for supper, she might not choose such a stickery bed."

"Mrs. Farmington seemed very ordinary to me. She behaves just like the other ladies. A little gaudy, maybe, and inclined to talk too much. But a lot of them do that."

"That's just what I say. Ain't you got it drummed into your head by this time?" Viola leaned towards me, whispering intensely. "You mean after fourteen years you still don't understand what I tell you? That's the point! They act like other folk, them Macafees. They ooze their way into everybody's company. But they rotten as sin inside. It just don't show."

"Perhaps." I turned it over in my mind. The long tradition of secret trysts between Macafee and Ransom might have convinced me, even had I not absorbed Viola's fierce belief, that Mrs. Farmington and Uncle Bert had once been intimate. By now Viola was as firmly convinced as if she had witnessed the event. Nevertheless, it was hard for me to see Mrs. Farmington as a nemesis, with her brassy hair and chipper epigrams. She seemed too banal to be evil. Her rings had glittered and flashed, as she slapped her hands over her mouth and crowed at Mother's witticism. She looked the perfect part of the middle-aged Southern matron, choicely fleshed as a fryer, winking broadly.

"You know what I done heard now?" Viola stuck out her lower lip as I glanced towards Bessie again. "She ain't got the faculties to listen no more. But when I passed out the champagne cocktails at your mama's party last week, I hear Mrs. Farmington claim how she sent her boy off to school. You know about that Randall."

I stared steadily into her eyes.

"Well, he went off to military school way year before last. And you know where he went, her late baby that she don't have till she was old?" Her lids narrowed. "Even though she strut round like she just come out the nest! She sent him to Sauter!"

Still I said nothing.

"Sauter Military Academy in Kerrville! Now what do you reckon about that?"

"I know. I heard about it today." I spread jam on a biscuit. "As you pointed out, I was hiding in the angle of the double door, and watching through the crack between the hinges."

"You be mighty sly, Victoria."

I looked away; another cookie sheet slid into the oven. I could smell the perfume. My mouth watered.

"She thought she was flattering Mother."

"Huh!"

The tables had been placed around the drawing room off center to form diamonds, my mother's favorite suit, her "lucky sign." I could see Mrs. Farmington in three-quarter profile, and the profile of Mrs. Deloache. Mother faced me directly in the light from the window. Mrs. Farmington dealt the cards.

"I remember the day soon after I was a bride. You would have only been a schoolgirl then, Anabelle," she said, giving my mother a playful nudge, "I'm old enough to be your big sister. But that day, soon after I had moved to Bernice from Maypearl for Otis to take over the hat factory, I met your lovely gallant father-in-law in the courthouse square. We were introduced by his old schoolteacher. Mrs. Burley was her name. She died just a few months after.

"He had the three boys with him at the time, one of them your very own husband, Anabelle! Shy as a mouse. Anyhow, we all chatted back and forth, and Mr. Ransom asked me about Cousin Grant. I didn't know about the old business ties at the time, how those two go way back. Then old Mrs. Burley asked him where the boys were attending school. One of them piped up—no, it wasn't Bert, I don't think, and surely not Willie Junior, knowing him. Anyhow, *one* of them piped up and said, 'Sauter Military Academy.' Mrs. Burly was so impressed! The finest boys' school in Texas. Oh, I may have been green, but I was all ears. I took it in. That very day I swore to myself: 'If it's good enough for the Ransom boys, it'll sure be good enough for my son when I ever have one.' So soon as Randall got old enough, whoosh! Straight to Kerrville he went. Just loves it, too." Her bracelets tinkled above the buzz from the other tables. "Is it my bid already? All right then—two hearts!"

Mother had dimpled, while Mrs. Montgomery studied her cards, murmuring, "This girdle is too tight."

"I can't say Willie is any kind of a recommendation, to tell the truth," said Mother.

"Why, don't you malign that sweet man, Anabelle!" Mrs. Farmington turned to Mrs. Deloache. "Cherie, you mark my words: when your little Jimbo gets old enough to send away to school, you just plonk him straight into Sauter. Randall's grades are way way up from what they were. He's the smartest thing, though!" And she chuckled and made a move. "Got a mind of his own? Whew! Just a barrel of trouble. His cousin Grant adores him, though."

I peered through the crack and took it all in.

"Ain't but one reason that Farmington boy's gone to that same school," Viola muttered now.

I gazed at her. "What is that?"

"He got sent there for one reason. And that is, to get Mr. William's goat."

I pondered. "Possibly."

"'Possibly!'" she exclaimed in a whisper. "Huh! They done it to remind your granddaddy. They done it to keep him in line."

"Perhaps they are grooming him to take over. If Grant Macafee is so old, and cannot do what he would like anymore."

"You'd better count on it. And there's your mama, drinking it up like she's thirsty on a dry day—that's when she let fly with her joke, like she make a present of it! Lord, lord. That boy Randall Farmington's going to take over for sure."

THE NEXT afternoon Bessie's dill bread browned in fragrant loaves, sending forth a spirit of plenty on the kitchen air. Father had not come home since before the bridge party. Nowadays he often stayed gone for two or three days at a time. Mother was in Dallas shopping.

Except for us, and Grandfather locked in his library, the house was empty.

Viola had nodded off, her head pitched back, her mouth hanging open. Through the kitchen window I could see the gardener pruning back roses, his skin matte black, hands caged between thorny branches, and the spark of the shears.

I had just got up to use the bathroom when Viola awoke with a start.

"What time is it, Bessie?"

"Reckon it's going on for three."

"Three! Already!" She dabbed her pendulous lip. "She's late, then."

"Who's late?"

"That new one's late. Her first day, too."

"Oh, you mean the iron girl."

"Yessum."

"This her first day? I forgot all about it."

"It surely is."

"What time is she due?"

"Mrs. Ransom said two-thirty. That's all I know."

"Expect she had to wait on the bus. I hear they're real slow through the East Side, since the roads gone bad with the rain."

"Who are you talking about?" I asked.

Both faces turned to me.

"The ironing girl your mama done hired," said Viola.

Bessie watched me impassively. The black bosses of her cheeks shone with faint mist.

"Oh."

Bessie snapped a glance to Viola. It was returned.

"You know your mama done hired a girl to do the ironing instead of poor old Bessie?" Viola's voice was doctored with the new glibness that she used when she and Bessie spoke together in front of me.

I did not admit; no, I had not known. I met her mineral gaze.

"Yessum," she went on. "First time in forty years we'll have us another girl to help even part-time. It's a grand day in the morning, when we have somebody else to fiddle with that backache truck."

"Oh."

"She'd best be able to iron a fine seam," Bessie proclaimed. But still she watched me, her hands fisted in the small of her back.

"Nyla, Mrs. Ransom say her name is. You hear of any girl called Nyla, Bessie? I been studying, but I can't feature her."

"Reckon she must have just come to town." Bessie shot me a gaze, and turned back to the counter to buff a silver candelabra. "Ain't nobody know a girl name Nyla. I asked in church on Sunday. Could be she just moved here. Reckon she maybe go to First African Methodist. If she go at all."

"Hmm."

"How long have you known she was coming?" The need to urinate held me halfway between the stove and the pantry door.

"Your mama told me last week."

So they had both known for several days. I looked at them blandly.

"I hope she ain't one of them young flighty girls," Viola pursued. "Coming in here, rousting the peace, simpering around. I ain't said nothing to Mrs. Ransom, but—" She sniffed; we knew whose business it was.

"What gets me is how Mrs. Ransom say, 'Be nice to her.' You know, when she told you this Nyla girl kind of special?"

"Uh-huh."

"I ain't figured why she said that. 'Be nice to her, she's kind of special.' What call Mrs. Ransom got to tell us how some colored gal's special?"

"We take the instruction, that's all." Viola tilted to the ceiling, her eyes hard in silent surmise.

"Huh! I been working in this house forty year, and she sent me that word. I'm glad some other fool's going to stand over that old board for a change, but if I got to 'be nice', it's going to strain. Specially to some uppity gal who sashays in here full of airs."

I stepped through the pantry door, bladder aching. As I levered onto the reinforced steel stool that Grandfather had had installed just for me the year before, the perturbation took over.

Another person was to enter the stone world of the Ransoms, and see its secrets.

It had never occurred to me that someday Mother might find it necessary to hire more servants. So hermetic was our life in the kitchen and the back halls that I took Bessie's old age, Viola's growing infirmities for granted.

I considered Viola's craft, the shrewd avoidance of my eye.

I was too inured to resent the glance between Viola and Bessie. But this news smoldered with subtle menace. I realized what their conspiracy meant. The previous day, the slot of light between darknesses, the heady omniscience, and the women, unaware, shuffling their cards, stirring their Bloody Marys, returned; the spring sunlight through the drapes, occasionally spurting Mother's hair with a gout of gold. But they had not seen me.

This one would.

All the last years of espionage, the cautious concealment, the fear lest I be caught outdoors by a workman as he went about his business, the hugging to staircases, walls, disappearing acts down a corridor as a guest's voice drew near: now useless.

Eventually I struggled up. The pantry was quiet, but I put my ear to the louvers in the door.

"Some nigger flaunting in here," Bessie grumbled. "I may be tired, but I ain't too tired. That gal best watch out."

"She only going to come in three days a week," Viola said. "Afternoons. Mrs. Ransom say she want to try her out. It won't hurt you to find a little kindness."

"Suppose she try to take over. You going to find kindness then? It ain't nothing to me, you know I don't care what happens. Ever since the morning Ezra died, I just get through the day, cook fancy food for them. But I won't take no backtalk. What you going to do, she call you Granny?"

"She'll show respect. We can make it plain who been here longer."

"Suppose she don't care? Suppose she just come, get her money, do her job—suppose she the kind like to mess with the men?" Bessie paused. "Did Mrs. Ransom say is this gal marry or single?"

"Say she's single."

"Huh! That means she's wild."

"You ain't got a generous bone in your body, Bessie. You already putting her down on the ground."

"We'll see what we see. I aim to take it easy, no matter what. I just don't like that talk of Mrs. Ransom's, 'Be nice to her, she's special!' That woman, she so sugar and much obliged, and then says what we tell a fresh nigger gal." Bessie drummed the table, her fingers rapping down on the wood.

"We been here too long to—"

But suddenly both women went silent. I pressed my eye to the louvres. The back door was opening. Its closeness prevented me from seeing much but a midsection view, so as the person entered the kitchen I could observe only her upper midriff, a faded green gingham dress, the curve of a bicep hanging from the short sleeve. But I watched Viola's and Bessie's heads lift, their faces slam close. A gasp escaped Bessie.

The arm was the color of oatmeal.

The woman moved forward, in a slow tread. Her hands dangled

empty; her head swung gently on the neck. I could see lines of grime in the creases. When her head moved, her hair glistened, yellow strands against her fine-boned skull.

"I come to iron," she said. Her voice was meek, lying on the kitchen stillness. "Mrs. Ransom told me to come to the back door and ask for Viola."

After a long pause, Viola said, "That's me."

"Well. I come to iron." Her twang sounded strange, crisp. I listened for the flattened vowels and stilted consonants. She was not a Texan. "Where do I do it?"

Bessie skittered to the counter.

"There's a board in yonder and a board in here," Viola mumbled. "This one's back behind that little door. Reckon you can do the ironing in here or in the wash room."

The woman began to walk toward the built-in door. She raised her pale hand and twisted the knob. The ironing board dropped out.

I jerked. Viola rocked violently backwards. The woman did not blink. When the ironing board stopped bouncing, I pushed the pantry door wide and stepped out.

For one second, she turned her eyes my way. They were blue, crystalline with disinterest. She stared again at the ironing board, fingering the silvery cover.

I went to my chair and sat down.

"This here is Victoria Grace Ransom." Viola rocked in short stubborn rhythm. But a strange smile transformed her face. "She's the daughter of the house. Miss Victoria, this is—Nyla." She twisted her head around to the ironing board. "I don't recall your last name, ma'am."

Nyla did not look up.

"Ma'am?"

I watched the fine skull revolve, slow as a rusty gear. "What?"

"I said, I ain't recall your last name."

"Nyla Arlene."

"Nyla Arlene. Excuse me, but is Arlene your last name?"

She nodded. Her tilted round eyes seemed to take nothing in, nor react with the light.

"Uh-huh! Well, now." Viola cleared her throat. "We be glad to have you. Hope you're happy here and spend lot of time keeping us company. Miss Victoria like a little company, too.

Nyla ducked her head towards the wash room, and then crossed the floor and passed through the portal.

Instantly Bessie whipped around from the counter, glaring from the door to Viola. Her stare fixed in baffled outrage.

Viola put a finger to her lips and shook her head.

"It don't matter none," she whispered. "Sshht! It don't matter if she's white. Don't you see? That must be how come Miss Ransom say she's special. She ain't right in the head."

Bessie stood trembling.

"Feebleminded," Viola pronounced. Then she waggled the hand before her lips; we heard the sibilance of Nyla's slippers as she entered. Towering above her was a bank of trailing cloth; she had lifted two baskets at once. She staggered to the ironing board and dumped them. Laundry toppled across the floor. She stared at it for a moment, sighing and scratching her ear. Bending, she retrieved a shirt. Her eyes wandered over the three of us, settling blankly on me.

Then she turned and went back to fetch the iron.

NYLA COULD not be tempted into commonplaces.

"Why don't you just set down with us and rest a spell," Viola would invite. "Come have a piece of this cake Miss Victoria's enjoying. We're mighty proud of Bessie's cake in this house, sure would appreciate if you try a bite."

"No, ma'am," she would reply. Each time the answer was a small shock. A white woman addressing a black one this way made Viola uncomfortable.

"You come on the bus this morning? Where you got to catch it? I hear tell it makes folk wait a long while if you got to catch it in some parts of town—can't count on it the same time from one day to the other."

Nyla shrugged.

Eventually the day came when Viola dismissed her as a hopeless case. Autumn rolled in. Nyla ironed obliviously, there at the board the way a boulder might be there, or a lump of salt. She was like the presence of a table seen dimly in a room when the lights are out. No personality emanated from her, no glow of intention; and for the first time in my life, I took the chance to observe a person at close quarters who had nothing, nothing at all, to do with the Ransoms, and who seemed incapable of noting me.

This was the greatest single thing about her. While Viola's voice dipped over the episodes of Sarah and Grant, the Pinkertons and William, I watched the long, slim back in the gingham dress and wondered. She was the exception, the being with no history at all. It was possible to surround her with all kinds of minutiae, to imagine a life for her that existed in an untouchable purity. I envied her anonymity, her lack of alliances. Should she choose, she could walk out the back door and leave us all behind: take a bus to Dallas, rove through the streets, eat in a diner, sit through a late-night movie, without exciting the least notice from the strangers who passed her. She was unpolluted by kinships, untrammeled by beauty or vivacity. No networks of tradition held her in place; she could hardly (or chose not to) speak a clear sentence. She seemed to me immeasurably blessed. And she fascinated me, long after Bessie and Viola had stopped greeting her; the freedom to shop in a dimestore and then leave, the glass doors separating her face from the clerk's forever, was miraculous. I spent many hours merely trying to determine her age. She could have been twenty-five or fifty, with the chiseled features, the skin that looked like plumped rolls, with the sudden surprise of the nose thrust like a beak out from the soft saddles of her cheeks.

Each day she wore the same faded clothes, stained under the arms. A belt circled her waist, like a string around a wineglass stem. She took no food with us, refused coffee and iced tea. Viola decided one day that Nyla must belong to a religion that eschewed caffeine. But I did not agree. She was a woman of no commitment whatsoever. How could she give heart and soul, much less wits, to spirits she could not apprehend, or clasp an idea when she had trouble clasping a pay envelope? But I privately invested her with other pastimes. She meant only to starch our napkins, iron my muu-muus, and go home. Therefore, she must live somewhere.

I invented for her a boardinghouse such as I had read about, and then discarded it as too hectic. After that I pictured a little clapboard cottage, tucked in a dusty yard down a gravel backstreet near the cemetery Viola had described to me so often. Nyla rose early in the morning. She tossed back her quilt and carefully folded it on the end of her iron bed. She shuffled into the kitchen, poured out some corn-flakes or cold fried grits into a chipped Woolworth bowl, and sat at an old pine table to eat slowly. She ate as if chewing a cud. Then she put a dented saucepan on the burner, lit the gas, and made herself a cup of instant coffee, scrubbing the sleep out of her eyes with a bunched fist, knuckling the corners while her hair hung over the pan, while the mockingbirds chirped outside the one window, in a mimosa. They would flick their tails, dart up and down in the sun-light, as Nyla swallowed her coffee from the blue willow cup veined with brown and paid them no attention. That must be how she lived, I imagined: she rinsed the cup in the sink and straightened her cotton dress, and ran fingers like long pencils through her hair. "Now, what do I do next?" she would wonder, in the luxury of her singleness. "Oh, yes. Now——" But I could not fill in the gap. It was hard to see Nyla planning ahead. But soon she would go outside, stepping into the dust of the yard, and onto the sidewalk that led to the supermar-ket. Once there (I could not picture the supermarket, never having heard Viola describe it) she would buy some bananas and some

Bisquick and fatback pork for the butter beans. In the back of her mind would be, "Two o'clock, go to the Ransoms," but it was still only ten or so, and she placed our house where it belonged, in a niche of other stops to make. (Did she iron elsewhere?) She would keep us at ironing arm's length. She might go to Sopwith's and linger in the dry goods, wishing for another cotton dress, or take a picnic lunch to the cemetery. Eventually she would board a bus, listing in her seat until it let her out in the suburban street that lay beyond our woods and meadows. Then she would trudge past the stone monument, past the lone cactus, past the thick trees and mirrored lakes, around the house with its turrets of stone. Her feet would lift over the steps of the back gallery, her hand touch the knob, and then, like an epiphany, she would enter my life.

Which was of so little account to her, or so I thought. The bliss of playing such a small part—solely a contractual part—to be the only different face I saw at near scope, and think nothing of it, endowed her with marvels. Her indifference to me made her magnificent.

One day in late autumn Mother came into the kitchen as usual to pay Nyla her wages. It was the end of the week, a Friday; Mother seemed distracted and sour.

"Here you are, Nyla." She held out the envelope, biting her lower lip when Nyla, as usual, fumbled and dropped it on the floor. "I've been talking with Mr. Ransom," she said, "and we've decided to have you start coming every day for the full day from now on. Would you like that?"

Nyla was on her knees, fishing the envelope from under the ironing board. She did not answer until she stood up. Her blank blue eyes rested on Mother's chin.

"Well, Nyla?"

"Yes, ma'am," she said.

"It means you'll be doing other work besides ironing. Cleaning, polishing the furniture like Viola does, sweeping and mopping, doing the vacuuming. All that stuff."

Nyla nodded slightly.

"Do you think you could do that?" Mother persisted with forced brightness, her charity voice.

"Yes."

Viola sat up straight in her rocker. Bessie paused over the steaks; I huddled in my chair, listening, throwing a glance to Viola.

"Cleaning bathrooms. You'll have to do everything Viola's been doing. I want you to be a big help to her." Mother tried to smooth. "Do you understand what I mean?"

Nyla nodded. Her eyes did not blink, and I noticed something I had never noticed before, something I knew Viola had not yet perceived: a certain enigmatic mask, molded over thought.

Nyla was understanding. Nyla was thinking it through.

Mother stared at her dubiously. "It was Mr. Ransom's idea, to tell the truth," she said. "But it'll mean you get paid more, of course. Mr. Ransom feels he wants you to—to join us here, maybe move in eventually. There's a spare bedroom on the second floor. Oh, goodness, I don't think I'm doing this right. Viola—"

But Viola sat stock-still.

So did I.

Mother stood, her head cocked beseechingly, for a few seconds unable to realize the sensation she had created.

"What's wrong with you-all? You look hamstrung or something."

Viola stirred. "I'm sorry, ma'am. I didn't quite catch—you say Mr. Ransom wants her working regular here?"

"That's right. He felt you could use more help. I mean, with—your age getting—and Mavis bedridden more, such a burden—anyway," Mother cried. "We want Nyla to settle in here with us. To help you."

But Viola still gaped at her.

Several thoughts occurred to me at that moment. The fact of my father, taking the initiative over a servant, or even with my mother; the fact of him expressing an opinion; that they had discussed the household at all; that—

"Viola, if you have anything you want to say about this, you can go talk to Mr. Ransom yourself. He's in the library, same as always." Mother looked angry, with some private fatigue. But then I realized: it was not Father she referred to.

It was Grandfather.

The stillness in the kitchen seemed to exasperate Mother even further. She wheeled back to Nyla. "Do-you-want-to-work-here-all-the-time?" Finally, when Nyla stared at the round creamy chin, her hooded gaze flickering: "Do! You! Want! T—"

"Yes, ma'am. I do. Every day."

Mother stopped, winced, and sighed. She pursed her lips as if to retort, and then let them fall primly into position. "Fine. That's fine. I'll go tell Mr. Ransom myself."

Nyla nodded.

She continued to nod to Mother's retreating back, as Mother stalked on down the hall to the library.

Then she turned to us, and gave us the benefit of her blue stare. The thin jaw balked below her mouth, that mouth so like an unhealed bruise, and she seemed to be challenging us.

"Well," said Viola. "I declare." She looked at Nyla. She had not been so suspicious for months. She settled uneasily into the rocker's pad. "Miss Arlene," she said slowly, "you ever met Mr. William Ransom before?"

Nyla lowered her head. A tic twitched above one eye, but she did not blink. "No, ma'am," she said.

Viola regarded her. "Seem like he mighty concerned about you. Or me, one." Her voice was deceptively light and gay, and she looked out the window.

I OPENED the library door without knocking.

When Grandfather heard me, he looked up. "Why, Victoria! Come on in, I've just been—" He patted a book of check stubs. "Just a little business I've been putting off all day. My accountant called and—" He rose from his chair and stood uncertainly, smiling. "This is a pleasure. What can I do for you?"

"I just dropped in," I said.

"Come sit down." He looked about, eyes alighting on the settee. His thinning hair fringed the tonsure; his paunch bulged over his waistband. Incarnate, he bore no trace of the boy he had been at twenty-one. But the photograph stood on the shelf above his head, and that boy's tight shoes still hurt; the touring car still loomed; the two sisters sat on either side of his arms. He saw me glance at it, and smiled again, as removed from that boyish grin as a saint. As he eased down into the leather chair I peeped sideways at the white hands, the plump virginal knuckles, the thick fingers hooked over the chair arms.

"Must be supper time. Am I late? I've been so—" He waved at the desk top.

"No. They have not even set the table yet. It is only dark because of the season."

"Hm. Yes. Dark early these days. Funny thing, how fast the years go. Winter already. Seemed like spring just this morning." He blinked.

"We have someone new moving in with us, I hear."

"Do we?"

"Yes. Mother told us this afternoon. Nyla Arlene, the—lady— who has been coming in to do the ironing." I worked to contain my voice.

"*Oh*, yes. He looked at me then, smiling gently. "We talked about that this afternoon. Seems like a good idea. Poor Viola's getting on, and your mother's been telling me how well it's worked out so far. No home to speak of, living in that—"

I caught my breath. The revelation dwindled into nothingness. "Um," he said.

I sat back, disappointed. "Will she move onto the second floor with us?"

"Hm? Oh. Yes. I think it could work out that way." He laced his fingers together, across his chest.

"I cannot vouch for how Viola will feel, if Nyla moves onto the second floor like—like family."

"Is that so?" He shook his head. "That's a pity. I had hoped—"

After a pause, I said, "She is a bit troubled about how Nyla came to be invited here. You see, Mother told us it was your suggestion."

"Uh-huh." He nodded. A moon was hanging on the blackness beyond the window; his eyes strayed to it, held by the frail white glow.

"We have not known how Mother came to hire her. She never said, and it has always seemed odd. I mean, a stranger coming in, from nowhere. And it seemed unlike Mother, to take on someone who, well, had certain problems. She said Nyla was 'special.'" I gave the word a dainty stress. "Grandfather—"

"Yes, Victoria?"

"Oh, nothing."

"You see," suddenly he leaned forward, "what I really had in mind—that is, when she's been trained a bit more—I've been hoping that she'll take care of Mavis."

"*Nyla?*"

He nodded. "I've been a little concerned about her lately. You know she hardly ever leaves her room these days. Not even for dinner. Have you noticed that?"

"Yes."

"Well, it would be good, a wonderful thing. Viola has so much on her shoulders, and I was hoping that the spare bedroom next to Mavis's could be fixed up. That way, in the night or whenever she's really needed—and she's not really mentally defec—that is, according to my lawyers—"

"Yes, sir?"

"Your mother's been very helpful. I was able to tell her the circumstances. Orphanage and so forth. When they told me *that*, you see——" He paused. "I want the best for Mavis. My sister, almost the last thing I have. Excepting Viola, of course. There has always been Viola." He lapsed.

"Grandfather. Have you actually met Nyla before?"

He gazed at me. "No, I haven't——met her. I haven't been able to." He gave a small shrug and frowned. "And who else would she have in this world? After all was said and done?"

"Who else would *who* have, Grandfather? Mavis?"

He coughed, looking at me sharply. "Why, surely."

The grandfather clock whirred, popped, sawing out a chain of notes.

"Now *that's* dinnertime, I know," he smiled. "Well, I better go freshen up."

"All right."

He got up from his chair. But I remained on the settee, rubbing the old balding velvet under my fingers.

I had not learned enough. I still felt empty.

Outside the window, night gathered. I hoisted up and moved to the desk. Beyond the lawn, the trees stood dark and clear against hollow blue. The grass in the pool of light below the window was still. Even the lamplight seemed cold on it, a pale yellow. Where the lamplight ended, the lawn spread out and out beyond an indigo lake towards the far black boles. No owl called.

The telephone rang on the desk. I let the jangle repeat. Perhaps someone upstairs, or in the kitchen, would answer. No one did. Finally its drill overcame me; I put my hand on the receiver, and with the ineptitude of a novice, lifted and held it to my ear.

"Hello?"

A voice on the other end spoke. "Hello! Hello, there?"

"Hello." My echo came faint, untrustworthy. The receiver curved around cheek, several inches from my mouth.

"Is that the Ransom residence?"

"Yes."

"Could you speak up, please? I can't hardly hear you."

"This is the Ransoms'."

The contact, a twanging from out of the darkness, caused my fingers to squeeze. The voice was male, gruff, impatient. "Who'm I talking with?"

"Uh—Victoria Ransom." I breathed it out.

"Well, this here's the Greyhound bus station. We have a car here belonging to one of y'all, blocking the bus lanes."

"Car?"

"Yes, *ma'am*." He snorted. "I'll say. Been setting here since early this afternoon. Sure would appreciate it if y'all'd come over and get it."

"A car."

A momentary buzzing on the line. "Yes, ma'am, that's what I said." Then the sound muffled, as if he had covered the mouthpiece; I heard a blurred shout. "Listen, we're waiting on the New Orleans bus, and this here thing's smack dab in the lane. Rolls-Royce. Registration's in the glove box, plain as can be: Mrs. Anabelle Ransom. I'll have to have it towed if y'all don't hustle. Don't mean to offend, but that's the problem."

I stared at the circle of numbers in its metal wheel. I had never before dialed a series, I was unfamiliar with its operation. Sticking my finger through a hole, I touched the 6, PQR, R for Ransom. "Who is this, please?" I asked.

A gust exploded on the line. "Ma'am, you ain't *supposed* to park cars in the bus lanes, I don't care if it's a damn Sputnik. It'll cost you ten dollars to bail her out at Pomeroy's. He says call him in the morning. I'm sorry, Mrs. Ransom. Gotta go."

I heard the click, and the purr on the line as darkness closed in.

Abandoned

W hen the last thing you remember about someone is the look of her back, flexing towards an unknown destination, the memory might be expected to weigh.

If it were possible to recast that memory, I would imbue Mother's back with special purpose, like a pioneer's cutting forward into the wilderness. As she was, silk-clad, scissoring down the hall in high heels to attend to the last-minute duties of her family, she was only usual. The riddle of Nyla's hiring is what stays with me: a brief glimpse of Mother, and then the closer view of Nyla's face, fastened on the corridor. It is that face which swells to fill the moment.

Sitting next to Father at dinner (who was in fact drunker than usual, swaying dangerously over his soup), I looked around the table. Who was left? The men. Mavis, stoop-shouldered, scarcely eating. And me. Of the four people poised above the tablecloth, only one could be said to be awake; as Grandfather sat immutably beguiled, the old dream sensation descended: I moved slowly among the petrified shapes of former lives.

I did not mention the Greyhound station.

The next morning Father left the house. When he returned, he was driving Mother's Rolls. I watched from the playroom window as he nosed it into the stable. That night we did not speak of her absence; and for several months afterwards, he was usually comatose with liquor.

On the third night after her disappearance, Grandfather asked, "Willie? Where is Anabelle?"

Father did not answer. He tipped the bourbon into his open mouth. But I thought, Well. At last—someone has missed her.

On the fourth morning of her absence, I stepped towards the kitchen for breakfast.

"What you mean, you don't blame her?"

A voice, pitched loud and sharp, cut through the stuffy hall. I stopped. The kitchen was still four yards away; I listened, swaying backwards on my heels.

"Hmph," the voice went on. "It ain't no man, I guarantee. She's got no truck with men. It's something else. Just like Bert did when he skittered off to Europe. But she ain't got no business—"

There was a low mutter. Again Viola cried out. "I tell you why. Because she married into it. She's married in the eye of the Lord, and no matter how low-down she feel, she got to stick by it. If it's hard, then all the more call to stick. Just because that Vic—"

Bessie's mutter rose: "—dead drunk all the time, carrying on fit for a cathouse—sluts from all over town, the nights he don't come home—taking up where Mr. Bert left off—"

"That's her own fault! Now she's got this feeble-minded—" Viola's voice, in turn, sank; I caught only snatches. "—she'll take over— some kind of slave."

I sauntered forward.

Bessie leaped up from the table and ran to bang pots on the stove. Viola's mouth snapped closed. She looked at me once, quickly, and then turned.

"Is breakfast ready?" I asked.

I ate with leisure, sopping my biscuits with molasses, browsing over my toast and bacon. Viola would not even say good morning. Their argument hung like a fog over the table. After a short while, Viola began to rock, her face set balefully in the direction of the back door. Bessie smote the skillet, knocking off egg crusts.

After I left the room, closing the door behind me, I pressed an ear to the wood.

They waited a little. Then came an outburst from Viola.

"She ain't took no clothes. You know that? Not one tiny little scrap. What you reckon that means?"

"Shoo, I'm not saying," Bessie replied. "If it ain't a man, according to you, then I don't reckon nothing. That's all."

"It ain't no *man*, for sure," Viola said in her darkest tone. "But maybe I've figured who it is."

"What do you mean, who it is?"

I had to strain against the door to hear above the rhythmic *chonk*.

"No clothes, the car left setting where Willie Junior had to pick it up. It ain't the first time. Only two people, maybe only one, might be able to say where Mrs. Ransom's gone."

"Who's that?"

No answer.

"Who says, Viola?"

The silence went on, except for a scrape of metal on metal. When Viola spoke again, her voice was low and flat. "She's a Ransom, ain't she? She's a Ransom."

"She was something else first. Besides, what's that got to do with it?"

But Viola did not need to answer.

I walked deliberately up the hall. As I passed the Venetian mirror, the trapped Leviathan of reflection prowled alongside me. I gave no heed, but climbed the staircase. Reaching the landing I had to stop for breath. It was as if Viola's implication had added to my bulk already, draining the heart of power. But I plowed on. When I reached Mother's bedroom, the door was ajar.

The drapes hung drawn over the windows. A chill emanated from the satins and brocades, although the thermostat on the wall was turned up high. A stale musk seemed to rise from the carpet with every step. Mother's perfume blended with it. The tidiness, the neat dresser top, the stark bulbs above the mirror, all seemed prepared. I could sense her presence still, like the ghostly pulse of a missing limb.

There was something to find out. I stepped to the closet and opened it.

The stuffiness ebbed out. All her clothes hung inside; the evening gowns, gleaming with sequins, filmy chiffon; the sable coat; the suits and dresses, linen and tweed, taffetas and velvets; and the rows of shoes, arched insteps ready to receive her narrow feet. I touched the sleeve of a raincoat. A plume, deep purple, curved down from the shelf above and brushed my cheek. It was joined to a pillbox hat. I recalled Mother's face, framed by the dotted veiling, and the plume's sweep towards her throat.

Next I pulled open a drawer filled with nightdresses. The one below it held underwear. I stared at a corsetlike garment, inlaid with lace, and topped with two hard molded breasts. Other items, some just as strange, lay folded underneath it. The drawer was crammed to the brim.

Now Viola's theory began to work in me like yeast. Hastily I ransacked the other drawers: scarves, stockings, bits of batiste, gossamer handkerchiefs. My hands felt grubby touching the stuff. Drawers slid open and slammed. A silk scarf trailed. Leaving the highboy, I ran over to the dressing table. Her crystal vials released scent into the air; my fingers smeared cream across the plate-glass top. Faster and faster I rummaged, overturning jars, scattering scissors, files. When I had finished, I stood panting over the devastation. Mother's artifacts lay everywhere, tumbled or strewn; a dune of pink powder covered the porcelain ballerina's toe.

Slowly I rocked from side to side, wrapping my arms around myself. Had Grant himself kidnapped her, or had he used an accomplice to trick her? If someone—Father, Grandfather—or if I, yes, I, went to Mrs. Farmington and challenged her, would she laugh, or merely act surprised, and then wink broadly as the defeated Ransom slunk away?

I could not keep standing; my legs trembled. I sank to the bed. The mattress hammocked. A tape of light bound the drapes, and I gazed vacantly at the bedside table, illuminated by the glow. Nothing was on it except a rosewood chest. There was a single drawer, which I pulled. A black velvet mask, cut in the shape of a butterfly, was all it contained; the plush wings were spread in flight, and on each was painted a pink petal, the closed lid of a sleeper's eye. I stroked the spokes of paint: lashes like cilia, the species' camouflage. I closed the drawer, and lay back on the bed.

I must have slipped into a doze as the sun rose higher outside. Once I heard Father's voice down in the foyer. Another time I sank into dream, and Mother was standing over my crib, smiling down at me, her face soft as a peony, her eyes dark green jewels, dark from lack of sleep. I knew I was in the hospital; my hand reached out across the crib and fumbled for the pink dog Paddy, but did not find it. All I could do was yearn out to her, stricken with loss and loneliness, while she bent over the bars and said, "What is it, Victoria? What do you want, darling?" and patted my head. I grabbed her pink hand, mashing it against my mouth, sucking on the palm. She frowned and pulled it away.

When I woke, the room had grayed. I struggled up and sat on the bed's edge, staring once more at the rosewood chest. It reminded me of something, some other memory. Hesitantly I touched the carved lid, summoning up an old pleasure that belonged to the childhood before my illness.

Mother smiling: "Victoria, come here to Mama. Come to me, and I'll show you something pretty." Mother seated on this bed's edge, her long legs crossed at the ankles, her hair smooth like lacquer, her skin coraline. The lilting voice: "Victoria, you come to me, now. Look what's inside this magic box." I looked from her face to the carved wood. Her tapered fingers prised the catch. And inside, nested on purple velvet, the frozen dewdrops glittering, flashing; coiled beads shaded like dawn, pearls flushed with pink; a square blue stone licked with cold fire. "See? Mama's jewelry. Isn't it beautiful?" She cupped a blood drop framed in gold. "That's a ruby," she said. "Rubies will be very becoming to you when you grow up, with your coloring. See? Pretty. Slip it on your finger, like that." I looked down at my knuckles; the blood glistened across them. "Here's a necklace." And she giggled as she wrapped the string around my neck. I stared at her, filled with wonder. She seemed made of beauty, all the earth at her command; her tender flesh glowed as she crushed a diamond chain to her throat. She laughed with delight. "Pretty!" she cried. "They're real. Real, Victoria! You'll see." She shoved one, two, three bangles up to my elbow, admiring their settings. "And this one for me." A snake of green and blue cells slithered around her wrist. "Now we're ladies. We're the princesses." Her eyes smiled; she tilted her head before squeezing me close. "Pretty girl," she cooed. "Now back into the magic box until next time," and she gathered the jewels together. The chest swallowed them; the lid dropped. I stared at her, warmed with love.

I had forgotten. Through the years since, I had let it disappear, replaced by Viola's tales.

Until now.

I reached to the catch. With one stumpy nail I popped it open.

Inside was velvet, deep as fur. But nothing else.

For a moment, a feeling welled up, more painful than the hunger in my belly; I pounded a fist into my thigh and groaned with rage. But then I looked again at the chest. Empty, completely empty. What rose then, like a bitter acid, was worse than pain. I felt a taste on my tongue, stinging.

I closed the lid.

Grant did not steal her away.

I hated the missing jewels.

I hate them still. Oh, God, I can feel her yet, sliding the bracelets up my arm. I had never wanted them.

I only wanted her.

THE FOLLOWING morning I met an apparition on the stairs.

For a minute we stood still, confronting one another. She had a blue vinyl suitcase in her left hand, small and peeling. Her face looked pale in the early morning light. She would not gaze at me directly, but kept her eyes on my neck like a refugee. But she was a refugee from the world Mother had joined, and I felt I recognized her for the first time. She belonged here after all.

"Hello, Nyla." I moved aside so she could pass. "Are you moving in now?"

She nodded.

"Did Viola tell you which room is yours?"

I was not ashamed to see that this time she was taking me in, staring without judgment at the necklets of fat, the rolls of my chest, the arms. She went over me to the waist, and then lifted her eyes to mine. They were more candid than they had ever been in the kitchen. I felt a new detachment surge like power. She would do.

"She said to go to the one next to Miss Mavis's. If she's awake, I'm supposed to help her get dressed. Miss Viola told me where her clothes are." Her strange twang sounded less unpleasant to me now.

"Well, I will leave you to it. Good luck." I went on past her. As I reached the stair foot, I turned. Her skull from behind, flat hair and all, looked familiar suddenly. I puzzled over its rounded dome as her foot rose and took the next step.

TWO MONTHS later, Mavis died.

Pneumonia killed her. Doctor Middleton told Grandfather 't was quick and painless, death at a gallop. How could a life invisible t. the naked eye move her to such speed, when she had been so truculent in her solitude?

Grandfather did not attend the service in town. Father got into his car and followed the undertaker's hearse to the mortuary, and went back the next day for the funeral. I wondered where in the Bernice cemetery they would put her. Finally I settled on a spot beside Baby Boy, a few scant yards from the Macafee plot and the heir's phantom grave, parenthesized between fiction and reality.

I went outside into the spring sunlight. Waddling across the arched lake bridge, in the French style that Mother and Grandfather had designed together, I looked down at the two swans lazing in its shadow. Bright molten arrowheads trailed behind them. The wind slapped at my arms and cheeks. New buds pricked the branches with silver; redbuds and dogwoods bloomed. The air smelled sweet. The grass was so green it glowed pure emerald.

"Bun? Is that you?"

I said nothing, but waited there. Father stepped up onto the bridge.

"It's nice to see you out here. Pretty day, isn't it?"

I maintained my silence.

"Would you like to take a walk?"

I turned and stared. He was not drunk, only warmed up.

"Hey. Why don't we get comfortable? Take a seat." He waved vaguely toward the rustic chairs under the trees on the bridge's far side, framed by roses. "Come on, Bun. Let's be sociable."

I stood a moment, dumbfounded. Then I crossed the width of stone to an iron bench.

"That's better." He followed me, reached for the hip flask in his back pocket, and unscrewed it. "You know, Bun, seems like we hardly ever do anything together. It doesn't seem right."

My jaw dropped.

"I was just thinking as I drove home——" He took a sip from the flask. The wind battened his hair. "Funerals aren't something I particularly enjoy. You know? But somebody's got to do it. Now, what kind of a day have you had today?"

"Ah——a pensive day, Father."

"A what?"

"I have been thinking."

He peered hard at me, head cocked. "Is that a fact?"

"Yes, sir."

He marveled. "Well, that's not something I do a whole lot of myself." He scratched his nose. "Today I have been. Coincidence, huh? Us both at it. But mostly it just gives me a headache. A day like this, though, is just bound to make you think. What do you figure?"

"It does prompt unwonted cerebration."

He looked pleased suddenly, and astonished. "You sure seem to know some big words, Bun."

"Grandfather makes books available to me."

"Well, of course he would. Surely. What else have you done today?"

"Nothing, really. I came out here." Perhaps he did not realize how extraordinary this was.

"I guess you must know these grounds as well as I did when I was a child." He smiled, looking around at the formal gardens, the Greek summerhouse at the lake's wider end, the oak copses. "Of course, it's changed some. Additions everywhere. Do you stroll around much, run through the pastures and all?"

"No."

"Oh. What stops you?" He blinked, smiling.

I shrugged. "Weather," I said drily.

"Is that a fact?"

I winced slightly and looked down at my lap. "You do the same. Does it not make a difference, say, if you plan to play golf and it looks like it might rain?"

"Well, I suppose so." He sighed. "Your mother was like that, too. Couldn't hardly tear herself out of bed in the morning if she thought her hairdo might get rained on." He raised the flask.

I said nothing.

"She was a real stickler for good weather," he mused.

I waited. My breath seemed to have stopped somewhere in my chest. He had not mentioned Mother since she had left.

"What she liked best was to open her drapes just a tad, to check on the sky. Then if everything was to her liking, she would get all primped up and go out to lunch somewhere. She was like that back when I first knew her, too. I came by her sorority house one day, me and Bert I mean, to pick her up, and she met us in the vestibule. 'Boys, I'm not sticking one toe out in that mess, even to go to classes—it's going to pour cats and dogs.' We couldn't budge her." He smiled fondly. "She used to call Bert a lunatic who didn't know enough to get out of the rain, because one time he'd carried her through it, whooping like an Injun and making her scream, and then he'd threatened to hold her down and not let her go inside. It was a spring storm—rain in sheets and blankets. She like to had a fit, her hair all hanging down in rat's tails."

"Oh."

"She was—she had a lot of personality back then. Prettiest girl on campus. You can just imagine how honored I felt when she consented to become my wife. Like to bowl everybody over. Except for Bert, he didn't seem too surprised somehow. But then, him and me, we always did everything together. I guess Bert figured if I was marrying her, he'd be kind of marrying her too." He swished whiskey around in his mouth. "You know the funny thing about that was, that was kind of how I figured it too. I just kind of believed it, deep down—never crossed my mind it would be otherwise. But of course, that's not the way it turned out. Bert was best man, of course. After the wedding he stood in front of Anabelle and me and said, "I'm off to Europe this afternoon." You could have knocked me down with a feather. Anabelle didn't say a word, just watched him march out of the church, her hand where Bert had stuck it in mine. We couldn't hardly look at one another." He chuckled and yawned. But then he stared straight at me. His eyes had the bright sheen of the reckless tippler. "I'll bet you didn't know any of that stuff, about your Mother and me. Did you, Bun?"

I swallowed the lump in my throat. "No."

"See what I mean?" He dwelled sentimentally on my face. "Now we've just got each other. My little girl. My little raisin bun. You remember when I used to call you that, when you were just a baby?

When I used to snuggle you up in my lap and say, 'You're my little raisin bun, I'll eat you right up.' Remember that? And then your mother would yell that I was spoiling you. You were—you were what I had been given to love, out of this whole world. Look at you now. You don't seem spoiled to me." He sighed.

The wind snatched the new clover at our feet.

Father closed his eyes.

"My very own daughter. Who'd have thought I could have a daughter of my own? If it had been Bert, now, that got you going, well, I wouldn't have been so surprised. But it was me. Nobody else but me.

"I was never so amazed in my life, when your mother told me what was going to happen. She was kind of mad about it—oh, not that she didn't want you, of course. Just right at first, just when she found out what was making her feel kind of sickish in the mornings. Couldn't hardly believe it. Well, neither could I, considering. I guess we were both ignorant. Then when you came, I was just thrilled to death. Me, a daddy? Me, getting a fine pretty woman like your mother with a baby?"

He shook his head, still baffled after all those years. His eyes opened. "You just name it. I'll do anything for you, Bun. Anything in the world. Especially now she's—funny I haven't thought of it before." He nodded deeply. "Only thing I ever did in my whole life, having you get born. A half-breed for sure."

I sat in wonder.

"Maybe you'd like to go into Bernice."

My breath halted.

"We were ten or so when we left the house and went to Bernice. No, more like eight. And Baby Boy, he was—" But suddenly he frowned. "Anyhow," he said quickly, "never mind that.

"I reckon you're old enough to leave the house yourself now if you want to. How old are you, Bun? Ten? Eleven?" He began to count on his fingers, elaborately, while I sat back, watching the sunlight play over his thin face.

"Eight," he said. "No, that can't be right. Let's see, eleven, twelve." He started on the first hand again. His innocence seemed to wrap around him like a pale soft shroud.

"Thirteen!" he cried, and lifting, smiled at me. "That's right, now, isn't it, Bun?"

"No, Father," I said, carefully and clearly. "I am fifteen."

"You're not!"

"Yes. I will be sixteen in seven months' time, in October."

"Oh, my," he murmured. "Oh, my."

"To tell the truth, Father," I said, "I would prefer not to go into Bernice—downtown."

"You—is that a fact, Bun?"

"Yes," I said gently. "It is."

"Oh." He spread the ineffectual fingers on his thighs. "You know what? I would like to give you something . . . something special. Tell me. What would you like more than anything in the whole world?"

What can one answer to such a question? I gazed around at the glinting lake, the red roses, the iron bench beneath me.

He scrubbed his hands together, helplessly.

"Your offer is very kind," I said.

"No, it's not—kindness," he said. His eyes were imploring, but not pitying. "I just want to make you happy."

I could not imagine "happiness." He needed my request more than I needed anything.

"There is something you could give me that I would like very much," I said slowly. His shoulders relaxed from their hunched position.

"What, Bun? You name it."

"Well, there is a room I am very fond of. Now that Moth—I like to sit in it. But because the furniture is—a little flimsy, I have always to sit on the rim of the fountain, which is brickwork and grows uncomfortable and chilly. The conservatory, you know." I drew a breath, to see how he would react; but he listened, staring into the clover. "Nyla has been taking care of the plants since—for the last two months. She waters them every day, and does a bit of pruning. I often join her there. I enjoy it."

"I've only been there a few times," he mumbled. "Not lately, though."

"It is a very beautiful room. It receives the best of the light, you see."

"Bun?" His voice sounded a little forlorn. "What if I got some carpenter to build you your very own seat, right there in the conservatory? It could be strong enough—you know what I mean? He could build it right there, not even have to get it through the door. Then you'd be able to go in there anytime. Hey, Bun! What do you think of that idea, eh?"

"That would be splendid."

"You'd like that? So you could use that room whenever you wanted—no problems?" His gradual brightening touched me, his face beaming.

"It would be a lovely gift, Father."

"Well! Seems like I remember one or two things from the woodworking classes down at Sauter. I'll pick over the old brain, see what I can come up with."

I hid my smile, glancing down at my lap. The smile felt strange in its spontaneity, and I realized why. I was smiling with happiness, the pleasure of having done something for him. I was a fact.

NOW HE always came home. No longer did the assignations in town lure him away for days at a time. The pendulum of the grandfather clock would swing in its wooden case and cancel out the endless half-hours, while I sat in the drawing room. The house would be so still that the sound carried through the library door and across the foyer.

Finally the front door would open. My father would shut it carefully. Then he would turn around and sway toward the sofa. He walked like a cow walks in a strong wind at those times, or as if he were swimming. But he talked more, and more clearly, as his coordination declined.

"You there, Bun?" he would ask.

"Yes, Father. I thought I would wait up for you."

"You should be in bed by now, Bun."

I would go to the sideboard and fetch the decanter for him.

"I am never in bed before one or two anyway."

After a short time, these preambles became unnecessary. I would have the decanter ready and waiting for him on the coffee table, and watch as he sank into the cushions.

"I told old Girt Taylor today what I thought. You know that, Bun?"

"What you thought about what, Father?"

He sighed and nudged off his shoes without untying them.

"Why, what I thought about the price of oil."

"Did he agree with you that monopoly control would force it to rise?"

"Yep, he did. Won't be long before it goes up to sixteen, eighteen cents a gallon. That's gasoline. Oil by the barrel, why, *that* would be—you mark my words."

He fancied himself a canny prophet.

"Nothing surprises me these days. Russians sending monkeys up in spaceships, those satellites whirling around the earth like tennis balls."

"Like what Jules Verne once wrote about."

"Jules who?"

"Never mind."

"You are a very smart child for your age, Bun." He spoke admiringly. "You must get it from your granddaddy. You sure don't get it from me; and your mother, wherever she is, is definitely not winning any sets of encyclopedias on a quiz program." He snorted lightly with laughter. "She was—is—a lovely woman, your mother. Don't you forget it. I married her for her loveliness, and her—lively grace. A real Southern woman." His voice grew reedy, thin with sentiment, and his bony arms gestured in air. "She was like a ripe peach when I met her. But no Einstein."

"No."

"Her mind was as gossamer as her being."

"Yes."

"When she crossed a room, she gave the impression that she was floating. Sometimes I said to myself, 'Well, William Garner Ransom Junior, you have married a creature of light and air—that is, if light and air can have curves—and you need to watch out that nothing burns her up or blows her away. Not even your own desires." The alcohol often released a streak of hidden poetry in him. "That is how I saw her, Bun. Oh, she appeared as a ripe peach. But light and air, was all. There are certain ideas a man must not entertain, Bun. Whether he's a gentleman or not. It simply wasn't practical." He hicupped.

"No?"

"You are, of course, too young yet to know what I mean. When you get married to some boy, you'll find out. The curse of Adam."

I pushed into the shadows of my chair.

"All men are made with one particular curse built into their systems. It can strip them of their nobler impulses."

I thought of Grant Macafee, and nodded.

"It can make them—betray the most beautiful, the finest, the most angelic of women." He paused. "I didn't watch out hard enough, did I, Bun?"

"What, Father?"

"Something blew her away after all."

"Oh." I let the darkness congest, peering through it at Father. His pecan-shaped head was touched by the gold from the foyer sconce. "Father, you must not blame yourself so. Mother was merely a woman. If she was frigid—"

"Bun!" He flinched with alarm.

"Well, one must face facts. Even when you were in college together, from what you have said—remember when you told me what she said, when she returned after she and Bert had disappeared at the same time at that sorority dance? About not forcing anything on a girl? Surely you can deduce—"

He wore a pained expression. "We decided to *marry* that night."

I said no more for a few moments.

"You must not blame yourself for not knowing how to love her, Father. It is not your fault. It was really always out of your hands."

"For not loving her, you say?" he repeated in a foggy voice. He poured some whiskey, lifting the glass carefully level. "You're wrong there, Bun. I loved her. I just didn't practice it on her. I couldn't ask her to satisfy such a base, a wicked—"

I rose from the chair, and knelt on the floor beside him, picking up one of his feet and massaging the sole. The foot was slender; the ankle bones jutted knobby and frail under the papery skin.

"My feet don't stink, do they?"

"No." I replaced the right foot on the floor and picked up the left. "Are you still going deer hunting with Girt Taylor and your other friends next week?"

"I reckon so." Father had a deer lease in the hills near Kerrville, to which he repaired every year with his cronies. He had described it to me many times, lovingly and in detail, a landscape that possessed a rare reality for him. But my reading of *African Game Trails* had filled my mind with the sight and sound of other images: the crisp hollow shot from the gun, the tawny pelt spangling with red, the knees buckling forward under the weight of a rack of antlers.

Abruptly I said, "You know, Father, I do not think I have much of a bloodlust."

"Is that a fact?" His chin rose a little into the pale sconce light. "Why, that's mighty strange. Everybody else in this family—well, except Baby Boy, he didn't like killing things. But your great-grandmother Arliss Ransom was a crack shot. You ever hear anybody mention her?"

My hands froze on the foot. I put it gently down. "Was she? I did not know that."

"She was famous. She could hit anything, anything at all. She'd go traipsing out in the fields with the men. Knock the eye out of a rabbit at two hundred yards if she wanted to. But she died long before I was born, before Daddy got his wife. Daddy and Aunt Mavis used to talk about her." He shook his head. "She even taught Mavis to shoot."

"What?"

How was it Viola had never revealed this factor?

"You'd never credit it, would you? Of course Mavis couldn't take very good aim, on account of her back and all. My grandmother Arliss taught them how to shoot, and Daddy taught me and Bert."

"Uncle Bert could shoot?"

"He sure could. If he'd been awake with a gun in his hand when that burglar——" He drifted to silence. I heard the clock winding up.

"When we went off to Sauter Academy we took all the top prizes on the rifle range every single year. Bert was Class Sharpshooter."

"Did you win medals?"

"Yep. I did." He mused a moment. "We're going to have another Sauter boy hunting with us this year, I hear. A young'un. What did his daddy say? A junior at Sauter? Well, Bun. I reckon I should stumble on up to bed. A little bit teetery, but I reckon the old boy can make it."

As he lurched up the stairs, one step at a time, his long stork legs seemed weighted at the feet, and his oval face shone out of the stairwell dusk.

"Father?" I called. He turned.

"Bring back some venison for Bessie to barbecue."

"I'll do that, Bun. I know how you like it."

I watched until he had disappeared around the landing. Then I locked the front door and turned off the single sconce. The drawing room swelled around me, into a cavern of night, and then the night itself, starless, a reach of space that went on and on. The chair made no sound as I came to rest on its still point. Above my head in the void, Grandfather slept; Nyla slept; Viola dreamed of long-dead children or her obsession. But now I had Father.

I would sit until dawn pearled the sky, assimilating the new parts of myself, acquainting my being with the tales of hunting, Mavis's shooting lessons, Father's desire for Mother, the interactions with the citizens of outside that I would never meet; weaving the fresh information into my flesh and sinews, intent on my solitary appointed profession. It seemed there was a great deal Viola had left out. I could feel my blood spin through the arteries to the different zones, taking the knowledge with it.

There is so much that is tenuous in life: a crumb of phrase, a half-remembered chill; faint webbed patterns that lie invisible in the mist until you begin to track them strand by strand.

TWO DAYS after Father went off to Kerrville deer hunting, I sat in the conservatory drying in the sun from my bath.

The fountain pool had been cold. I wrapped a blanket around myself and collapsed on Father's gift. Behind the nymphs the pool lay flat, and a soap scum opalized the surface. I was tired from floundering in and out of the water. But it had been several years since I could squeeze into a bathtub, and on the day I had got wedged in the shower stall, and Nyla had had to bring a can of shortening from the kitchen to grease me out, I had abandoned dignity. Usually Nyla dried me off afterwards and rubbed the chafed places I could not get to, the spots under my heavy breasts and crevices absorbing us both. It was through an Archimedean experiment with the fountain, in fact, that I had lately ascertained a calculation of what I now weighed: according to water displacement, roughly five hundred pounds. I was still expanding.

Certain thoughts led to certain others as I sat drying: the water, the season, my trouble to keep clean among the rank sweetnesses of hot-house blossoms—and suddenly I was remembering a summer years before Mother left—a day of blanched skies, too hot to endure outdoors. I was twelve years old. I stood in the playroom, looking out over the lawns. The sprinklers spun round and round, lacing the yellow with arcs of crystal. The sun seemed like a hole burned into the sky.

I caught sight of movement: two men, no more than boys, were walking towards the ornamental lake. For a second I thought they must be visitors. Then I realized they were two carpenters from the workshop, stripped to the waists. As they neared the lake, I saw one of them fumble at his fly. Then they climbed onto the bridge. With a swift motion one skinned down his pants, shucking them off his feet. The other did the same. Then together, in a sinuous double brown curve, they dove forward into the waters.

Two heads, moisture darkened, bobbed up a few yards apart. They swam straight for the bridge, silver shattering behind them. Under the arch they stopped and dog-paddled in place; the shadows all but hid them in black gauze.

I ran from the window.

There had been no provision in Viola's stories for this.

Now, suddenly, as the memory came back, a pang of something I could not identify came with it. I shuddered, clutching the blanket, quaking uncontrollably. For awhile the shivering ache of loss made me mumble my own name out loud: "Victoria. Victoria," until I overheard myself and stopped. So for once, the distraction of those longings stifled my hearing, and caused me to miss what I should have known might come.

Someone had entered the conservatory.

I felt the presence before I glanced up. Through the fern, I saw Grandfather, blinking myopically. He stood uncertainly, out of his element; his shoulders hunched. I had never seen him look so random, as if bits of his misered thoughts had come loose. What little hair he had left stuck out like a zinnia. His tie was askew, the cardigan gaped over his paunch. One hand raked his jaw.

"Victoria?"

The whisper was dust, scattering from his lips.

"Are you—Victoria?"

I gathered the blanket tight, and stood up.

"Ah, there you—" He shuffled, eyes round.

"What is it, Grandfather? What has happened?"

The familiar tension numbed. I felt nothing, nothing. My voice was cool as the water.

"They called up to tell me. I thought it was the accountant at first, you see—"

"Who did?"

"Oh. That Girt Taylor. Couldn't be a thing done. I never have—"

I stood still, seeing him pass through a transformation of stages: youth, middle age, childhood, all with this one state in common, fixed to its blind helplessness.

"I did not hear the telephone. I can hear it through the wall."

"Well. Girt Taylor, he—" Grandfather pitched a little, righting himself. "I don't know where Viola's got to. Can't seem to grasp what—"

"Father," I stated, knowing now.

"Yes. In the hospital down there. I don't know what we can do. There's not a thing—never has been. They're operating now, Girt Taylor said. Cutting his arm off. I don't even know Girt Taylor, can't recollect who he could be, unless one of the Taylors from the old house on Sycamore. . . ."

"He is not dead," I said.

"No, he was using the telephone, so he must be—"

"Father, I mean."

"No." He seemed to struggle, to pull himself intact. "He's not dead." He paused. "He's badly hurt, though."

"Shot."

"Yes."

The silence fell, in the weak watery sunlight.

"How?" Father, I thought. *Father*.

He rubbed his ribs, unconsciously straightening the cardigan. "It was an accident. They don't know rightly who—fired the—some hunter, but they can't figure out which—it got him right below the elbow. It splintered the bone."

"He's losing it," Grandfather said. "They're operating on him now. Cutting it off."

It was a few moments before I could speak.

"Do you know who was on the hunting trip?"

"Why, the usual bunch, I guess. Don't know who all your daddy— Girt Taylor. I believe that Farmington fellow, you know, the one who's—the Rutherford boys. That crowd he grew up with. . . ." Then in my mind, I bent down; and fishing through the mist, retrieved the word I had missed, the one that had been hidden from immediate sight and hearing.

"Mr. Farmington," I said softly. "Oh, yes. The junior from Sauter. Of course."

"Junior?"

He came forward a little, squinting. The sun had grown stronger. The cloud cover must have dispersed.

"Randall Farmington. He went on the hunting trip this time with Father. The son of Mary Sue Farmington."

Then I said, "He is Grant Macafee's young cousin and heir."

Grandfather did not move.

A fern leaf stabbed against my throat. I sidled away from it. Somewhere inside me, from a place I had not known of, a cold bulb of anger smoldered, igniting as I stared at him.

For a moment his face retained the fuzzed look of an old man groping through brambles. His lips opened and closed, working on something they could not finish.

Then, as I watched, the stupor fell away.

His shoulders set inside the cardigan. The plane of his jaw solidified, cut square above the pillared neck. His eyes suddenly focused

380

on me, wonderingly, as if recognizing my entirety for the first time.

"Grant, you say.

"His heir, you say," he said.

I nodded.

"I didn't know he had one."

There was about him the poise of the carpenters, pondering the water before they got ready to dive.

"Oh, yes," I said.

The anger and ruthlessness flamed.

Then I said, into the silence, "Apparently Grant has taught him how to shoot."

The sunlight gathered and glowed around us, on the brick floor, on the plants, striping Grandfather with gold bars.

"I'll take care of it." His voice rang full and firm. Before he turned to go, he said, "Tell Viola about it, will you, please?" Without waiting for my answer, he walked away.

IT WAS, in fact, an hour before I saw Viola again.

I was still in the conservatory when I heard the long shrill wail. But I did not hurry. Instead I peeled the blanket slowly and emerged from the cocoon. Then I put on the muu-muu, already getting too small: last year's dress. Then, with a measured pace, I went towards the unwinding banner of sound.

At the kitchen's threshold, I paused.

Viola's face was thrown backwards towards the ceiling. The scream had become convulsive gasps; her eyes rolled in her head, white rimmed. Her mouth made a round O of darkness. Bessie stood at her side, trying to wrench her down into the rocker. Her hands were ashy; she was snatching at Viola's apron, flecked with what looked like vomit, and the toes of her tennis shoes were stained red.

When Bessie saw me, she began to gabble. Through Viola's pants and shrieks, I caught some of what she said. "He just kneeling there, kneeling—down on his knees—oh, Viola!—kneeling there on the sawhorse—saw motor still going! Oh, my God—saw blade still spinning around—" She began to whine, high up in her throat. In between she went on wrenching Viola's apron. "—couldn't see— nothing—till we went on around. His head," she moaned, "his head—"

"Sit down here," I commanded. "Sit down now, while I call the doctor. It is all taken care of now. Both of you," I said sternly, "sit down."

Valedictory

The years revolve in a circle, around and around, and just as you think the circle must be complete, you discover you have been deluded.

"WHAT ARE you going to do?" she had asked him once in the balm of a summer night, when he put Sarah's letter away. Her voice came at him almost dreamily, trusting, still bemused with his new adulthood—the boy she had raised. "What are you going to do?"

He answered her, and the answer was the primary choice of that new manhood, fostering decades to come. He squinted up at a cluster of stars above the black treetops. "All we can ever do in this life is to leave each other alone."

Out of love, he had said. That's the main thing.

Another time, and now there was bewilderment in the question. She was finding him consistent. "What are you going to do?"

Nothing, he said. Nothing.

And still she did not leave off asking, goaded presently by anger, indignation, the sting of the victim. *There would never be enough payment.* "What are you going to do now?"

And the answer stayed the same. Then the price climbed, the blackmail of a monstrous ego suffering its humiliation. Now there was blood. And her question rang with anguished rage. "What are you going to do?"

This time there was no answer at all.

But he had not known I understood.

AFTER THE doctor had come and sedated Viola, he conferred briefly with me. Then he was gone, out to the workshop, to lower Grandfather's body to the floor. I sat alone in the library, mulling over the crowning act of William's life: his one response to his enemy.

The phrase that kept returning to me was the initial one, spoken so long ago in the first flush of confidence between him and Viola. Out of love, he had said. Out of love.

The leather chair would not bear me. I had to sit on the settee. Above my head rose the tiers of books, bound in cloth and leather. Galleries of philosophy, centuries of history: Voltaire, Goethe, Tocqueville, the Bible, Jung, Rousseau, Nostradamus, on and on. Suddenly they tore me with impatience—for *this* he had allowed the sacrifices, for his pathetic peace he had let it happen, over and over, until now it was Father, and the anger drove me to spur the truth, bring his death. Love! Love for whom?

I studied the framed photographs. The most recent was one of myself as a baby. The tiny girl in a frilled bonnet stared back, solemn, delicate, her minute features like parings arranged on a saucer. She waved a fist at the onlooker, in tranquil pastlessness.

Mother and Father cutting the wedding cake; Bert and Father as boys (all images of Baby Boy were stored in Mavis's albums); William's cap and gown; Sarah in her ball dress; Arliss snapped in an arbor. The last one to catch my eye was the picnic shot taken that summer of 1920. Sarah again, on the day of her proposal: the day that had started it all; her hat sloping over her eyes. There sat Mavis, snugged across her brother's arm, begging for a pat. William's white face cast forever in the amicable grin, the squint, the lazy posture.

And somewhere behind the car, the unseen picnicker hanging back, refusing to come out and declare himself. As I stared at the photograph, I thought: Grant is the only one still alive. He, of all the people in it, can still change. Perhaps he is changing already, his gaunt face registering surprise that the war is now over.

I left the pictures and gazed at the window.

The anger and scorn dissolved, leaving me empty. Bereft. Out of love, the words repeated. Love for all of us.

Now I comprehended.

He alone, besides me, would have understood Grandfather's martyrdom. He alone could have perceived the gesture of love and respect and guilt, a final rendering of the bill, which defeated and yet failed to defeat. No one else in the family, or Bernice, or the world, would know what Grandfather's suicide had meant. All was paid. All was consummated.

Father was safe at last.

A KNOCK sounded on the door. I called, "Come in." I steeled myself for the ordeal of the doctor's sympathy. But the door opened, and instead of the doctor I saw Nyla.

Her face could have been a mirror, so completely did I feel the lack of expression on my own. For a moment she said nothing; we stared at one another with wary stillness: two fugitives come to rest.

"I was upstairs cleaning," she said then. "I was upstairs when I heard."

And then I recalled her absence from the kitchen, as Viola screamed and panted. I had felt at the time that something was missing, but the confusion had overridden its identity.

I nodded.

"Miss Bessie and me put Miss Viola in bed." She jerked her head towards the stairs.

"Good. Thank you." Still she waited.

"He's killed himself," she stated.

"Yes."

"It's him I have to thank, isn't it?"

"What?"

The words seemed to bring on a dream; I could not for a second decode their meaning, and felt myself sinking into dizzy fatigue.

"It's him I have to thank," she said. "When I was working in the orphanage. I was too big and growed to be an orphan anymore. A growed woman, nowhere to go." Her head thrust forward. "It was him and his lawyers that brought me here."

"Oh. I see."

"He tell you where he'd got me from?"

"Well . . . he just suggested. That was all."

She pondered. "I was glad." Steadily she stared at me. "I'm real sorry now he's gone."

"Yes." I thought of Father, sleeping safe now, one-armed. The grandfather who had always loved me—

"I like it here." She nodded slowly. "You won't make me leave and go back to live in that State Home now he's gone, will you?"

"No."

She gave me a last stare, of surprising penetration.

"Thank you."

She turned away. For an instant she stood staring into the foyer. Her shoulders squared up within her gingham dress. The back of her skull had that peculiar round curve; it struck me again, seeming once more inevitably familiar. Then she went out and shut the door behind her.

V*iola*

"Long time after your granddaddy put up that stone," Viola began, "the day you and me walked over and saw it bitting on down, I said to him: 'I seen what you did when you got it carved. I went over it real good this afternoon, and you know what I find?'"

"He smiled at me over his book. 'What did you find, old lady?'"

"'I find a crack plumb down the back of it, that's been there ever since it was first drug out the quarry. It's got the carver's name on the back. And those letters are split on purpose, and planned that way from the start.'"

"He say to me, 'What are you trying to get me to admit? You reckon I got any secrets from you?' I look at him real sharp.

'Nawsuh. There ain't nothing you can hide from Viola. Seem like to me, though, if you want to make folks welcome, you got a right to let the welcome fall to pieces after while. Like maybe that's what you had in mind, when you picked out a great big old rock you know was bound to break and carry your word right down with it.' He say, 'Well, this is how it is. If folks can't get used to the good intention after a few years, then it isn't going to take. And if they do get used to it, then they won't need a stone to spell it out to them.' He smiled. 'I never desired to fix any conditions as permanent, Viola, even an invitation. That would be hubris. Time and the nature of things wouldn't let me get away with it. The gods punish us for pride.'

"I jumped up then and hollered, 'You got punished anyhow. That's what your old "invitation" done invite—you know how. You asked the devil to come to this house, and you lost Baby Boy.'

"He don't answer me. He just let the smile go, and then after while he went back down buried in his book, like I ain't there at all."

She scowled at the air conditioner vent. "Why ain't you turn that thing down, Victoria? It's too cold on my old bones, you go over to the doodaddy and switch it low."

"It is more comfortable for Father," I said. "But I will lower it a few degrees until he comes down."

I rose and fingered the thermostat.

"Did he say anything else?"

"How come you asking for? All you done for over a year now is ask me questions."

"Only because you are willing to tell me."

A change had come over her after Grandfather's death. She attended the funeral as chief mourner, and came home in the mortuary limousine, stupid with grief. It was months before she could tell me that Grant Macafee had not attended the service. She had spoken with me ever since, sometimes freely, sometimes with caution. She still suspected me of an alien nature, but she no longer recognized that she had instilled it. But these days I was goaded always by the family curse, and I had to pump her for every particle she could express.

"He say one thing about that stone. He say he reckon it's the only thing we got a right to mess with, the thing that ain't perfect in the first place. That's before he went back to reading, there in his chair."

I nodded, and sat on the table.

Nyla was mopping the floor, ignoring us as usual. She had not said more than a few words to anyone since the day more than a year before, when she had found me alone in the library and got my assurance that she would never have to leave. "Father will be waking soon," I said. "Is his lunch ready to take up?"

"I thought he's coming down to lunch this day," Bessie grumbled from the counter.

"He had a headache."

"Again!" She twisted around to me. "That's the third day running. You best get the doctor out here." With painful motions she patted the top of a meatloaf smooth; her hands had grown increasingly arthritic lately, and I knew she wanted a chance to see the doctor for a pain prescription. Bessie took mild morphine now.

"No. Father prefers to battle the headaches himself. A doctor cannot really help. You know what causes them."

"All that liquor!" Viola slammed the rocker forward. "He like to salt himself away."

"It keeps the aching at bay."

"Hmmph." She gnawed her lower lip. "There's better ways to do that."

"He has not discovered any."

"It's a crying shame he lost that arm. It ain't so bad he done stopped tom-catting round and fooling on the golf course all day. But taking his whole entire arm clean off! I ain't never understood how come they ain't figured out where the shot come from. It don't mystify me."

"Don't mystify you!" Bessie exclaimed. "There's plenty mystery in this house. They ain't caught Mr. Bert's killer in all these years, have they?"

"It don't mystify me," Viola said somberly, and fixed her dark gaze on me.

I took a hunk of bread and jelly from the plate. Silence fell on the kitchen, broken only by the swish of the mop. Then Nyla finished, and disappeared through the hall. Bessie sighed, rubbed her hands, and went out to her little house for an afternoon nap. "You daddy's tray ready when he wake up," she said. We watched the back door swing closed.

"I'm getting too old," Viola said. "I just sit waiting, waiting for change to come, and dreading it."

"What could you expect to change?" I asked.

"Oh, I don't know." She heaved back on the pad. "Something fine, maybe. Something different from what I always seen."

"But there has always been change here."

"Guess it's not rightly just change I'm talking about."

"There were times when you could have . . ." I did not finish.

"Could have what, Miss Smarty?" She scowled. "Don't you go telling me what I could have done."

"I suppose you mean a change authored by someone else besides Grant Macafee."

"Hmmph. He don't always get the last say no more." She ruminated, in her face a trace of bewilderment. "Last thing that happened, he didn't have a say. That's what got me dogged." Her frown deepened. "Time was, I could always figure on it. It ain't right that the main thing be different. Mr. William. My own boy."

"It is interesting, what you said a few minutes ago about the stone." I wanted to change the subject; her distress bothered me, and I had no intention of relieving it with the truth.

"Honey, your granddaddy was always an interesting man."

She had not called me honey in years. I put the bread down on the plate, and for a moment could not speak.

"Viola. Do you not like things the way they are now?"

She shrugged. "They all right."

"I mean, living here as we do, you telling me of your life—"

"Ain't *my* life I tell you about."

"Oh, yes," I said quietly. "Yes, it is. You have given me your life the same way you gave me everyone else's. Do you not know that?"

Her eyes widened and then narrowed. "I ain't never done. You don't know what I come from, what my own mama and daddy be like—you don't know nothing about it."

"I did not have to."

She remained silent for a long while. Her eyelids lowered, brooding.

"You was my child once, same as the others." Her voice dragged. "Then somehow you changed. Not like the others. You changed inside yourself, and got me all—I ain't never known what to make of it."

I said nothing.

She twisted her hands fretfully in her lap. "Could have just let you be. But you was what the Lord give me, after Baby Boy was gone, and your daddy and Mr. Bert grow up."

"Yes."

"So I tried to make it all right for you. All I could do."

I said nothing.

"You give me back something for a bit. But then directly—"

She shook her head tiredly.

For an instant, no more, I considered giving her something. The words were on my tongue: the few scant words which would give her back her sense of coherence and pattern. I remembered the scene under the ferns, Grandfather standing in just this frail hapless attitude, befuddled with a fresh disaster; and then the drawing up, the calm purpose in his eyes.

"I recollect when Baby Boy first come," she said.

"Yes?" I answered softly.

"When Mr. William first seen him, how it come over him what the truth was. That baby laying there on the bed in the early morning."

Her yellow eyes kindled, the pupils dilating. She put out a foot to shove the rocker backwards. "'In the midst of death we are in life,'" she repeated. "That's what he say, there on the stair. Then he climbed on up to see the very same baby the flowers come for." She laughed richly.

"What do you think he meant by it, exactly?"

"Why, honey, it's a joke—can't you see?"

"I realize that. But he meant something more, beyond a joke. Do you not think so?"

Her forehead wrinkled. She mulled this. "Could be. He was always a deep one, my Mr. William. Had him a fine sense of humor, though."

"It is not very humorous, to cut off your own head with a buzz saw," I observed, and Viola frowned.

"You don't talk disrespectful about him. You quit that."

"I am sure his sense of humor was well honed," I said. She glanced at me, with the look of doubt and estrangement. "That is a kind of joke, also. The saw . . ."

"I don't got to like it, do I?"

"Anyhow, I have always been intrigued by what he said about death and life. I remember his sense of humor when he would bother to talk. But those last few years he did not do much of that."

"I ain't *never* understood just why he done what he did with that saw," she said tiredly.

Now the moment had come, if it ever would. I assessed her carefully, thinking in my arrogance that I would be able to tell. "Yes, you have."

She looked at me sideways. Her mouth set.

"We both know why he did it," I insisted pleasantly, but there was entreaty behind the pleasance. "Or one of the reasons, at least."

She swung straight and faced me full on.

"No, ma'am, Victoria." Her voice was loaded, intense. "I ain't seen what you driving at."

"You're avoiding it," I said, pleading, "the same way Mavis tried to avoid you, that first night of the baby. You told her she did not know what she was taking on. Obviously she did. She simply did not want to know."

"That's a long time back now." She hedged away, from the great long fatigue that had followed her to the present moment, sick of the war, sick of the terms she had lived on throughout the decades of siege.

A resentment flooded me, goading me on. "Not for me. When I

hear you talk about it, it is the same as if it were yesterday, or today." The anger prickled under my skin, like blood stinging in the veins.

"It's just a story," she said, turning away. "I just tell you the stories, that's all I do."

"But it happened! I can see it happening." The anger held with it a strange elation, a fury of discovery. I would make her admit at last what she had done. "It is as real as this bread and jelly to me." You have made me what I am, Viola! Do you not understand? "You will not admit that you know why Grandfather killed himself. You do not wish to admit that Grant Macafee finally won."

"*Won?*" Her head flew up. "He ain't got nothing to do with it, that Grant Macafee!" Her eyes looked helpless, even as they narrowed down.

"Did he not?"

"Won!" But suddenly she was electrified with suspicion. "That old hound, sitting out there on his ranch." She glared. "You getting too smart for your britches, Victoria." I had finished the bread. She hesitated; then, as if reminding me of what I was, shoved the plate of cookies towards me.

"I ain't telling you no more," she declared.

I saw how completely she chose not to know. "Do not get angry. I am not smart. I am merely interested." It was too late, all too late. I saw now. She would have to be spared.

I reached out for a cookie, and noticed with surprise that my hand trembled.

"Your stories are much more interesting than the books I read," I placated her. "I am sorry I interrupted. Would you please go on with the rest?"

She paused, and thought for a moment, head cocked up. "Did I ever tell you about what Dandy said, that time I seen her at the funeral—about how Mr. Grant carried on, and wouldn't let the coffin be open for the service—how he told Mrs. March when she come running back from San Antonio on the train that he don't want nobody looking down on his dead child?"

"You told me." The thousands of repetitions swung in my head, and I settled back in that dark revolving voice, a cookie in my hand.

"Well, then——" she said.

SHE REACHED the part where the band stood on the depot platform. The cicadas buzzed in the stubbled grass; Viola was walking past, her head held high, looking at the amazing sight standing in the August sunlight from the corner of her eye. The men in their dark foreign glamour grinned as she approached. Behind her was the courthouse square, the patch of land she had known all her life; ahead of her, under the sycamores and elms, was the cemetery. The funeral waited, the panoply of Macafee pride. But the grins were flashing and gleaming at her from the platform. And suddenly another gleam struck her: the sunlight glancing off nickel silver.

"Hey there, pretty sister. Where you high-stepping to so fast?"

For a second the words joined the flashing trumpet.

She flung back her head.

"Whooee!" The call came from his mouth, and it hit her in the same place.

The sound of his chuckle followed. He nudged the man next to him. But she would not look; not yet. "Them Texas gals look mighty fine to me," he cried, and his cry was sweet as a mockingbird. "Come on, pretty baby. You give us some time."

She was nearly past. Suddenly her feet felt heavy, with a weight she could not have accounted for. A glimpse of the trombonist, the plump penguin man, affected her like a poignant drug; her head swam. He was blinking and squinting. Perhaps she slowed her step; she could never have said. But when she heard the next words, in their lost notes, she felt like weeping.

"Say there, sister. Can you please tell us how to get to the Baptist church in this town?"

She turned with an effort. Her fists rose to her hips. "How come you wanting to know?"

"We got to get there quick as we can. There's a funeral at that church, we suppose to play it down to the cemetery."

"You what?" In the dazzle, she could only think of one thing: they were connected to her, they were part of her drama. "Ain't no funeral I know of, except a poor little white baby. That can't be the one you mean."

"That's the one! That's the one!" The trumpeter ran his finger over his throat, grinning at her, his grin as intimate as if he had found her life.

"You going to play that funeral?" The light beat down, making them shimmer. He grinned from another world.

"Yes, ma'am," the other horn player said. "Reckon we going to be late, too, if you don't tell us how to find it."

"It's that way," she pointed towards the square. Her arm felt light as cornsilk. "You just walk on down there two blocks, past the hotel and the courthouse, you'll see it."

"Why, thank you kindly," the trombone player cried.

Then the trumpeter began to swagger towards her. Slowly, sinuously, he moved through the waves of heat, until he was near enough to touch, and she could see his wide lips curl, the deep cleft of his throat where he had loosened the shirt.

"What are you doing tonight, with your fine proud legs?" he murmured.

What are you doing tonight, he murmured. The whisper brushed against her. What are you doing . . .

"Hush your—" Viola cried; and then she stopped, her mouth hanging.

"Viola?"

I stared at her from the table. She was stretched forward, eyes round and blank.

"Viola?"

Her neck was strung taut, jutting out. No sound of breathing disturbed the silence. She stared straight ahead at the wall.

"What is it? What—"

A noise ground from the skimpy chest, in little bursts, like a motor turning over, trying to start.

"Viola!" I leaped off the table and ran to her side. Her hands wrapped around the rocker arms and clutched tight. One last sound came out of her mouth. Then, with a long sigh, she sank back into the rocker pad.

She had left me alone and gone.

Bessie

"R eckon I'll take this old skillet with me. Reckon I cooked enough bacon in it now, it'll be mine by right."

Bessie would not look at me, but tossed her words defiantly into the cupboard depths.

"You know that is fine with me," I said.

"Forty years frying bacon in the same pan. You got these fancy new-fangled copper skillets your mama bought. You don't need some old black cast iron what's nearly wore out."

"Take whatever you like."

"Don't want nothing else, especially," she grumbled. But still she squatted and glowered at the stacks of kitchenware.

"Will you have a stove to use where you are going?"

"That's my business."

"Oh."

She puckered her lips balefully.

"I sure ain't intend to cook for no more *folk*," she said after a pause.

I watched her in silence, as she scraped a speck of burnt stuff off a cake pan.

"Had enough of that in my time. That's for sure."

"I will miss your cooking."

"Hmph."

I shrugged.

"Fed enough Ransom stomachs now to keep me till the Judgment."

"You have done us proud."

"It's just my work." She seemed dissatisfied with the arrangement of the pots; she continued to shift them about in the cupboard, straightening them in a row. "Be glad to leave off at last."

"Your cooking suited me."

"I don't care a doe. You all got that Nyla, that suit you now."

"She cannot make fried chicken."

"Well," she mocked to the cupboard hole, "guess she best learn."

"No need to worry. I am not trying to convince you to stay."

"You surely ain't." Stiffly she drew to her feet, staring at me with frigid spite. "Because you best not. You imagine I'd stay here now Viola's gone, you got to think again."

I met her eyes evenly.

"Forty years, did I say? Huh, it's more like fifty. Fifty years beating biscuits for you-all, my Ezra slaving in the yard. 'Ezra, do this.' 'Ezra, tote that.' 'Rake, drive, clean the stable.' That's what he got from Miss Arliss, then he turn round and get it from Miss Mavis. Then she killed him dead." She drew a trembling breath. "The cooking part ain't so bad, except when that old nurse Mrs. Joiner was here. But Ezra he got treated like a fool." She sniffed. "Only reason I stay once he was dead was Viola. Now there ain't none at all."

She stuck her arms akimbo, and pondered the skillet. "Cooking for you now would be like cooking for the Bottomless Pit," she said to it. "You and you daddy, who eats like a bird. It's all out of kilter. Nome. I just sashay right on to that old folks' home your daddy fixed for me, and put up my dogs on the footstool and spend my days laying in the breeze. Reckon they even got a hammock. That Nyla, she tend to you all. I am through."

"I know."

"You best go fetch your daddy, tell him I'm ready."

"All right."

"He can come get me and my box out back in the shack."

She bent and picked up the skillet. Then without another word she moved towards the back door.

"Good-bye, Bessie," I said. But the door slammed; her shuffling step sounded once more on the gallery, and then vanished.

THAT NIGHT Nyla cooked our dinner: canned soup, lukewarm peas from a package, tuna fish. Father and I glanced at each other over the plates. We ate in silence; Father drank his whiskey slowly. The funeral had been the week before. He had had Viola, against all precedent, interred in the Ransom family plot. There was plenty of room. It was plain that the other lengths of turf would never be filled with more descendants.

When Nyla came in, bearing the tray of dessert, he suggested she sit down and join us. But she refused with a shake of her head, and went back through the swinging door. Together Father and I gazed at the plates she had put before us: two black cupcakes each, firm and neat as little flower pots, with squiggles of white icing across the top, still in their cellophane wrappers.

Father sighed. "It's against my principles, Bun, you being a young girl and all, but would you like a little drink tonight?"

I hesitated.

"Just a drop of sherry or port, mind. To—to cheer things up."

"Yes. All right."

"Allow me," he said. He grabbed the chair seat with one hand and hoisted up. His skinny stump wavered back and forth in its sleeve, balancing him, as he stepped to the sideboard.

"What'll it be?"

"I do not know. I will leave it to you. I have never tasted alcohol before."

"Ah," he said. "Something sweet, maybe." He selected a crystal decanter filled with garnet, poured a small glassful, and raised his whiskey. "Here's to you."

"Here is to you," I echoed; we drank them down.

AFTER GRANDFATHER'S death the gardening boy had quit. Then the grounds spread wild and untrimmed, the grass never mown, the trees and bushes left unpruned to hang over glass and stifle the day.

Since Father's accident, I had ceased going out at all. Father himself occasionally left the house to go to town. But even his trips to the end of the drive for the mail grew sporadic. He always drove Mother's Rolls-Royce, rescued that Saturday long back from the tow yard. Since his "accident," he had had a special turning knob riveted on the steering wheel for his stump. He grew deft at spinning the wheel around; I would watch him as he waved farewell through the windshield and headed down the drive. Then I would turn away from the leaded side-light, and stroll through the foyer to my seat among the humid flowers, switching the fountain on as I passed the panel by the door.

It was during these years that I discovered my secret friendships.

Sitting in the chair, reading one of Grandfather's books (Heidegger, Husserl, Hegel—a chain of Teutonic sighs) I would forget where I was for hours at a time. The fern shadow shawled across my knees, slipping down to the floor as the sun traveled. The book in my hands grew heavy from the tortuous German phrases rendered into tortured English, until the weight of it would sag.

I could trace Grandfather's journeys in a trail of coffee spots and cigar ash through the long library nights and days, turning the page as pulpy as a soft old cheek, until I reached a place of rest. His quest had been time itself. Time as a necklace string, moments as translucent beads knotted into position by limited human perception; time as rivers or brief explosions. Grandfather had lost himself in the medium of time, and never emerged until the pause came to commit a final act. That lonely beach he crawled out onto must have seemed strange to him, overly bright, a landscape of burning outlines and absolute arrest. I would close my eyes to imagine his fear and resolve. The empathy I would feel then, and the grief at our mutual curse, drew me closer to him. Sometimes I sat for the the day, with the sound of the fountain trilling in my ears.

That is how I first noticed the private lives going on around me.

It came as a slow awakening. I cannot cite the moment when they decided to make themselves plain; or rather, when I grew sentient enough to find them out. The temperatures, dawning gradually as differences on my body, appealed for my attention. I think it must have been winter, because this would be when they could declare their variations against a background of chill gray. The Boston fern was first. My special seat rested directly under him. The climate near him, I began to notice, was much warmer than that of the smaller ferns, and the longer I sat (very still, without a twitch) the more it extended, glowing finally with a deep heat, welcoming, benevolent—very much like Grandfather's fondness when I had been a child. If I leaned slightly forward, the warmth enclosed me completely. Whereas the smaller ones merely laid light fingers on my cheeks, and the bromeliads, on their log trestles, did little more than breathe the memory of heat towards my chest.

Alerted, I began to realize how each species of plant emitted a different nature, expressing itself or even resisting according to its choice. Some were flirtatious: there was a slipper orchid, which teased with mild waves of temperature that wafted to and fro. Its mate on the same log grew in dainty silence; no amount of patience would coax its friendship. I would sit for an hour, listening with my skin. The longer I remained, the more they solicited me—all except for the African violets, who squatted against the wall in their pots, coolly apart. But the shyness of the camellias and gardenias soon changed to lush curiosity, and the inquisitive nervousness of the Japanese wisteria amused me. Mother had planted it only a few months before she left. Even now, as I write this, it droops towards the page with languor, trying to enter into my spirit of endeavor.

But then—as now—the real presiding character of that self-contained world finally revealed himself. One day as I sat waiting for the fern's first advances, he preempted them with a bold leap of incandescence, and I was stunned by the fervor of his revelation.

I had been resting quietly enough, only for a few minutes, waiting until I felt them salute me, when suddenly a shaft of heat like an opening oven flowed straight across the brickwork floor.

My eyelids flew up. As I looked about, the force was failing. Seven feet away from my chair stood a terra-cotta tub. In it grew the Ficus lyrata, an old citizen, chosen by Mother because of his size. The gnarled trunk was whorled and twisted, with knobs along the stem. He was not completely erect; the nearby miniature palms crippled him by their airy stance and smooth boles. Yet he burned. I could tell now it was from him the profession came, fierce and clear.

I stared at him, while his labor ebbed back to the feeble radiation. He was like an old weathered soldier simmering with tuberculosis, whom nothing could cure. I did not know what to make of it. But then I knew nothing of the species Ficus lyrata, except that he was telling me a crucial secret, no less a confidence about himself than a truth about me. I sat up straight in alarm.

The wisteria sent out curls of laughter. The Boston fern wrapped me in kindly affection.

I thought: Oh, my.

But I would not have dreamed of offending him, the gallant old admirer who had dared to confess. I was dogged by ignorance: how does the admired respond to such a compliment?

Towards evening I finally went to dinner. Several thoughts knocked in my head: the hours of oblivious reading I had done under his observation. The friendship of the other plants, the clamor of the gardenias and their rich, fragrant consent when we conversed; the little gossipy violets, who spoke only among themselves, and peeped with their magenta and purple tabs at the rest of us. And at him. Had the others known? Was the fern trying to reassure me, speak for the Ficus lyrata's good character? Had he now earned the fatuous wisteria's contempt?

At dinner Father talked of the lawyers, who were saying that we were richer than we had ever been. But I could not reply. I was too overwhelmed, as I munched Nyla's frozen French fries, by the thought that now, just like Estella in *Great Expectations*, I had reached the courtship age.

The next day I again seated myself in the conservatory, wary and somewhat self-conscious.

For a little while nothing happened.

The fern hung above me as if in a doze. One slight query shivered from the slipper orchid, but his mate aloofly chilled it.

Then slowly, as if with the dignity of his old age and the awareness of his presumption, the Ficus lyrata approached. Now the warmth was humble, an homage paid with courtly tact. There was no fever. The other plants seemed to wait, hesitant and breathless, to see how he would be greeted. I wondered: what after all could he do to me? Why was I so perturbed? How does one accept love?

Then suddenly I felt moved.

If nothing had ever prepared me to be beloved this way, was it any reason to want to escape?

> ". . . *Our vegetable love should grow*
> *Vaster than empires, and more slow.*"

I could see the tree, ridged with old scars in his terra-cotta prison. He seemed to bend, impatiently but with calmness.

Perhaps the love of a tree is purer, lacking in expectation, more— dare I suppose?—sublime than that of a human counterpart. The Ficus lyrata asks nothing of me. It does not even ask that I, too, be a tree.

After a time, I grew aware of the other plants, whispering heat in my direction. Their offertories mingled with the Ficus lyrata's fires, until the room defied the winter outside with Edenic pleasance.

The Big Present

had continued to grow, even after Viola ceased to feed me. At first this puzzled me—where was the new material coming from? But then I realized that every book I read covering the familiar themes (*Paradise Lost*, austere Ahab and his murderous feud, my nightmare) added dimensions to my body of knowledge. And this last held the real fear, after all: now that every Ransom had one way or another been picked off or eliminated, I was the only one left. The ultimate object of revenge. The Great White Whale.

For after all, whether Grant knew it or not, I contained the entirety.

Sometimes, as I stared out of the unlighted conservatory windows at night, from darkness into darkness, I thought I saw movements too high up for racoons or nutrias or other forms of game to make among the trees. In the woods a bush might shudder; a riffle of leaves chart more than the wind's progress; dark shapes blot out the spaces between branch and earth, and then clear. Then one night I caught a flicker of pale phosphorus at the foot of the bridge, behind the gazebo's latticework. I froze beside the glass. For a moment the thing hung still, as the moonlight reflected upon its plane. My heart seemed to stop. Then it glided forward. It was Nyla's head, I realized: Nyla out for what I would have considered to be an unprecedented stroll in the spring evening. But then, perhaps it was not unprecedented. What did I really know of her habits these days?

I had not realized that she stood so tall.

Sometimes I understood that fear itself was now feeding me.

NYLA HAD made a dress for me out of Arliss's fine French brocade bedspread, and Father had purchased bolts of fabric from Sopwith's. Deep green linen—*they* would like that, the ficus and wisteria and my other allies. Blue cotton chenille. Ten yards of gray wool flannel for winter. Nyla surprised me again, this time with a clumsy skill on the sewing machine in the third floor room that had once been Mavis's dressmaker's workplace.

But still I continued to burgeon.

"Father," I began one evening. "It has become very difficult lately for me to—well, for me to climb upstairs."

I trained my eyes downwards, to avoid his little flinch.

"Is that a fact?" There was no pleasurable lilt.

"Yes. Almost impossible." I looked up, searched him calmly. "Last night it took me twenty-five minutes."

"Oh, Bun. No."

"Yes."

He spoke into his glass. "I had no idea."

"It is true. So if you are interested in giving me something—" His eyes began to glint. I could never ask him for as much as he wanted to give me; he had brought the fabrics home with touching delight. I reached out for his foot, massaging it, consoling him against the truth. "What I need is an elevator. One that will carry great loads. I am sure they must make such things. One that would be used in factories, hospitals. You know the sort I mean?"

He stared at me, eyes wide. "An industrial elevator? Oh, but Bun! Surely you don't need—I mean you surely aren't that—"

"I must think of the future, Father," I said primly.

"Bun. Tell me. Are you counting on getting any—I mean, is the swelling—"

With smooth dispatch I dropped the foot and took up the other. "It will be all right, Father." Then, "We are what we are. You must not think I mind."

Even today I cannot account for the calm jubilation that flooded me as I said it.

WEEKS LATER, on a beautiful morning, I sat after my bath.

The sun rose high among fronds and vines, strewing gold wafers on the floor. The overgrowth bushed outside the windows. I watched through half-open eyes the patterns of light on my lap, printing the towels with leaves, paisleys, fishbone fern. Then suddenly the air cooled. Father was standing in the foyer. I saw him look up at the staircase, assessively, and then turn to the conservatory door.

"Well, it's done, Bun. The men will be driving out here in a day or two to start getting the place ready."

"Ah," I murmured. "You have bought it?"

He nodded, head faltering a little. He seemed unhappy. "The best Otis elevator I could find. They come in a range of sizes. I bought the——one of the middle-sized ones. I mean, you don't really need——"

"How large?"

He gazed down at his feet. "It'll hold one ton."

I nodded. "That should do."

"I can't imagine why you would need——"

"Better to be thrifty now, Father."

"Oh," he sighed. "Well——"

"Thank you."

"They tell me they'll have to make structural changes to get the thing installed."

"Do you mind that?"

"Why, heck, no. I don't give a durn——but——"

"Where are you thinking of putting it?

He considered me, as I sat camouflaged by towels and jungle shadow. "I figured maybe behind the staircase. It could open up in the paneling on the wall upstairs."

"Yes, Father. That will be fine."

"Okay." He sighed again.

"Father—when they come, I plan to stay up on the third floor until they have finished."

"What do you mean, Bun?"

"I can stay in Viola's old room. I will sleep on the floor. How long did they say it would take?"

He grimaced. "You mean you're going to hide out?"

I smiled.

He shook his head dolefully. "It's a crying shame, Bun. That you feel that way. Of course, I'll come see you. It'll be two weeks. But how will you—I mean, what about—see what I'm driving at?"

"Nyla and I will make arrangements. You are not to worry, Father."

"Whatever you say, Bun."

After he went away, the Ficus lyrata was first. I felt his protests roll, beckoning, reproaching. Soon the others joined him.

"It will only be for two weeks," I said aloud. "Then I will be back. You can wait for me."

It was the first time I had addressed them this way. The air grew hotter. I looked about, from pot to pot, from rack to lattice. The very bricks warmed under my feet, and soon I realized that the temperature was climbing as it never had before. Yet the sun was autumnal. A curious thought occurred to me. I went behind the pool to the bay windows, and with one palm pressed against the glass, tested the room's ardor. The pane was burning hot. Beyond it, two live oaks and a bower of hearty hibiscus sheltered the grass; no sun penetrated here at all.

So I discovered how they had all conspired.

"Even there," I murmured aloud. "Even outdoors, you are related."

A wave came from the hibiscus.

"I had not realized." I glanced at the still prisoners, their roots forever hostage in the walled pots and tubs. If they had been planted outdoors, would they have spread and stretched? The Ficus lyrata sent one intense volley; I felt it clear across the room.

"I am surrounded." I chuckled despite myself. An effervescence buzzed in my forehead. "Well, now you need never worry again. I will be back, and then for always."

THE NEXT morning I stood sentinel at the front window. I did not want to be caught off guard.

The drive stretched through platinum white light; shadows lay like cavities on the gravel. Sure enough, soon I saw the metal spin around the curve. "Ah. Here they are." With the thought, I felt suddenly weightless. But I stayed, thinking, "A moment more. Just a glimpse, perhaps," knowing what that glimpse would mean. It would not come to me ever again. The metal changed, became dense and dull; it was painted yellow.

Then I saw it was not a truck at all.

Dumbfounded, I leaned against the window. Oil smudges clouded it when I took my nose and forehead away. I peered, trying to decode the car. It wore a comb stuck to the roof; it flickered in and out of the shadows, flinging them back like scarves, growing larger, until it had reached full size and stood, humming and ticking, a few yards from the door. The motor cut dead. I heard silence; the panes cooled as I pressed against them, the azaleas secluding themselves. Then I saw the letters. "Taxi Cab," they said, "Ph. 48266."

A woman in black emerged from the back seat and stepped out onto the drive.

The Return

Mother. Mother. The years of my childhood slide together in the split second of her pirouette, their distillation suddenly sears my brain. Soft black casing, long pale stockings on her legs, handbag crushed like a glove between her hands. The small hat on her crown is bowing, lifting; my vision seems to fail as I search for her face. Darkness, hidden, nothing but a black scrim where her face should be: am I going blind? I stood frozen, heart thumping inside the fat like a gong, as she took her first step towards the door.

It was then I realized the truth: the black extended from head to hem. Her face was covered by a veil. Not the palest pearl of skin showed through; not the tiniest cheek, nor glint of eye. The thick veil fell from her hat brim to her collarbone.

In the second it took for her to lift her foot another step, my body slowed. I watched her ascend to the porch, disappear around the curve of house under the portico. I was still at the window when the front door wheezed open. I heard her footfall on the parquet, the pause before the Venetian mirror. Her uncertainty vibrated; her bewilderment at the silence, her doubt. I saw, before it actually occurred, my appearance at the conservatory door like a monstrous gargoyle. Caliban. The giant walking vegetable. I gauged her shock, still trying to manage my own: the intake of breath, the fluttering hands stopped in midair, the pain coursing unseen beneath the veil, or over the cream and coral face as she lifted it. I turned and stepped out into the foyer.

"Mother."

My palm, glazed and rubbery with sweat, slid down the door frame. She turned. The black crepe shuddered on her gasp. Fingers like white feathers lifted the air before her; winging hands, glittering with rings, escaped from the long sleeves and then retreated once more down to her sides.

"Victoria?" The voice sounded different. Harshened, throatier.

"Yes." I glanced down at my bulk. "Welcome home."

"Victoria?"

Then she came towards me. Her arms reached out, hot in their black material. Through the shock, I felt the veil, like a whisper of fur, touch my cheek and nose. She was hugging me to her, holding me against the small neat framework of bones and black wool. "Victoria!" she wispered. "My baby. Victoria Grace." She embraced me with hunger, tenderness. My throat tightened; I was breathing through my nose in fear.

"Mother?" Her elegant body on mine felt unbearable. Something inside began to melt.

"My darling. My baby," she whispered. "You're here."

Tears scalded my eyes.

"Mother." I couldn't believe it. "Let me look at you. Let me see your face." The veil extended to the back of her head. There were gray streaks in the tawny hair, which she wore clipped short on the nape.

"No!" she cried out, whipping back. Her arm swooped up, holding the veil in place.

"No," she said more quietly, in the voice I remembered. "No, darling. I'm sorry, Victoria. But not now. There are—reasons." Her hand shook on the black edge, tugging it onto her throat. Then she stood for a moment, still close enough for me to inhale her scent, and slowly let the veil go. She stroked my hand, patted it. "I'll explain later, maybe—oh, Victoria. You've grown up."

"Yes, Mother. I have."

"It didn't stop, did it, darling?" The endearment was like a soft touch. I heard the tears in her voice. "It never did get any better."

I could not reply. My tears were burning, coursing down. "Never mind," she sighed, trembling, and the material blew gently out. "Never you mind," kirtling the arm around my waist. "I've missed you. And Daddy."

I fumbled for air.

"Would you like to sit down?" I asked awkwardly. "Are you tired?"

She sighed once more, nodded.

"I would absolutely cherish a cup of coffee, to tell you the truth. If you could just go back and let Bessie know, or Viola? Coffee for two."

She took a tremulous pace towards the drawing room.

"Oh. Bessie is not here, Mother."

"She's not?" Her voice fell.

"She retired three years ago. She lives in an old folks' home somewhere near Dallas."

"Oh."

The smallness of the word, with its broken hopes, moved me. "Viola, then. Ask her." I saw the limber spine straighten.

"She is dead."

Another breath, fluttering the veil. Then she moaned. "Oh, no."

I looked down.

"How—when?" Before I could answer, she said, "What in the world am I going to do, then?"

"How do you mean?"

"I need them, Victoria," she said, low. She lifted her hand to the veil, touching it, shrinking within the black dress.

"Well, there is Nyla. Nyla is here."

"Her," she whispered.

Then, "Ahh. Nyla." The darkness swung towards the double doors. "Tell her, then. She will do." A choked sound came out of the veil's mystery.

"Shall I go tell her now?"

"Wait a minute." She paused. Without turning, she said, "Victoria. Your father?"

The upturned note held the edge.

"He is upstairs. Having an afternoon nap."

"It's morning." We stared at each other.

"He often starts early."

"I heard he had—an accident. I heard about his arm."

"Yes."

"And your poor granddaddy. What he did after it happened."

I waited.

Then with a tininess strange to hear, coming from that hidden mouth: "Do you think he's missed me any—at all?"

Silence hung for a long moment.

"Oh, yes. He has missed you." Something squeezed inside me then, pushing out breath.

"I must go up to him."

I clenched my hands, waiting.

"But not quite yet. Coffee." She smoothed her hips. "In a few minutes. I'll just rest first."

"All right."

I turned and lumbered to the kitchen, while she stood in the foyer like a mother from my oldest dreams.

NYLA WAS ironing Father's shirts.

"Mother is home," I said.

"Mrs. Ransom? She's come back?"

"She would like some coffee. Also, I think she wants to ask you something. She wants you to help her."

"Help her."

"Yes. She seems to have a problem."

There was no reaction in her face. "Okay." She thumbed the lever on the iron. "She want something to eat?"

"Perhaps some cake or—no." I thought of the sleeve of cellophane wrapping a store-bought pound cake. "Cookies, I think. That would be best. Oreos will do. Then we shall see what else."

"Okay." She twisted the instant coffee lid.

MOTHER STOOD at the mirror, a black shape in dim aquamarine. She had removed the little hat, but the cerements hung anchored from bobby pins. She raised a hand, correcting their folds. The gesture was so feminine, an echo of the old days when she would check her makeup, that it nearly brought tears again. I coughed.

She turned around and patted my hand. Hers quivered slightly. "I'm afraid my eyesight isn't what it used to be." The veil was a thick material.

"Would you like me to turn on some lights?"

"That would be nice." Anything could be made of this shrouded head. Sockets appeared and vanished at a movement. The illusion of a mouth arranged itself, and I watched it as she spoke, only to see it a second later as a dark pleat to the left of where her mouth must be. Indeed, everything she had said so far had the air of mirage. Why? What had happened to her?

"I wonder what you're thinking. Me coming back home."

I touched the switches and the hall blazed into sharp relief. "I mean, it is kind of unexpected, I know." She laughed hesitantly, searching for inner control. "I could hardly believe it myself, driving up that old drive. Why has your daddy let it go to rack and ruin like that? The garden is a mess, weeds every whichaway, the windows choked with shrubbery. And my roses—ah!" She sighed. "What all have y'all been up to? Why, it looks just like that Sleeping Beauty story I used to read you at your bedtime."

"You never read me that," I said carefully.

"Why, Victoria! Shame on you. Of course I did."

I shook my head. She wagged a finger. "You just simply don't remember, darling." The word sounded even more tender. "Nearly every single night, when I tucked you in. Don't you remember?"

"No. I cannot."

"Well, it was before you had the measles—and afterwards as well, for a little while. . . ." Her voice caught.

"Some things I remember. Once, you showed me the jewels in your jewelry box."

"Did I?" The voice dropped sadly. "Yes. I remember. Those things. All sold."

I said nothing.

"Well! That coffee's just about due now, don't you think? Come keep me your good company. Oh, but honey—" she said as she glided away. "I'm going to have to speak with Nyla awhile in private. Just for a little. Then—but let's just plop down now, and have a chat."

"All right."

She sat down. The white hands writhed gently in the black lap.

"You know what I'm wondering?"

"What?"

"I'm wondering if you ever have forgiven me?"

"For what?"

"Why," she laughed nervily, "for just up and flying the coop the way I did. Just—scooting!"

I stared down at my legs.

"There was nothing to forgive, Mother. Do not worry anymore about it."

"Victoria," she blurted, "you are not—*not*—what I expected!" The hands twisted hectically. "I mean, you're not—you're not at all—"

"Simple?"

She nodded; the hands went limp.

"No."

"I'm sorry," she whispered. "Oh, darling, I'm so sorry. For all of it. I don't know why I thought—but I guess I had forgotten, or avoided—"

A footfall interrupted her.

Slowly she turned to the doorway.

"Hello, Mrs. Ransom." Nyla stepped into the room, and set the tray on the coffee table.

The veil sucked in softly, a little gasp. "Hello, Nyla."

"I made the coffee for you," said Nyla.

"Thank you, that looks very nice." She reached for a cup. "Well! How are you, Nyla?"

"Okay."

"What nice cookies." She did not take one; nor did she raise the veil to sip. "Won't you have some, Victoria?"

"I've got hers coming soon," Nyla said.

"Surely she can try these with me. Or don't you eat this kind, darling?"

"Actually, I eat a bit more than this," I said. "Actually, I think today I might just excuse myself and go eat in the kitchen. No need to get up, Nyla. I can forage for myself."

"Why, Victoria, I know you don't mean to be rude, but—"

Suddenly she realized that this was a diplomatic gesture. "It's all right. I think Nyla and I can find something to talk about."

I pulled to my feet.

"Nyla, would you like to sit down?" She plumped up the sofa cushion next to hers.

Mother, I wanted to say. Mother. Lift up your veil a moment.

"We'll see you in a little bit, darling," she said brightly. "You go on back and have your dinner." Nyla lowered herself, expressionless, onto the sofa. I looked from yellow hair to the black cloth.

"Yes," I said. "All right." And I trundled away.

I opened every can in the pantry. I could have eaten much more— Nyla would have to go back out to shop for dinner. I gave them more than time for Mother to say to Nyla what she had to, or strip her concealments away. Soon the counter was littered with cracker boxes, torn packets, crumbs, dry cake mix scattered over the top. Chocolate powder, cornmeal. At last I paused. The counter now resembled — what was it? Mother's dressing-table, two days after she had left.

Oh, I thought. Then I sank onto the table.

Finally Nyla appeared in the doorway. Now, perhaps, I could go back. I looked at Nyla, to see what Mother had shared. She walked straight to the ironing board and turned on the iron. Her blue eyes scanned the shirt, finding the place she had left off. But now I noticed something behind the blank expression, as I had the day Mother abandoned us: the masked cognition.

"Has Mother finished with you for awhile?"

"Yes, ma'am."

"Did she say what she wanted you for?"

"Uh-huh. She said."

She licked her thumb and touched it to the iron. Her face was as closed, as reverential, as a nun's.

I STOOD behind the stairwell, girding myself to cross the foyer to her. Now; now would be the moment.

The click of her heels sounded. She glided through the foyer, the executioner's hood pivoting from left to right. She didn't see me. Her head set back, and she mounted the stairs. At the fifth tread, she paused. I saw the articulation of ankle through sheer stocking.

She was going to my father.

BACK AND forth I paced among the nymphs, blindly. There was no doubt in my mind now. She had made herself plain. If the old repugnance was gone, I could at last take my place, parents and daughter, a unit beginning a new life. Change was not only possible; it was imminent.

I did not even ponder on where she had been, what she had done, for the past five years. I did not care. Whatever had befallen her had saved us all. Grant Macafee was not the sponsor of this resurrection. Or was he? Had he, in some way inconceivable to me, tampered with

Mother during her wanderings? But no; out of the question. Nor could he affect what was about to happen, when Mother and Father came down and beckoned to me, enticing me at last from the chrysalis Viola had manufactured, nourishing me with something other the idea of evil. I would burst through to their waiting embrace; and with no further thoughts I willed the evening to come.

Finally, Nyla came plodding through the house to water the plants.

As she filled the watering can at the sink, I said, "Have Mother and Father come down yet?"

"No, ma'am." Dusk had fallen outside the leafy windows. She dragged the hose over the bricks.

"Is dinner ready?"

"Yes, ma'am. I already put it on the table. It's sitting there now."

I did not wait for more, but heaved through the foyer and up the stairs, heading for my mother's door.

It was standing wide open.

For a moment, I felt uncentered, flying apart. The room lay empty. The stillness of cold satin, the dark window drapes, told of years' neglect. The only smell within was that of dust.

But then I heard a noise.

It came from somewhere ahead. It was unlike any sound I had ever heard. Up the corridor the doors stood closed, vanishing in darkness. The sound seemed to rise and sift down: a long whimper. It teased at my ear, yet dimmed as I listened. Then it surged. It was as if the upstairs had swallowed Mother and Father whole. They had disappeared into a void; and yet this ghostly sound repeated, a piercing, tiny cry on the hush.

I was afraid.

I stumbled forward, groping. Past one door, two: my own bedroom, Nyla's, Mavis's. Nearly at the end of the corridor, the sound swelled, drawing me on; but still I could not locate it. Then, suddenly, just as I reached the end, it pitched high. A wail trembled on the air.

I was standing outside Father's room.

I gripped the knob and turned. Nothing happened. The door was locked.

The wail died. Through the panel I heard gasps, "Ah! Ah! Ahhh—" Bewildered, I tried the knob again. It did not budge. Was someone tortured? What were they doing, what—? I lifted my hand to knock, to stop the terrible sound; yet my hand did not touch wood. The gasps changed to a soughing pant, struggling whispers. Mother's or Father's: was this why she had come home? What was she doing to him?

Then they too died. Through the quiet, I heard a faint giggle.

Then Father laughed.

Mother and Father at Last

Over the next two years, Mother and Father spent all of their time together, and when we three were in company they behaved very kindly to me. Mother remained veiled. Father was happy at last. I could see that. All the things he had ever dared to desire were now fulfilled. At the dinner table he glowed with a satisfied lover's confidence at the black veil opposite, and watched the fork rise and slip underneath the hem, and come back out empty with the same admiration he had once given to her creamy bright-eyed beauty. Except now, of course, there was no hunger in his gaze. Occasionally Mother even jumped up from her chair and ran around to stoop, whispering in his ear, the drapery swaying outward. Often they would leave the table before dessert arrived. I would eat theirs from the bowls.

Mother offered me her old room.

"I don't use it anymore," she said, with her new gay contentment. "That old bed would be just perfect for you, sweetie. Much more comfortable than the floor in your room, it's just plain silly to let it go to waste. I don't ever want to sleep in it again, to tell you the truth. I always did have bad nights in it."

"Thank you, Mother."

"We could have it redecorated for you if you like."

"Oh, no. No." I knew she would not welcome people into the house any more than I would. The two weeks of elevator installation had been agony.

"Well, we can haul out all my old things. Goodness me, all those old dresses—and the drawers full of—gracious, I don't want to even look at it all. You get Nyla to help. Tell her she can burn it, that is, unless she'd like to keep it herself."

"I can't feature Nyla wearing your party dresses somehow," Father said, smiling.

"Well, maybe not. Anyhow, I'd just as soon not have to watch." She stroked the arm of her black dress, and hesitantly touched the veil. "Got no use for it at all."

It was good to sleep in a real bed again. And Mother was right. It bore me surely, without a protest: the bed that Arliss had died in; the bed I had been conceived in, I, the end of the Ransom line. How could it not?

M*other*

One day Father came downstairs alone.

"I'm kind of concerned," he said. I looked at him, standing meager and quiet, his face with its gaunt eye sockets and bonework a pale polished yellow.

"Your mother's kind of seedy. And she won't let me call a doctor—says she absolutely refuses to see one, she made me swear up and down not to touch the telephone. So of course I can't do a thing."

"Why will she not see a doctor?"

"She's decided she doesn't like doctors anymore, says they lied to her, made her feel bad. She says they handed her a lot of bull about her condition being permanent and—unfixable." He frowned. "Frankly, Bun, you know I sometimes get the feeling that she wants to believe it has been fixed, that there's nothing there at all. Of course, I just act like it's gone. This is just between you and me, understand."

"Yes.

"Is the veil still on?" I asked after a moment.

It was the first time I had used the word aloud, to him or anyone.

"The—well, yes. It is."

"Father." I studied him. "Have you ever seen underneath it?"

"Why, Bun." He grimaced. "Yes, well, naturally I have." The grimace, I recognized, had to do with his modesty rather than the secrets the veil hid. "I mean, I could hardly help it." He blushed and stared down at his toes. "We're man and wife, you know."

"She has let you? Willingly?"

"Oh. Well, yes, she has. I mean, she knows how I love her, and she knows she can trust me, and this here," he waved the stump ruefully in the air, "makes us a pretty good match now."

"But you say she wants to imagine that it conceals nothing. Just her usual face, that is."

"Bun," he sighed in perplexity, "how can I explain it to you? I think she would like to believe that that piece of material *is* her face."

"Yes," I said gently. "And we have all cooperated."

"It's changed her. I mean, deep down." He sighed again. "It's been the greatest blessing that ever occurred to me."

I began to conjecture the possibilities his words evoked. For over two years now I had pondered the riddle of the veil. All kinds of images swarmed through my mind: burn scars, vitriol splashes; for one brief time I had even entertained the idea of a brand, such as they use on cattle ranches. I had imagined the splayed *M*, with the small *ac* beneath, puckered on my mother's lovely cheek.

"Father—"

He glanced up.

"Please tell me. What is it?"

"You mean—what—?"

I nodded.

"Well, Bun, she took sick towards the last of the—the time out there. And she went to the doctor, and he had to look up in books and get second opinions and all, and then put her in the hospital. The doctors told her it was called 'rosacea'; they said it was incurable. She didn't believe them. But between you and me, of course she did, way down deep. That's why she came home." He paused. "But when she got here, she said to me, 'See, Willie, they were nothing but a pack of fools and liars after all.'" He shook his head. "That's why I can't possibly call the doctor now."

"Yes," I answered. The wild speculations crumbled to dust, blew away.

"Her face was always just like a rose to me," he murmured.

I thought of the blighted rose. "What is it now?" I whispered.

"Well, you could say it's just bloomed deeper. That's all. Just deeper. And red as blood."

After a while, I asked, "What are you going to do?"

"Nurse her as best I can, I expect." He looked dismally about him. "Wish I knew how to, though. Nyla's the one helps her wash and so forth. She doesn't like to—touch it herself. I just stand by feeling helpless. But now she's got a real bad cough, can't seem to get out of bed. Wish I knew if it was because of this thing she came home with. It could be something else. She hasn't said whether it affects the rest of her, or whether it's just the skin and stuff right underneath."

I watched him go. So I was the only one in the house who had not known the truth of her disfigurement. I dropped my head in my hands; some things did not change, after all.

MOTHER DIED a few days later.

Doctor Middleton came out to sign the death certificate. "I'm sorry, Willie," he said to Father, who stood in the hall sobbing, and seemed not to hear. Doctor Middleton turned to me. His liver-spotted hand reached out and patted my arm. "I'm so very sorry, Victoria. It was pneumonia, like your great-aunt Mavis. And your great-grandmother too, come to recall. If she had seen me, perhaps—" He shook his white head. "This house must be damper than most. The stonework, maybe. I don't know, though. It wasn't the rosacea. I can tell you that. Are you—"

"I am all right," I said.

He looked hard at me, pursing his mouth. "I can give you a little something to take, if you're too upset." We both gazed to Father, leaning weeping against the door to their room.

"No. I need no sedations, thank you." I said firmly. "I do have one request. I know I—we—can count on your discretion, regarding Mother's appearance. It was something she did not want known."

His smooth manner deserted him for a moment. "Really, child, I

423

have no intentions whatsoever—your family has always been able to trust—" He collected himself. "Considering the unusual misfortunes of this household, I might suggest you take your daddy away for awhile. For a change of scene. I truly don't believe this house is healthy."

I forced myself to remember that he was the one who had attended me during the bout with measles; he imagined he knew the source of my own condition.

"Sanitariums always look different to those on the outside," I said.

RECENTLY, RANSACKING the house for the documents and papers, photographs and letters with which to detail this history, I came across the curious contract drawn up between Father and the undertaker.

I, Lewton Summerall, bachelor, do hereby agree, that after I have embalmed the deceased wife of William Garner Ransom Junior, to wit, Mrs. Anabelle Lacey Ransom, and committed her to burial, I will never disclose the state of her visage, or break confidence as to said condition to another human being; and I will never discuss her appearance or defame the memory of her beauty, as this is according to her dying wish, or refer to the mortification I have witnessed on her body in any context whatsoever, so long as I shall live.

And I hereby swear and agree, upon payment of one million dollars, to be paid in a manner agreed upon by myself and Mr. William Garner Ransom Junior, to remove my residence to another state of my choice, to wit: (and here the undertaker's scrawl filled in the blank) *Little Rock, Arkansas*; whereafter I will never contact or correspond with, or have any communication whatsoever with, any resident of the town of Bernice, Texas, as long as I shall live, so as not to be tempted to defy that dying wish. For the span of my lifetime I will not return to the said town of Bernice, Texas, or impart my address to any resident of said town: nor will I ackowledge any personal knowledge of Bernice, to new friend, acquaintance, business associate, or any human being. No assistant shall accompany me when I embalm said body. I understand that these are the explicit wishes of the deceased, and that they are the explicit wishes of the deceased's husband, William Garner Ransom, Junior.

Signed this day February 27th, 1969, by me: *Lewton Summerall. William Garner Ransom, Junior.* Witnessed by: Nyla Arlene *X*

It was to be Father's magnum opus. I had had no idea he could construct something so articulate; but I suspect that he studied the legal documents in Grandfather's desk before attempting to compose; and the grief would have inspired him to those glorious heights of prose.

OVER THE next few months Father's drinking grew worse.

Eventually he grew delirious, tossing in his bed, groaning. He often cried out names: Bert or Anabelle. Once I heard him scream "Viola!" and add an incoherent spate of mutters. He did not call out for me.

His skin grew slowly to be the color of saffron. His eyeballs changed to that color, also. His body was wasted, and the pajamas hung like sails over his breastbone and the rigging of his ribs.

After a certain point, he ceased to drink. The decanter by the bed was left untouched; he asked for water. But a day came when he ceased to ask for anything. It seemed he could no longer talk, even when I stood over his bed, holding the glass to his lips. His eyes did not focus, nor did they swivel from side to side as they had earlier. One small space in front of his face engrossed him, and whatever strength he had left was concentrated on a perusal of that square foot of air.

When I saw what was to happen, I made plans with Nyla.

On the afternoon he died, I went to the ducal bedroom and sealed myself in. Nyla telephoned Doctor Middleton, met him at the door, and led him to Father's room. I did not have to do a thing. I certainly was not going to suffer the good doctor's reproaches once more, or listen to his condemnation of our choices. The mortuary men were too quiet for me to overhear them; the carpet muffled their tread. I sat propped in the ducal bed, surrounded by Mother's and Arliss's relics, listening for the sound of Father's departure. Only in my mind was there a final vacuum, filling gently after awhile with stillness.

MY FATHER died the day before my twenty-second birthday. On the morning of that day I wrote a letter to the lawyers, giving instructions for Father's funeral and burial, leaving most of the details to their judgment. I made it clear that I would not be meeting them in person at any time, but that if they had questions regarding the estate, the businesses (which I ordered to be liquidated or sold), or their positions with me, they could write. I entrusted them with everything.

I also took Grandfather's letter opener, and as an afterthought, sawed through the telephone wire.

The anger which seemed to seize me more and more often in recent years was churning in my bowels as I cleared the drawers of Grandfather's desk of his and my father's papers. They had left them all to me. They had left me here alone, abandoned, to serve as their monument. I shoveled up sheaf after sheaf of titles, deeds, stocks and share certificates, ledgers, and dumped them in Nyla's arms so that she could store them in trunks on the third floor. I wanted to scour the desk out, pack away the written traces of my betrayers. I had emptied most of the drawers when I came to the lower left one, and discovered to my astonishment that it was locked. Then, suddenly, a comment of Viola's, secreted in the midst of one of her stories, came to mind. This must be where Grandfather had kept the journal of his youth. The book he'd blacked out with ink, except for Sarah's epitaph at the end. And it was where he had put the papers he had been working on after the lawyer's visit, that day Grant Macafee sent him to dissolve the ice house partnership. I recalled what she had described to me: the neat stack inscribed in his close handwriting set on the polished wood; the key in his hand, as he bends towards the lower left-hand drawer: "I've been listening to all you said," he tells her. "You said what I needed to hear. Don't worry, it'll be all right on Monday."

It had not been all right on Monday. It would never be all right again.

I put the key in the lock and tried to turn it. But it was stiff. I was just about to send Nyla for oil to loosen it when it sluggishly eased round to the right.

The pages were crisp but not yellowed with age. They were written on the same fine writing paper that he had used for all the documents now in the trunks.

"We are born knowing our lives. . . ." I began.

"Nyla, bring me something to eat." She glanced incuriously at the papers and left the room.

We are born knowing our lives.

"The mode in which we know them is not a function of smell, touch, sight, hearing. Yet it informs all these, just as our dreams inform our waking hours of something we cannot quite remember. Sometimes it may arrive in the form of a 'premonition,' a feeling that something specific is going to happen, and we know what it is. Yet when it comes (or we arrive at its moment—which? they are the same) it takes us by surprise. We have seen it from afar. We receive it freshly, charged with what it brings us. It is not destination, but process. *IT HAS ALL HAPPENED BEFORE; IS HAPPENING NOW; IS ALREADY THE PAST AND THE FUTURE.* All we have learned of our lives before it transpires contributes to it, just as its aftermath will. So we merge with the experience, *JUST AS WE ALWAYS HAVE AND ALWAYS WILL.*

"All our lives are the recovery of what truths we already knew. That is what memory is. That is discovery. The joy and pain, which cannot be separated, are what give our lives value.

"This is why we fear death. Not only as an end to joy, pain, but as a different kind of recovery which will require all our strength and learning to meet with grace. When we submit to it, unafraid, we actually choose death. At that moment I believe we fully remember all that has been and is to come; at last we learn everything. We must go on to the next path, which is beyond memory."

I threw the papers down in disgust. Words! Hypnotic, seductive— shit! "It has all happened before, is happening now, is already the past and the future." How did that differ from what Viola had murmured and hummed into me over all the years? I was walking proof of what he said—and look what brewed in me! I could see his precognition of death, but failed to see the dignity or inevitability of sawing off one's own head. "I have a bone to pick with you, Grandfather," I cried. "It is easy to predict death. I am living its prelude now."

I felt the urge to scream, to hate. The last bequest from the Grandfather who had "loved" me, who had helped to make me what I was! At least Viola had woven her philosophy into the tangible, the hard and visible, the warmth of a child in her arms, waking from a trip to a city in the rain—the icy coldness of Baby Boy when the farmer brought him home.

There were more pages, but they were more of the same. I put them back in the drawer, locked it, and cried out: "Grandfather! Grandfather! Where is my joy? Where is my truth?

"I am not ready to die in this condition!"

The Advent

"The joy and pain, which cannot be separated from one another, are what give our lives value."

I thought Grandfather had left me nothing, but long after Father's death, this sentence beat in my mind like a trapped bird.

Then, one autumn, I heard a dove call out in the woods. It shocked me—I do not know why. I took a close look at the calendar kept on the clean desktop in the library, the days marked off automatically each evening by my hand, and found that the day before had been the anniversary of Father's death. Three years. My twenty-fifth birthday.

My life/death, by ordinary gauges of mortality, was one-third over.

I took Grandfather's papers out of the locked drawer and reread them. Suddenly I understood what I had to do.

I had never answered Viola's question. But perhaps in beginning a chronicle of all I knew, I could recover the truth, discover why all these people that composed me—my family, my flesh—had allowed this to happen; why Grant's hatred burned unabated against us, why we were sacrificed. Even if the truth did not appear like a genie from Grandfather's formula, at least the process might give what was left of my life value.

Nyla and I continued as always. We had grown so used to each other that it was no longer necessary to speak. She knew all my needs by rote, so that the slightest cough or fart would summon her.

I spent my days in the conservatory, the heavy iron table pulled up to my chair. Sometimes the events I recorded seemed to write themselves. Story followed story, and yet truth did not come. The days closed, the lives of the Ransoms summed up in paragraphs, and I rose, aching, fed on myself, no longer hungry for meals. And now, if it had not been for the plangent stirrings on the air, almost inaudible to me in this lush crypt, I would have closed as well. Accepted my death as it might come, as I was.

But about the time that I recorded Mother's return, a change began to waft in the house. So gossamer, so skittish was it that I told myself I merely imagined it: I was preparing myself for the end of this archive. That was all. Its end would be mine. The change could be no more than this.

Yet something sifted through the air around me, deepening the atmosphere where I wrote with an increasing sense of perturbation.

Nyla knew of it. She was the agent.

All the irrational fears that I had kept to myself before and during Mother's final tenure here, of the tall man's shape lurking under the darkened trees, returned to me. He was out there, and somehow Nyla was connected to his presence. I must be mad, I thought. Grandfather's death had settled the debt; logically I knew that there could be no more reason for Grant to go after me. The Ransoms and the Macafees were now square. And to suspect Nyla of any mentation, any activity demanding a cerebral challenge, much less threat, was ridiculous. And yet the very stones breathed it, in a gentle indrawn pause.

I had believed that everything that could happen in the Ransom history had already taken place. Everything but the one final thing.

Something was afoot.

WEAK SUNLIGHT steeped the room. The plants brooded. All the African violets ranked along the wall seemed to huddle, their little blossom mouths nested deep into the leaves.

Nyla helped me to my chair, tucked my robe around me, shoved the table forward, and then gave the manuscript a long, careful look before she left me. I watched her walk across the foyer, through the drawing room. I had never indicated to her the character of my project, nor the near completion of it. Yet on this morning I noticed a new alacrity in her step. And her head seemed set higher on her neck, as if she held it towards a purpose.

After a time, a door slammed in the distant reaches of the kitchen, and then a flurry of noise, pans banging just as Bessie used to do. It was very unlike Nyla to cause such a racket. Sometimes lately she served me food straight out of the brown store bag as soon as she returned from a shopping expedition. On one such occasion I noticed that the bag bore a new legend: 7-Eleven. Certain items dropped off the menu, but I did not care; everything she prepared tasted the same. I wondered what the proprietor and the other shoppers made of her, the plain pale woman who appeared and speechlessly filled her basket each day. Did they know where she came from? But perhaps Bernice had grown too large to be curious anymore, or to contemplate the ragged drive past the weathered gate and stone, and its mysterious owner.

Or perhaps there still remained one exception to this truth.

Sometimes a plane droned over, causing the plants to retract with alarm. But that could not account for their sullenness today. And if Nyla once more flitted through the foyer unseasonably, I thought, as she had for the past two weeks or so, I would have to break the habit of three years' long silence, and speak to her about it.

After inscribing my fears, however, I felt somewhat silly. Nyla— . in cahoots with Grant Macafee?

But the next morning I was not so sure.

Nyla! Each evening she grew more erratic, scuttling down the upstairs hall like a chased thing, and at the oddest hours. Then, on the other hand, she took to disappearing for two-thirds of a day at a time. It must have been she that jolted me awake at some black hour one night about this time, for I had had no dream. But when I looked around the room, all was still. Then I could not get back to sleep. I shifted on my pillow mountain; my lungs felt choked. Finally the sky lightened, and I fell into a doze.

When I woke up, the sun was bright. It was not until I looked towards the foot of the bed that I saw Nyla. She had been so silent I did not realize she was there. She stood over the footboard, staring at me with her blue crystal eyes, motionless. What was she thinking? She watched me for another ten or fifteen seconds, and then turned and walked out of the room.

Perhaps she was watching me with calculation.

Then one day she did not even appear to help me dress. I had to do it myself.

My skin was loose. It had begun to sag in places, and it frightened me. And yet I could not speak to Nyla to ask about this.

Later on that morning, I heard her stomp heavily through the foyer, to bring me a very late breakfast tray. What was she up to? I wondered.

The following morning I came downstairs, resolved to be indifferent that she had not come to my room at all. I had eaten nothing since breakfast yesterday. I went straight to the conservatory, and sat in the heat, feeling the plants send their radiance, the fern, the miniature palms, the gardenias. Until suddenly they stopped. They stopped as abruptly as if they had been wrenched from their soil. Even the Ficus lyrata snapped off; and when I looked up in surprise, the gang of violets seemed to shrivel within their silvery stems. Nothing had stirred. No leaf quivered in the slightest air current.

Perhaps Nyla was somewhere nearby, I thought. I looked towards the threshold. We were alone. Then I heard it, and understood. From the kitchen, floating down the long hall, came the sound of Nyla's voice. It began as an indistinguishable mutter, and then grew louder. She was speaking in a dull singsong, sentence after sentence.

The volume increased until I could almost hear what she was saying. But not quite. She has gone mad, I thought. Her voice wound through the hall into the soft conservatory air, where it touched me with ice. Then she paused.

And in the pause, someone else answered her.

Panic

Three days went by. Since I had last written in my manuscript, three full days had passed in frozen terror. Three nights (Jonah in the whale, Christ in the tomb) since I heard the voices insinuate themselves, like a wisp of smoke, through the rooms to my ears. The house is on fire! I wanted to cry out. Help! Someone help me!

Someone's in the kitchen with Nyla.

ANOTHER DAY came and went. The plants had withdrawn completely, even the loyal fern. There was no way to write, or do anything except listen to silence, and then the sonorous morning outbreak. I could sit here, in the conservatory, and hear the voice at the same time every day. I could calculate what it might be saying by the inflection, even though the words were muffled by doors and furniture. Who was it? Could it be he?

Nyla: "Nebble or too."

The Stranger: "Foll sss. Ef go snow——"

And so on, until they finally fell silent for awhile. I had forgotten how deep a man's tones could sound. I wanted to ask her. But my own voice locked in my throat, so long ago had I left it. To ask Nyla: had she found a friend? Her new employer?

TWO WEEKS passed. It was like a tune that would not leave my head, boring steadily through the brain. I was no longer afraid. I was getting used to it.

She had not failed to tend to me every morning during that fortnight. And the food was improving. She behaved as if nothing had happened. One night she rose with me in the elevator the way she did the first year after Father's death. I did not question her by so much as a look. But a new current passed between us now, when she dressed me or brought me a meal. When we did glance at each other, it was reflected in our faces like mutual images. She was not what she seemed, walking up the stairs in an old seersucker dress, hair flat as always. She bore the secret like a pregnancy, in the fashion I once saw one of Mother's bridge friends carry her body through a door: a woman nurturing unknown possibilities. When I caught her slanting a look towards me, it said, "You are different to me now. You are not the same as you were." And she contemplated me as I ate. Which I hardly did at all.

Something else, that evaded me while we rode the elevator, but dawned on me the next morning as I pondered it. There was a more concrete manifestation to Nyla's change. I could still hear the elevator cables whir, see the sideways glance of those blue eyes. I felt her nearness, the potency of her secret. And a smell emanated from the shapeless cotton dress, a climate familiar and at first lost to me. In all the registry of changes, I had forgotten it: a scent I knew, my mother's smell of mimosa. Nyla was wearing perfume.

A Reckoning

T he next day he came out of the kitchen.

He appeared through the double doors between the dining room and the drawing room. Sun dazzled me. At that distance he was a black stroke moving through a well of light, growing denser, and then taking form—a man, walking slowly, pacing his way across carpets and rugs. For one fleeting second I thought, "He walks the way Father did when he was drunk. It is Father, back from the dead." Then I could see that he had something long and white in his hand. A stick. He tapped the carpet with it, as if killing bugs. "Cockroaches," I thought in my delirium. "Nyla has hired an exterminator." Then I saw his sunglasses, like the ones Mother wore during her heyday.

From across the drawing room floor and foyer he came to me. It might as well have been an ocean. And he was alone. He stood at the threshold, seeming to scent the air, to take its measure with his long thin nose. Then he lowered it directly towards me. I had the brief sensation of a leveled gun. His free hand rose to the long square jaw, a young man's jaw, and drew a thoughtful line along its bevel. Then he pulled the sunglasses off.

His eyes were two scarred lids.

Curiously enough, I did not think he did it to shock. The gesture was meditative, preceding his words.

"Miss Estella Havisham, I presume." He smiled, dryly and precisely.

I tried to answer, and could not. It had been three years since I had last spoken. My mouth felt dry. My throat scorched. Then a tremendous effort began, deep down in my chest, building, building, until suddenly the words cranked themselves out: "And you, I take it," I said, "must be Pip."

IT HAD finally happened. All unfolded as if foretold in a dream, and yet it was all new, a revelation. Grandfather had been right. The invasion had begun.

"How is it that you have come here?" I asked.

He shrugged. His lids reflected nothing back. "I let myself in. The door wasn't locked."

"Why? What do you want?"

Again the smile. Behind its curve, the white teeth glinted. "As to that—" He held out one empty hand.

"You could tell me. Then, whatever it is, you can have it and go."

"It's not something I can take away with me."

He glanced sightlessly about him, and then placed the sunglasses above his brow. I could see now what he wore: I was paying close attention. He stood tall, slender and loose hanging; that was why he reminded me of Father. A plaid shirt, open at the neck, bloused around the wiry waist. Below that were white corduroy pants, well fitting and well cut. His hair was light brown, almost blond. It lay on the pale wall of forehead in a glossy drift, and covered his ears, lengthening his face. It looked newly washed, soft. He could be twenty-two years old, or thirty-two, or forty-two. I could not tell. But no more than that.

"So you are not a thief?" An aimless question, buying time.

"A thief?" He laughed shortly. "Oh, no. No. Just the opposite."

"Then to what"— my voice, rough and atrophied, grated on the air; I cleared my throat "do I owe this pleasure?"

"I was invited."

This stopped me for a moment. He smiled.

"By Nyla?"

"By your granddaddy."

My God, I thought. Have the lawyers done something?

The smile widened. "The stone by the gate, you know. Or do you know of it? It has always been there. I've waited a long time to answer it."

I looked at his closed eyelids. "You could not have seen it," I said at last. "You are lying."

"I read it." His voice fell light and cool.

"That is impossible. It was overgrown long ago with weeds and moss and lichen. You have no eyes."

The thrust did not seem to bother him. He held up long white fingers, and I saw their tips were stained with dirt.

"I read the invitation," he said.

"It says not to approach the house."

"Time has erased that dictum."

He was the first for decades who could have, I thought with angry futility.

"How do you know Nyla?" I demanded, suddenly cunning.

But he merely ran a thumb up and down his shirt front, then hooked it into the belt loop. "She's—a friend."

"Of yours?" I pondered a moment. "Do you shop at Seven-Eleven?"

"Ah. Perhaps." Then he said, "You know, I've waited a long time, Victoria. A long, long time. To meet you at last."

The sigh expelled, deep and expressive, as if he had been holding it in for years.

There must be a flaw in my hearing, I thought. It has been too long since people spoke around me—I must have misunderstood what he has just said.

But what was he planning to do?

He leaned against the door frame, negligently, with an absent patience, as I looked him up and down again. He seemed so familiar, and not just because of Father. Why? But it was pointless. Finally I broke the silence.

"What is your name?"

But he gave his easy shrug. "Just call me—Lazarus."

And then it hit me.

The implication of his words quivered with full force. I shrank back on my seat, hearing the meaning reverberate throughout the walls of the house, strike against the roofbeams, shiver the ghostly memories, with their terrible finality of purpose. Yes, I thought. It had come at last. Clearly, Grant Macafee intended this to be his *coup de grâce*.

The final battle had begun.

But I, unlike Grandfather, unlike all the other victims—I, the last of the Ransom line, would not give in without a fight.

I mustered my courage. "That is rather a grand boast," I parried, when my voice returned. So now, I thought, we were squaring off, crouched mentally, as it were, for the spring.

"Just let it rest that I've come here to—" He stopped, frowning. He seemed to muse, to weigh his next attack. "To know you."

"*What?*"

"Yes. Or shall I say, to talk."

I had to remind myself: *I* was having this experience—*I* was. Not Grandfather. Not Father, nor Bert, nor Baby Boy. It had now come down to me.

"Preposterous!" The whisper was strained through my outrage.

His hands clenched around the stick, the knuckles nearly as pale. He had readjusted the look of cautious detachment, and suddenly it struck me as familiar also. Why?

Then I recognized it. Who should know better? I had seen it in the Venetian mirror. And from the leviathan's face reflected before me above Mother's dressing table.

"I'll sit down, shall I?" he suggested.

I shook my head. Then I realized I had no choice but to speak. "No. You shall certainly not!"

The blind lids seemed to probe.

"Victoria—"

"Go. *At once!*"

He smiled once more, sweetly regretful, turned on his heel, and started to tap his way back across the foyer.

"Wait!" My voice cracked.

He halted. His back, rigid with the concentration of finding his way, relaxed momentarily. He did not turn around.

"Yes?"

With what resentment did I give in to the weakness of the next, necessary question. How I disliked conceding that first advantage!

"Are you real?"

From the space before him I heard a slow strangled sound rise, and broaden. His back hunched with the force of it; the plaid shirt drooped against his shoulder blades. "Yes, Victoria," he said finally. His voice was thin, ironic with breathlessness. "Oh, yes. I am real, all right. Only too real."

Then he half turned to me.

"Out. *Now!*"

He lingered a moment. I could scarcely bear it. Then, turning back, he continued the slow tapping until he had successfully dodged past sofas and tables and disappeared through the double doors.

The following day I timed my entrance to the conservatory, so that I sank into the chair at the exact half hour, no more, no less, than I had the day before. Not to fix his entrance. I already knew he would come. But now that the rhythm of my days was destroyed, I clung to any consistency. Yes: consistency, regularity—in the midst of such an assault I depended upon any vestige of my former life.

The night previous I had gone to bed racked with indigestion. His arrival had evoked a frenzy of appetite; I devoured Nyla's sausages in seconds, gulped the pudding down, and accused her silently over the tray when she returned for it. She brought more: canned spinach, cottage cheese, French fries still soggy with ice, raw carrots, chili. I scooped it all in, and then suddenly could hold no more. I got sick.

It had been too long. Plainly, I thought, this was not the way to prepare for mortal combat.

She left me to find my own way upstairs. Later, of course, I could not sleep. The room boiled in my ears all night; Mavis's wraith cooed from the far black corners. I wanted to swat it. When the sun rose, I had not yet slept. I hoped for a day of hard clarity. Instead, a bronze fog, turning milky, lay between the window and the sky. It soaked up the light. Outside, the lakes looked like pools of mutton fat, the trees smudges, the tall grass a smear of ochre.

After breakfast, I bided my time. It would not be long now, I knew. It crossed my mind to offer him some refreshment, coffee or tea, or even to have Nyla open the sideboard where Father kept the liqueurs and ports. That would be a clever gambit. I could poison his choice, perhaps. But with what? And how did I ask Nyla?

What could I fear from a blind man? my rational mind insisted. Wait. Wait.

I felt he had come to toy with me before wielding his blow, that he was probably cruel. But there was an evenness of advantage. He could not see. I could not run.

So I sat and waited.

When he appeared, his thin form slid into half-view at the threshold. He had entered through the front door (I heard the wheeze, so long silent) and patted along the wall of the foyer with his hands. Nyla had unbolted the door. Conspirators! I thought. Then he reached the doorway. One arm pushed through the denser air inside. The arm was long, strong, neatly haired with down like silver sparks. Where was his coat? It was winter outside. The clip of radius and ulna, with its covering of golden skin, made the forearm look like a beautiful instrument, reminding me of a scythe, or Samson's ass jaw gleaming clean and fatal above a doomed head.

A rolled-up sleeve, pale blue, followed. His tawny neck was ringed in blue material. I fretted for the lack of good strong light. For now he stood before me, full frontal, and I could not study his features carefully enough. The day fixed his face in a twilight, increasing as he stood there. The milky glow was fading, doused by—what? The air outside shimmered with motion. Rain.

He did not wear his sunglasses. Neither did he carry the stick. His hands were empty.

"Victoria?"

I held my breath.

"I'm back."

"I trust you're well." He tilted his head high, one ear cocked.

"It's such a dreary day out there. I hope you don't mind if I dropped my coat in the vestibule."

I did not feel ready to reply. I thought, with sudden mischief, Could it be that if I do not answer, he will begin to doubt himself? If I stay absolutely still, will he perhaps think he addresses nothing but air?

"I'm glad you don't have to suffer the inconvenience of inclement weather. This house is built like a fortress."

Did I detect the tiniest hesitation? I waited, not breathing. Sure enough, no lack of hopefulness, but a sigh threaded through his tone.

"It's not exactly politic, for me to gloss over your dismissal yesterday. I know you're so used to being alone that a visitor—" His head swung slowly around the room. The long nose took a delicate sniff. Then, suddenly, the face turned directly to me.

He had smelled me out.

Now consternation shackled my tongue.

"I realize I'm audacious in doing this. But I'm determined as well."

"Indeed?"

He smiled. There was a change in his face, below the deliberate casualness. "Yes. You see, I've always known the invitation at the gate was meant for me."

He stood as he had the day before, lolling against the door frame. His head inclined. "I believe I will sit down this time, if you don't mind." He straightened up and took seven steps forward until his shins nudged into the chaise lounge. He must accomplish such things with an instinctive part of his brain, I thought; for while he maneuvered himself, he continued to speak.

"We have a great deal to say to each other. I don't want that to sound impertinent. I mean, it's my hope that you may choose to share what you know—what you have—with me." He groped out with his hand, lowered himself, sat sideways, resting his chin on one upturned palm. "Your . . . solitude." The other hand extended, open.

"Your presumption awes me." I heard a choked, gritty voice.

He sat silent a moment. "Ah."

"How dare you say such things!"

"Which things?" He looked genuinely puzzled.

"Do not be ridiculous! You know perfectly well." My anger exploded at this mockery. But we both seemed to be engaged in avoiding the truth behind his presence, as if, by not using the word "asassin," we could prolong the time before it actually became applicable. "You are a presumptuous person who has come here uninvited. You have seduced that poor half-wit Nyla into letting you in. Heaven knows how you did it. That stone is obsolete, which is why it has been allowed to decay. As for the *arrogance* that it was meant for you—!"

"What better proof that the stone was meant for me alone? And no one else?" he said, touching his eyes.

I paused. "And for what it is worth, I have nothing to share with anyone. My own company is quite enough!"

"Victoria—" He sighed heavily. "How can I make you understand? I wouldn't offend you for anything in the world. You! I've waited years— a lifetime—for this chance!" He tapped a cigarette out of a pack from his pocket, and brought out a gold lighter. At this remove it looked to be real gold. "It's a test," he concluded, mumbling to himself. He tucked the cigarette between his lips, flicked the lighter with a thumb pad, and, behind the smoke streamers, frowned slightly. A stitchery of small coughs darned the air in front of his mouth. "I come here humbly, and in good will," he said carefully. "And if I may be so frank, envy."

"*Envy!*"

I could hardly speak.

"Plus what I mentioned before. As an——an ally. I long to talk with someone. Someone who could be above what I had to live. Someone—— unpolluted, you might say. Untainted. Unbesmirched by worldly concerns. By the horrors, the . . ." He scowled. Slowly it began to dawn on me now, the way in which he planned to toy with me. He wished to use me. I was to become, in the manner of the victim to whom the torturer opens his soul, his confessor. "Victoria. You're who I've dreamed for all my life. I mean that quite literally," he said in tones of deepest sincerity. It occurred to me that anyone not knowing the situation might have found him quite credible. "I've thought so long about you, sealed up in this house. I know more about you than anyone in Bernice could, no matter what they buzz about. More than you could imagine. And one thing I know"——he dropped the cigarette half-smoked onto the mossy brickwork——"is that, whether you know it or not, you could be a friend. To me."

Dumbfounding.

I took a long look at his body, sitting stiff on the chaise lounge.

"How do you imagine that I could be your friend? Why do you want it?"

His hand caressed the jaw. When he answered, his voice fell so low I could scarcely hear. "Because I cannot be at rest without it."

Then he collapsed back, lying full length. His hands folded wearily on his chest. He turned his face to the ceiling.

"How do you know about me?" I asked slowly.

"Oh. Ways. I've used my ears. Eyes, too, while I still had them."

Now my guard returned; I did not like his enigmatic manner. Obviously, Grant had succeeded in hiring a local person to deal his final cut. "What exactly do you want from me?"

He waited too long before answering.

"Is it money? Will that do it?" Will it suffice to buy your mercy? I meant.

The wince came quick as a slap.

Then he grinned wryly. "Victoria. I will tell you one thing. I do not need money."

"Good!"

"What do you think I am?" Anger sharpened the grin. "A con man or something?"

I did not reply.

"Do you know what a con man is? And why 'Good'? Money doesn't mean anything to you, does it?" He lifted his head towards me. "Does it?" The anger was changing to something else. He knows his craft, I thought; he was very convincing. "How can I reach you? I tell you, I *know* who you are. I understand you. I understand your life. Nobody else does. Stop playing with me this way, with your masquerade questions. You don't need them! You don't even have the faintest idea what a con man is. You couldn't." He rolled his head away, then back to me. "And I know perfectly well you don't give a hang for the Ransom millions. Money! I have more money than I'd need in two hundred years. Money. Christ." He crunched the cigarette pack in his hand. "The stuff makes me sick." The grin turned bitter. "That you would ask that question. Of all people—Victoria Grace Ransom. Grace. Yes." He smiled, frowned, and let out a long breath, exhausted. I wondered what Grant was paying him with, if not money.

After a little, I said, "Who are you?"

"Does it really matter?" He tensed. "Does it really matter who I am?"

"Of course it does," I said, surprising myself, wishing suddenly for it to come out and get stated, for him to admit clearly that this was death, that he was Grant's emissary at last. "Consider how much you have made of your presumption of knowing me."

His face went calmer, less rigid.

"If we are to be friends," I murmured, "I would like to know."

There was a long silence. The muscles relaxed; he seemed to go boneless.

"Victoria. I was hoping you would say that. Thank you."

I stared. Somewhere within I felt lightning; had I in my trickery actually said something the meaning of which I could not even imagine?

"Well?"

"I am a man who's come from too much. That's who I am."

"Yes?"

"I've come—as I've said—to be your friend."

The stillness trembled between us.

"To join you here."

"What did you say?"

"Yes," he whispered. "Oh, yes. Here."

"Why?"

"Because this is sanctuary."

I said nothing. My throat hurt. All at once I realized I was not equal to this duel. I did not know the rules.

"Because the whole world is full of horror. Evil. There is no place to escape it. But you have. You, and your family before you. I know that for a fact." He sighed again. "This place is a haven. Out of time. The Ransoms created it—they alone could do it. They refused to play. Do you see? They refused. Then they created you, and kept you here. Safe. Safe from everything. Untouched. You don't even know what evil is. And you never will."

In the dead silence, my jaw began to ache. I touched it softly.

"You can't," he said reasonably. "Can you?"

I know no rules, I thought in despair. But now I felt I saw an inkling of how he would achieve his goal. He meant to do me to death with sarcasm.

"That's why I know your question about money was just a blind. To fool me, to protect your solitude. You've never even left this house. No school, no Bernice, no Texas, no United States. No North America. No world. Not for you. Isn't that so?"

For a brief moment, I could not reply. "No. It is not so," I said then. "I *have* left here. When I was a very young child." It was the only defense I could think of. Prove him wrong, I thought. Show him he is in error, his advantage is not whole.

"Really?" He sat up, curiosity on his sightless face. "When? To go where?"

But the moment passed. I fell silent again, the early memories paling before me, gone. I only thought: What next? His form was drowning in darkness. Outside, the rain lashed against the panes, a hopeless sound, going on into eternity.

"You are wrong," I said after a little. "You do not know who I am."

"Yes, I do."

My face stretched tight; but he, of course, could not see the frozen smile.

"I've known most all my life who you are," he said. His voice drifted low across the beating rain, almost dreamy now. "I used to watch you. You were just a little girl in those years. I'd sneak into these grounds. Not through the gate, I didn't want to be seen. When I first started doing it, nobody had a clue where I'd go. Mother gave me all hell for disappearing back then, for hours at a time. I chased rabbits, and hunted up the squirrels, and picked the spikes off that one big cactus down the drive and made darts with them. I knew every inch, every single tree in the woods. As well as if I'd mapped them. It's one of the only things I still know perfectly. I can find my way around anywhere. Even since the place has been allowed to run down."

The smile had gone. He pondered, not expecting me to speak.

How could it be true?

"You were this pretty little dark-haired girl, dawdling around the edge of the lawns and stirring sticks in the lakes. With that black woman who came with you sometimes. What was her name?"

"Viola," I whispered; and suddenly the name rippled away from me across the conservatory, like a sighing wave of water.

"Of course. Viola. I should have recalled, I've heard it so often. Your maid. But it wasn't important, like you were. She had nothing to do with you, not really."

I closed my eyes.

"Not for me, anyhow," he added.

I began to feel as if I was slowly falling into a trance, embracing what lay waiting for me, the way I had read that people succumb to the fate of freezing.

"Naturally I never came close to the house. I knew better than that. But those azalea bushes along the drive, they made good hiding places when a car went past—your mother or father. I must have played Indian a thousand times. And spent whole afternoons waiting in the hopes that you might come out of the house. At least, until— but never mind that."

"Did you—did you live close by?" The whisper rose, vanished.

"Oh, fairly close. After we moved. We had lived across town, over on Ficklin."

"Oh."

"See, I was something of a loner too. Until I got sent away, that is, and had no more choice."

"When did you go away?"

But he did not answer. "Every square inch. . . ." he mused.

"Then," I said, "you did know the stone. Grandfather's stone."

"Oh, yes. By heart. I scraped all the lichen off it one time and memorized it."

"That was what I—" I trailed away.

"Like I said," he grinned, "I always felt it was meant for me. Calling me in." He scratched his jaw in thought. "I was fascinated with this place. And with all of you—your mother, your father. Your granddaddy. You especially."

"Why?"

But once more he did not answer.

"Once I was gone, I used to long to come back. I'd have dreams about it at night. To these woods—stuck here smack dab in the middle of a Bernice neighborhood! It seemed strange to me, you understand. Not out in the country, like a ranch. Or a farm. But like an enchanted place. And I was very homesick. I didn't fit in where I was, I didn't fit in anywhere. Not in my family. Certainly not in the army."

"Oh—"

So Bernice had not forgotten us after all. There had been an anonymous boy, the son of some merchant or lawyer, perhaps, who focused his obsession . . . probably his father had scolded him for it, if he knew.

"And when I'd come home, which I did occasionally, I'd always wait for the chance to slip back into the woods. I'd creep up to the house—never close enough, though—and lurk around, in the possibility that you might come out. But it's a funny thing. A day came—it was one summer—when I realized how long it had been since I'd seen you. Years. You'd been living in my mind inside this house, I just pictured you here whether I saw you or not. But then I realized. And I got the feeling that you'd stopped coming out. It wasn't just that I came at the wrong times. There weren't many opportunities by then; I got here when I could. But I realized you never came out anymore. Not at all."

He rested quietly back on the cushion flecked with mildew.

"Why was that, Victoria?"

I said nothing.

"It was as if the house was holding you in. As if even the outdoors, the Ransom grounds, weren't safe enough anymore. Like Rapunzel. Only you were being held inside because you were too pure for the world. It was the world's evil that hovered outdoors, and the house was all that could preserve your innocence." He paused.

"Your state of perfection."

A numbness, a cold terror, stole through me now.

"Sometimes," he grinned ruefully, "I used to be afraid that I myself had somehow brought the contamination in with me. That it was my fault the place wasn't safe anymore."

"Ah——" A whisper escaped me.

"I had dreamed about the lives lived inside here for so long. I'd imagined what it must be like to grow up in this enormous stone house, among these——lofty people. Their fineness. You were all elevated over us somehow, like beings who couldn't dare mingle with lower forms of life. And I thought, Oh, no, what if I've leaked the bad stuff in? Especially after that thing happened when I was sixteen."

The numbness stopped my mouth.

"But that was just imagination. I know that now. It was the rest of the world that prevented you."

"What happened when you were sixteen?" I whispered.

He sighed deeply. "Oh. Something horrible. The first of the horrors." His tongue touched his lips. "Something I saw."

"What was it?"

"I'd rather not say right now. It's a memory I try to lose. But I'll tell you this. I went on to see a lot worse while I was in Vietnam."

"Ah."

He sagged down into the cushion. Then he shook his head. "You know, it's a strange thing. Vietnam was bad. Unspeakable, in fact. Yet whenever the memories come back, of all the blood and mess I saw there, that first one stands out with more clarity. It's that one that hangs above. That one which haunts at night."

"Haunts——"

"Oh, yes." He clasped his hands tightly together on his stomach. "Actually," he murmured, "you're what got me through those years in Vietnam." His face flushed in a grave smile.

The scope of his cruelty seemed petrifying.

"What do you mean, 'Vietnam'?"

He sat up. "What?" A flash of bewilderment altered his face.

"The war," he said. "The war there."

"Oh." Any moment. It had to be—any moment, it was coming. We were just putting it off, delaying.

"You don't know," he said, slowly marveling. "Do you?"

"No."

"You don't even know about that." His whisper filled with wonder. "My God. Is it possible? That somebody—" For a second, silence fell.

"I apologize," I said stiffly, "for my ignorance."

"No TV," he whispered, locking his sightless eyes straight ahead. "No papers. No radio news. No word from the outside."

"No."

He turned to me. "You see? That's what I mean. Oh, Victoria—I can hardly believe it. I can hardly believe—after all these years of hoping, of trusting—" A chuckle of spontaneous joy burst from his smooth golden face gleaming in the dusk, eyelids flickering.

"I used to think of you there. I used to hold you in my mind, everything you meant, while I did what they told me. Shot. Threw the grenades. Set the torches. You were what kept me alive."

I stared at him.

"And that this place existed as well."

There was nothing to say. The horror began to swell once more, tinged with misery.

"I used to think, If I ever get out of this alive, I will find her." He drew a deep breath. "It's taken me longer than I planned. It has taken me years." One finger reached up to rub his temple. "This is why."

I stared and stared at the pale scar traceries.

"But while I learned to get around—deal with the problem, as it were—I realized something else. It is better this way. Better. Because—I have seen too much. Seeing is what nearly destroyed me. And this way I come to you clean. Purged. Like you are. I don't need eyes to see you. I know what beauty is better without them."

No.

"The blind prince," a voice muttered. But then I recognized it was his.

"No," I whispered.

"What's that?"

"No." But it fell silently.

"Rapunzel."

I was cold, cold all over.

"Do you know the story?"

"Yes."

"Yes," he said gently. "Exactly. I have heard your song everywhere. And now I've found you. In the desert. Safe."

It took all I had to speak. "But I have not been singing." I felt as if now, at last, I was pleading for my life.

"Yes. Yes."

"You must leave here."

"What?" He sat up, rigid. "Oh, Victoria. Don't—"

"I want you to go. Now. Immediately."

"You can't mean that."

"Yes."

"No. Victoria." The emotions mingling in his face frightened me more than what had come before. Determination ruled them all. "I know that as a child I violated this place. I didn't know any better. And it must appear to you now that I still violate you—your solitude, your safety—"

"You will go. Now."

"But why?" he whispered.

"There are reasons." My voice choked. I could not breathe. Dear heaven, help me, I begged. "Reasons," I gasped. "Nyla!"

The call was enough. He jumped up from the chaise, nearly stumbling.

"There can't be reasons," he started to argue frantically. "You know I'm not going to harm you. I'm not going to ruin this. I've waited too long, too—"

"Get out!"

The cry boomed around us, on the stone walls and humid air.

"Victoria," he said low as he stood to go. "Even today I have heard you singing."

THERE WAS nothing to be done, I thought. About any of it.

Over the following days, I found myself wishing deeply that he had never entered. I wished he had not made things worse. I had never fancied, even in my darkest brooding, as I sat anticipating death by his hand, that they could actually get worse.

Three nights went by. Nyla neglected the conservatory. The Ficus lyrata looked a little sickly, and some of the fern's fronds were turning brown.

What had wrenched more than his revelations was what he had brought with him. Not the world. Not even his sad dreams, or his outside acknowledgement of the evil. But he had brought me a new way in which to consider myself.

I did not like what I saw.

When Nyla served my lunch, she paused, and gazed at me. Her face was expressionless, yet beneath its surface lay something that I knew at last I had avoided or denied for many years now. It was not calculation. It was not threat. It was kindness.

She turned and looked long and steadily at the pile of manuscript on the table before me, almost as though she could penetrate it and read after all.

ON THE day he came back, it was a bright morning. He stood at the threshold. I could see his features perfectly; the shaved cheeks, hollow under the prominent bone, the carved mouth. They made me flinch. Now the horror and numbness had left; even in my surprise that he stood there, all I felt was the tired, toneless misery, sifting through. He must have come from the kitchen, through the hall, past the sitting room and Grandfather's library, for I had heard no sound.

"Victoria." His voice rang peremptory. He marched through the room, seven steps, and gripped the edge of the chaise. "I have something to say to you."

Even in defiance, he had a dignity that I respected.

"I understand that I've really told you nothing. I didn't know how. But today I want to try to speak."

He set himself on the chaise, erect, his feet planted side by side. "Will you listen?" There seemed to be no more doubt left in him. But why was he here? With such stubborn tranquility in his expression?

"I will listen," I said.

And thus he began to explain to me how this house, which he called a retreat, was the only sane place left for him in a universe of insanity. Only here could he become nothing.

"You understand nothing," I said to him. He lighted a cigarette. His every movement had solidity, purpose. Then he began to tell me about his childhood.

He had had a preceptor, he said. There was someone into whose hands he had been put. He took a happy, ordinary boyhood and taught it a vision.

"What kind of vision?" I asked.

"Of infamy."

He waited, perched stiffly on the chaise's edge. The silence lay for long minutes.

"I won't try to describe the details of what he tutored. You'd never grasp them," he said. But on Saturday mornings he would be playing with his friends, bicycling around the block, climbing trees, flying his kite in the back yard, and then his mother would come to the door and call him. "Come inside, honey," she would cry. "We have a special visitor! Come in and say hello." And the teacher would be in the living room, waiting. She wanted them to get to know each other, his mother told him. She wanted them to be close. She admired the teacher, and said he was a good example for him. She knew very well he had a lot to offer. There was the outdoor life of horses and cattle; and of course, all the money up for the bidding.

"But one day," he said, drawing on his cigarette, "he found out I had a secret place I liked to go explore. And from then on, his lessons were about war."

"War?"

"Yes. Until at last, when I'd graduated from high school, and already seen my first concrete evidence of the kind of evil he was always talking about, I went to war myself. To a literal war. Vietnam."

I said nothing.

"The war was awful. So awful that you, thank God, will never understand it. Because you don't know such things exist. Then I lost my eyes."

"How?"

He touched the tender right lid with a fingertip. "Never mind how," he said. "Let's just say that I had seen enough. Whatever the case, after that I was spared any further visible proof."

"Oh." A dozen possibilities flackered through my mind.

"But you see, Victoria——" he went on. "I'd traded one war for another. And I reached a conclusion."

"And this was?"

"War is everywhere."

"Even outside," he added, when I remained mute. "In Bernice."

"Why?"

He gestured around the room. "You surround yourself with beauty. And I have touched the books in the library. You're well educated, I know that. But you can't have known the truth of things, no matter how many books you've read, or what you have written."

"What I have——"

"Nyla has told me that you write. She said that's what you spend your time doing. Working on a huge stack of papers."

I dragged myself up to meet this disclosure, tearing away momentarily from his blindness, the despair he had opened in me without even recognizing it. "She did not say what they were, I presume?"

"No." He looked puzzled. "I suspect I know, though."

"What could you know?"

"Poetry." He produced it as if he dared another breach of privacy. "I figured you write poetry."

"I see."

"I was thinking—maybe—someday perhaps you'll read it to me." My grin grew black.

"You have not answered my question," I said. "You've told me the truth now, about how you went to war. But you have not said why."

"Oh," he muttered, lying back on the chaise. "Victoria," sighing deeply.

For a moment, there was silence. "I went because he made me," he said.

"He made you."

"Yes."

Because that was the nature of evil, he explained. He was forced to join the army by his teacher. He had understood his teacher's infamy only too clearly. His teacher did not like what he knew.

"Because *his* version was different, and I wouldn't accept it. You'll never credit this, how could you?—but he actually was deranged with the notion that true evil lay here. Within this very house. Decay, he called it. Inwardness and corruption. He called this house a living example of death." For years his teacher preached this obsession to him. All during his childhood the lesson was drilled home repeatedly. I pictured this teacher as I listened: some rabid Baptist church deacon, intoning his lower-middle class disgust with the Ransom money and habits—a pharmacist, perhaps, like Mr. Sloane of all those years past in Bernice. I tried to connect him to Viola's Bernice, the only Bernice I knew. But I already suspected the truth. I was merely fooling myself one last time.

"But I saw through him. *His* was the evil, all right. And then, when

I thought I'd escaped his vision, I went away only to see it made flesh. After that there was only this place left. This house was somewhere he couldn't reach."

"Why?"

"He couldn't touch it. It was too good for him, and he knew it. He didn't like that, believe me."

"Why are you doing this to me?" At last I forced myself to ask him. "Is this revenge?"

"Victoria!" he said. Then, faintly, "What do you mean? What do you mean, doing what?"

I summoned all my strength. My voice rasped. "Who—are—you?"

He tilted his head at the floor.

"Have I wrecked it? Is that it?

"You have to realize," he said, low, "you were what sustained me through all that. And the knowledge that he was wrong, he was a part of what I was seeing. I knew that by the time I was sixteen. The first time. I knew, absolutely, the day I heard him laugh."

"Oh, dear God." I closed my eyes. "I know who you are."

His face lifted.

"You can't!"

The invasion was complete. The suspense was over, the final revenge had arrived. My breath charged with fear.

"Do you want to know what I know about evil?" I asked softly.

Even in gravity, he looked bewildered.

"Do you? Would you like to hear?"

"Victoria—" He held up his palms.

"Because I will tell you." My tone was hushed, lethal. He heard.

"Would you like to hear what I have been writing for the past few years? Trying to dredge up from the mire? Would it satisfy you to learn something about war?" I laughed. "It is not poetry. Oh, no. Unless history is a kind of poetry."

"I don't see what—"

"Quiet!" I stared at the long carved features. At last I knew what seemed so familiar. Something within me lifted. Elation, poised for attack. He did not move, or open his lips.

"Randall," I said, "let me tell you now about true evil. Let me tell you the stories of our families."

His face lay blank. He cocked it toward nothingness. I began to talk.

I told it all.

It took a long, long time. It seemed I spoke for many hours. I started with the ice business partnership, with Sarah and Grant. When I neared the end of the complicated twinings, the vendetta payments, the deaths—all I had absorbed into myself since my con-ception—night was falling.

He did not move, except for his spine bending ever lower, until he sagged over the chaise's edge. My tongue, my jaws, my throat were burning, but I went on. Once—as I recounted the story of Grand-father's suicide—I heard a stirring at the room's threshold. I glanced over, and glimpsed a flutter of gingham hem, disappearing around the door frame's line in the twilight. I did not care.

But I recognized I had left one important thing out: his participa-tion in the Macafee revenge. My father's lost arm. I did it deliberate-ly; I was saving it. At last, when I had finished, I asked, "Do you com-prehend now what I am?"

He sat, speechless, sightless, his face so creased with pain that it looked beyond pain.

"Do you understand what your family has made of us? Of me?"

"You're wrong," he whispered. "Part of what you say may be right. My God!—even Baby Boy. But part of it is wrong."

"Do you realize, then, what a paltry and deluded idiocy it was that led you here? Do you see now what my father was? What Grandfather's life was like? Because of you and yours?" I did not add: And how I had deluded myself into thinking that you would kill me outright with an instrument, rather than in this slow, more terrible way?

"You're wrong." He sounded drained of air.

"No. I was here. And you do not even know what I look like." I laughed. "'State of perfection' indeed!"

"I . . . know what you look like."

"How could you?" The scorn burned now.

"Nyla has told me."

"*What?*"

"You're tall. Long hair, dark. With large dark eyes."

I stared. Then it snapped. "You know who Nyla is, do you not? A childlike, half-witted stray, an orphan from nowhere that my grandfather had his lawyers hunt up to take care of my great-aunt Mavis?"

"Yes. Well, not half-witted, of course, but yes. I knew who she is—or suspected it—already. Although I wouldn't call Joliet, Illinois, nowhere, exactly."

I said nothing, stopped short.

"I guess an orphanage in Illinois must seem like nowhere to you," he added.

"Illinois?"

"Joliet. The Catholic orphanage there. That's where the couple put her when they decided they couldn't look after her anymore. Then, apparently, the couple took the stipend that your grandfather sent them every month, and moved to California. Had it forwarded, I guess. I don't really know. Anyhow, Nyla says the nuns were kind to her. But they weren't quite sure what to do with her once she grew up. And it was cold up there in Illinois. She didn't like that. She is childlike, no doubt about that."

"Are you saying—" The revelation struck with the clang of a bell; instantly I saw before my mind's eye that familiar dome of skull under the blond hair. So she had not taken after her father, I thought. She had taken after the Ransom side—my grandfather's head. Sarah's head.

Grandfather had done one other thing, after all.

"I was already acquainted with most of what you told me. I just didn't think you had any idea of it all," Randall was saying. I turned on him. "I thought they had let you be."

"Let me be?" I whispered. "Let me *be*?"

"I was his heir. The one he had to talk to. He had no son."

No, I thought. No; only a daughter.

"He poured out all the details. Then he saw I refused to accept them. So he accused me of being enamored with Ransoms. With their corruption, and cowardice. He blamed them all."

It had been like an itch Grant could never scratch hard enough. Because here we all were, safe inside this house, out of harm's way. And after the accident, Randall said, he began to understand.

"And which accident was that?" I inquired. My voice, I could hear, rang rich in irony.

"Your father's," he answered.

And now, everything within me revolted.

"How dare you mention that to me?" I cried. "How dare you bring up such a subject? Did you not notice that I had left it out of my own story? Have you Macafees not crammed yourselves enough? Are you still not sated?"

"I thought you were the one nobody got to," he said, aghast. His face had gone pale in the twilight with shock.

"Do you not see, even now, that somebody did?"

"No," he whispered. "I'm sorry. But Victoria, you're wrong. I've got to show you. Listen. I'll tell you what I know, the thing I saw, that provoked him into telling it all to me."

"I do not want to hear it! Just leave this house. Get *out*!"

"Your father—he wasn't what you thought."

And then, despite my command, he told me.

His parents had sent him to Sauter Military Academy. Grant had helped pay for this, it seemed; he was always a willing sponsor when it suited his purposes. But Randall continued to come home for holidays. And one Thanksgiving, when he was sixteen, his father took him deer hunting with some of his friends. My father had been there. He had asked Randall to call him Willie.

At this point Randall squinted, as if he would smile. But apparently he could not.

"No adult had ever asked me to do that, to call him by his first name. Oh, I had met him before. I had been introduced to him when he was drunk and, yes, a little incompetent. But it didn't matter. He was Mr. Ransom, that was enough for me."

But on that occasion, the time of the deer hunt, my father had been in his full stride. It had intrigued Randall, to see him suddenly so authoritative and at ease in his surroundings, as if he knew exactly what he was doing. He had conducted himself with a hunting craft that Randall thought smooth and swift and proper—unlike the other men, who blundered about through the bushes, making a lot of noise, and scaring everything away within miles. Father moved like an Apache. I could see him as Randall spoke, imagine his boots treading so carefully among the twigs and leaves, watch the flare and quench of his jacket in the brush as he took his position, waiting for the buck. He had described it to me so often before. All through those long nights as we sat alone together, he had shared the sharp autumn mornings, the crisp air on his face, the scent of gunpowder. I closed my eyes, remembering. I could see the boy, young, a novice, following Father under the trees, the son he had never had hoisting the gun to his shoulder. "Like this?" he had asked. "Like this?"

"That's right," Father said. "Hold the stock a little bit tighter against your palm. Now aim your eye down the sight. Easy. Easy does it."

The boy obeyed. He took aim. A rustle sounded in the brush. Father held up his hand, touched a finger to his lips for silence, pointed—

"I wanted to ask him about you," said Randall.

"I beg your pardon?" I opened my eyes.

"But I didn't dare. Not that first day. Then, later, when they carried him in, I couldn't. I had never seen blood, except for a rabbit or a dove shot down. My own father never really hunted, he just enjoyed playing poker. He was a hat factory executive, for Christ's sake. But your father . . . it was because I had caught the flu." He stopped.

"What?" I said blankly. I was sitting so quietly that he did not notice my stun.

"I had caught the flu. I came down with it the night of that first day. I had to lie in bed in the cabin, tossing around with a compress on my head, while all the men went on hunting without me. And it was my first deer hunt, too."

The silence expanded around us.

"I was very disappointed. But mostly because your father had set such an example. I wanted to prove myself to him. He was a genius with a rifle. That second morning, before they started, he came to my bed and patted my shoulder. 'Don't worry, son,' he said. 'Tomorrow's another day. I'll take you out then.'"

Again the hush prolonged, fell away in darkness.

"So when they came back to the cabin, I thought, 'Wonder why they're back so early?' And then I heard shuffling, and the voices rising, and they were carrying him through the door."

I stared, blinked.

"And I saw his arm."

They had carried him in. Two men had carried him between them: Wirt Taylor and a friend. He lay limp, unconscious, the arm dangling like a broken stick. Bone jutted out through cloth, a wreckage so complete that as Randall sat up in bed and saw it he thought for a fleeting second that it wasn't an arm at all, it was some bloody debris from the hunt that had got entangled with Father's coat. A trail of red spattered the floor; Randall heard the drops fall. Leaves patched the wound, stuck with clotted blood. Even from his bed Randall could see the closed eyelids, like wax, the face in its swoon seamed against the pain. The fever racing through his head rarified the scene, lending an eerie radiance like a halo in the dim, dusty shadows of the cabin. Staring at the body while they lowered it onto the table, Randall could think only one thing: that he and Father would not go hunting together tomorrow. That Father would never hunt again. Then Randall began to weep. The tears streamed down his face, into his open mouth, until his own father told him to shut up, and they bandaged the arm and drove Willie Ransom off to the hospital.

I said nothing.

"I couldn't get over it," he whispered. "Victoria, I couldn't get over it."

"Yes," I muttered.

The silence lengthened. It was not until a moment later that the truth of his story reached home.

"You did not do it." A strange sensation began to fill my head. Doubt, mistrust, a jarring of time itself, of event, held me frozen.

"What did you say?" he said.

It took a few seconds to speak. "I said, Who did it?"

"Oh," he sighed, "don't you remember? They never figured it out. Which one it was. From that group of teenagers across the valley. A bunch of kids from Johnson City. They'd been drinking. They thought they saw deer and they all shot. No one ever knew which of them actually hit him. But—you heard all about that too, didn't you? The investigation and all. From the Johnson City sheriff's department." He rubbed his forehead, and raised towards me. "Didn't you?"

I could not reply.

"Victoria— didn't you?" he asked.

Something overturned within me and went still. I felt a tearing, and at the same time my head trembled, light as glass.

"Well, Victoria." He spoke jerkily. "Well. There it is."

"Yes," I said.

Something was happening.

It was when Randall returned home from the deer hunt, and told Grant about the accident, that he saw definitively for all time his teacher's true nature. Grant listened to the account of the accident, sitting upright and slightly back on a hard wooden chair in Randall's mother's kitchen. His thin face, grown thinner and wattled below the chin with age, flexed as he listened. The jawline hardened, released. He raised a hand to comb back the hair which he wore plastered against his skull as if scalped. When Randall reached the climax description of Father's wound, Grant smiled.

"*Smiled*, you understand," said Randall. After he had described the horror, the terrible sight of Father's mangled arm, Grant sat back with a bizarre smile upon his face. And then, he laughed.

For him it was the hand of God, smiting down the despised weak. That much he made clear to Randall. And when, a few days later, he had caught Randall coming out of these grounds, he made it clearer. He must have followed in his car, tracking by stealth the errant nephew, recognizing the first hint of soft corruption. Randall had spent the afternoon trying to see through the windows, to catch some glimpse of me. He wanted to know if I was all right. But I was not visible anywhere. It had been years since he had seen me by then.

So when Randall came through the fence, scrambling between the wires, there Grant stood. His face looked withered, twisted into something unrecognizable. Like a piece of mesquite that had grown into a dry distortion, it glared downwards.

"What do you think you're doing?" he said. One hand rose towards Randall's collar. He made as if to seize it. But then he held back. Instead he merely pointed to the car. "Get in." He had not shouted; there had been none of his usual signs of anger. As he drove home, he repeated once more, venomously, what he felt for all the Ransoms.

Then, the day after Randall's graduation from Sauter, Grant took him aside. "Are you still besotted with that rotten breed?" he asked.

"They're not rotten, Grant." That was all Randall would answer;

he was too old now to argue. He knew Grant had found his evil, and insisted it be Randall's also.

"In that case, I think we'd best get you far away from here and make a man out of you," said Grant. A tiny froth of spittle lined his lower lip as he spoke. "I worry about you, Randall. You're inheriting everything I own. I want you to use it right—there's too much here in Bernice to deprave and sap you." His old man's hands shook.

And looking at him, Randall realized that he wanted only to get as far away from Grant as he could.

Leaving Bernice seemed like an adventure then. He imagined coming home eventually from his journeys, entering this stone house, presenting himself to the remaining Ransoms as a figure of romance. His mother had always considered him a problem, interfering as he did with her youthful image. His father was pleased when he saw him in uniform. It had been a simple expedient to join the army with a commission, thanks to Sauter. He was going to a real, openly declared war, to extricate himself from this one. And it was what Grant wanted.

But he had come home blind.

"I guess it's all been a mistake after all," he said now. "A delusion." He coughed hard against his hand. He was heaving to his feet. "They should have let you alone, at least," he muttered. "They should have left us both alone. We've been talking just like them." He headed slowly for the door. His feet picked the way, crossing the brickwork, the felted moss.

I tried to stand up. I strained to rise out of the seat. "Randall! Wait!"

But the cry rebounded on stone.

He was gone.

AFTER THAT the days slid by. I sat in the conservatory, with the mute, rebuking plants. I would have paid any price now to have them come out and warm me, send away this cold, but they would not.

He did not arrive.

Ever since the last visit, and its hopeless conclusion, he stayed away.

I knew now what I had done to deserve it. What we all did; our error. But there was no place to use this salvation. All I had was the dead pile of paper. Nyla drooped through the house, tossing me a glance of sadness. She blamed me, I knew. No longer did she wear that blank, dull mask; life gleamed from the blue Macafee eyes, but one which had risen too late. It was like the life waking in Grandfather's eyes, that day below the fern when I prompted his beheading. That had been my error too. But the responsibility was his, and he did not take it. None of us took it.

Until now.

Oh, Viola, I thought: I can at last answer your question, "Why."

I remembered other things: the flash of pain and sorrow that had crossed his face when he spoke of Father's arm. How does a cripple not recognize her fellow?

The house seemed to sink daily on top of me. I was completely alone now. Mother, Father, Viola, Grandfather—I had lost them all, yet never learned to mull over loss, to mourn my vacant arms and lay my fingers on a face that had fled elsewhere. My appetite had vanished, I could not eat, living now upon air, upon understanding, upon the rolls and layers of the past's accretion. And how had he taught me about loss in this way?

There was plenty of time to contemplate how.

Then one day I heard myself declare: "It is all too dear. The price is too dear. I will not pay with this pain." I thought, Where on these pages have I inscibed that I will not die enraged, marooned in this house?

Oh, God. I want to live.

After awhile I cried out: "It costs too much to let yourself be touched. It is a good thing it will not happen again."

And I thought, How curious. To think that I *could* have been.

Then I was weeping, and the hot drops smeared on my hands.

WHY, I wondered, did Grandfather waste his life thinking he had to hide from his enemy?

Where had Randall gone? Where was his false home?

If I ventured out into the open air, into the streets, to find—but no, I thought, I must be crazed to think of it!

Why had he started what he would not let me complete?

AND THEN he came back.

One morning he strode in through the front door. I had scarcely heard it swing open when he was standing at the threshold, his face flushed. Then, slowly, he crossed the room to the chaise lounge, and lowered himself onto it.

I could scarcely breathe.

He sat, face intently towards me, visibly in the throes of something. At last he spoke. "I'm sorry, Victoria."

"It is all right," I whispered. "Randall, it is all right."

He nodded. We sat there in silence. Then he rose to go.

Not yet, I wanted to cry. Give me a chance. Do not apologize and vanish, not you.

He paused before my chair, on his way to the door. The long brown hand reached out. He touched my cheek, softly, cupping its curve in his palm, feeling the moisture on it. He rubbed his fingers together, raised them to his mouth, tasting. His face lifted to the ceiling. I sat very still.

"Ah," he sighed; just a brief sound.

Then, in a clear, firm voice, he said, "I'll see you tomorrow."

The foyer swallowed him. Then the front door, closing gently.

MY BODY began to do strange things. I explored this new casing that held me: the skin of my arms, for so long stretched to bursting, hung slack. There could be little question. The belly was shrunken; I palpated it with my fingers. My hands felt more lithe, nimbler. I suddenly remembered their fluency when I was a child. The night of Randall's return I took a thorough bath. I did not even need Nyla afterwards. Later I could not sleep, but paced back and forth across the conservatory floor, discovering a new looseness in the steps, an ease that I had not known for years. At last I went to bed, tired out, but began the pacing the next morning. I could walk.

Farther.

During my engrossment with the discovery, I found myself standing before the front door.

The foyer and stairs rose behind me, through finite distances.

One hand moved forth, and tentatively fondled the brass knob. Then I knew.

I opened the door, and stepped into winter sun.

HE CAME from far off, up the winding drive. As I watched him approach through the vista of dogwood trees and wild azaleas, the blue of the sky seemed to scour my eyes. Deep gusts of air, so long unsmelled, untasted, filled my mouth; yet the day stood still, there was no wind. So long, it had been. It took no time at all to climb down the porch steps; and then the house was at my back, and all that lay before grew out of the plane of earth: a boundless world. The trees I had seen through glass, the shrubs that had clustered around me with their thick leaves—now clear cut, little fragments of a picture that included lakes, drive, and the sky. I had forgotten its enormity.

One glance I spared at the house front, before turning back to watch him draw nearer; the blank stone white in the light, unfamiliar in its reality as a photograph of some historical mansion. He walked slowly, his stick tapping ahead for potholes. The other hand gripped the handle of a suitcase. He seemed so small under that vastness, his lone figure the only movement on the landscape. A dove burbled in the woods. I could scent leaf mold, damp greenery; I could smell the odor of the sun's faint warmth.

I waited until he reached the head of the drive.

"Randall," I called quietly.

He halted. "Victoria?"

THE FOLLOWING day I started reading this aloud.

I had not got very far when I realized there was an audience. Nyla stood in the doorway, her hands fallen at rest to her sides. When I met her eye, she came in, sat down on the fountain's rim under a nymph, and neatly crossed her ankles.

I read throughout the morning. After a lunch break of soup and bread, I waited for Nyla to come back from the kitchen, and then resumed. She listened like a bird, perched on the brickwork, her gaze set straight ahead. Without a word she had joined us; we were all here together now.

SUMMER IS nearing its zenith. The days grow brighter, brassier. The lawn thickens with green weeds and wildflowers.

For six months I have sporadically read this chronicle aloud, beginning every other morning after breakfast. At first I read on through until supper, watching what was left of its legacy drop away from my body all the while. (I sit lost in my giant chair now, a loose pebble rattling around in its warehouse.) But for the last six weeks we have spent our afternoons otherwise. In the long hours Randall and I roam the grounds together, hiking over the meadows, poking around in the woods, listening to lake frogs. We rummage through the stables, or dig among the old tools heaped in the workshop's corners. Randall has started cleaning and oiling the hand tools. He wants to work wood. Clearly my family never threw anything away; even the fatal buzz saw still squats in its dominion, unplugged now forever. But I am more fascinated by the engines inside the automobiles we found stored in the horse stalls—the intricacies encased within the Pierce Arrow's enameled shell, the Lincoln roadster, the twins' blue Mercury and the two Rolls-Royces. I plan to take them apart for study, then gradually put them back together again. Nyla has found leather cleaner with which to begin work on the interiors. Perhaps she can help me gather the parts we will need to make them start.

The weather here is lovely. Yesterday evening I saw a beaver.

I would like to explore the Hill Country around Kerrville.

This morning I went into the library to find an envelope. I have written to the lawyers, asking them to increase the household money they send. Nyla wants a new vacuum cleaner. Randall is teaching her how to cook a French menu, from escargots to rack of lamb to fresh vegetables. I need new clothes, socket wrenches, and timing lights.

When I had found the envelope, closed the drawer, and turned to go, I happened to catch sight of the photographs in their orderly array on the bookshelves.

There was the touring car among the silver frames, with the Ransom siblings stamped by sunlight. I studied it a moment, the way I had always done, wondering about the hidden figure: watchful, uneasy, shy, obsessed. But I thought, Now he will be there forever. He cannot change anymore.

I thought, And now I know the hinge of his and Sarah's secret. Bemused, I turned to go.

Then, with a clean bolt of realization, I looked back.

The touring car. How could I never have noticed before? The car had been built as a high chassis with no side windows. The canvas roof stood supported by thin steel frames; only the windshield enclosed the passengers.

Through all the years I pored over it, how could I have imagined that a man could be lurking invisible on the other side of that empty space?

PERHAPS EVEN now, Dandy is out there, pulling the Johnsongrass off his grave. But it is an odd thing: even after Randall told us, and named the date it happened (the same year Mother came home), I found it hard to imagine the world without him. Somewhere he must be ranging yet, nursing his ire, or recalling the past with a dim irascible effort. Or perhaps it faded for him right before he died: a dream of many years ago, abolished by the life intervening. When did that war finish, the siege grow to be imaginary? When did he cease firing and leave us to make ourselves? Therein lies the true evil, after all; but it is no longer relevant whether Bert was killed by some irate husband, or a spurned lady friend, or a burglar.

I would like to think that the only thing which finally returned to him, there at the end, was the first: a thin pale image, set now by time, of the girl who had left him far behind.

I will not send this to the lawyers. I have thought about leaving it wrapped like a surprise present under the shade of a live oak. But I do not think so. Perhaps tonight, before we go on our first experimental stroll through the gate, Randall and Nyla and I might carry these pages out to the pile of old lumber and rotten junk we have cleared from the stables, and place them on top. The blaze would make a good signal fire if anyone in Bernice should happen to be watching.